Writers' Association prize for best debut. Its sequel, *The Blood Spilt*, was chosen as Best Swedish Crime Novel. She was shortlisted for the 2007 Crime Writers' Association International Dagger for *The Savage Altar*, and again in 2012 for *Until Thy Wrath Be Past*.

MARLAINE DELARGY works as a translator and an adult learning support teacher. Her translations include crime novels by Åsa Larsson and Johan Theorin.

"A superior example of Scandinavian noir" JULIA HANDFORD, *Sunday Telegraph*

"Another enormously successful Swedish import, Larsson is a remarkably good writer who has been well served by her translator" JESSICA MANN, *Literary Review*

"The growing friendship between Mella and Martinsson is one of the best things about Larsson's novels, which grow in confidence with each book"
JOAN SMITH, *Sunday Times*

"Among the current female Scandi crime authors, I think that Åsa Larsson is one of the best . . . I look forward to the next Åsa Larsson novel, as she really is 'the one to watch'" KATHERINE ARMSTRONG, *Shotsmag*

"This book reminds me of Ruth Rendell's psychological thrillers . . . Overall this series is really amongst the cream of recently translated Scandinavian crime fiction" LAURA ROOT, *Eurocrime*

"A breath of fresh cold air in the seething squad of Swedish sleuths . . . This double act has a dangerous edge to gladden fans of Lisbeth Salander"
BOYD TONKIN, *Independent*

"Larsson's laid-back style makes her unflinching probing of the icy depths of the human heart all the more chilling" JAKE KERRIDGE, *Daily Telegraph*

"The new Larsson is to be followed with the most minute attention"
BARRY FORSHAW, *Independent*

Also by Åsa Larsson in English translation:

The Savage Altar (2007)
The Blood Spilt (2008)
Until Thy Wrath Be Past (2011)

Åsa Larsson

THE
BLACK PATH

Translated from the Swedish by
Marlaine Delargy

MACLEHOSE PRESS
QUERCUS · LONDON

First published in Sweden as *Svart stig*
by Albert Bonniers Förlag, Stockholm, in 2006
First published in Great Britain in 2012 by MacLehose Press
This paperback edition published in 2012 by

MacLehose Press
an imprint of Quercus
55 Baker Street
7th Floor, South Block
London W1U 8EW

This edition published by arrangement with Dell Books,
an imprint of The Random House Publishing Group,
a division of Random House Inc.

A CIP catalogue record for this book is available
from the British Library.

ISBN 978 0 85705 033 5

2 4 6 8 10 9 7 5 3 1

Typeset in Minion by Patty Rennie
Printed and bound in Great Britain by Clays Ltd, St Ives plc

The Black Path

NORWAY

Torneträsk

Narvik

Riksgränsen Ski Resort

Abisko

Nuolja Mountain

E10

Kiruna

Gällivare

ARCTIC CIRCLE

NORWAY

Luleå

SWEDEN

Umeå

GULF OF BOTHNIA

FINLAND

Åland

Uppsala

Regla Estate

Lake Mälaren

STOCKHOLM

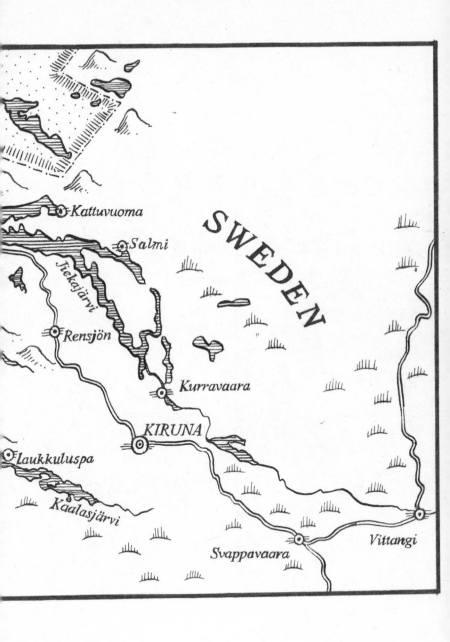

Do you remember what happened?

Rebecka Martinsson saw her dead friend lying there on the gravel in Poikkijärvi. And the world shattered. And they had to hold onto her to stop her walking into the river.

This is the third book.

Extract from case notes 12 September 2003
regarding patient Rebecka Martinsson

Reason for contact: Patient admitted to Kiruna hospital with facial injuries after a fall & trauma to head. On admission found to be in acute state of psychosis. Surgical treatment of facial injuries necessary; patient therefore sedated. On waking, clear psychotic symptoms still present. Decision made to section patient under 3 § L.P.T. Transferred to psychiatric clinic at St Göran's hospital, Stockholm – secure unit. Preliminary diagnosis: psychosis U.N.S. Treatment: Risperdal mix 8 mg / daily plus Sobril 50 mg / daily.

This is the last time.

Behold, he comes with the clouds, and every eye shall see him.

This is the final hour.

This is the time of the fiery steed. She who comes with the long sword, so that men shall slay one another.

And here! They seize me by the arms! They will not listen! Stubbornly they refuse to turn their eyes to the heavens, opening up before them.

This is the time of the pale steed.

And he paws the ground with his sharp hooves. He kicks earth out of his way.

There came a huge earthquake, and the earth turned as black as ink, and the moon was the colour of blood.

And I remained behind. Many of us were left behind. We fall to our knees before our journey into the darkness, and we empty our bowels in fear. On the way to the lake burning with fire and sulphur, and this is the second death. Only a few minutes remain. We must take hold of whatever we can. Hold fast to what is closest to us.

I can hear the voice of the seven storms. At last the words are clear.

It says. The time. Is up.

But no-one here will listen!

Extract from case notes 27 September 2003
regarding patient Rebecka Martinsson

Patient responsive, answers when spoken to, able to give an account of events which triggered depressive psychosis. Displays signs of depression: weight loss, listlessness, disturbed sleep pattern, waking early. High risk of suicide. E.C.T. treatments to continue. Cipramil in tablet form 40 mg / daily.

One of the nurses (I have nurses, imagine that) is called Johan. Or maybe Jonas? Jonny? He takes me for a walk. I'm not allowed out on my own. We don't go far. It still makes me incredibly tired. Perhaps he notices as we're walking back. He doesn't show it, though. Keeps talking the whole time. That's good, it means I don't have to bother.

He's talking about Muhammad Ali's title fight against George Foreman in 1974 in Zaire.

"He took so much punishment! Leaned against the ropes and just let Foreman keep hitting him. Foreman, well, he was cruel. We're talking heavyweights here, and most people have probably forgotten, but people were worried about Ali before the fight. Thought Foreman might actually kill him. And then Ali just stood there like a bloody . . . stone! And took the punishment for seven rounds. Completely psyched Foreman out. In the seventh he leaned against

Foreman's shoulder and whispered 'Is that all you got, George?' And it was! Then in the eighth, Foreman could hardly keep his guard up any longer, and then the opening came. Ali just went: bam! He made a right hook in the air. Foreman goes down like a pine tree! Crrrash!"

I walk in silence. Notice that the trees are starting to smell of autumn. And he's talking Rumble in the Jungle. I am the greatest. Thrilla in Manila.

Or he talks about the Second World War (is he supposed to do that with me, I wonder quietly to myself, aren't I sensitive, fragile, what would the consultant say?)

"The Japanese, now they're real warriors. You know, when their fighter pilots ran out of juice in the middle of the Pacific, if there was an American aircraft carrier within range they flew straight into it. Pow! Or they did an elegant belly landing on the surface of the water, just to show what incredibly skilful fliers they were. Then when they were sitting there having survived, they jumped into the water and stabbed themselves. Wouldn't let themselves be taken alive by the enemy. Same thing when they were fighting at Guadal Canal. They jumped off the cliffs like lemmings when they realized they were beaten. The Americans were standing there with their megaphones telling them to give themselves up."

When we get back to the ward I'm suddenly afraid that he'll ask me if I enjoyed the walk. If I liked it? If I'd like to do it again tomorrow?

I can't manage to answer "yes" or "that would be nice". It feels like it did when I was little. When some of the older ladies in the village bought you an ice cream or a drink. They always had to ask: "Was that nice?" Despite the fact that they could see. You were sitting there devouring it, in silent bliss. But you had to give them something. Pay the price. "Yes", and preferably "thank you" from the little girl, the poor little soul with the crazy mother. I have nothing to give now. Not even a squeak. If he asks me I'll have to say no. Although it was so good to breathe the air. The ward smells of medication sweated out through every pore, smoke, dirt, hospital, the cleaning fluid they use on the vinyl floor.

But he doesn't ask. Takes me for a stroll the following day too.

Extract from epicrisis October 30th re. patient Rebecka Martinsson
Patient has responded well to treatment. Suicide risk no longer regarded as likely. For the past two weeks has been nursed according to H.S.L. Low, but not seriously depressed. Transfer to residence in Kurravaara, village outside Kiruna, where patient grew up. To keep in contact with clinic in Kiruna. Continued medication Cipramil 40 mg / daily.

The consultant asks me how I'm feeling. I say: fine.

He looks at me in silence. Almost smiling. Knowing. He can keep quiet for as long as it takes. He is an expert at it. Silences don't provoke him. In the end I say: not too bad. That's the right answer. He nods.

I'm not allowed to stay here. I've taken up a place for long enough. There are women who need it more. The kind who set fire to their hair. Who come onto the ward and swallow pieces of broken mirror in the toilets, and have to be rushed into the emergency department all the time. I can talk, answer questions, get up in the morning and brush my teeth.

I hate him because he won't force me to stay here forever and ever. Because he isn't God.

Then I'm sitting on the train travelling north. The landscape hurtles past in a series of snapshots. First there are the big deciduous trees in tones of red and yellow. Autumn sunshine and lots of houses. People living their lives in every single one. Getting by somehow.

After Bastuträsk there's snow. And then at last: forest, forest,

forest. I'm on the way home. The birch trees shrink, standing black and skeletal against the white background.

I press my forehead and my nose against the window.

I feel fine, I say to myself. This is what it's like to feel fine.

SATURDAY, 15 MARCH, 2005

An early spring evening, Torneträsk. The ice was thick, more than a metre. All along the lake, some seventy kilometres long, lay arks, small cabins on runners, four square metres in size. At this time of year the inhabitants of Kiruna made their pilgrimage up to Torneträsk. They came up on snowmobiles, towing the arks behind them.

Inside the ark there was a hole in the floor. You drilled a hole through the thick ice below. A plastic pipe linked the hole in the ice to the hole in the floor, and that prevented the freezing wind from coming up into the ark. And then you sat inside fishing through the hole.

Leif Pudas was sitting in his ark in just his pants, fishing. It was 8.30 in the evening. He had cracked open a few beers, it was Saturday night after all. The Calor gas stove was hissing and whistling. It was lovely and warm, more than 25°C. And he had caught some fish too. Fifteen mountain char, only small, but better than nothing. And he had saved a few sprats for his sister's cat.

When it was time for a pee it felt like a kind of liberation: he was much too hot, it would be good to get outside and cool down a bit. He pulled on his boots and clambered out into the cold and dark in his pants.

As soon as he opened the door, the wind seized hold of it.

During the day it had been sunny and calm, with no wind. But in the mountains the weather changes constantly. Now the storm was tugging and snapping at the door like a rabid dog. One moment there was hardly any wind at all, it was as if it were lying there growling and gathering its strength, then it was pulling at the door for all it was worth. Would the hinges hold? Pudas took hold of the door with both hands and closed it behind him. Maybe he should have put some clothes on. Oh what the hell, it only took a minute to have a pee.

The gusts of wind carried loose snow with them. Not soft, fine fresh snow, but sharp diamond slivers of compacted snow. It whirled across the ground like a white cat o'nine tails, flaying his skin with a slow, evil rhythm.

Pudas ran around the ark to shelter from the wind and got ready to pee. He might be out of the wind, but it was cold so far up north. His scrotum contracted. But at least he managed to pee. He half expected it to freeze on its way through the air. To transform into a yellow arc of ice.

Just as he finished, he heard a kind of bellowing through the wind, and all of a sudden the ark was at his back. It almost knocked him over, and the next instant it was gone.

It took a little while for him to understand. The storm had taken the ark. He could see the window, the square of warm light in the darkness, travelling away from him.

He ran a little way, but now its mooring had come loose, the ark was gathering speed. He had no chance of catching up with it, it was hurtling away on its runners.

First of all he thought only about the ark. He had built it himself out of plywood, then insulated it and covered it with aluminium. Tomorrow morning when he found it, it would be firewood. All he could do was hope it did not cause any damage. That could lead to difficulties.

All of a sudden there came a powerful squall. It nearly knocked him to the ground. Then he realized he was in danger. And he had

17

all that beer inside him, it was as if his blood was just beneath the surface of the skin. If he did not manage to get inside somewhere very soon, he would freeze to death.

He looked around. It had to be at least a kilometre up to Abisko tourist station: he would never make it, it was a question of minutes now. Where was the closest ark? The whirling snow and the storm meant he couldn't see the lights of any other arks.

Think, he said to himself. You do not take one single bloody step until you have used your head. Which direction are you facing now?

He used his head for three seconds, felt his hands starting to stiffen, and tucked them under his arms. He took four steps from where he was standing and managed to walk straight into the snow-mobile. The key was in the disappearing ark, but he had a little toolbox under the seat, and he got it out.

Then he prayed to someone up there that he was going the right way, and set off in the direction of his closest neighbouring ark. It was no more than twenty metres, but he wanted to weep with every step. He was so afraid of missing it. And if he did, he was a dead man.

He searched for Persson's fibreglass ark. The wet snow covered his eyes; he tried to peer through, but it was as if a slush kept forming over his eyes and he had to wipe it away. It was impossible to see anything, darkness and snow.

He thought about his sister. And he thought about his ex-partner, about the fact that things had been good between them in many ways.

He had nearly walked straight into Persson's ark before he saw it. Nobody home, the windows dark. He took the hammer out of his toolbox, had to use his left hand; the right one was useless, pain shooting through it after holding the cold steel of the toolbox handle. He fumbled his way through the darkness to the small Plexiglas window and smashed it.

The fear made him strong, and he heaved his hundred kilos in through the window. Swore as he scraped his stomach on the sharp metal frame. But what did that matter? Death had never been so close before, breathing down his neck.

Once he was inside, he had to get some heat going. Even if he was protected from the wind, it was still bitterly cold inside the ark.

He rummaged in the drawers and found some matches. How can you hold something so small when the cold has made your hands completely useless? He pushed his fingers into his mouth to warm them until they were working well enough to allow him to light the lamp and the stove. His entire body just wanted to shiver and shake, never in his life had he felt this cold. Frozen to his bones.

"Bloody hell it's cold, fuck me it's cold," he said to himself over and over again. He spoke out loud; it somehow kept the panic at bay, as if he were keeping himself company.

The wind howled through the window like a malevolent god; he took a big cushion that was leaning against the wall and managed to wedge it fast between the curtain pole and the wall.

He looked around and found a red padded jacket, probably one of Mrs Persson's. He also found a drawer full of underwear, pulled on two pairs of long johns, one pair for his legs and the other for his head.

The warmth came slowly, he held his arms and legs out towards the stove, pain shooting through his body; it was agonizing. He had no feeling at all in one cheek and ear, which was not a good sign.

There was a heap of blankets on the bunk bed. They were ice cold, of course, but he could wrap himself in them anyway, they would provide some sort of insulation.

I've survived, he said to himself. What does it matter if I lose an ear?

He pulled a blanket off the bed. It was covered in big flowers in different shades of blue, a relic of the '70s.

And underneath it lay a woman. Her eyes were open and had

frozen to ice, so they were completely white, like frosted glass. Something that looked like porridge, or maybe it was vomit, on her chin and hands. She was wearing sports clothes. There was a red mark on her top.

He did not scream. He did not even feel surprised. It was as if his emotions had been completely erased.

"What the fuck," was all he said.

And the feeling that washed over him was like the feeling you get when your new puppy pees in the house for the hundredth time. Exhaustion at how tiresome everything is.

He resisted the impulse to simply put the blanket back and forget about her.

Then he sat down to think. What on earth should he do now? He had to get to the tourist station, of course. He was not too keen on going up there in the dark. But he had no choice, did he? And he didn't much like the idea of sitting here thawing out with her.

But he needed to sit here for a little while longer. Until he was not so damned cold.

It was like a kind of companionship between them. She kept him company as he sat there for an hour, tortured by the pain in various parts of his body as the warmth brought the feeling back. He held his hands out to the stove.

He didn't say a word. And neither did she.

Inspector Anna-Maria Mella and her colleague Sven-Erik Stålnacke reached the scene at quarter to midnight on Saturday. The police had borrowed two snowmobiles from Abisko tourist station. One of them had a sledge. One of the mountain guides had offered to help out, and he drove them both down. Storms and darkness.

Pudas, who had found the body, was sitting in the tourist station and had already been questioned by the squad car unit who had been first on the scene.

When Pudas arrived at the tourist station, the reception desk was closed. It had taken a while before the staff in the bar took him seriously. It was Saturday night after all, and they were more than used to unconventional dress at the tourist station; people would take off their snowmobile overalls and sit there drinking beer in their underwear and all sorts. But Pudas had come stumbling in dressed in a ladies' padded jacket that reached just below his navel, with a pair of long johns wound round his head like a turban.

It was not until he burst into tears that they realized something serious had happened. They had listened, then treated him somewhat warily while they contacted the police.

He had found a dead woman, he said. He had repeated several times that it was not his ark. They had still thought it was probably a matter of a man who had killed his wife. Nobody had wanted to look him in the eye. He had been sitting there all alone and weeping, disturbing no-one, when the police arrived.

It had proved impossible to seal off the area around the ark; the wind simply snatched the police tape away. Instead they had tied the black and yellow tape around the ark, wrapping it up like a parcel. The tape was flapping angrily in the wind. The technicians had arrived, and were working on the small surface area in the beam of the spotlights and the muted Calor gas light afforded by the ark itself.

There was not room for more than two people inside the ark. While the technicians were working, Mella and Stålnacke stood outside and tried to keep moving.

It was more or less impossible to hear each other through the storm and their thick hats. Even Stålnacke was wearing a hat with ear flaps; he did not normally wear anything on his head, even in the middle of winter. They yelled at each other and moved about like Michelin men in their snowmobile overalls.

"Look," Mella shouted. "This is ridiculous."

She spread out her arms, standing like a sail against the wind. She was a small woman and did not weigh a great deal. Besides which, the snow had melted during the day, then frozen again in the evening and turned shiny and icy, so when she positioned herself like that the wind had taken her and she began to glide slowly away.

Stålnacke laughed and pretended to hurry over to catch her before she slid off to the far side of the lake.

The technicians emerged from the ark.

"She wasn't murdered here, at any rate," one of them bawled at Mella. "Looks like she was stabbed. But as I said, not here. You can take the body. We'll carry on here in the morning when we can see what we're doing."

"And when we're not freezing our balls off," yelled his colleague, who was not dressed nearly warmly enough.

The technicians climbed onto the sledge and were driven off to the tourist station.

Mella and Stålnacke went into the ark.

It was cold and cramped.

"But at least we're out of that bloody wind," Stålnacke said as he closed the door. "That's better, we can talk normally."

The small folding table attached to the wall was covered in a wood-patterned material. Four white plastic chairs were stacked on top of one another. There was a small hotplate and a place to wash the dishes. A red and white checked café curtain and a vase of artificial flowers were lying on the floor beneath the Plexiglas window. A big cushion fixed in front of the window provided a reasonable amount of protection against the wind, which was desperate to get in.

Stålnacke opened the wardrobe. The equipment needed for distilling alcohol was inside. He closed the door.

"We didn't see that," was all he said.

Mella looked at the woman on the bed.

"One seventy-five?" she asked.

Stålnacke nodded, snapping small icicles from his moustache.

Mella took the tape recorder out of her pocket. She fought with it for a while, because the batteries had got cold and it did not want to work.

"Oh, come on," she said, holding it close to the stove, which was doing its best to warm the inside of the ark despite the broken window and the many gaps in the door.

When she got it going, she put the description in first.

"Female, blonde bob, in her forties . . . She's attractive, isn't she?"

Stålnacke mumbled something.

"Well, I think she's attractive anyway. About one metre seventy-five, slim build, large breasts. No rings on her fingers. Eye colour difficult to establish in the present circumstances, maybe the pathologist . . . Light-coloured tracksuit top, looks windproof, stains on it which are probably blood, but we'll find out soon enough, matching tracksuit bottoms, running shoes."

Mella leaned over the woman.

"And she's wearing make-up, lipstick, eye shadow and mascara," she continued into the tape recorder. "Wouldn't that be a bit odd, when you're going out to exercise? And why hasn't she got a hat?"

"It's been a lovely day, really warm, and yesterday was the same," said Stålnacke. "As long as you don't get that wind . . ."

"It's winter! You're the only person who never wears a hat. Her clothes don't look cheap, and neither does she. She's kind of elegant."

Mella switched off the tape recorder.

"We'll start knocking on doors tonight. The tourist station and the eastern side of Abisko. And we'll ask the shop owners if it's anybody they know. You'd think somebody would have reported her missing."

"I've got the feeling there's something familiar about her," Stålnacke said.

"Maybe she lives in Kiruna, then. Think about it. Maybe you've seen her somewhere? Dentist? Behind the counter in a shop? In the bank?"

Stålnacke shook his head.

"Leave it," he said. "It'll come to me if it wants to."

"We need to go round the other arks as well," Mella said.

"I know. And in this bloody storm."

"Still."

"Right."

They looked at each other for a while.

Stålnacke seemed tired, Mella thought. Tired and depressed. Murdered women always had that effect on him. The women lay there dead in their kitchens, their husbands in floods of tears in the bedroom, and you just had to be grateful if there were no small children who had seen it all happen.

It never really affected her that much, unless it involved children of course. Children and animals, you never got used to that. But a murder like this one. Not that it made her happy. Or that she thought it was a good thing, nothing like that. But a murder like this . . . it gave you something to get your teeth into, somehow. She needed that.

She smiled inwardly at Stålnacke's big, wet moustache. It looked like roadkill. Recently it had been more or less growing wild. She wondered how lonely he really was. His daughter lived in Luleå with her family. They probably rarely saw each other.

And then about eighteen months ago that cat of his had disappeared. Mella had tried to persuade him to get another one, but Stålnacke refused. "They're nothing but trouble," he said. "They're such a tie." She knew exactly what that meant. He wanted to protect himself from the anguish. God knows he had worried about Manne and pondered over what might have happened to him, until in the end he had given up hope and eventually stopped talking about him.

It was such a shame, thought Mella. Stålnacke was a good man. He would make a fine husband for someone. And a good master for any animal. He and Mella got on well, but it would never occur to them to spend their spare time together. It was not just that he was much older than her. They simply did not have that much in common. If they met by chance in town or in a shop when they were not working, it was always difficult to make conversation. But at work they would chat away and get on really well.

Stålnacke looked at Mella. She really was a little woman, no more than one metre fifty. She almost disappeared inside her big snow-mobile overalls. Her long blonde hair was flattened by the hat. Not that she cared. She wasn't one for make-up and that sort of thing. Probably didn't have the time either. Four kids and a husband who didn't seem to do much around the house. That aside, there was nothing wrong with Robert, things seemed to be good between him and Mella; he was just lazy.

Although how much had he actually done at home himself in the years he and Hjordis had been married? He didn't remember, but he did remember not being used to cooking when he was first living on his own.

"O.K.," Mella said. "What if you and I fight our way through the snowstorm and go round the arks, while the others take the village and the tourist station?"

Stålnacke grinned.

"Might as well, Saturday night's ruined anyway."

It wasn't really ruined. What would he have been doing otherwise? Watching T.V. and maybe taking a sauna with his neighbour. Always the same old routine.

"True," Mella said, zipping up her overalls.

Although she didn't actually feel like that. This was not a ruined Saturday night. A knight can't just stay at home nestling in the bosom of his family, he would go mad. He needs to get out there and draw his sword. To come home, tired and sated with adventures, to the family who have no doubt left their empty pizza boxes and fizzy drinks bottles in a heap on the living room table, but it did not matter. This was life at its best. Knocking on doors out on the ice in the darkness.

"Hope she didn't have kids," Mella said before they went off into the storm.

Stålnacke did not reply. He was a little ashamed. He hadn't even thought about children. He had only hoped there wasn't a cat shut in an apartment somewhere, waiting for its mistress.

NOVEMBER 2003

Rebecka Martinsson is discharged from the psychiatric clinic at St Göran's hospital. She takes the train up to Kiruna. Now she is sitting in a taxi outside her grandmother's house in Kurravaara.

Since her grandmother died, the house has belonged to Rebecka and her Uncle Affe. It is a grey stone house down by the river. Worn linoleum on the floors, damp patches on the walls.

The house used to smell old, but lived in. A permanent background aroma of wet Wellington boots, the barn, cooking and baking. Grandmother's own, safe smell. And Daddy's, of course, at that time. Now the house smells abandoned, closed up. The cellar is stuffed full of glass wool to keep away the chill that strikes up through the ground.

The taxi driver carries her suitcase inside. Asks if it's to go upstairs or downstairs.

"Upstairs," she says.

She used to live upstairs with her grandmother.

Daddy lived in the flat downstairs. The furniture is standing in there in a strangely silent, timeless sleep beneath big white sheets. Uncle Affe's wife Inga-Britt uses the ground floor as a storeroom. More and more banana boxes full of books and clothes are being gathered here, along with old chairs Inga-Britt has picked up cheaply and is intending to restore one day. Daddy's furniture beneath the sheets has to shuffle even closer to the walls.

The fact that it does not look the way it used to is no help. For Martinsson, nothing changes the flat on the ground floor.

Daddy has been dead for many years, but as soon as she walks through the door she can see him sitting there on the kitchen sofa. It is time for breakfast, upstairs with Grandmother. He has heard her coming down the stairs and has sat up quickly. He is wearing a red and black checked flannel shirt and a blue Helly Hansen sweater. His blue work trousers are tucked into the long thick socks that Grandmother knitted. His eyes are slightly swollen. When he catches sight of her, he runs his hand over his stubbly chin and smiles.

She can see a great deal now that she did not see then. Or perhaps she did? Running his hand over his stubble – she can see now that it was a sign of embarrassment. What does it matter to her? The fact that he does not shave? That he has slept in his clothes? Not one atom. He's handsome, handsome.

And the beer can standing on the draining board. It is so battered and scuffed. It is a long time since it held beer. He drinks something else out of it, but he wants the neighbours to think it is ordinary beer.

I never cared about that, she wants to say to him. It was Mummy who went on about it. I loved you.

The taxi has gone. She has lit the open fire and switched on the radiators.

She is lying on her back in the kitchen on one of grandmother's rag rugs. Following a fly. It is buzzing loudly, in distress. Thumping against the ceiling, as if it is blind. They get like that, the ones that wake up because the house is warm. A tortured, tense noise, its flight slow and erratic. It lands on the wall now, wandering listlessly and aimlessly. It has no ability to react. She could probably swat it with her bare hand. Then she wouldn't have to listen to the noise any more. But she cannot summon the strength. Lies there watching it instead. It will die soon anyway. Then she can sweep it up.

DECEMBER 2003

It is Tuesday. Every Tuesday, Martinsson goes into town. Has a session with her therapist and collects her weekly dose of Cipramil. The therapist is a woman in her forties. Martinsson tries not to despise her. Cannot help looking at her shoes and thinking "cheap", and at her jacket and thinking it doesn't fit properly.

But despising another person is a treacherous thing to do. It suddenly turns around: What about you? You haven't even got a job.

The therapist asks Martinsson to tell her about her childhood.

"What for?" Martinsson says. "That's not why I'm here, is it?"

"Why are you here, do you think?"

She is so tired of these stock questions being fired back at her. She looks at the carpet to conceal her expression.

What could she say? The least thing is like a red button. If you press it, you don't know what might happen. You remember drinking a glass of milk, and then everything else comes flooding in.

I have no intention of wallowing in all that, she thinks, glaring at the box of tissues that is always there at the ready, just in case, on the desk between them.

She looks at herself from the outside. Can't work. Sits there on the cold toilet seat in the morning popping the tablets out of the box, afraid of what will happen if she doesn't.

There are many words. Embarrassing, pathetic, feeble, disgusting, revolting, a burden, crazy, sick. Murderer.

She has to be a little bit nice to the therapist. Meet her halfway. On the road to recovery. Not always such hard work.

I'll tell her about something, she thinks. Next time.

She could make something up. She has done that before.

She could say: My mother. I don't think she loved me. And perhaps that really is not untrue. More of a small truth. But this small truth is hiding the big truth.

I didn't cry when she died, thinks Martinsson. I was eleven years old, and cold as ice. There is something wrong with me, something fundamental.

NEW YEAR'S EVE 2003

Martinsson is celebrating New Year's Eve with Sivving Fjällborg's dog, Bella. Sivving Fjällborg is her neighbour. He was a friend of her grandmother's when Martinsson was little.

He asked if she would like to go with him to his daughter Lena and her family. Martinsson wriggled out of it, and he did not push it again. Instead he left the dog behind. It isn't usually a problem to take Bella along. He said he needed a guard dog, but in fact it is Martinsson who needs guarding. It doesn't matter. She is glad of the company.

Bella is a lively pointer. She loves her food like all pointers, and would be as fat as a sausage if she were not always on the move. Fjällborg lets her run off the worst of her restlessness down on the river, and he usually manages to persuade some of the villagers to take her hunting from time to time. She paces about in the house, winding herself around your legs – it's enough to drive you mad. Jumps up and barks at the least sound. But the constant activity keeps her as thin as a rake. You can see her ribs quite clearly beneath her skin.

Most of the time, lying down is a punishment. But at the moment Bella is lying on Martinsson's bed, snoring. Martinsson has been skiing along the river for several hours. At the beginning she had to drag Bella with her. Then she let her off the lead, and Bella scampered here and there kicking up the snow around her. For the last few kilometres she trotted along happily in Martinsson's tracks.

At about ten o'clock Måns Wenngren rings; he used to be Martinsson's boss at the office.

When she hears his voice, her hand moves to her hair. As if he could see her.

She has thought about him. Often. And she thinks he rang and asked about her when she was in the hospital. But she is not sure. She remembers things so hazily. She thinks she told the nurse in charge of the ward that she did not want to speak to him. The electric shock treatment made her so confused. And her short-term memory disappeared. She became like an old person, saying the same thing several times in the course of a few minutes. She didn't want anything to do with anyone at the time. And certainly not Wenngren. She didn't want him to see her like that.

"How's it going?" he says.

"Fine," she says; she feels like one of those automatic pianos when she hears his voice. "How about you?"

"Bloody great, fantastic."

Now it is her turn to say something. She tries to come up with something sensible, preferably something funny, but her brain is not working at all.

"I'm sitting in a hotel room in Barcelona," he says at last.

"I'm watching television with my neighbour's dog. He's gone to celebrate New Year with his daughter."

Wenngren does not answer straight away. It takes a second. Martinsson listens. Afterwards she will sit and analyse that silent second like a teenager. Did it mean anything? What? A stab of jealousy about the unknown male neighbour with the dog?

"What kind of man is he, then?" Wenngren says.

"Oh, it's Sivving. He's retired, he lives over the road."

She tells him about Fjällborg. How he lives down in the boiler room with his dog. Because it's simpler. He has got everything he needs down there including a refrigerator, a shower and a hotplate.

And there is less housework if you don't spread yourself all over the place. She tells him how he got his name. That his real name is Erik, but that his mother, in a fit of pride, had his civil engineer title added to the telephone book: "civ. ing." And that the retribution had swiftly followed in the village, where it was not done to regard oneself as better than anyone else: "Oh, yes, here comes civ.ing himself."

Wenngren laughs. So does Martinsson. And then they laugh a little more, mostly because they haven't got anything to say. He asks if it is cold. She clambers up onto the sofa and looks at the thermometer.

"Minus thirty-two degrees."

"Bloody hell!"

Silence again. A little too long. Then he says quickly:

"I just wanted to wish you Happy New Year . . . I mean, I'm still your boss after all."

What does he mean by that, wonders Martinsson. Is he ringing the whole office? Or just those he knows don't have a life? Or maybe he actually cares?

"Happy New Year to you too," she says, and since the words are bordering on the formal, she allows her voice to soften.

"Right . . . well . . . I'll probably go out and take a look at the fireworks . . ."

"And I've got to take the dog out . . ."

When they have hung up, she sits there with the receiver in her hand. Was he alone in Barcelona? Hardly likely. It was all a bit quick there at the end. Did she hear a door open? Did somebody come in? Was that why he ended the conversation so abruptly?

JUNE 2004

It was fortunate that Rebecka Martinsson did not witness Chief Prosecutor Alf Björnfot begging to be allowed to give her a job. If she had, her pride would have made her turn it down.

Chief Prosecutor Björnfot is in a meeting with his boss, head of chambers Margareta Huuva, over an early dinner, and he chooses a place with real linen napkins and real flowers on the tables.

This puts Huuva in a good mood; what is more, the boy who is serving them pulls her chair out for her and pays her a compliment.

You would have thought they were out on a date. A couple who got together late in life; both are over sixty.

Huuva is a short, rather stocky woman. Her silver-grey hair is cut flatteringly short, and her lipstick matches the pink polo-neck jumper she is wearing under her blue jacket.

As Björnfot is sitting down, he notices that the corduroy at the knees of his trousers is more or less worn away. The flaps on his jacket pockets are always pushed halfway in; they get like that because they are in his way when he stuffs things into his pockets.

"Stop shoving a load of crap in your pockets," his daughter scolds him as she tries to smooth the crumpled flaps.

Huuva asks Björnfot to tell her why he wants to take on Martinsson.

"I need somebody in my area who knows about financial crime," he says. "The mining company, L.K.A.B., is contracting out more and more work. We're getting an increasing number of firms up there, and that means more and more financial entanglements to sort out. If we manage to persuade Martinsson to work for us, we'll get a lot of lawyer for our money. She worked for one of Sweden's top business law firms before she moved up here."

"You mean before she became mentally ill," Huuva says sharply. "What actually happened to her?"

"I wasn't involved, but she killed those three guys in Jiekajärvi a couple of years ago. It was a clear case of self-defence, so there was never any question of a prosecution. And then . . . when she was just getting over that, there was the incident in Poikkijärvi. Lars-Gunnar Vinsa locked her in the cellar, then shot himself and his son. And when she saw the boy, she just went to pieces."

"Ended up in a secure unit."

"Yes. She didn't even know what day it was."

Björnfot falls silent, thinking about what Mella and Stålnacke told him. How Martinsson had screamed like a lunatic. Seen things and people that did not exist. How they had had to hold onto her to stop her walking into the river.

"And this is the person you want me to appoint as a special prosecutor."

"She's fine now. This opportunity won't come again. If this hadn't happened to her, she'd have stayed down there in Stockholm earning a ton of money. But she's come home. And I don't think she wants to carry on working in an office."

"Calle von Post says she didn't do a particularly good job when she was representing Sanna Strandgård."

"But that's because she wiped the floor with him! You can't listen to him. He thinks the sun rises out of his bloody arse in the mornings."

Huuva smiles and looks down at her plate. Personally, she has no problem with von Post. He is the kind of man who is always nice to those higher up the chain. But it's true, deep down he is a self-obsessed little shit; she is not so stupid she doesn't realize that.

"Six months, then. To start with."

Chief Prosecutor Björnfot groans.

"No, no. She's a lawyer; she earns more than twice as much as I do. I can't offer a provisional position."

"I don't care whether she's a lawyer or not. Right now we don't even know whether she can manage to sort out fruit in a supermarket. It's provisional, and that's the end of it."

And so the decision is made. They move onto more agreeable topics of conversation, exchanging gossip about colleagues, police officers, judges and local politicians.

A week later, Björnfot is sitting with Martinsson on the steps outside the house in Kurravaara.

The swallows slice through the air like knives. There is a clattering noise as they hurtle down beneath the roof of the barn. Then they are off again. You can hear their young, tweeting imploringly.

Martinsson looks at Björnfot. A man in his sixties, horrible trousers, reading glasses on a cord around his neck. He seems like a nice man. She wonders if he is good at his job.

They are drinking coffee out of mugs, and she offers him a digestive biscuit out of the packet. He has come to offer her a job as a special prosecutor in Kiruna.

"I need somebody good," he says simply. "Somebody who'll stay."

As she is replying, he sits with his eyes closed and his face turned up towards the sun. He hasn't much hair left; you can see the age spots on the top of his head.

"I don't know if I can do that sort of job any longer," Martinsson says. "I don't trust my head."

"But it's such a waste if you don't even try," he says, without opening his eyes. "Try it for six months. If it doesn't work out, then it doesn't work out."

"I went crazy, you know that?"

"Yes, I know the police officers who found you."

She is reminded of it once again. The fact that she is a topic of conversation.

Björnfot still has his eyes closed. He is thinking about what he has just said. Should he have said something different? No, best to be straight with this girl.

"Were they the ones who told you I'd moved back up here?" she says.

"That's right, one of them has a cousin who lives here in Kurravaara."

Martinsson laughs. It is a dry, joyless sound.

"It's only me who doesn't know anything about anybody."

"It all got too much for me," she says after a moment. "Nalle, lying there dead on the gravel. I really liked him. And his father . . . I thought he was going to kill me."

He grunts in reply. Eyes still closed. Martinsson takes the opportunity to look at him. And it is easier to talk when he is not looking at her.

"It's the sort of thing you think is never going to happen to you. At first I was so scared it would happen again. And that I'd be stuck there. Living the rest of my life in a nightmare."

"Are you still afraid it'll happen again?"

"At any moment, you mean? You're just walking across the road, and then . . . kapow!"

She clenches her fist and opens it out, spreading her fingers, as if to illustrate a firework of insanity.

"No," she says. "I needed the insanity just then. Reality was too heavy for me."

"Anyway, none of that concerns me," Björnfot says.

And now he is looking at her.

"I need good prosecutors."

He falls silent, speaks again. Much later, Martinsson will remember his words and think that he knew exactly what he was doing. How to handle her. She will discover that he really does know about people.

"Although of course I do understand if you're not sure about it. The position is in Kiruna, after all. So it'll be bloody lonely. The other prosecutors are based in Gällivare and Luleå, and they only come up here when the criminal court is sitting. The idea is for you to take most of the sessions. A secretary will come up one day a week and deal with applications for summons, that sort of thing. So it'll be pretty isolated."

Martinsson promises to think it over. But that business about working alone seals the deal. No people around her. That, and the fact that somebody from her insurance company had rung up just a week earlier and talked about training and a gradual return to working life. It had made Martinsson feel sick with fear. Being shoved together with a load of burnt-out no-hopers and being made to take her driving licence or join in some positive-thinking course.

"The respite is over," she says to Fjällborg that evening. "I might as well give the prosecution service a go as anything else."

Fjällborg is standing by the stove, turning over slices of blood pudding.

"Stop giving the dog bread under the table," he says. "I can see you. What about your lawyer's job, then?"

"Never again."

She thinks about Måns Wenngren. She will have to resign now. She has felt like a burden on the firm for a long time. He will disappear forever.

It's fine, she says to herself. What would a life with him be like? You'd be going through his pockets while he was asleep, searching for receipts and yellow credit card slips to check that he hasn't been out drinking. His past would certainly put you off. Is it possible for anybody to be worse at maintaining relationships? Sporadic contact with his grown-up children. Divorced. Nothing but short-term relationships.

She makes a list of his faults. It doesn't help in the slightest.

When she was working for him, he would touch her sometimes. "Well done, Martinsson," and then the touch. His hand around her upper arm. Once, a brief caress of her hair.

I'm going to stop thinking about him, she tells herself. It just drives you bloody mad. Your whole head is full of some man, his hands, his mouth, what he looks like, and all the rest of it. You can go for months without thinking a single sensible thought.

SUNDAY, 16 MARCH, 2005

The dead woman came sailing through the darkness towards Inspector Mella. She was floating in the air as she would have done if a magician had waved his wand over her and made her rise, lying on her back with her arms pressed closely to her sides.

Who are you? thought Mella.

Her white skin and those eyes of frosted glass made her look like a statue. Her features were also reminiscent of a marble statue from antiquity. The bridge of her nose was set high up between her eyebrows, her forehead and nose forming an unbroken line in profile.

Gustav, Mella's three-year-old, turned over in his sleep and gave her a series of kicks in the side. She got hold of his small but muscular body and turned him firmly so that he was lying with his bottom and back towards her instead. She drew him close and stroked his tummy with circular movements, nuzzling his night-sweaty hair with her nose and kissing him. He sighed contentedly in his sleep.

It was just so blissful and so sensual, this time with the children. They grew up so quickly, and that was the end of the nuzzling. Mella dreaded the time when they would no longer have a small child in the house. Hopefully there would be grandchildren. She could always hope that Marcus, her eldest, would start early.

And there is always Robert in an emergency, she thought, smiling at her sleeping husband. There are advantages to hanging onto the same man you've had from the start. However wrinkly and saggy

I get, he will still see the girl he got to know at the dawn of time.

Or else you have to get a load of dogs, she thought. Who'll be allowed to sleep on the bed with filthy paws and slavering jaws and all the rest of it.

She let go of Gustav and groped for her mobile, looked at the clock: 4.30 a.m.

One cheek was burning. She had probably got a touch of frostbite the previous evening when she and Stålnacke were knocking on doors out there on the ice. But nobody in the arks close by had seen anything. She and her colleagues had asked around up at the mountain centre, woken up the tourists who were there for the skiing and kept the people in the bar behind. Nobody could tell them anything about the woman. The owners of the ark where she had been lying had also been traced. They had seemed genuinely shocked, and did not recognize the picture of the dead woman.

Mella tried to picture likely scenarios. Obviously it is possible for a person to go out running along snowmobile tracks while wearing make-up. Or maybe she was running along Norgevägen. A car stops. It is somebody she knows. Somebody who asks if she would like a lift. And then? She gets in the car and somebody hits her over the head? Or she goes along and takes a sauna, gets raped, fights back, gets stabbed.

Or it might have been somebody she didn't know. She is running along Norgevägen. A man drives past her in a car. He turns around a little way ahead. Maybe he runs into her with the car and drags her into the back seat; that would make her easy to handle. And not a soul in sight. He drives her to a cottage . . .

Mella turned her pillow over and told herself to try and get back to sleep.

Maybe she wasn't raped, she thinks. Maybe she was jogging along in the snowmobile tracks on the lake. Met some bloody lunatic with his body full of drugs and a knife in his pocket. There are people like that everywhere. Up on the marshes too. Every woman's nightmare. Just happening to come across the wrong man at the very moment when the madness strikes.

Stop it, she says to herself. No fully formed images in your head before you actually know anything.

She needs to talk to the Medical Examiner, Lars Pohjanen. He had travelled up from Luleå the previous evening. The question was whether they had managed to do anything with the frozen body.

Staying in bed was completely pointless. And why should she go back to sleep, anyway? She wasn't tired, after all. Her head was full of adrenaline-pumped brain cells playing guessing games.

She got up and dressed. She was used to doing it in the dark, so she was quick and silent.

It was 5.05 in the morning when Mella parked her red Ford Escort outside the hospital. The Securitas guard let her into the culvert that ran beneath the building. The ventilation pipes humming on the ceiling. Deserted corridors. A scruffy vinyl floor and the sound of automatic doors opening ahead of her. She met a caretaker, whizzing along on a kick scooter, otherwise everything was peaceful and quiet.

The lights were out in the autopsy room, but in the smoking room Lars Pohjanen, the medical examiner, was lying on the battered 1970s sofa just as she had hoped. He was lying with his back to the room, his thin body moving up and down in time with his laborious breathing.

A few years ago he had undergone an operation for throat cancer. His technician, Anna Granlund, took care of more and more of his work. She sawed open the chest cavity, lifted out organs, took the necessary samples, put the organs back, sutured stomachs, carried Pohjanen's bags, answered the telephone, put the most important calls through, which effectively meant those from his wife, made sure his lab coat was washed between shifts and wrote up his reports.

By the side of the sofa, his battered clogs stood neatly. Once upon a time they had been white. In Mella's imagination, Granlund tucked the medical examiner in with the checked blanket that lay over him, placed his clogs tidily beside the sofa, removed the cigarette from his mouth and turned out the light before she went home.

Mella took off her jacket and settled down in an armchair that matched the sofa.

Thirty years of accumulated dust, and thoroughly permeated with smoke, she thought, pulling the jacket over her like a blanket. Nice.

She fell asleep at once.

Half an hour later she was woken by the sound of Pohjanen coughing. He was sitting on the sofa leaning forwards, and it sounded as if half his lungs were due to end up on his knee.

All at once Mella felt stupid and uncomfortable. Sneaking in like that and sleeping in the same room. It was almost as if she had crept into his bedroom and got into his bed.

There he sat with his morning cough and the Grim Reaper's arm around his shoulders. It was not the sort of thing just anybody should witness.

He is angry now, she thought. What did I come here for?

Pohjanen's attack of coughing ended with a strangled clearing of his throat. His hand automatically patted his jacket pocket to reassure himself that his cigarettes were there.

"What do you want? I haven't even started on her yet. She was frozen solid when she came in last night."

"I needed somewhere to sleep," Mella said. "Home's full of children sprawled across the bed kicking their legs out and enjoying themselves."

He glared at her, amused despite himself.

"And Robert farts in his sleep," she said.

He sneezed to hide the fact that he was mollified, stood up and jerked his head to indicate that she should go with him.

Granlund had just arrived. She was standing in the sluice emptying the dishwasher, just like any housewife. The only difference was that it was knives, pincers, tweezers, scalpels and stainless steel bowls she was taking out instead of cutlery and crockery.

"She's such a *hätähousu*," Pohjanen said to Granlund, nodding towards Mella.

"Stress pants," he supplied, when he saw that Granlund didn't understand.

Granlund gave Mella a restrained smile. She liked Mella, but wished people wouldn't come in here and stress out her boss.

"Has she thawed?" asked Pohjanen.

"Not completely," Granlund said.

"Come back this afternoon and you can have a preliminary report," said Pohjanen to Mella. "Some of the tests will take a while, but that's always the way."

"Can't you tell me anything at this stage?" Mella said, trying not to sound like a *hätähousu*.

Pohjanen shook his head, as if he had given up completely when it came to Mella.

"O.K., let's take a look," he said.

The woman was lying on the fixed autopsy table. Mella noticed that fluid had run out of the body and down into the drain beneath the bench.

Down into the drinking water? she wondered.

Pohjanen caught her expression.

"She's thawing out," he said. "But it's going to be difficult to examine her, that's obvious. The muscle cell walls split and become loose."

He pointed at the woman's chest.

"This is an entry wound here," he said. "You could assume that's what killed her."

"A knife?"

"No, no. This is something else, although probably something pointed."

"Some kind of tool? An awl?"

Pohjanen shrugged.

"You'll have to wait," he said. "But it seems to have been perfectly placed. You can see she's bled comparatively little onto her clothes. Presumably the blow went straight through the cartilage in the thorax and into the pericardium, so you end up with a cardiac tamponade."

"A tamponade?"

Pohjanen became snappy.

"Haven't you learned anything over the years? If the blood hasn't run out of the body, where has it gone? Well, presumably the pericardium has filled up with blood, so that in the end the heart couldn't beat any longer. It happens quite quickly. The pressure drops too, which also means that you don't bleed so much. It could be a pulmonary tamponade too, a litre in the lungs, and that means it's curtains. And it has to be longer than an awl, there's an exit wound on her back."

"Something that went right through! Bloody hell."

"Furthermore," Pohjanen continued, "no external signs of rape. Look here."

He shone a torch between the dead woman's legs.

"No bruises or scratches there. You can see she's been hit in the face, here and . . . look here, there's blood in her nostril and a slight swelling above the nose, and somebody has wiped blood from her upper lip. But there are no strangulation marks, no sign of restraints around the wrists. This, however, is strange."

He pointed at one of the woman's ankles.

"What is it?" Mella said. "A burn mark?"

"Yes, the skin is very obviously burned. A narrow, circular injury around the whole ankle. And there's something else that's odd."

"Yes?"

"Her tongue. She's chewed it completely to pieces. Very common in serious road traffic accidents, for example. With a shock of that kind . . . but from a stabbing, I've never seen that. And if it was a tamponade and it happened so quickly . . . No, that's a little mystery, that is."

"Can I have a look?" Mella said.

"It's just mincemeat," said Granlund, hanging up clean towels by the sink. "I was going to put some coffee on, would you both like a cup?"

Mella and the medical examiner accepted the offer of coffee as Pohjanen shone his torch into the dead woman's mouth.

"Ugh," Mella said. "So maybe the blow didn't kill her? What was it, then?"

"I might be able to tell you that this afternoon. The stab wound is fatal, I must emphasize that. But the sequence of events isn't clear at all. And look at this."

He turned one of the woman's palms towards Mella.

"This can also be a sign of shock. You can see the marks. She's clenched her fists and driven her own nails deep into her palms."

Pohjanen stood there with the woman's hand in his, smiling to himself.

That's why I like working with him, Mella thought. He still really enjoys it. The trickier and the more difficult, the better.

She realized with a twinge of guilt that she was comparing him with Stålnacke.

But Stålnacke has become so half-hearted, she defended herself. And what am I supposed to do about it? I have enough to do injecting enthusiasm into the kids at home.

They drank their coffee in the smoking room. Pohjanen lit a cigarette, pretending not to see the look Granlund gave him.

"The business with the tongue is very peculiar," Mella said. "It's often a result of shock, you said? And then that faint mark around her ankle . . . But the stab wound went through her clothes, so she must have been dressed when she was murdered?"

"Although I don't think she'd been out running," Granlund said. "Did you see her bra?"

"No."

"Top of the range. Lace and underwiring. Aubade, that's a really expensive label."

"How do you know?"

"One might have treated oneself from time to time, in the days when one still had hopes."

"Not a sports bra, then?"

"Not even close."

"If only we could find out who she was," Mella said.

"I keep thinking there's something familiar about her," Granlund said.

Mella perked up.

"Stålnacke thought so too," she said. "Try to think where you've seen her. In the supermarket? At the dentist's? *Big Brother*?"

Granlund shook her head thoughtfully.

Pohjanen stubbed out his cigarette.

"Right, go and disturb somebody else," he said. "I'll open her up later on today, then we'll see if we can find out more about that mark around her ankle."

"Who am I going to disturb at this time?" Mella said. "Twenty to seven on a Sunday morning. There's nobody up but you two."

"Excellent," Pohjanen said dryly. "Then you'll have the pleasure of waking them all up."

"Yes," Mella said seriously. "I'll do just that."

Chief Prosecutor Björnfot stamped the compacted snow off his boots and carefully scraped the soles clean when he entered the corridor of the police station. Three years ago he had been in a hurry, slipped on his icy soles and banged his hip. He had been on painkillers for a week after that.

A sign of old age, he thought. Being afraid of falling over.

He did not usually work at the weekends. And certainly not this early on a Sunday morning. But Inspector Mella had telephoned the previous evening and told him about the dead woman who had been found in an ark up on the marshes, and he had asked for a briefing the following morning.

The prosecution offices were on the top floor of the police station. The Chief Prosecutor glanced guiltily at the stairs and pressed the button to call the lift.

As he passed Martinsson's room he had the feeling that there was somebody in there. Instead of going into his office, he turned, went back, knocked on the door and opened it.

Martinsson looked up from behind her desk.

She must have heard me in the lift and the corridor, he thought. But she doesn't let on. Just sits there, quiet as a mouse, hoping not to be discovered.

He did not think she disliked him. And she was not shy, even if she was a lone wolf. She wanted to hide how hard she worked, he supposed.

"It's seven o'clock," he said as he walked in, removed a pile of documents from the visitor's chair, and sat down.

"Hi there. Come in. Have a seat."

"O.K., O.K. We operate an open door policy here, you know. It's Sunday morning. Have you moved in?"

"Yes. Would you like a coffee? I've got a flask. Instead of the old water from the L.K.A.B. pelletizing plant that's in the machine."

She poured him a coffee.

He had thrown her straight into the job as special prosecutor. She was not the type to start off gently, observing somebody else for weeks on end, and he had realized that from day one. They had gone to Gällivare, sixty miles to the south, where the rest of the district prosecutors were based. She had gone round politely saying hello to everybody, but had seemed restless and ill at ease.

On the second day he had dumped a pile of files on her desk.

"Small beer," he had said. "File the prosecution and let the girls in the office do the processing. If you're not sure of anything, you have only to ask."

He had thought that would last her a week.

The following day she had asked for more work.

Her work rate made her colleagues uneasy.

The other prosecutors joked with her, asking if she was trying to put them out of a job. Behind her back they said she didn't have a life, and in particular that she didn't have a sex life.

The women in the office were annoyed. They explained to their boss that the new woman could not possibly expect them to keep up with processing the summons applications in all the cases she was raining down on them, they did actually have other things to do.

"Such as?" Martinsson had asked when the chief prosecutor explained the problem as delicately as he could. "Surfing the net? Playing Solitaire on their computers?"

Then she had held up her hand before he could open his mouth to reply.

"It's O.K. I'll do it myself."

Björnfot let her carry on working that way. She could be her own secretary.

"It'll work out fine," he said to the office manager. "You won't have to come up to Kiruna so often."

The office manager did not think it was fine at all. It was difficult to regard oneself as indispensable when Martinsson seemed to be managing perfectly well without a secretary. She took her revenge by handing three criminal court sessions a week to Martinsson. Two would have been too many.

Martinsson responded by not complaining.

Björnfot did not like conflict. He knew it was the secretaries, led by the office manager, who ruled his district. He appreciated the fact that Martinsson didn't moan, and found more and more reasons to work in Kiruna rather than Gällivare.

He turned his cup around. It was good coffee.

At the same time, he did not want her to work herself to death. He wanted her to be happy here. To stay.

"You work hard," he said.

Martinsson sighed and pushed back her chair. She kicked off her shoes.

"I'm used to working like this," she said. "You don't need to worry. Hard work wasn't my problem."

"I know, but . . ."

"I have no children. No family. Not even pot plants, actually. I like working hard. Let me get on with it."

Björnfot shrugged. He felt relieved; at least he had tried.

Martinsson took a gulp of her coffee and thought about Måns Wenngren. In the law firm you just worked yourself to death. But that was fine by her, she had had nothing else to do.

I must have been out of my mind, she thought. I could work all night just for a curt "good" from him, or even a nod of approval.

Don't think about him, she told herself.

"What brings you here today?"

Björnfot told her about the woman they had found in the ark.

"I don't think it's all that strange that she hasn't been reported missing," Martinsson said. "If somebody's killed his wife or partner, he'll be sitting there drinking himself under the table, crying and feeling sorry for himself. And nobody else has had enough time to miss her yet."

"Could be."

There was a knock, and Inspector Mella stuck her head round the door.

"Oh, so this is where you are," she said cheerfully to the Chief Prosecutor. "We're ready to go over the whole thing. Everybody's here. Are you joining us?"

The question was addressed to Martinsson.

Martinsson shook her head. She and Anna-Maria Mella bumped into each other sometimes. They said hello, but not much more. It was Mella and her colleague Stålnacke who had been there when she cracked up. Stålnacke had held onto her until the ambulance arrived. She thought about it sometimes. Somebody holding onto her. It had felt good.

But it was difficult to talk to them. What would she say? Before she went home from work, she usually glanced out of the window at the parking lot below. Sometimes she saw Mella or Stålnacke there. When that happened, she would hang about for a little while until they'd gone.

"What's happened?" Björnfot said.

"Nothing since we last spoke," Mella said. "Nobody saw a thing. We still don't know who she is."

"Can I have a look at her?" Björnfot said, reaching out his hand.

Mella passed over a photograph of the dead woman.

"I think I recognize her," Björnfot said.

"May I?" said Martinsson.

Björnfot passed over the photograph and looked at Martinsson.

She was wearing jeans and a jumper. He had never seen her like that since she had started working for him. It was because it was Sunday. She normally had her hair up, and wore well-tailored suits. It made him think she was a kind of strange, exotic bird. Some of the other prosecutors would put on a suit if they were involved in proceedings. He himself had given that up long ago. Made do with pulling on a jacket if he had to go to court. He ironed only the collars of his shirts, and wore a jumper over the top.

But Martinsson always looked expensive, somehow. Expensive and very simple in her grey and black suits with white shirts.

Something stirred in his mind. That woman. He had seen her wearing a suit.

Like Martinsson. A white shirt and a suit. She was an exotic bird too.

Different from the others.

What others?

A picture of a female politician came into his head. A suit, with the shirt collar on the outside. The hair in a blonde bob. She is surrounded by smartly dressed men.

The thought was lurking just out of reach, like a pike among the reeds. It could feel the vibrations of something approaching. The E.U.? U.N.?

No. She wasn't a politician.

"Now I remember," he said. "I was watching a news item. They were filming a gang of executives who had got together for a group photo in the snow here in Kiruna. What the hell was it about? I remember laughing because they weren't dressed for the weather at all. No overcoats. Thin black shoes. They stood there in the snow lifting their feet up like storks. They just looked so funny. She was one of them . . ."

He beat his forehead as if to force the coin to drop down into the machine and pay out.

Martinsson and Mella waited patiently.

"Got it . . ." he said, clicking his fingers. "It was that former resident of Kiruna who has one of those new mining companies. They were having their company meeting or something like that up here . . . Oh, what's the matter with my brain?"

"Come on!" he said pleadingly to Martinsson and Mella. "It was on the news before Christmas."

"I fall asleep on the sofa after the children's programmes," Mella said.

"Oh!" Björnfot said. "I'll ask Fred Olsson. He's bound to know."

Inspector Olsson was thirty-five, and completely indispensable as the unofficial computer expert for the whole building. He was the one everybody rang when the computer had frozen or when they wanted to download music from the net. He had no family, so he was happy to come over in the evening and help his colleagues with their electronics at home if need be.

And he kept an eye on people in town. He knew where the villains lived and what they were up to. Bought them a coffee from time to time and kept himself informed. He knew the fine-meshed net of power. Knew which of the important people in town were watching each other's backs, and whether it was because they were related, because they had something on each other, or because they were doing each other a mutual favour.

Björnfot got up and plodded along the corridor and down the stairs to police headquarters.

Mella gave Martinsson a signal, and both women hurried after him.

On the way to Olsson's office, Björnfot suddenly turned back to the women and shouted:

"Kallis. Mauri Kallis, that's his name. He was born here, although it's a long time since he moved away."

Then he carried on towards Olsson's office.

"What's Mauri Kallis got to do with anything?" Mella muttered to Martinsson. "It was a woman we found."

All three of them were standing in the doorway of Olsson's office.

"Fred!" puffed the prosecutor. "Mauri Kallis! Didn't he have a meeting up here with a load of bigwigs in December?"

"He did," Olsson said. "Kallis Mining has a company here in town called Northern Explore Ltd, one of the few companies of theirs that's listed on the stock exchange. A Canadian investment company sold all their shares at the end of the year, so there were a lot of changes on the board . . ."

"Can you find a picture of the meeting?"

Olsson turned his back on the three people in his doorway and switched on the computer. The three waited patiently.

"They elected somebody from Kiruna, Sven Israelsson, onto the board," said Olsson. "I'll do a search on him. If I look for Mauri Kallis I'm bound to get thousands of hits."

"I've got a vague memory of a gang of suits standing in the snow having their picture taken," Björnfot said. "I think the woman in the ark was in that picture."

Olsson tapped away at his keyboard for a little while. Then he said: "There. Looks like it is her."

On the screen was a picture of a group of smartly dressed men. In the centre of the picture stood a woman.

"Yes," said Mella. "She's got that antique nose, it kind of starts up between her eyebrows."

"Inna Wattrang, head of information," read Björnfot.

"Bingo!" said Mella. "Get her formally identified. Inform her next of kin. I wonder how she ended up on the marsh."

"Kallis Mining has a cabin in Abisko," Olsson said.

"You're joking!"

"It's true! I know because my sister's ex is a plumbing and heating engineer. And he was working up there when they built it. And it isn't really a cabin. More like a proper house with top sports facilities, something like that."

Mella turned to Björnfot.

"No problem," he said before she could get the question out. "I'll sign a search warrant straight away. Shall I ring Benny the locksmith?"

"Please," said Mella. "Let's go!" she shouted, racing to her room to pick up her jacket. "We'll do the briefing this afternoon!"

Her voice could be heard from inside her office.

"You come too, Fred! Sven-Erik!"

A minute later, they had all disappeared. There was a sudden Sunday silence in the building. Björnfot and Martinsson were still in the corridor.

"So," said Björnfot. "Where were we?"

"We were drinking coffee," smiled Martinsson. "It was just time for a top-up."

"Isn't it beautiful," Mella said. "Like a tourist brochure."

They were driving along Norgevägen in her red Ford Escort. To the right of them lay Torneträsk. Clear blue sky. Sun and sparkling snow. Along the length of the lake were arks in every conceivable colour and shape. On the other side of the road the mountains stretched away into the distance.

The wind had dropped. But it had not turned warm. Mella looked in among the birch trees and thought the snow had formed a solid crust. They might be able to use kick-sledges in the forest.

"Try looking at the road instead," said Stålnacke, who was sitting next to her.

Kallis Mining's mountain cabin was a large, timbered house. It was situated in an attractive spot down by the lake. In the opposite direction Nuolja mountain towered above.

"My sister's ex told me about this place when he was working up here," Olsson said. "His father was involved in the building. It's actually two chalets from Hälsingland that they've transported here. The timber is two hundred years old. And the sauna's down there by the shore of the lake."

Benny the locksmith was sitting outside in his van. He wound down the window and shouted:

"I've opened up, but I've got to go." He raised his hand in a quick salute and drove away.

The three police officers walked in. Mella thought she had never seen anything like it. The hand-hewn silver-grey timber walls were sparsely decorated with small oil paintings featuring motifs from the mountains, and mirrors in heavy gilded frames. Enormous Indian-style wardrobes in pink and turquoise contrasted sharply with their simple surroundings. The ceiling had been opened up, with the beams exposed. The broad wooden floor planks were covered with rugs in every room but one: in front of the big open fire in the living room lay a polar bear skin with its mouth gaping open.

"Good grief," Mella said.

The kitchen, hall and living room were open-plan; on one side were huge windows giving a view over the marsh, sparkling in the late winter sunshine. On the other side of the room the light filtered in through small high-set leaded windows with hand-blown glass in different colours.

On the kitchen table stood a carton of milk and a packet of muesli, a used bowl and a spoon. On the draining board dirty plates were piled high, with the cutlery sticking out in between.

"Ugh," Mella said as she shook the carton of milk and heard the soured lumps clunking around inside.

Not that her house was ever tidy. But to think that somebody could stay in such a grand place all by themselves, and not keep it nice. That is what she would do if she ever had the chance to live like this. Strap her skis on outside the door and go for a long cross-country trek over the marsh. Come home and cook dinner. Listen to the radio while washing up, or just enjoy the silence and think her own thoughts with her hands in the warm water. Lie on that inviting sofa in the living room and light a fire, crackling in the hearth.

"Perhaps these people aren't the kind that wash up," Stålnacke said. "There's probably somebody who comes in and cleans up after them when they've gone."

"In that case we need to get hold of that person," Mella said quickly.

She opened the doors to the four bedrooms. Big double beds with Sami covers. Above the bed heads hung reindeer skins, silver-grey against the silver-grey walls.

"Nice," Mella said. "Why doesn't my house look like this?"

There were no wardrobes in the bedrooms; instead big American trunks and antique chests stood on the floor to store things in. Coat hangers hung from beautiful Indian folding screens and elegant hooks or horns on the wall. There was a sauna, a laundry room and a big drying cupboard. Next to the sauna was a large changing room with space for ski wear and boots.

In one of the bedrooms was an open suitcase. Clothes lay in a heap both in and out of the case. The bed was unmade.

Mella poked about among the things.

"A bit of a mess, but no sign of a struggle or a break-in," said Olsson. "No blood anywhere, nothing unusual. I'll check the bathrooms."

"No, nothing has happened here," Stålnacke said.

Mella swore to herself. It would have been helpful if this had been the scene of the murder.

"I wonder what she was doing here," she said, eyeing up a skirt that looked expensive, and a pair of silky hold-ups. "These aren't exactly clothes for a skiing holiday."

Olsson reappeared behind them. He was holding a handbag. It was made of black leather, with a gold-coloured chain.

"This was in the bathroom," he said. "Prada. Ten to fifteen thousand kronor."

"Inside it?" Stålnacke asked.

"No, that's how much it costs."

Olsson tipped out the contents onto the unmade bed. He opened the wallet and held up Inna Wattrang's driving licence to Mella.

Mella nodded. It was definitely her. No doubt about it.

She looked at the rest of the things that had fallen out of the bag. Tampons, nail file, lipstick, sunglasses, face powder, a load of yellow credit card slips, a pack of painkillers.

"No mobile phone," she established.

Olsson and Stålnacke nodded. There was no phone anywhere else either. That might mean the perpetrator was somebody the victim knew, somebody whose number was programmed into the phone.

"We'll take her stuff to the station," said Mella. "And we'll seal this off anyway."

Her glance fell on the handbag again.

"It's wet," she said.

"I was just coming to that," said Olsson. "It was in the basin. The tap must have been dripping."

They looked at each other in surprise.

"Strange," Mella said.

Stålnacke's substantial moustache came to life beneath his nose, moving in and out and from side to side.

"Can you take a walk around the outside?" Mella said. "I'll just look about in here one more time."

Olsson and Stålnacke disappeared outside. Mella walked around slowly.

If the woman didn't die here, she thought, the killer has at least been here. And he was the one who took the phone. But of course she might have had it with her when she went out running, or whatever it was she was doing. In her pocket.

She looked in the basin where the bag had been. What had it been doing there? She opened the bathroom cabinet. Empty. Typical for a place that is going to be used by guests and employees or rented out; nothing personal left behind.

I can assume that anything here was hers, thought Mella.

There were a few microwave meals in the refrigerator. Three of the four bedrooms were completely untouched.

There's nothing more to see here, she thought, walking back into the hallway.

On a white chest in the hall stood an old lamp. It would have looked kitsch anywhere else, but it fitted in well here, thought Mella. The base was made of porcelain. It had a painted landscape on it that looked as if it might be from the German Alps, with a mountain in the background and a magnificent stag in the foreground. The shade was the colour of cognac, with a fringe. The switch was just below the light bulb fitting.

Mella tried to switch it on. When it didn't work, she discovered that it was not because the bulb had gone, but because the flex was missing.

In the base of the lamp there was just a hole where the flex had been.

What have they done with it? she wondered.

Maybe they had bought the lamp at a flea market or in an antique shop, and it was already like that. Perhaps they had put it on the chest thinking they would fix it soon, that it could stand there for the time being.

Mella had thousands of things like that at home. Things they were going to repair any year now. But in the end, you just got used to the defects. The front of the dishwasher, for example. It had been made in the same style as the kitchen cupboards, but it had come loose about a hundred years ago and now the door was too light for the spring. The whole family had got used to loading and unloading the dishwasher with one foot on the door so that it wouldn't close by itself. She did the same thing in other people's houses without even thinking about it. Robert's sister always laughed at her when she helped load their machine.

Perhaps they had just moved the lamp and the flex had got caught between the wall and a piece of furniture, and been pulled out. But that could be dangerous. If the flex was still plugged in, but not attached to the lamp.

She thought about the fire risk and then she thought about Gustav, her three-year-old, and about all the plastic covers on the sockets at home to keep them child-safe.

She got a fleeting picture in her head of Gustav when he was eight months old, and crawling everywhere. What a nightmare. A plug in a socket with a broken flex lying on the floor. The copper wires clearly visible inside the plastic covering. And Gustav, whose main method of investigating the world around him was putting things in his mouth. She quickly pushed the image aside.

Then it struck her. Electric shock. She had seen several during her career. God, there was that guy who had died five years ago. She had gone to confirm that it was an accident. He had been standing on the draining board in his bare feet, fiddling with a ceiling light. The skin on the soles of his feet had been badly burned.

Inna Wattrang had a circular burn around her ankle.

You could imagine someone ripping an ordinary flex out of a lamp, thought Mella. A lamp with a stag on, for example. Opening it up and removing the plastic covering and winding one of the copper wires around someone's ankle.

She flung the door open and shouted to her colleagues. They came quickly through the deep snow.

"Bloody hell! She died here! I'm sure of it! Call in Tintin and Krister Eriksson."

Krister Eriksson, inspector and dog handler, arrived at the scene an hour after his colleagues had rung him. They had been lucky; he was often out on duty with Tintin.

Tintin was a black Alsatian bitch. An excellent tracker dog, good at finding dead bodies. Eighteen months ago she had found a murdered priest in Nedre Vuolusjärvi; someone had wound an iron chain around his body, then sunk it in the lake.

Eriksson looked like some kind of alien. His face had been badly burned in an accident when he was young. He had no nose, just two holes in his face. His ears looked like a mouse's ears. He had no hair, no eyebrows, no eyelashes. His eyes looked very strange, because his eyelids had been reconstructed in plastic surgery.

Mella looked at his shiny pink skin, like a pig's, and her thoughts bounced back to Inna Wattrang and her burned ankle.

I must ring Pohjanen, she thought.

Eriksson put Tintin on the lead. She was dancing around his feet, whimpering with expectation.

"She always gets so excited," Eriksson said, disentangling himself from the lead. "You still have to hold her back, otherwise she searches a bit too quickly, and then she might miss something."

Eriksson and Tintin went into the house alone. Stålnacke and Olsson ploughed around the corner and looked in through the window.

Mella went and sat in her car and rang Pohjanen. She told him about the missing flex.

"Well?" she said.

"The burn mark around her ankle could certainly be the result of a wire conducting electricity through her body," Pohjanen said.

"The end of a flex, split and wound around her ankle?"

"Definitely. And you use the other end of the flex to transmit the electricity."

"Has she been tortured?"

"Maybe. It could also be a game that got out of hand, of course. Not very common, but it has happened. There's one more thing."

"Yes?"

"There are traces of stickiness on her ankles and wrists. You should get the technicians to check the furniture in the house. She's been taped, it could just be that her hands and feet were taped together. But she could have been bound to a piece of furniture, bed posts or a chair or . . . Just hang on."

It took a minute. Then she heard the doctor's hoarse voice again.

"I've just put my gloves on and I'm looking at her now," he said. "There's a tiny but distinct mark on her neck."

"The mark from the other part of the electric cable," said Mella.

"A lamp flex, you said?"

"Mmm."

"Then there should be traces of copper where the epidermis has melted. I'll take a tissue sample and do a histology test, then you'll know for sure. But that's probably what happened. Something certainly interrupted the rhythm of her heart. And she ended up in a state of shock. That would explain the fact that she'd chewed her tongue, and the marks of her own nails on her palms."

Stålnacke knocked on the car window and pointed at the house.

"I've got to go," Mella told Pohjanen. "I'll call you later."

She got out of the car.

"Tintin's found something," Stålnacke said .

Eriksson was standing in the kitchen with Tintin. She was tugging at the lead, barking and scrabbling madly at the floor."

"She's marking something there," Eriksson said, pointing to a

63

spot on the kitchen floor between the sink and the stove. "I can't see anything, but she seems convinced."

Mella looked at Tintin, who was now howling with frustration at not being allowed to get at her treasure.

The floor was covered with turquoise linoleum with an Oriental design. Mella walked over and looked closely at it. Stålnacke and Olsson accompanied her.

"I can't see anything," Mella said.

"Nope," said Olsson, shaking his head.

"Could there be something underneath the floor covering?" Mella wondered.

"There's definitely something," Eriksson said; it was all he could do to hold onto Tintin.

"O.K.," Mella said, checking her watch. "We've got time to have lunch at the tourist station while we're waiting for the technicians."

By 2.30 in the afternoon the scene of crime team had taken up the linoleum floor covering. When Mella, Stålnacke and Olsson got back to the house it was lying in the hallway, rolled up and wrapped in paper.

"Look at this," said one of the technicians to Mella, pointing at a tiny nick in the wood that had been underneath the linoleum.

In the little nick there was something brown that looked like dried blood.

"That dog must have one hell of a nose."

"Yes," Mella said. "She's very good."

"It has to be blood, given the dog's reaction," said the technician. "Linoleum is such fantastic stuff for floors. My mother had it on her floor, and it looked good for over thirty years. It heals itself, if it's damaged."

"What do you mean?"

"Well, if it's damaged in some way, cut or something, it pulls itself back together so that it doesn't show. It looks as if something sharp and pointed, a weapon or a tool, went straight through and cut into the wood underneath. Then the blood ran down into the nick. The linoleum knitted itself back together, and once you've cleaned the floor, there's no trace. We'll send the blood, if that's what it is, for analysis and then we'll know if it's Inna Wattrang's."

"I'd put money on it," Mella said. "This is where she died."

It was 8.00 on Sunday evening when Mella pulled on her jacket and rang Robert to tell him she was going to call it a day. He did not sound tired or annoyed, just asked if she had eaten and said there was food ready to be warmed up for her. Gustav was asleep, they had been out playing on the sledge. Petter had been with them too, despite the fact that he usually stayed indoors. Jenny had gone to a friend's, he said, adding quickly that she was on her way home right now before Mella had even managed to think "school tomorrow".

Mella was almost ridiculously happy. They had been out in the fresh air having fun. They had been enjoying themselves. Robert was a good father. It didn't matter at all if everyone's clothes were lying in a heap on the hall floor and dinner had only been half cleared away. She would tidy up after them with a cheerful heart.

"Is Marcus home?" she asked.

Marcus was their eldest. He was in his final year at senior school.

"No, I think he's staying over at Hanna's. How did it go?"

"Fine. Really good. It's only twenty-four hours, and we know who she is: Inna Wattrang, a bigwig in Kallis Mining. It'll be in the papers tomorrow. We've found the scene of the murder, although whoever did it tried to clean up after themselves and hide any traces. Even if the national crime squad ends up taking over, nobody can say we didn't do a good job."

"Was she stabbed with something?"

"Well, yes, but that's not all. The killer electrocuted her as well. The technicians were there this evening and they've found traces of sticky tape on one of the kitchen chairs, on the arms and the legs. And the same stuff on her ankles and wrists. Somebody taped her to the chair and gave her electric shocks."

"Shit. What with?"

"With an ordinary lamp flex, I think; they've opened up the end of it, split the wires, wound one round her wrist, and placed the other on her neck."

"And then he stabbed her to death."

"Yes."

"What's it all about?"

"Don't know. It could be a madman, or a hate crime. Could be a sex game of some kind that's gone wrong, although there doesn't seem to be any semen inside her or on her clothing. There was something white and slimy around her mouth, but it was just vomit."

Robert made a distressed noise.

"Promise you'll never leave me," he said. "Just imagine being in a bar looking for somebody new . . . and then when you get home, she wants you to electrocute her."

"You're better off with me, I'm happy with the missionary position."

"Good old honest boring sex."

Mella cooed at him.

"I like good old boring sex," she said. "If all the children are asleep when I get home . . ."

"Don't give me that one – you'll have something to eat, then you'll fall asleep on the sofa in front of *Six Feet Under*. Perhaps we ought to spice things up a bit."

"We could buy a book, maybe the *Kama Sutra*."

Robert laughed on the other end of the phone. Mella was pleased. She'd made him laugh. And they were talking about sex.

I ought to do this more often, she thought. Flirt and joke with him.

"Exactly," said Robert. "Positions like The Flight of the Crane over the Vault of the Heavens or something like that, where I have to hang upside down and you do the splits."

"O.K., forget it. I'll be straight home."

Mella had barely hung up when the telephone rang again. It was Björnfot.

"Hi there," he said. "Just wanted to let you know that Mauri Kallis is coming up tomorrow."

Mella had to think for a second. She had expected it to be Robert again, remembering to ask her to pick something up from the shops on the way home.

"Mauri Kallis as in Kallis Mining?"

"Yep. His secretary just rang me. Our colleagues in Stockholm called too. They've informed Inna Wattrang's parents. Who were shocked, of course. Didn't know she was up in Abisko, they said. But Inna Wattrang and her brother Diddi both work for Kallis Mining. And he owns some big place on Lake Mälaren where they both live. Her parents said they had let her brother know and asked Mauri Kallis to come up and identify her."

"Tomorrow!" Mella groaned. "I was just on my way home."

"Go home then."

"I can't go home. I need to speak to him. About Inna Wattrang and her role in the company and so on. I don't know a damned thing about Kallis Mining. He'll think we're idiots."

"Martinsson is in court tomorrow, so she's bound to be in her office. Ask her to read up on Kallis Mining and give you a half-hour summary first thing in the morning."

"Oh no, I can't ask her. She . . ."

Mella broke off momentarily. She was going to say that Martinsson had a life too, but then again . . . People said she lived out in the country all on her own, and didn't socialize.

". . . she needs her sleep just like anybody else," she said instead. "I can't ask her."

"O.K."

Mella thought about Robert, waiting at home.

"Or can I?"

Björnfot laughed.

"Well, I'm going to park myself in front of *Six Feet Under*," he said.

"That's another thing," Mella said, feeling rebellious.

She finished her conversation with the prosecutor and looked out of the window. Yes, Martinsson's car was still in the car park.

Three minutes later, Mella was knocking on the door of Martinsson's office.

"Look, I know you're really busy," she said. "And this isn't your job. So it's perfectly O.K. if you want to say no . . ."

She looked at the pile of documents on Martinsson's desk.

"Forget it," she said. "You're up to your eyes in work."

"What is it?" Martinsson said. "If it's to do with Inna Wattrang, just ask. It's . . ."

She broke off.

"I was going to say 'it's cool working on a murder,'" she went on, "but that's not what I meant."

"It doesn't matter," Mella said. "I know exactly what you mean. There's something special about a murder investigation. I absolutely don't want one single person to be murdered. But if they are, then I really want to be involved in solving it."

Martinsson looked relieved.

"That's what I used to dream about once upon a time, when I decided to join the police," Mella said. "Perhaps you did too, when you took up a career in law?"

"Oh, I don't know about that. I moved from Kiruna and started studying because I'd fallen out with my church. The fact that I went for law was more or less chance. Then I worked hard and the jobs just came along. I slipped into things. I don't think I ever made a real choice until I moved back here."

They had quickly got close to a serious topic of conversation. But they did not know each other well enough to carry on along that particular route. So they stopped, and neither spoke for a little while.

But Martinsson noticed gratefully that the silence did not feel awkward.

"So," said Martinsson at last, with a smile. "What did you want to ask me?"

Mella smiled back. There had always been a kind of tension between her and Martinsson. She had not really given it much thought, but sometimes it occurred to her that you weren't necessarily close to another person just because you'd saved their life. But all of a sudden it felt as if that tension had evaporated.

"Inna Wattrang's boss, Mauri Kallis, is coming up here tomorrow," she said.

Martinsson whistled.

"It's true," Mella went on. "And I have to talk to him, but I don't know anything about the company or what Inna Wattrang's job involved."

"There must be loads of stuff on the net."

"Exactly," said Mella, with a pained expression.

She hated reading. Swedish and Maths had been her worst subjects at school. She had only just scraped the grades she needed to get into the police training college.

"I understand," Martinsson said. "You'll have a summary in the morning. Let's say 7.30, because I'm in court all day and they start at 9.00."

"Are you sure?" Mella said. "It's a lot of work."

"But that's my thing," Martinsson said. "Turning a great pile of rubbish into a two-page A4 summary."

"And then you're in court all day. Have you finished preparing for that?"

Martinsson grinned.

"Now you're starting to feel guilty," she teased. "First of all you want me to do you a favour. Now you want absolution as well."

"Forget it," Mella said. "I'd rather have a guilty conscience than do all that reading. And it's one of those company things too . . ."

"Mmm, Kallis Mining's an international company. Not a group as such, you could call it a sphere. But I'll explain the company structure as well, it isn't that complicated really."

"Yeah, right! As soon as you say company and group and sphere I come out in hives. But I really appreciate your doing this. And I'll think about you as I'm flopping down on the sofa in front of the T.V. this evening. But seriously – shall I go and get you a pizza or something? I assume you're staying here?"

"I'm going home, I have every intention of flopping down in front of the T.V. as well. I'll get this done first."

"Who are you? Superwoman?"

"That's right. Off you go now, home to the T.V. Haven't you got lots of children to kiss goodnight as well?"

"Mmm, the eldest two don't kiss Mummy any more. And the little girl only kisses Daddy."

"But there's your youngest."

"Gustav. He's three. Oh yes, he wants to kiss his old Mummy."

Martinsson smiled. It was a warm, kind smile with a fleeting hint of sadness. It made her look softer.

I feel sorry for her, thought Mella a while later as she was on her way home in the car. She's gone through a lot.

She felt a pang of conscience over talking about her children; Martinsson had none.

But what can I do? They're a huge part of my life. If mentioning them is taboo, it's going to be impossible to talk.

Robert had put everything away, and even wiped the kitchen table. She warmed up fish fingers and mashed potato in the microwave and drank a glass of red wine to go with it. Enjoyed the fact that the mash was home made, real potatoes. Felt that she had the best life anybody could possibly wish for.

That's right, thought Rebecka Martinsson as she got out of her car by the house in Kurravaara. I am in fact Superwoman. I was one of the best lawyers in Sweden. Heading that way, at any rate. Although you mustn't say that to anybody. Or even think it about yourself.

She had downloaded material on Kallis Mining from the net to her laptop. It would actually be quite good fun, she thought. A change from the steady stream of traffic offences and theft and abuse cases.

The moonlight shone like silver, painted onto the shining crust of snow. And above the silver the blue shadows of the trees. The river was sleeping beneath the ice.

She placed a wool blanket over the windscreen and tucked it into both the front doors so she wouldn't have to scrape the ice off the next morning.

There were lights shining in the windows of the grey cottage that had once belonged to her grandmother. You could almost imagine there was somebody in there waiting for her, but it was just that she had left the light on herself.

They were here once, she thought. Daddy and Grandmother. I had everything then. And that's more than a lot of people have. Some never have it.

She stood there leaning against the car. Grief overwhelmed her. As if it were some creature that had been lying in wait for her to get out of the car. That's how it always was. She was always unprepared.

Why can't I be happy? Happy that I had them for as long as I did. Nothing is forever. God, it's so long ago. You can't grieve forever. There really is something wrong with me.

The therapist's words echoed in her ears: Perhaps you've never grieved properly. Perhaps it's time.

She was glad she had given up seeing the therapist. But she missed the Cipramil, perhaps she should not have come off it. Musings of this kind had been easier when she was on medication. The most difficult feelings never quite made it to the surface. It had been nice not to feel as fragile as an eggshell.

She pulled off one glove and felt beneath her eyes; no, she was not crying. It was just her breathing. As if she had been running fast. Bitterly cold air in her lungs.

Just calm down, she told herself. Calm down. Don't go hurrying across to Fjällborg and Bella, they can't help you.

She thought of going in, but stood there, unsure if she was about to lock the car, if she had left a bag somewhere, and what the key in her hand was for.

It'll pass, she said to herself. You're not to lie down in the snow. It always passes.

But not this time, said a voice inside her. This time the darkness is coming.

It was the car key she had in her hand. She locked the door. She managed to pick up her laptop and her Mulberry briefcase, they were by her feet. She walked over to the house.

On the way up the steps she grabbed a fistful of snow from the railings and held it to her face. The key to the house is in the bag. Put it in the lock. Turn it. Take the key out. Open the door.

She was inside.

Half an hour later she felt much better. She had lit the fire, and she heard it suddenly catch as the chimney drew and the wood began to crackle.

A cup of tea with milk. The laptop on her knee on the sofa.

She tried to think all the thoughts she had had in her head before the attack. She felt absolutely fine. She could not bring back the difficult feelings however hard she tried.

And she did try. Played her highest card. Allowed her mother to take shape inside her head.

But nothing in particular happened. Martinsson could see her in front of her. The pale grey eyes, face powder that smelled good, nice hair, white, even teeth.

When she got the sheepskin coat, thought Martinsson, with a crooked smile at the memory. The villagers ground their teeth and wondered who the hell she thought she was. An animal skin coat, for goodness' sake.

What on earth had she actually seen in her father? Maybe she thought a safe haven was what she longed for. But she was never made for that. Her mother should have hoisted every single ragged sail and set off into the storm with her hair flying. The safe life wasn't for her.

Rebecka Martinsson tried to remember how things had been when her mother left the family.

Daddy moved back to Grandmother's in Kurravaara. He lived on the ground floor and I lived upstairs with Grandmother, running up and down between the two of them. And Jussi. He was a clever dog. As soon as I moved in he saw his chance of improving his sleeping arrangements. He lay down on the end of my bed. Grandmother didn't allow the dogs on the furniture. But what could she do? The child slept soundly with the dog on the bed, lying there chattering to him while Grandmother took care of the milking in the evening.

Mummy made beds on the trains, and moved up to work in the restaurant car. She swapped our three-room apartment in town for one with two rooms. I must have stayed there with her sometimes even before Daddy died, but I don't remember it at all.

And those memories that you do have. Do they really help? It's just a few pictures in an album in your head, after all. In between the scenes you do remember there are hundreds, thousands you've forgotten. So are you remembering the truth?

Grandmother in Mummy's little apartment. She is wearing her best coat, but Mummy still thinks Grandmother ought to buy a new one, she has told Rebecka that. However, now it is Mummy's turn to feel ashamed. Grandmother is looking around. From where she's standing, you can see right into the bedroom. Mummy's bed is unmade. There are no bedclothes on Rebecka's bed. Mummy is exhausted all the time. She has phoned in sick to work. In the past Grandmother has turned up and cleaned the whole place. Washed the dishes, done the laundry, done the cooking. Not this time.

"I'm taking the girl with me," she says.

Her voice is friendly, but there is no contradicting her.

Mummy does not protest, but when Rebecka tries to give her a hug to say goodbye, she pushes her away.

"Hurry up now," she says, without looking at Rebecka. "Grandmother hasn't got all day."

Rebecka can see her own feet on the way down the staircase. Thud, thud. Her feet are heavy. Big as blocks of stone. She should have whispered in Mummy's ear: "I love you the best." Sometimes that helps. She collects good things to say. "You're just the way a Mummy ought to be." "Katti's Mummy smells sweaty." Look at her for a long time, then say: "You're so lovely."

I'll ask Fjällborg to tell me, she thought. He knew them both. Before I know it, he will be gone as well, and then there will be nobody left to ask.

She opened the computer. Inna Wattrang in yet another group

photograph. This time wearing a helmet and standing in front of a zinc mine in Chile.

Peculiar job. Getting to know dead people.

MONDAY, 17 MARCH, 2005

Rebecka Martinsson met Anna-Maria Mella and Sven-Erik Stålnacke in the conference room at the police station at 7.30 on Monday morning.

"How did it go?" said Mella by way of greeting. "Did you manage to watch T.V. last night?"

"No," Martinsson said. "How about you?"

"No, I fell asleep," Mella said.

In fact, she and Robert had done something completely different in front of the television, but that was nothing to do with anybody else.

"Me too," Martinsson lied.

She had sat up and gone through the Kallis Mining group and Inna Wattrang until 2.30 in the morning. When the alarm on her mobile rang at 6.00, she had felt that familiar faint nausea that comes with too little sleep.

It did not matter much. In fact, it didn't matter at all. A slight lack of sleep was nothing. Today she had a packed schedule – first the meeting with the two police officers, then the criminal court all day. And she liked to be busy.

"Mauri Kallis started with nothing," Martinsson said. "He's the American dream, but in Swedish. He really is. Born in 1964 in Kiruna – when were you born?"

"In '62," Mella replied. "But he must have gone to a different school. And at senior school you don't know the younger kids."

"He was taken into care when he was little," Martinsson went on, "foster home, arrested for a break-in when he was twelve, too young to be charged, but that's where things turned around; the social worker got him to start studying. He started at the business school in Stockholm in 1984, and started speculating on the stock market while he was still studying. That's when he got to know Inna Wattrang and her brother Diddi. Diddi and Mauri were on the same course. Mauri Kallis worked for a firm of stockbrokers for a while after he graduated, and during those two years his own share portfolio grew; he bought H. & M. early, sold Fermenta before the crash, one step ahead all the time. Then he left and devoted all his time to trading for himself. A hundred and ten per cent high-risk projects, first of all trading in commodities, then more and more buying and selling concessions, both in oil and in mining."

"Concessions?" Mella said.

"You buy permission to drill for some natural resource, oil, gas, minerals. You might find something, but instead of starting a mine yourself, you sell the concession."

"So you could make a lot of money, but you could also lose a lot?" Stålnacke said.

"Oh yes, you could lose everything. So you need to be a gambler if you're going to do that kind of thing. And sometimes he really was way down. But Inna and Diddi Wattrang were already working for him at that time. They seem to have been the ones who attracted the finance for different projects."

"So it's a question of persuading somebody to put up the money," Mella said.

"Exactly. The banks don't lend money for this sort of thing, so you have to find investors who are willing to take a risk. And the Wattrangs seem to have been very good at that."

Martinsson went on:

"But over the last three years they've hung onto some of the concessions in the company, and they've also bought a number of mines and started to work them. All the Swedish newspapers are writing about the leap from stocks and shares into mining as the big step, but I don't agree. I think it's a much bigger step to go from speculating in concessions to starting up mining operations, working on the industrial side . . ."

"Perhaps he just wanted to take things a little easier," Mella said. "Not to take such big risks."

"I don't think so," Martinsson said. "He hasn't chosen to start up mines in straightforward locations. They're in Indonesia, for example. Or Uganda. A while ago the media turned against just about every company that has mining interests in developing countries."

"Because . . . ?"

"Because . . . well, just about every reason you can think of! Because poor countries dare not create environmental laws that might scare off foreign investors, so the water is poisoned and people get cancer and incurable liver diseases and so on. Because companies in countries like that co-operate with corrupt regimes; there might be a civil war going on, and they're using the military against their own people."

"Was there anything in it?" asked Stålnacke, who had a police officer's instinctive distrust of the media.

"Definitely. Some of the companies in the Kallis group have ended up on various blacklists with organizations like Greenpeace and Human Rights Watch. For several years Mauri Kallis was a pariah, and had no interests in Sweden. No investor was willing to risk being linked to him. But about a year ago, things changed. A year ago he was on the cover of *Business Week*; the article was about mining. And shortly after that *Dagens Nyheter* did a big profile on him."

"Why did things change?" Mella asked. "Had they mended their ways?"

"I don't think so. I think it's that . . . well, there are just too many companies with interests in these countries that are doing more or less the same thing. And if everybody's dodgy, in the end nobody's dodgy. And they get fed up of the painting the same picture as well. All of a sudden they need to write about this incredibly successful, energetic entrepreneur."

"Like the reality shows," Mella said. "At the beginning there's one particular character everybody loves to hate, and the newspapers write about how Olinda makes her fellow contestants cry: "hate shock attack" on all the billboards. Then it's as if they get fed up of hating her, and she suddenly turns into Madonna, she isn't a bitch, it's just girl-power."

"And it's easy to write about his successes too, because it's such a fairy-tale," Martinsson said. "Built up his fortune from precisely nothing. The worst start in life imaginable. And now he owns an estate in Södermanland and is married to a woman from the aristocracy, Ebba von Uhr. Well, she isn't aristocracy any more, not now she's married to Mauri Kallis."

"Aha," Mella said. "So the nobility gene is dominant only on the male side. Children?"

"Two, one's ten and the other's twelve."

Mella suddenly came to life.

"We need to check the national vehicle database," she said. "I want to know what car he drives. Or cars."

"We're not playing games here," Stålnacke said, turning attentively towards Martinsson. "What you were saying about mining . . . what do you mean by saying mining is different from all this business of concessions and experimental drilling?"

"Running a mine is a completely different matter. You have to be aware of another country's environmental laws, company laws, employment laws, administration laws, tax laws . . ."

"O.K.," said Mella, holding up her hand.

"In certain countries you come up against problems because the systems don't run smoothly, or simply don't work the way they do in the western world. Problems with unions, with entrepreneurs, with getting all the permissions you need from the authorities, it can be difficult to deal with the corruption, you don't have the necessary contacts . . ."

"Permission to do what?"

"Everything. Permission to mine, permission to pollute the water, to build roads, construction – just about everything, in fact. You have to build up a completely different kind of organization. And you have an employer's responsibility. You become . . . how shall I put it . . . you become part of a society, of the country where you're starting up your business. And you also create a society, around your mine. Usually there's nothing there, a stony desert or a jungle. And then a little town grows up around your mine. Families. Children who need to go to school. It's interesting that he suddenly turned into that kind of entrepreneur . . ."

"What was Inna Wattrang's role in the company?" Mella wondered.

"She was employed by the parent company, Kallis Mining, but worked across the entire group. Sat on a lot of the company boards. She was a lawyer, and had read a good deal of company financial law, but I don't get the impression that she worked on legal issues affecting the company. They've had a Canadian company lawyer working for the parent company; he's spent more than thirty years in the mining and oil industries, and he takes care of that sort of thing."

"She was a lawyer. But you didn't know her from before?"

"No, no, she was older than me and there are several hundred who start every year. And she studied in Stockholm. I was in Uppsala."

"So what exactly did she do?" Mella said.

"She dealt with information about the company, and with the financing."

"What does that mean?"

"O.K., let's say Kallis finds an area where he can buy concessions, that is the right to do experimental drilling for gold or diamonds or whatever. That can be very expensive. Because drilling for minerals is such a high-risk project, he might have a lot of money one day and very little the next, so perhaps he himself can't release the capital he needs. And as I said, there's virtually no bank in the world that's willing to lend money for this kind of activity. So he needs finance. People or investment companies who want to buy shares in the project. Sometimes you need to go on promotional tours, trying to sell ideas. It's also important to have a good reputation within the industry. She helped him to build up a good reputation and goodwill, and she was obviously very good on the finance side. Her brother Diddi works on finance as well. Kallis himself is more involved at the heart of things: sniffing out interesting projects, negotiating, closing deals. And recently on the industrial side too, the actual mining."

"I wonder what kind of man he is," Mella said, suddenly feeling nervous at the prospect of meeting him in just a few hours.

Stop it, she said to herself. He's only a person.

"There was an interview on the net that I downloaded, have a look at that," Martinsson said. "It's good. Inna Wattrang's there too. I haven't found much information about her otherwise. She isn't a celebrity in industrial circles, unlike Kallis."

The programme lasts an hour. An interview from September 2004. Malou von Sivers meets Mauri Kallis. Von Sivers should be pleased. She is interviewed herself before the programme and stresses just how pleased she is. It is a marketing ploy. The viewer is told that T.V.4 has sold the programme to no fewer than twelve overseas media companies. Many people have wanted to interview Mauri Kallis, but he has turned them all down since '95.

Von Sivers is asked why he agreed to be interviewed by her? For many reasons, she believes. Partly because he probably felt he had to give an interview; his growing celebrity status demanded it. And even if you work on the principle 'Work but don't be seen', you have to be seen sometimes. Otherwise it looks as if you're afraid to come out in the open. Partly because he wanted to do a Swedish interview. To show some kind of solidarity with his homeland.

And von Sivers treats her interviewees with respect; that probably played its part.

"I know he feels I'll be well prepared and take it seriously," she says candidly.

The journalist interviewing her is provoked by this self-confidence, and asks if von Sivers thinks the fact that she is a woman is significant. Perhaps it was a tactical choice? A way of bringing a softer element into the company's goodwill profile? Mining is recognized as a male dominated area, and a little . . . how shall we put it . . . coarse in some way. Von Sivers says nothing for a while. And she is not smiling.

"Or perhaps it's because I'm very good," she says at last.

When the programme begins, von Sivers, Inna Wattrang and Inna's brother Jacob "Diddi" Wattrang are sitting in a reception room at the Regla estate, which has been owned by the Kallis family for thirteen years.

Kallis has been delayed; the company's Beech B200 was not able to take off in time from Amsterdam. Von Sivers has decided to begin the interview with Inna and Diddi; it will give the programme a good dynamic.

The brother and sister are sitting in armchairs, leaning back comfortably. Both are wearing white shirts with the sleeves rolled up, and men's watches. They are very alike with their distinctive noses, the high bridge of the nose between the eyes, and their pale blond hair cut in bobs. They move in a similar way too, have the same way of distractedly brushing the hair out of their eyes.

Martinsson watched them and thought there was a faint but clearly perceptible sensual signal in that way of pushing aside the hair, the fingers following the strand of hair to the very end. On their way back to the knee or the arm of the chair, the tips of the fingers fleetingly brushed the chin or the mouth.

Mella watched the same movements and thought they were always bloody fiddling with their faces, like junkies.

"Shall I get you some coffee before I go?" Martinsson said.

Stålnacke and Mella nodded, their eyes fixed on the monitor.

I ought to work on that kind of body language, thought Martinsson on her way to the coffee machine. That's what's wrong with me. No sensual signals at all.

Then she had to smile. If she carried on like that in front of

Måns Wenngren he would think she was picking at her spots.

Von Sivers' hands are not moving. She is a professional. Her copper-coloured fringe has been sprayed, and stays exactly where it is meant to be.

Malou von Sivers: So you live here on the estate.

Diddi Wattrang [laughing]: Oh, that sounds terrible – like some sort of commune.

Inna Wattrang [also laughing and placing her hand over von Sivers' in a friendly way]: You can move in if you like!

Malou von Sivers: But seriously, isn't it difficult sometimes? You work closely together. And you live close together.

Diddi Wattrang: Not that close, in fact. The property is large. My family and I live in what used to be the farm foreman's house – you can't even see it from here.

Inna Wattrang: And I live in the old laundry.

Malou von Sivers: Tell me how you two met Mauri Kallis!

Diddi Wattrang: Mauri and I were at business school together in the '80s. Mauri belonged to the small group of students who'd started speculating on the stock market, and used to hang about under the stock market monitor outside the pub as soon as trading started.

Inna Wattrang: That was unusual at the time, trading in securities. Not like nowadays.

Diddi Wattrang: And Mauri was very good.

Inna Wattrang [leaning forward with a teasing smile]: And Diddi talked his way in.

Diddi Wattrang [giving his sister a playful push]: "Talked his way in!" We became friends.

Inna Wattrang [pretending to be serious]: "They became friends!"

Diddi Wattrang: And I put in a little capital . . .

Malou von Sivers: Did you get rich?

Half a second of silence.

Oops, thought Mella, trying to drink the coffee Martinsson had sneaked in with. It was far too hot. You must not talk about money. It is bad form.

Diddi Wattrang: By student standards, yes of course. He had such a good instinct, even in those days. Bought big in Hennes & Mauritz in 1984, hit the bullseye with Skanska, Sandvik, S.E.B. . . . his timing was perfect nearly always. At the end of the '80s a lot of the market was about commodities, and he was a demon for finding the next thing that was going to go up in value. Property became important when we were about halfway through our studies. I remember when Anders Wall came and gave a lecture, and advised us all to buy property in inner city Stockholm. By that time Mauri had already moved out of his student room, bought a rental contract, converted it to a tenancy agreement, and had a two-room apartment that he lived in himself and two one-room apartments that he rented out, and the difference between them gave him the money to live on.

Malou von Sivers: The press calls him the whiz-kid, the prodigy, the financial genius from nowhere . . .

Inna Wattrang: He's still the same. Long before China got involved, he was prospecting for peridot in Greenland. Then he had both L.K.A.B. and China begging to buy the deposits.

Malou von Sivers: Perhaps you could explain to those of us who are not familiar with the story.

Inna Wattrang: Peridot is needed to make iron into steel. He realized before anybody else that the steel market here was going to go through the roof when China got involved.

Diddi Wattrang: He was absolutely sure of China. Long before everybody else was.

*

In February 1985, Diddi Wattrang is in his first year at business school. He is not a natural student. But the pressure from home has been considerable, both on him and on his teachers. His mother has invited the ladies of the area to the summer concert which is held at the beginning of August every year, outdoors of course: you do not let just anybody inside the house. For those who have been invited it is still one of the high points of the year; they are happy to pay the small amount for their ticket, after all the money goes towards the maintenance of the cultural and historical value of the house. It is almost a charitable cause, there is always a roof that needs repairing and walls to be re-plastered. And as they are mingling afterwards, Mama makes a point of saying firmly to her son's French teacher: "The family regard him as a very gifted student." Papa is on excellent terms with the director of the school, but the director knows that it is a question of give and take. It is nice to be friends with the lord of the manor, but of course it does not come free.

Diddi has got through senior school somehow, cheating a little here, borrowing there. You can always find hardworking but dull people who will exchange help with essays and exams for a little bit of attention. A mutually beneficial deal.

Diddi does have one talent. He is easy to like. Tilts his head to one side so that his long blond fringe is not in his eyes when he is talking to someone. Genuinely seems to like everyone, especially the person he is talking to at the time. Laughs with both his mouth and his eyes, reaching out and touching people's hearts with such care and ease.

Now it is Mauri Kallis' turn to feel chosen and special. It is a Wednesday evening and they are hanging out in the student bar. It is as if they have been friends for ages. Diddi ignores a pretty blonde girl who is sitting with her friends a little way off, laughing a fraction too loudly and glancing in their direction. He says hi to loads of people who come over and want to chat. But that is all; this evening does not belong to them.

Mauri is drinking a bit too much, the way you do when you are nervous. Diddi is keeping up with him, but he can tolerate it better. They take it in turns to buy. Diddi has a little coke in his pocket. Just in case the opportunity arises. He is playing it by ear.

But actually, this guy is not completely without interest. Diddi relates highlights of his childhood. The pressure from his father to study. The outbursts of rage and the humiliating speeches when the exams had gone badly. He admits with a laugh that unfortunately he is just a ditsy blond, and does not belong here.

But then he defends his father. He has his own baggage, of course. Brought up in the old school, had to stand at the door and bow to his own father, Diddi's grandfather, before he was granted permission to come in. There were not many cuddles, not much sitting on Daddy's knee.

And after offering these initial confidences, he begins to dig and to ask questions. And he watches Mauri, this skinny guy whose trousers are too big, who wears cheap shoes and a beautifully ironed shirt made of such thin cotton you can see the hairs on his chest through it. Mauri, who carries his course books in a supermarket carrier bag. He does not spend his money on material things, that much is clear.

And Mauri talks about himself. He got caught doing a break-in when he was twelve. He talks about the social worker who made him pull himself together and start studying.

"Was she pretty?" Diddi says.

Mauri lies and says yes. He does not know why. Diddi has to laugh.

"You really are full of surprises," he says. "You don't look much like a criminal."

Mauri, who tells half truths, does not say a word about the fact that it was a gang of older boys, his foster brother and his mates, who sent him and some younger kids who were not old enough to be charged to do the crap jobs.

"What does a criminal look like?" he asks instead.

Diddi looks impressed.

"And now you're the student star," he says.

"Just about passed Business Studies," Mauri says.

"But that's because you study the stock market instead of anything else. Everybody knows that."

Mauri does not reply. Tries to attract the barman's attention to order two more beers, feels like a dwarf who's being ignored, trying to be seen over the top of the bar counter. In the meantime Diddi takes the opportunity to smile at the blonde and gaze into her eyes. A little investment for the future.

They end up in a club, in the packed bar, paying three times as much for their beer.

"I've got a bit of money," Diddi says. "You should invest it for me. Seriously. I'm willing to take the risk."

Diddi does not have time to work out what it is he sees in Mauri. A split second where he kind of straightens up, switches to a sober section of his brain, checking, analysing, reaching a decision. In time Diddi will learn that Mauri never loses his judgement. Fear keeps him alert. But it passes so quickly. Mauri gives a drunken shrug.

"Sure," he says. "I take twenty-five per cent, and as soon as I'm tired of it you can take over yourself or sell, whichever you want."

"Twenty-five per cent!" Diddi is dumbfounded. "That's profiteering! How much do the banks take?"

"Go to a bank then, they've got good brokers."

But Diddi says O.K.

And they laugh, as if everything is just a joke.

*

The programme editors have included Mauri Kallis' arrival at the interview. In the lower right-hand corner of the picture you can see von Sivers' hand rotating briefly, "keep rolling", to the person behind the camera. Kallis is slender and short, like an uptight schoolboy. His suit is a perfect fit. His shoes are shiny. His shirt is white; these days it is tailor-made in heavy, top-quality cotton, anything but see-through.

He apologizes to von Sivers for his late arrival, shakes her hand, then turns to Inna Wattrang and kisses her on the cheek. She smiles and says: "Master!" Diddi and Kallis shake hands. Somebody produces a chair, and all three of them are sitting with von Sivers in front of the camera.

Von Sivers goes in softly to begin with. She saves the difficult questions for the later part of the interview. She wants Kallis to feel comfortable, and if the interview goes wrong it is best if it happens at the end when they are done.

She holds out the copy of *Business Week* from spring 2004 with Kallis on the cover, and a centre spread from the financial section of one of the major dailies. The newspaper article's headline is "The boy with the magic touch".

Inna looks at the newspapers and thinks it is a miracle those articles were ever written, since Kallis refused to give interviews. In the end she got him to agree to the photographs. The photographer from *Business Week* chose a close-up shot with Kallis looking down at the floor. The photographer's assistant dropped a pen and it rolled away. Kallis followed it with his eyes. The photographer took a lot of pictures. Kallis looks lost in thought. Almost as if he is praying.

Malou von Sivers: From problem child to all this [she moves her head to encompass the Regla estate, his successful business empire, the whole shebang]. The image we have of your life is from a fairy-tale. How does that feel?

Kallis looks at the pictures and hardens himself against the self-loathing they bring out in him.

He is everybody's property. They use him to prove their ideology is the right one. The national confederation of Swedish industry, *Svenskt Näringsliv*, invite him to speak. They point at him and say: "Look. Anybody can succeed if they want to." Göran Persson mentioned his name on television recently during a debate on youth crime. After all, it was a social worker who put Kallis on the right path. The system works. The Swedish welfare state is still there. The disadvantaged have a chance.

It sickens Kallis. He wishes they would stop using him, pawing at him.

He lets nothing show. His voice remains calm and friendly. Perhaps a little monotonous. But he is not sitting there because he is charismatic. Diddi and Inna can take care of the charisma.

Mauri Kallis: I don't feel . . . like a character in a fairy-tale.

Silence.

Malou von Sivers [trying again]: You've been described in newspapers abroad as "The Swedish Miracle", and been compared with Ingvar Kamprad.

Mauri Kallis: Well, we both have a nose in the middle of our faces . . .

Malou von Sivers: But there's something in that, surely? You both started with nothing. Succeeded in building up an international company in a Sweden which is regarded as . . . difficult for new businesses.

Mauri Kallis: And it is difficult for new businesses, the tax laws favour old money, but there was a chance to build up some capital in the transition from the '80s to the '90s, and I took it.

Malou von Sivers: Tell me about that. One of your contemporaries at the business school said in an interview that you did not like the idea of just using up your student finances, "eating them up and then shitting them out".

Mauri Kallis: That was rather coarsely put. And I wouldn't wish to use language like that in this context. But yes, that's true. I'd never had so much money at once before. And I suppose that brought out the entrepreneur in me. Money ought to work, be invested. [He allows a glimpse of a fleeting smile.] I was a real stock market nerd. Always had a copy of the latest stock exchange reports in my briefcase.

Diddi Wattrang: And you read the Swedish version of *Business World*, *Affärsvärlden*.

Mauri Kallis: At that time it had edge.

Malou von Sivers: What did you do next?

Mauri Kallis: Well, then . . .

Mauri's student corridor consists of eight rooms with a shared kitchen and two shower rooms. A cleaner comes in once a week, but you still would not want to walk on the kitchen floor in your socks. You can feel crumbs right through them, and here and there you get slightly stuck to something tacky that hasn't been wiped up. The chairs and table are made of yellow pine. Clumsy and heavy. The kind you are always bumping into, for some reason. You end up with bruises on your thighs, keep stubbing your toes.

There are some girls living on the corridor; they hang out together and go to parties he never gets invited to. Anders, who lives opposite Mauri, wears trendy glasses and is studying law; you see him in the kitchen sometimes, but he is nearly always at his girl-friend's.

Håkan is tall and comes from Kramfors. Mattias is big and fat.

And then there's Mauri himself, who is a skinny little scrap. What a collection. None of them goes to parties. And there is no point in organizing one themselves – who would they invite? They sit in front of the television in Håkan's room in the evenings gazing mindlessly at porno films with cushions on their laps, like teenagers.

That is the way things have been, at any rate. But now Mauri has turned into a stock market nerd, and at least that means you are somebody. And not because he hangs out with the others who stand around just inside Kopparporten beneath the monitor.

He has become a real player, skipping lectures, sitting up at night with dry eyes reading *Dagens Industri* instead of studying.

It is a fever, and he is in love. The rush you get when you've got it right.

That first coup. He can remember how it felt, he will never forget: it's like your first girl. He bought five hundred shares in Cura Nova before the merger with Artemis. Then the price shot up. First the leap, then a steady climb as others caught on and bought. They were a long way behind him; he was already thinking of selling. He did not say a word about how much he had actually earned, not to anyone. Went outside. Stood under a street lamp with his face turned up to the falling snow. The certainty. The feeling. I am going to be rich. This is my thing.

And as a bonus he has become friends with Diddi Wattrang. Diddi, who stops beneath the monitor, checks the prices and chats a little, sometimes sits next to Mauri in lectures.

Sometimes they go out on the town. Mauri takes twenty-five per cent of Diddi's profits; he does not do anything for nothing.

He is no fool either. He knows it is money that gives him his entry ticket into the Other World.

So what? he says. For him, money is the ticket. For another person it's their face, for another their charm, for yet another it's their name. You have to have a ticket of some kind, and any ticket can be lost. It's a matter of holding onto what you have found.

There are rules. Unspoken rules. For example: it is Diddi who gets in touch with Mauri, Diddi who rings and asks Mauri if he fancies going out. It would not work the other way round; it would never occur to Mauri to take the liberty of ringing Diddi.

So Mauri waits for Diddi to call. There are voices inside him. They talk about a different circle of acquaintances that Diddi has, a circle to which Mauri is not admitted. Beautiful people. Cool parties. Diddi calls Mauri when he has nothing else on. Something like jealousy stirs in Mauri. He sometimes thinks he'll stop trading for Diddi. The next minute he consoles himself by remembering that he is making money out of Diddi, it is a reciprocal exploitation.

He tries to study. And when he cannot manage either that or share dealing, he plays cards with Håkan and Mattias. Thinks that Diddi's bound to call. Runs to his room when the phone rings, but it is nearly always the room next door where one of the girls lives.

And when Diddi calls, Mauri says yes. Every time, he thinks he is going to say no next time. Pretend to be busy.

Another rule is that Diddi chooses the company. It is absolutely out of the question for Mauri to take somebody along, Håkan or Mattias for example. Not that he would want to anyway. There is no friendship there, no solidarity or whatever the hell it is supposed to be. They're outsiders, that's all they have in common. But not any longer.

And Mauri and Diddi get wasted. Wide awake and high on cocaine. He sometimes wakes up in the morning without the slightest idea of how or when he got home. He has got slips and tickets in his pockets, stamps on his hands, all clues as to how the journey went. From the pub to Caféet to a club to a late-night party to some girls.

And he is allowed to screw the less attractive friends of the prettiest girls. And that is absolutely fine, and so much more than Håkan and Mattias get.

Six months pass. Mauri knows that Diddi has a sister, but he has never met her.

Nobody can shrug like Diddi Wattrang. They fail an exam, both of them. Mauri turns his anger inwards; it chafes and eats away at him inside. A voice tells him he is worthless, that he is just a fraud, that he will soon slip over the edge and fall down into the world that is really meant for him.

Diddi curses too, but then he turns his failure outwards. It is the invigilator, the examiner, the guy who was sitting in front of him farting silently . . . it is everybody's fault except his. And he only broods about it for a little while. Then his habitual insouciance returns.

It is a while before Mauri realizes Diddi is not rich. He has always thought that upper-class people, especially those from the aristocracy, have plenty of money. But that is not the case. When Diddi gets to know Mauri he is managing on virtually nothing, just a small student grant. He lives in an apartment in Östermalm, but it belongs to some relative. His shirts have come from his father's wardrobe; they are the ones his father grew out of long ago. He wears them casually buttoned over T-shirts. He owns one pair of jeans and one pair of shoes. He is always cold in the winter, but he always looks good. Maybe he looks best when he is freezing. When he hunches his shoulders with his arms pressed tightly against his body, inviting you to throw your arms around him.

Where Diddi got the money to invest in Mauri's share dealing Mauri does not know. He tells himself it is not his concern. Later, when Mauri worked out how a pissed, slurring Diddi could go into the toilets in the bar and come out a short while later on top of the world, he wondered where Diddi got the money for his habits. He has his own ideas about that. Once when they were out, an older man came over and started chatting. He had barely got beyond hello when Diddi got up and disappeared. Mauri sensed that it was taboo to ask who he was.

Diddi likes money. All his life he has been surrounded by money, hung out with people who have money, but never had any himself. His hunger has grown. It does not take long before he starts to take out more and more of his profits from the trading. Then it is Mauri's turn to shrug. That is not his concern either. Diddi's share in their simple company falls.

Diddi starts to disappear for long periods, travelling to the Riviera and to Paris. His pockets are full of money.

Everybody has to be crushed at some point. Soon it will be Diddi's turn. And soon Mauri will get to meet Diddi's sister.

Malou von Sivers: You call him "master".

Inna Wattrang: We are his hounds, after all.

Mauri Kallis [smiles and shakes his head slightly]: They've stolen that from Jan Stenbeck, the financier. His employees used to call him "master". I don't know whether I should be flattered or insulted.

Malou von Sivers: Are they your hounds?

Mauri Kallis: If we're sticking with the animal theme, then of course I'd prefer to work with starving cats.

Diddi Wattrang: And we're fat . . .

Inna Wattrang: . . . and lazy.

Malou von Sivers: So, tell me about it. A very unusual friendship seems to have developed between the three of you. Inna and Diddi Wattrang were born with a silver spoon in their mouths, and you're what's known as a "superkid", succeeding against all the odds; is that a fair summation?

Mauri Kallis: Yes.

Malou von Sivers: So it must be you who's the starving cat. What is it that makes the three of you such a good team?

Mauri Kallis: Diddi and Inna complement me. A major part of this enterprise involves finding people who are prepared to gamble, who are prepared to take a big risk for the chance of bringing off a big profit. And who can afford to do that. Who don't have to sell stock when it hits rock bottom, but who can afford to stay in a company that's losing money until I've brought in a winning project. Because it always comes along. Sooner or later. But you have to be able to wait. That's why we never float our companies on the stock exchange; we prefer private investments so you have some idea of who's buying. It's the same thing with, for example, mining in Uganda. Just at the moment, things are so unstable down there that we can't actually do any business. But it's a long-term project, and I believe in it. And the last thing I need is a gang of shareholders breathing down my neck and wanting to see profits within six months. Diddi and Inna find the right kind of investors for different projects. And they're very good at selling. They find adventurous investors and gamblers for risky projects, and patient investors without liquidity problems for long-term projects. They're much more socially adept than I am. They have that financial magnetism. And now we're running a number of mines within the group, I am delighted to have them working with the people on the ground and with colleagues. They can move in high or low circles, effectively and without falling out with anybody.

Malou von Sivers [to Inna]: So what is Mauri's strength, then?

Inna Wattrang: Well, he's got a real nose for a good business opportunity. A built-in divining rod. And he's an excellent negotiator.

Malou von Sivers: What's he like as an employer?

Inna Wattrang: He's always calm. That's the most fascinating thing about him. Things can get really rocky at times, like during the early years when he was buying concessions before he'd got the finance sorted. He never betrayed the least hint of unease or stress. And that means that those of us who work around him feel enormously secure.

Malou von Sivers: But now you've been sounding off in the papers. Showing your feelings.

Mauri Kallis: You mean the mine in Ruwenzori? The A.I.D.S. business?

Malou von Sivers: You called Swedish A.I.D.S. a joke, among other things.

Mauri Kallis: That was a quote that was taken totally out of context. And I wasn't sounding off in the press, a journalist came along to a lecture I was giving. But obviously I get annoyed eventually when I'm pestered by Swedish journalists who haven't done their homework. "Kallis Mining builds roads for militia troops." And then they see me shaking hands with a general from the Lendu militia, and they write about what that particular group has done in the Congo, and all of a sudden my mining company in north-western Uganda is the work of the devil himself. And so am I. It's very easy to maintain your high moral values, simply by having nothing whatsoever to do with countries in crisis. Send in a con-tribution and keep your fingers out of it. But the population of these countries needs businesses, growth, employment. The gov-ernment, on the other hand, wants budgetary assistance, with no form of control at all. You only have to look at the situation in Kampala to see where a great deal of the money goes. Incredibly luxurious houses all over the mountainsides. That's where the members of the government live, and highly placed officials within the administration. And anybody who refuses to recognize that A.I.D.S. money is going to the military, who apart from terrorizing the civilian population spend their time plundering mines in northern Congo – well, they're just being naïve. Every year billions are pumped into Africa to combat A.I.D.S., but if you ask any African woman in any African country you care to name, she'll say: It doesn't make any difference. Where does all that money go?

Malou von Sivers: Yes, where does it go?

Mauri Kallis: Into the pockets of members of the government, but that isn't the worst of it. Better to build luxury houses than spend it on arms. But the A.I.D.S. workers have jobs they enjoy, and that's fine. I'm only trying to say that if you're going to run a company down there, you need to be prepared to interact with people who are dodgy in one way or another. You're going to get your own fingers a little bit dirty, but at least you're doing something. And if I build a road from my mine, then it's difficult for me to prevent troops from using it.

Malou von Sivers: So you have no trouble sleeping soundly?

Mauri Kallis: I've never slept soundly, but that isn't the reason.

Malou von Sivers [he has adopted a defensive stance now, she changes tack]: Let's go back to your upbringing then, can you tell us something about that? Born in Kiruna in '64. Single mother who couldn't look after you.

Mauri Kallis: No, she wasn't really capable of looking after a child. My half-brothers and sisters who came along later were more or less taken into care straight away, but as I was her first I lived with her until I was eleven.

Malou von Sivers: And how was that?

Mauri Kallis [fumbles for the right words, closes his eyes sometimes, it is as if he pauses to look at the scenes playing in his head]: I had to manage on my own . . . a great deal. She was asleep when I went to school. She . . . used to get very angry if I said I was hungry . . . She could disappear for several days at a time, and I had no idea where she was.

Malou von Sivers: Is it difficult for you to talk about this?

Mauri Kallis: Extremely.

Malou von Sivers: You have a family of your own now. A wife, two sons aged ten and twelve. In what way has your upbringing influenced you in that role?

Mauri Kallis: It's hard to say, but I have no internal picture of how to live a normal family life. In school I used to see, how shall we put it, normal people. They had nice clean hair . . . And fathers. Occasionally I would go to a friend's house, but not very often. And I'd see their homes. Furniture, rugs, ornaments, an aquarium with tropical fish. We had almost nothing at home. Social services once bought us a lovely second-hand sofa, I remember that. It had one of those holes in the back that you could open, and pull out a spare bed. I thought it was just the height of luxury. Two days later it was gone.

Malou von Sivers: Where did it go?

Mauri Kallis: I suppose somebody sold it. People were always coming and going. The door was never locked, as far as I remember.

Malou von Sivers: And you were finally placed in a foster home.

Mauri Kallis: My mother became extremely paranoid, and behaved in a threatening manner to the neighbours and people in town. She was taken into care. And when she was taken into care . . .

Malou von Sivers: . . . you were taken into care as well. And you were eleven at the time.

Mauri Kallis: Yes. And you can always think back and wish . . . that things had been different, that I'd been taken into care earlier and so on . . . but that's how things were.

Malou von Sivers: Are you a good father yourself?

Mauri Kallis: That's a tough question. I do my best, but of course I'm away from the family far too much. That's not ideal.

*

Mella shifted position in her chair.

"That drives me mad," she said to Stålnacke. "If you confess your sin it doesn't count, somehow. As soon as he says 'I ought to spend more time with my children', that makes him a good person. What's he going to say to his boys when they've grown up? 'I know I was never there, but I can assure you I had a guilty conscience the whole time.' 'We know, Daddy. Thank you, Daddy. We love you, Daddy.'"

Mauri Kallis: But I have a reliable wife who's always there. Without her I'd never have been able to run this company and have children as well. She has had to teach me.

Malou von Sivers [obviously charmed by his gratitude towards his wife]: What, for example?

Mauri Kallis [ponders]: Often really simple things. That a family sits down and eats together. That kind of thing.

Malou von Sivers: Do you think you appreciate "normal" life more than someone like me, who's had an ordinary upbringing?

Mauri Kallis: Yes, I do think that. I feel like a refugee in the "normal" world.

When Diddi is in his third term at business school, he is finally able to leave the normal world. He has always had looks and charm, but now he has money. He goes beyond Stockholm. Further than Riche. He totters along the Canal Saint-Martin with two Gisele-like models as the sun rises over Paris. Not because they're so drunk they cannot walk properly, but because they are pushing each other like playful children as they walk home. The trees droop over the water like abandoned women, dropping their leaves like old love letters, every one blood red. There is the smell of newly baked bread from the bakery. Delivery vans go tearing by towards the city centre, their tyres bumping on the cobbles. The world will never seem more beautiful than this.

He meets an actor at a poolside party and is invited along on someone's private jet to two weeks' filming in the Ukraine. Diddi is able to show the required generosity. He has ten bottles of Dom Pérignon with him on the plane.

And then he meets Sofia Fuensanta Cuervo. She is much older than him, thirty-two, distantly related to the Spanish royal family on her mother's side, and to St John of the Cross on her father's side.

She is the black sheep of the family, she says, divorced with two children who are at boarding school.

Diddi has never met anyone like her. He is a wanderer who has finally reached the sea, and he wades out up to his elbows and drowns. Her arms can cure anything. He can lose himself if only she smiles, or scratches her nose. He is even filled with thoughts about himself and her children. Vague pictures of flying kites on the beach and reading aloud to them at night. He is not permitted to meet them, and Sofia does not talk about them much. She goes to visit them sometimes, but he is not allowed to go with her. She does not want them to get attached to someone who might disappear, she says. But he is never going to disappear. He wants to stay there for ever, his hands entwined in her coal-black hair.

Her friends own huge boats. He joins them when they go hunting during a visit to the country estate of some friends in the north-west of England. Diddi looks just wonderful in his borrowed hunting clothes and felt cap. He is like a little brother to all the men, and all the women adore him.

"I refuse to kill anything," he tells everybody with all the seriousness of a child. He and a thirteen-year-old girl are allowed to go along and join the beaters, and they talk for a long time about her horses; in the evening she persuades their hostess to place Diddi beside her at the table. Sofia lends him out and laughs, claiming her nose has really been put out of joint!

Diddi takes Sofia out to dinner, he buys her ridiculously expensive shoes and jewellery. He takes her to Zanzibar for a week. It looks like a theatre set: the decaying beauty of the town, the intricately carved wooden doors, the skinny cats chasing little white crabs on the long white beaches, the heavy aroma of cloves drying in great heaps on red cloths spread out on the ground. And against this backdrop of beauty breathing its last: soon the doors and the façades will have crumbled away, soon the island will be exploited to death, soon the beaches will be packed with noisy Germans and fat Swedes; against this backdrop is their love.

People turn and gaze after them as they wander along, their fingers entwined. His hair has been bleached almost white by the sun, hers is the shining black mane of an Andalusian mare.

At the end of November, Diddi rings from Barcelona wanting to sell. Mauri explains there is nothing to sell.

"Your capital has been used up."

Diddi tells him there's a furious hotel owner after him who's very keen for him to pay up.

"I mean, he's bloody livid, I have to sneak out so he doesn't catch me on the stairs."

At first Mauri bites his tongue during the long, embarrassing silence while Diddi waits for him to offer to lend him money. Then Diddi asks straight out. And Mauri says no.

After the telephone conversation, Mauri goes out for a walk in a snowy Stockholm. The rage of a person who has been abandoned follows in his footsteps like a dog. What the fuck was Diddi thinking? Did he think he could just ring up and Mauri would just bend over with his pants around his knees?

No. Mauri spends the next three weeks at his new girlfriend's house. All these years later, sitting in an interview with Malou von

Sivers, he would not be able to remember her name even if somebody were holding a gun to his head.

Three weeks after their telephone conversation, Diddi turns up in the kitchen on Mauri's student corridor. It is Saturday evening. Mauri's girlfriend has gone out to dinner with her friends. Håkan, who lives on Mauri's corridor, looks at Diddi as if he were watching him on T.V. He forgets to look away and behave like a human being. Stares at him uninterruptedly, his mouth hanging open. Mauri feels an inexplicable urge to punch him in the face. Just so he will close his mouth.

Diddi's eyes are white ice on a red sea. Sticky snow is melting in his hair and trickling down his face.

Sofia's love vanished with the money, but Mauri does not know anything about that yet.

Inside Mauri's room it all comes pouring out. Mauri is a fucking con man. Twenty-five per cent? Fucking ridiculous. He is so fucking mean he screams when he has to go for a crap. Diddi can accept ten per cent, and he wants his money. NOW!

"You're drunk," Mauri says.

He sounds compassionate when he says it. He has gone through the school of life and learned how to deal with exactly this sort of thing. He slips easily into his foster father's stance and tone of voice. Soft on the outside, rock hard on the inside. He has his foster father inside him. And inside his foster father, his foster brother is waiting. It's like those Russian dolls. Inside his foster brother is Mauri. But it will be many years before that particular doll comes out.

Diddi does not know anything about any Russian dolls. Or he doesn't care. He drills his rage into the foster father doll, screaming and going crazy. He will have only himself to blame if the foster brother comes out.

*

Malou von Sivers: So you were placed in a foster home when you were eleven. How did that go?

Mauri Kallis: It was a significant improvement on the way things had been. But it was a way of earning money for my foster parents, this business of fostering. They both did a lot of different things, one way or another. My foster mother had at least three jobs at the same time. She called my foster father the old man, and so did my foster brother and I. And he called himself that too.

Malou von Sivers: Tell me about him.

Mauri Kallis: He was a con man who kept himself more or less within the boundaries of the law, but he lacked scruples. A really small-time businessman. [He smiles and shakes his head at the memory.] For example, he bought and sold cars, the whole garden was full of old wrecks. Sometimes he went to other towns to sell. He would put on a shirt and a dog collar, because after all people trust a man of God. "I've read the laws of the church from cover to cover," he said. "Nowhere does it say you have to be ordained to wear a collar like this."

Sometimes people who think they have been conned turn up at the house. Often they are angry, sometimes they are crying. The old man sympathizes, he is sorry. He offers them a coffee or something stronger, but business is a matter of honour. The deal stands. He will not let go of the money.

On one occasion a woman who has bought a used car from the old man comes to the house. She has brought her ex-husband with her. The old man can read him in an instant.

"Fetch Jocke," he says as soon as the couple get out of the car.

Mauri runs to fetch his foster brother.

When Mauri and Jocke get there, the old man has already been pushed around a little. But Jocke has a lump of wood in his hand. The woman's eyes grow big.

"Let's get out of here," she says, tugging at her ex-husband's arm.

He allows her to pull him along. That way he can give in with his pride intact. You only have to look at Jocke to see that he is crazy. And yet he is only thirteen. Still just a little boy, making mischief. Like the business with the dog. Such mischief. One of the neighbours in the village lets his dog run loose. The old man has been getting annoyed because it pisses in his front garden. One day Jocke and his friends catch it, pour kerosene over it and set it alight. They laugh as it runs across the meadow like a torch. It is almost as if they are competing to see who can laugh the loudest, who is having the most fun. Egging each other on with sneaky glances.

And Jocke teaches Mauri to fight. When he first arrives at the foster home, Mauri does not have to go to school, he is going to restart the year in the autumn. He hangs about in the village. There is not much to do in Kaalasjärvi, but he is not bored. He goes along with the old man in the car on his "business trips". A quiet little lad is an excellent accessory. The old man sells water purifiers to old people and ruffles Mauri's hair. The old ladies offer them coffee and cakes.

There is no hair-ruffling at home. Jocke leans over him at the dinner table and calls him cripple, spastic, retard. He knocks over Mauri's milk as soon as his foster mother turns her back. Mauri never tells. It doesn't actually bother him. Being teased is normal. He concentrates on eating! Fish fingers. Pizza. Sausage and mash. Blood pudding with sweet lingonberry jam. His foster mother watches him in fascination.

"Where do you put it all?" she says.

The summer passes. Then school starts. Mauri tries to lie low, but there are kids who have a nose for a compliant victim.

They push his head down the toilet and flush. He doesn't say anything, but somehow they find out at home.

"You've got to get them back," says Jocke.

Not that he cares about Mauri. Jocke just likes it when something is happening.

Jocke has a plan. Mauri tries to say that he doesn't want to do it. It's not that he is afraid of being beaten up. Being hit by his peers is . . . nothing. It's unpleasant, that's all. And he tries to avoid unpleasantness as much as he can. But that alternative is not available.

"In that case I'll beat you up instead, you get it?" Jocke says. "I'll make so much trouble they'll send you back to your mother."

Then Mauri agrees to go along with it.

It is three boys in another class who are the worst tormentors. They find Mauri in a corridor near the recreation room and start pushing him around. Jocke has stayed nearby, and now he comes over with two of his friends and says it is time to get things sorted out. Jocke and his pals are in Year 7. Mauri might think his three tormentors are big and scary, but next to Jocke and his buddies they're just little shits.

The leader of the bullies says:

"Sure. O.K.!"

He tries to look as if he is not bothered, but all three of them look rattled. It is an ancient reflex, the eyes are looking for an escape route.

Jocke leads them out of the recreation room where there are supervisors and teachers, to the storeroom outside the craft rooms. He shows Mauri and the leader of his tormentors into a corridor which is a dead end, with clothes cupboards along both sides.

The leader's two pals think they're going with him, but Jocke stops them. This is between Mauri and the leader.

The match begins. The leader pushes Mauri in the chest so that he falls into a locker, hitting his head and his back. Fear floods his body.

"Come on Mauri, get him!" Jocke's friends shout.

Jocke does not shout. His face is expressionless, almost inert. The leader's friends dare not call out, but their body language grows bolder. They are beginning to think that the only one who is going to get beaten up here is Mauri. And they have no problem with that.

Then it happens. A different system is switched on in Mauri's head. Not the system that gives in and backs away and puts its hands up to its head to protect itself. There is something shining inside his head, his body is moving of its own accord while he looks on.

It is everything Jocke taught him. And a little bit more.

In a single movement his feet dance forwards, his hand supports itself on top of one of the lockers and helps to give height and strength to the kick. A kick like a mule, hitting his opponent on the side of the head. Then a kick in the stomach, a fist in the face.

An insight: this is how he has to fight, distance, strike, distance. You cannot wrestle and push people around when they are bigger than you. Mauri is back inside himself, but he is alert, looking around for a weapon. He finds a loose locker door that the caretaker is going to fix any year now; he has got his cottage to do up after all, and he is hardly ever in school.

Mauri gets hold of the locker door with both hands; it is made of orange tin, and he slams it down. Crash. Bang. It is the leader of the bullies who is holding his hands up now. He is the one who is trying to protect his head now.

Jocke grabs Mauri's arm and says that's enough. Mauri has driven his opponent right into the corner. He is lying down. Mauri is not afraid he has killed him: he hopes he has killed him, he wants to kill him. Reluctantly, he lets go of the door.

He walks away. Jocke and his pals have already disappeared in a different direction. His arms are shaking with the effort.

The three boys from the other class do not tell a soul. They might have taken their revenge if it had not been for Jocke and his friends.

Jocke probably would not have bothered, but they think Jocke is on Mauri's side.

Mauri does not become king of the class. He does not win respect. He does not advance one single step up the status ladder. But he is left in peace. He can sit out in the school playground waiting for the bus and thinking his own thoughts, instead of being ever on his guard, ready to slip away and hide.

But the following night he dreams that he kills his mother. Beats her to death with an iron pipe. He wakes up and listens, because he thinks he might have been screaming. Or was she the one who was screaming, in the dream? He sits up in bed and tries to stay awake, afraid of going back to sleep.

Diddi is standing in Mauri's student room. His hair is wet, he is making a noise, he wants money. His money, he insists. Mauri says pleasantly, in his foster father's voice, that he is sorry things have turned out like this between them, but they had a deal and it stands.

Diddi says something contemptuous, then he gives Mauri a push in the chest.

"Don't do that," Mauri warns him.

Diddi pushes him again. He probably wants Mauri to push him back, then they can push each other harder and harder until it is time to give up and go home and sleep it off.

But the blow comes instantly. It is foster brother Jocke, who needs no warm-up time. Right in the middle of the nose. Diddi has never been hit before, he does not have time to raise his hand to his nose, the blood does not have time to begin flowing before the next blow falls. And then his arm is being twisted up his back and Mauri leads him out into the corridor, down the stairs, and throws him out into the wet snow.

Mauri takes the stairs back up to his room three steps at a time.

He is thinking about his money. He can take the lot out tomorrow if he wants to. It is just about two million. But what would he do with it?

He feels free. Now he does not have to wait for Diddi to get in touch.

Inspector Tommy Rantakyrö poked his head around the door of the interview room.

"Mr Kallis and company are here," he said.

Mella shut down the computer and went down to the main office along with her colleagues Rantakyrö and Stålnacke.

Mauri Kallis had Diddi Wattrang and his chief of security, Mikael Wiik, with him. Three men in long black coats. That alone made them stand out. Men in Kiruna wore jackets.

Diddi Wattrang kept shifting from one foot to the other, his eyes flicking everywhere. When he shook hands with Mella, his grip was fierce.

"I'm so nervous," he confessed. "When it comes to the crunch I'm a real wimp."

Mella was disarmed by his honesty. She was completely unused to men who admitted they were weak. She was overcome by the desire to say the right thing, but only managed to mutter something about understanding that it must be difficult.

Kallis was shorter than she had imagined. Not as short as she was, of course, but still. Seeing him in the flesh, she was struck by how sparse his body language was. It was so obvious with the restless Wattrang by his side. Kallis spoke in a calm, quiet voice. There was nothing left of his Kiruna dialect.

"We want to see her," he said.

"Of course," said Mella. "And afterwards I'd like to ask you a few questions, if that's all right."

"If that's all right", she thought. Stop creeping!

The chief of security shook hands with the police officers, and it quickly emerged that he himself had begun his working life in the police.

He gave them each his card. Rantakyrö put it in his wallet. Mella resisted the urge to throw it straight into the waste paper basket.

Granlund, the autopsy technician, had rolled Inna Wattrang's body into the chapel, since her relatives were going to come and see her. It was free of religious symbols. A few chairs and a bare altar.

The body was covered with a white sheet; there was no reason to reveal her stab wounds or burns. Mella folded the sheet back from her face.

Diddi Wattrang nodded and swallowed. Mella noticed that Stålnacke discreetly moved to stand behind him so that he could catch him if he fell.

"That's her," said Kallis sorrowfully, taking a deep breath.

Diddi dug a packet of cigarettes out of his jacket pocket and lit one. Nobody said anything. It was not their job to make sure the no smoking rule was followed.

The security chief walked around the bier and lifted the sheet, looked at Inna Wattrang's arms, looked at her feet, paused for a second when he saw the circular mark around her ankle.

Kallis and Diddi followed his actions with their eyes, but when he lifted the sheet where it covered her hips and pudenda, they both glanced away. Neither of them spoke.

"I don't think the medical examiner will appreciate your doing that," Mella said.

"I'm not touching her," replied the security chief, leaning over her face. "Relax, we're on the same side."

"Perhaps you could wait outside," Mella said.

"Sure," said the security chief. "I'm done here."

He left the room.

At a sign from Mella, Stålnacke followed him. She did not want the security chief roaming around the autopsy suite.

Diddi Wattrang blew his fringe out of his eyes and scratched his nose with the hand that was holding the cigarette. It was a thoughtless movement. Mella was afraid he was going to set fire to his hair.

"I'll wait outside," he said to Kallis. "I can't do this."

He went out. Mella moved to replace the sheet over Inna Wattrang's face.

"Could you leave it a moment?" Kallis asked. "Her mother wants her to be cremated, so this is the last time I . . ."

Mella took a step backwards.

"May I touch her?"

"No."

There were just the two of them left in the room.

Mauri Kallis smiled. Then it almost looked as if he were going to cry.

Two weeks go by. Mauri threw Diddi out in the snow, and there has been no sign of him at college. He tells himself he does not care.

"What are you thinking about?" asks Mauri's girlfriend. She is so simple he can hardly stand it. "I'm thinking about when we met," he replies. Or: "I'm thinking about how sweet you are when you laugh. You're only allowed to laugh at my jokes though, don't forget!" Or: "About your bum! Come to Daddy." An easy way to avoid her: "Do you love me?" That's where he draws the line at lying. He can lie and dissemble about anything else. But it is remarkable that it is so difficult to answer "yes" to that particular question and look her in the eye as if you mean it.

Then Inna Wattrang comes to call one evening.

She is so like her brother, the same distinctive nose, the same blonde bob. He looks almost like a girl and she looks almost like a boy. A young boy in a skirt and a white shirt.

Her shoes look expensive. She did not take them off when she came in. She is wearing pretty pearl earrings.

She has just finished her law studies, she says, sitting there on the edge of Mauri's bed. He is sitting on the desk chair, trying to keep a cool head.

"Diddi," she says, "is an idiot. He met the woman it's every young man's destiny to meet. The one who gives him an excuse to behave like a pig towards every other woman for all eternity."

She smiles and asks if it is O.K. to smoke. Mauri notices that she has a single dimple, only on one side of her face.

"Oh, I'm terrible," she says.

She has a voice like a '30s movie star, and blows out smoke like a little train. It is as if she has come from another time. Mauri has a vision of her surrounded by housemaids in black dresses and white aprons; she is driving a car, wearing gloves and drinking absinthe.

"I don't want to belittle his pain," she says. "That Sofia really crushed him. I don't know what happened between the two of you, but he isn't himself. I don't know what to do. I'm really worried. I know he regards you as his friend. He's talked about you lots of times."

Mauri wants to believe. He really does. Lord I believe, help thou my unbelief.

"I know he wants to put things right between you. Come with me and meet him. He needs to be able to say sorry. The last thing he needs is to ruin the good relationships he has."

This is not what Mauri had in mind at all. But they take the number 540 bus and then the metro into town and he tramps with her through the wet falling snow to Strix.

She walks a little close to him, her upper arm brushing against him from time to time. He would like to take her arm, like in an old film. She is easy to talk to, and she laughs often. It is quite a low, soft laugh. They have time for a few drinks before her brother arrives.

She insists on paying. She has done a job for a relative who owns a property company, and she just been paid. Mauri is interested and asks questions; she has asked him about so many things already, but she dodges them skilfully although he does not notice it at the time. They're just suddenly talking about something else. He is pleasantly under the influence and forgets himself and he is talking a little bit too much and his eyes become disobedient and slide down towards her heavy breasts beneath the man's shirt.

And when Diddi arrives it really is like an old film, where three best friends are finally reconciled. The snow falling outside on the dark Stockholm streets. Insignificant people walk along Drottninggatan like film extras, or raise their glasses, talking and laughing at the tables nearby, but they are simply nobodies.

And Diddi, who is the most beautiful ghost and wreck you can imagine, weeps openly there in the restaurant as the story of Sofia comes tumbling out of him.

"She had no problem squandering my money, as long as it was there."

And Inna fleetingly caresses her brother's hand, but her knee is touching Mauri's all the time, although perhaps that does not mean a thing.

And much later, when they are standing under a street light outside an all-night store and it is time to part, Diddi says he wants to carry on speculating on the stock market with Mauri.

Mauri does not say anything about the fact that he and Diddi have never speculated together, it has always been Mauri who does the job. But the hardness inside him begins to wake up; no Inna or Diddi Wattrang or any magic in the world can rock it completely to sleep.

"Fine," he says with a half smile. "Come up with the money and you're in again. But this time I'm taking thirty per cent."

The atmosphere immediately becomes less pleasant. Mauri takes great gulps of the awkwardness. Thinks he will have to get used to this. If you are going to do business, and do it successfully, you need to be able to put up with things. Unpleasantness, awkwardness, tears, hatred.

And the homeless dog that sits somewhere inside his chest, he will need to keep that on the leash.

Then Inna bursts out into her melodious laugh.

"You're wonderful," she says. "I hope we can see each other again some time."

Mella pulled the sheet over Inna Wattrang's face.

"We'll go down to the station," she said. "I'd like you to tell me a bit about Inna Wattrang."

What can I say? Kallis thought. That she was a whore and a drug addict? That she was as much like God as a human being can be?

And then he lied to the very best of his ability. And he could lie very well indeed.

Rebecka Martinsson finished her work at one o'clock. She microwaved something boring and went through the morning's post. Just as she had sat down at her desk, her computer pinged. An e-mail from Måns Wenngren.

Just seeing his name on the screen was enough to send a twinge through her body. She clicked on the message as if it were a reflex action.

> I assume all hell has broken loose up there. Read about Inna Wattrang this morning. By the way, everybody in the office is coming up to the Riksgränsen resort to go skiing this weekend. Three days, Fri–Sun. Come and join us for a drink.

Nothing else. She read the message several times. Pressed send / receive as if it might magic up something else, another message perhaps.

He would make me unhappy, she thought. I know that.

Because she had been his assistant advocate she had sat in the next office to him, listening to him talking on the phone, his "Look, I'm just on my way to a meeting", although she knew he was not. "I'll call you . . . no, really, I will . . . I'll call you tonight." Then the conversation would be brought to a close, or else the person on the end would not give up, and then the door of his office would slam shut.

He never talked about his grown-up children, perhaps because he had no contact with them, perhaps because he did not want to remind people that he was actually over fifty.

He drank too much.

He slept with newly employed lawyers, and even with clients.

Once he had made a pass at her. It was at an office Christmas party. He had been pretty drunk, and everybody else had given him the brush-off. His drunken groping was not even a compliment, it was an insult.

And yet she still thought constantly about his hand on the back of her neck. About all the times they had sat in court together, had lunch together. Always a little bit too close, just so that they happened to brush against each other now and again. Or was that just her imagination?

And that time she had been stabbed. He had sat by her bed watching over her.

This is exactly what it is, she thought. This is exactly what I am so tired of. This brooding. On the one hand, on the other hand. On the one hand, this and this mean he cares. On the other hand, this and this mean he does not care. On the one hand, I ought to forget him. On the other hand, I ought to cling to every scrap of love I can find, like a drowning man. On the one hand, it will be complicated. On the other hand, it is never simple. Love, that is.

Love is like being possessed by a demon. Your will softens like butter. Your brain is full of holes. You have no control over yourself.

She had done her best when she was working for Wenngren. She put on her straightjacket, muzzle and choke chain every morning. Watching herself all the time so that she did not give herself away. She climbed into a kind of stiffness and hid herself inside it. She did not talk to him any more than necessary. Communicated by way of yellow Post-its and e-mail, although she was in the next door office. Often gazed out of the window when he was talking to her.

But she worked like the devil for him. She was the best assistant he had ever had.

Like a pathetic dog, she thought now.

She ought to e-mail him back. She wrote a reply, but deleted it immediately. Then all of a sudden it became difficult. Writing one single letter was like climbing a mountain. She turned and twisted the words. Nothing sounded right.

What would Grandmother have said about him? She would have thought he was a boy. And that was probably true. He was like one of Daddy's hunting dogs that never wanted to stop playing. It never really grew up, racing into the forest and coming back with sticks for Daddy to throw. In the end it was shot. No room in the house for a useless dog.

Grandmother would have noticed Måns Wenngren's soft white hands. She would not have said anything, but she would have thought a great deal. Puppy's games instead of real work. Sailing and using the treadmill at the gym. Rebecka could still remember him moaning and groaning all the way through a two-day court case because he had turned his ice-yacht over out in the archipelago. He had been black and blue all over.

Different from her father and the other men in the village.

She could see Daddy and Uncle Affe sitting in her grandmother's kitchen. They are drinking beer. Affe is cutting off slices of raw Falun sausage for his dog Freja. He holds the slice of sausage in front of her and asks: "What do the girls in Stockholm do?" And Freya lies on her back with all four legs in the air.

Rebecka likes their hands. Capable of doing all kinds of skilful work. The tips of the fingers rough and black from something that no soap can shift; there is forever some machine that needs looking at.

It is always O.K. to sit on Daddy's lap. You can stay there as long as you want. With Mummy your chances are fifty-fifty. "Oh, you're so heavy!" she says. Or: "Let me drink my coffee in peace."

Daddy smells of sweat and warm cotton and engine oil. She nuzzles into the stubble on his neck. His face is always sunburned, as are his neck and hands. But his body is as white as paper. He never sunbathes. None of the men in the village does, only their wives. The women lie on sun loungers sometimes. Weed the garden wearing bikinis.

Sometimes Daddy might lie down on the grass for a rest, with one arm under his head and his cap over his face. Homeowner Martinsson. It was a man's right and privilege to take a little rest on the grass in his own garden from time to time. Daddy works hard. Drives the logging machine in the forest at night to make his expensive investment pay. Does the chores around the house and garden himself. Works for a pipe-maker in town when there is not much in the forest.

But sometimes he lies down for a while. On the kitchen sofa in the winter. Out in the garden in the summer. Their oldest dog, Jussi, often comes to lie beside him. And soon he has his daughter on his other arm. The sun warms them. There is a strong scent from the wild camomile growing on the poor, sandy soil. Otherwise there are not many plants like that. With a powerful scent. You always have to get close to them to smell anything.

Rebecka has never seen her grandmother lying down like this. She never rests. And she certainly wouldn't be doing it outside, right in front of the house. People would think she had lost her mind. Or even died.

No, Grandmother would have thought Måns very strange. A Stockholm boy who could not take an engine apart, fish with a drag-net or even rake hay. And rich. Uncle Affe's wife Inga-Britt would have been nervous and got out the serviettes. And everybody would have wondered about Rebecka: who does she belong to now?

Just as they had already done. You always had to prove you had not changed. People were always saying: It's nothing special . . . I'm sure you're used to much better. And then she would have to heap praise on the food, say it was a long time since she had eaten perch, how delicious. The others were allowed to eat in peace, in silence. And then it became even clearer that she had taken on those Stockholm ways, too much praise.

There was a kind of gravity in Daddy that is lacking in Måns Wenngren. She will not say a depth, it is not that Måns is superficial. But Måns has never had to worry about his finances, fretting that he is not getting enough work to cover the payments on the logging machine. And there is another difference too. Something that does not come from worrying. A streak of melancholy.

That melancholy, she thinks. Was that what made Daddy cling onto Mummy with such intensity?

I think she came into his life with her laughter and her simplicity, because in her good spells she was as light as the wind. And I think he grabbed her upper arms with both hands. Held onto her, firm and tight. And I think she liked that, but only for a while. I think she thought she needed that. Security and calm and his embrace. And then she slunk away like an impatient cat.

And what about me? Rebecka thought, looking at Mån's message. Shouldn't I find somebody like Daddy, but hang onto him, unlike Mummy?

A heart that is in love is an indomitable thing. You can hide your feelings, but, inside, your heart takes over. Your head changes jobs, stops reasoning or making sensible decisions, and starts painting pictures: pathetic, romantic, sentimental, pornographic. The whole damn thing.

Rebecka Martinsson prays in vain: God protect me from passion. But it is already too late. She writes:

Sounds cool. Hope too many of you don't end up with broken legs on the slopes. I might come up for a drink, might not – depends on the weather and work and so on. Be in touch.

R

She changes the "R" to "Rebecka". And then changes it back. The message is ridiculously short and simple, but it takes her forty minutes to write it. She sends it. Then she can't get anything useful done at all. Just moves papers from one pile to another.

"Is it O.K. if I switch the tape recorder on?" Mella said.

She was sitting in Interview Room 1 with Mauri Kallis.

He had explained that they did not have much time left, they were flying back soon. So they had decided that Stålnacke would talk to Diddi Wattrang, and Mella to Kallis.

The security chief was hanging around in the corridor with Fred Olsson and an impressed Tommy Rantakyrö.

"Of course," Kallis said. "How did she die?"

"It's a little early to release details of the murder at this stage."

"But she was murdered?"

"Yes, murder or manslaughter . . . at any rate, somebody else will . . . She worked as head of information? What did that involve?"

"It was just a title. She did all kinds of things within the company. But certainly she was the one who was good at dealing with the media and building the brand. She was generally very good at dealing with people, the authorities, landowners, investors, you name it."

"Why? What was she so good at?"

"She was one of those people that you just want to like you. You wanted to please her. Her brother's the same, although at the moment he's a little too . . ."

Kallis made a slight shaking movement with his hand.

"You must have been close to her, you could say she lived with you after all."

"Well no, Regla is a large property with several farms and houses.

There are a lot of us living there: my family and I, Diddi and his wife and children, my half-sister, several employees."

"But she had no children?"

"No."

"Who was close to her, apart from you?"

"I'd just like to point out that you're the one who's saying I was close to her. But I'd say her brother, of course. And her parents are still alive."

"Anyone else?"

Kallis shook his head.

"Oh, come on," Mella said. "Girlfriends? Boyfriend?"

"This is rather difficult," said Kallis. "Inna and I worked together. She was a good . . . friend. But she wasn't the kind of person who makes friends for life. She was too restless for that. She didn't feel the need to sit chatting on the phone to girlfriends going over this and that. And to be honest, her boyfriends came and went. I never met them. This job was perfect for her. She could go off to a conference or an international event, and at the party in the evening she'd pull in ten investors."

"What did she do in her free time? Who did she meet up with?"

"I don't know."

"What did she do on her last holiday, for example?"

"I don't know that either."

"I find that rather strange. You were her boss. I have a very good idea what my lads do in their free time."

"Oh yes?"

Mella stopped speaking and waited. Sometimes that helped. But not this time. Kallis fell silent and waited too, apparently unconcerned.

In the end it was Mella who spoke first. They were leaving soon, after all. The conversation was oddly terse.

"Do you know if she felt threatened in any way?"

"Not that I'm aware of."

"Threatening letters? Calls? Anything like that?"

Kallis shook his head.

"Did she have any enemies?"

"I don't think so."

"Was there anybody with a grudge against the company that you think might have done this?"

"What for?"

"I don't know. Revenge? A warning?"

"Who would that be?"

"That's what I'm asking you," Mella said. "You're involved in a lot of risky deals. A lot of people must have lost money because of you. Somebody who feels they've been conned, perhaps?"

"We haven't conned anybody."

"O.K., we'll leave that one."

Kallis allowed an expression of simulated gratitude to cross his face.

"Who knew that she was in the company house in Abisko?"

"I don't know."

"Did you know she was there?"

"No. She'd taken a few days off."

"So," said Mella, summing up. "You don't know who she hung out with, what she did in her free time, if she felt threatened, or if there's anyone who might have a grudge against the company . . . Is there anything you'd like to tell me?"

"I don't think there is."

Kallis looked at his watch.

Mella was seized by the urge to give him a good shake.

"Did you ever talk about sex?" she asked. "Do you know if she had . . . particular interests in that area?"

Kallis blinked.

"What do you mean?" he asked. "Why are you asking that?"

"Did you ever talk about it?"

"Why? Has she been . . . was there any . . . is there some sort of sexual element involved?"

"As I said, it's too early . . ."

Kallis stood up.

"I'm sorry," he said. "I have to go now."

And with those words he left the room, after briskly shaking Mella by the hand. She did not even have time to switch off the tape recorder before the door closed behind him.

She got up and looked out into the parking lot. At least Kiruna had had the sense to show itself in the best light. Thick snow and brilliant sunshine.

Mauri Kallis, Diddi Wattrang and their security chief came out of the station and walked towards their hire car.

Kallis was walking two metres ahead of Wattrang; it didn't look as if they were speaking to each other. The security chief opened one of the rear doors for Kallis, but Kallis walked around the car and got into the front passenger seat. Wattrang had to sit in the back on his own.

Interesting, thought Mella. And they seemed to be such good friends when you saw them on T.V.

"How did it go?" Stålnacke said five minutes later.

He was sitting with Rantakyrö and Mella in her office, drinking coffee.

"I don't really know what to say," Mella said hesitantly. "It was probably the worst interview I've ever done."

"I'm sure it wasn't," Stålnacke said.

"It would have been better if I hadn't done it, I can promise you that. How did it go with Wattrang?"

"Not brilliantly. Perhaps we should have swapped. He would probably have been happier talking to you. What did he say now . . . That she was his best friend. And then he cried. He didn't know she was in Abisko, but evidently that's how she was. Didn't say much about what she was doing. Probably had a few boyfriends, but nobody the brother knew of right now."

"Mikael Wiik was a good guy," Rantakyrö said. "We had a bit of a chat. He was in the paratroopers when he did his military service, then he went on to train as an officer in the reserves."

"But he was in the police force?"

"Well, somebody's not telling us everything," said Mella, who was still lost in thought about her conversation with Kallis. "Either Inna or the other two."

"Yes, he was in the police. But then he went for a post as a reserve officer in the Special Protection Unit. Should have made a bit more of an effort when I did my military service. Instead of just hanging about doing as little as possible. Although you can get a job in Iraq and places like that with private bodyguard firms and that kind of thing. With a police background, that is. You don't need to be a soldier. When Wiik left the S.P.U. and went over to the private side, he was making 15,000 euros a month."

"With Kallis?" Stålnacke said.

"No, that was in Iraq. But then he wanted to work in Sweden and take things a bit easier. That man's been everywhere . . . although not to the places you'd go on holiday with the kids."

By now Mella had tuned into her colleagues' conversation. The last sentence sounded to her like a direct quote from Wiik.

"You stay here with us, never mind running off and getting shot in the head by terrorists," Stålnacke said to Rantakyrö, who was sitting there with his eyes full of dreams of adventure and plenty of money in his pockets.

Mikael Wiik swung off the E10 towards Kiruna airport.

Kallis and Wattrang had sat in silence all the way. Neither of them had even mentioned Inna. Wiik had not seen either of them shed a tear; as soon as they were alone, they did not even look at each other. He noticed that neither of them asked for his observations. What he thought. What he had found out when he had spoken to Rantakyrö.

This was the beginning of the time after Inna, that much was clear. Everything had been more fun in her time.

After his spell with the S.P.U., Wiik had found Sweden difficult to cope with. When he had come for his job interview with Kallis, he had been a man who woke up at three o'clock in the morning fighting a feeling that life at home was meaningless.

Inna had helped him through that first year with Kallis Mining. It was as if she could sense how things were for him. She had always managed to find time for them to chat about Kallis' business affairs, who they were meeting and why. Slowly he had begun to feel a part of Kallis Mining. Us against them.

He still slept badly, woke up early. But not so early. And he was not yearning to go back to the Congo, Iraq, Afghanistan, places like that.

Suddenly Kallis broke the silence in the car.

"If it's a sex crime, the bastard will pay for it with his life," he said grimly.

Wiik stole a glance at Wattrang in the rear view mirror. He looked as dead as his sister, black circles under his eyes, chalk-white face, chapped lips and his nose eaten away. His hands were tucked into his armpits. Maybe because he was cold, maybe to stop them shaking. It was time for him to pull himself together.

"Where are we landing?" asked Wattrang. "Skavsta or Arlanda?"

"Skavsta," Wiik said after a while, when Kallis did not answer.

"Are you going home?" Wattrang asked Wiik.

Wiik nodded. He lived in Kungsholmen with his partner. He had a room for the night with a kitchen and toilet at Regla, but he rarely made use of it.

"Then I can come to Stockholm with you," said Wattrang, closing his eyes and pretending to try and sleep.

Wiik nodded again. It was not up to him to tell Wattrang he ought to go home to Ulrika and his seven-month-old son.

Trouble, he thought. Best to be ready for it.

Kallis was looking out through the window.

I would have liked to touch her, he thought.

He tried to remember the times he had done so. Properly, a real touch.

At that moment he could recall only one occasion.

It is summer 1994. He has been married for three years. His eldest son is two, the youngest a few months old. Kallis is standing by the window in the small drawing room sipping a whisky and looking down at Inna's house, the old laundry that they've finally finished renovating.

He knows that Inna is just home from a visit to a processing plant for extracting iodine in the Atacama desert in Chile.

He has just had dinner with Ebba. The nanny is putting Magnus to bed, and Ebba places Carl in his arms. He holds the baby, not knowing what she really expects of him, so he keeps his eyes on the child and says nothing. Ebba seems happy with that. After only a little while his shoulders and the back of his neck are aching, he wants her to take it away, but perseveres. After an eternity Ebba lifts the child.

"I'm going to put him to bed," she says. "It'll take an hour. Are you going to wait?" He promises to wait.

Then he goes to stand over by the window, and suddenly he is longing so desperately for Inna.

I won't be long, he lies to himself. I'm just going to find out how things went in Chile. I'll be back before Ebba's finished putting Carl to bed.

Inna has unpacked. She seems really happy to see him. He is pleased too. Pleased that she works for him. Pleased that she lives at Regla. She has a high salary and a low rent. In his bad moments this makes him angry and insecure. He is tormented by the feeling that he is buying her.

But when he is with her, he never feels like that.

They start with the whisky he has brought along. Then they smoke a little and get silly and decide to swim. But they lose the impetus and end up lying on the grass down by the old jetty. The slender disc of the sun shimmers on the horizon, disappears. The sky darkens, pale starlight shining down; it always brings dizzying thoughts of eternity.

It should always be like this, thinks Kallis. Just as if I'm single. Why get married? Not for the free sex, at any rate. Sex with your own wife is the most expensive sex there is. Fact. You pay for it with your whole life.

When he married Ebba, he stepped away from Inna. For a while, she even stopped being so important to him. Difficult to put your finger on it exactly, but the power base between him and the Wattrangs altered. He became less dependent. Stopped having to stress the fact that he would be working at the weekends so they would not think he cared if they didn't invite him along to whatever they were doing.

Now he is giving back what he took from Inna then. At this very moment he does not think it is something he has to defend.

He turns onto his side and looks at her.

"Do you know why I married Ebba?" he asks.

Inna is inhaling smoke and cannot reply.

"Or to put it more correctly, why I fell in love with her," Kallis rambles on. "Because she had to walk a kilometre to school every day when she was little."

Inna bubbles up with laughter beside him.

"It's true. They lived at Vikstaholm when she was growing up. They had to sell up later, but in any case . . . to somebody like me . . . in any case . . . to some upstart . . . But in any case!"

He is finding it so difficult to follow the thread of the story that Inna just lies there laughing beside him. He goes on:

"She had a lift to school, and once she told me how she had to walk a kilometre from the palace to the road. And she told me she remembered the wood pigeons cooing in the bushes as she walked along the track on her own early in the mornings. That just captivated me. The picture of that little girl, walking along towards the road with a bag that was too big for her over one shoulder. The morning silence, broken by the cooing of the doves."

He is a pig and he knows it as soon as the words leave his mouth. Chop off Ebba's head and serve it to Inna on a silver platter. That picture of Ebba has been a sacred little thing. Now he has screwed it up like a piece of rubbish.

But Inna never thinks the way he expects her to. She stops sniggering and points out some of the constellations she recognizes as they begin to emerge more clearly.

Then she says:

"Actually, I think that sounds like an excellent reason to marry someone. Perhaps the best reason I've ever heard."

She rolls over onto her side and looks at him. They have never had sex. In some way she has made him understand that what they have together is much greater than that. They are friends. Her boyfriends, or whatever you want to call them, they come and go. Kallis is never going to be an ex.

They are lying there face to face. He takes hold of her hand. It is because he has been smoking that he is suddenly filled with the feeling that love does not make you vulnerable. It costs nothing to love. You become Gandhi, Jesus, and the starlit sky.

"Inna . . ." he says.

And then his thoughts run around desperately looking for words he never uses.

"I'm glad you moved here," he says in the end.

Inna smiles. He likes the fact that she is smiling and not saying anything. That she doesn't say "I'm glad too" or "you're wonderful". He has learned how easily she uses words like that. He lets go of her hand before she has time to say anything.

Anna-Maria Mella sank down in Martinsson's armchair. It was 2.15 in the afternoon.

"How's it going?" she asked.

"Not so well," Martinsson said with a half smile. "I'm getting nowhere fast."

And I'm not getting any messages from Måns, she thought, glancing at her computer.

"Oh, one of those days. You sort out one pile and turn it into three new piles. But you were in court this morning, weren't you?"

"I was, and that went well. It's just this . . ."

Martinsson waved a hand at the documents and papers covering her desk.

Mella smiled mischievously at her.

"Damn!" she said. "This conversation's taken completely the wrong turn. I was going to ask you to carry on helping us with Inna Wattrang."

Martinsson was pleased.

"That's O.K.," she said. "Go ahead and ask."

"I'd really like you to check her out. The kind of thing that shows up on the financial records. I don't really know what I'm looking for . . ."

"Anything unusual," Martinsson said. "Regular payments. In or out. A sudden sale of personal property. Shall I check out her financial involvement in Kallis Mining as well? Whether she went in as a private investor? If she sold or made a profit in some particularly noteworthy way? What she's made or lost money on?"

"Yes please," Mella said, getting to her feet. "I've got to go now. I was thinking of going up to the house where she was murdered, so I'm going to get on the road now before it gets dark."

"Can I come with you?" Martinsson asked. "It would be interesting to see the place."

Mella gritted her teeth and made a rapid choice. She ought to say no, of course; Martinsson had no business visiting the scene of the murder. Plus there was the risk that she might relapse. What effect might the thought of a murder in that kind of location have on her? It was impossible to hazard a guess. Mella was no psychologist. On the other hand, Martinsson was being kind enough to help out with the investigation. She had a knowledge of financial matters that nobody in Mella's team could come close to. There was no chance of Mella finding somebody in the economic crimes squad who would be prepared to spend time randomly searching for something or other that she was not entirely clear about. Besides which, Martinsson was an adult who could take responsibility for her own health.

"We need to get a move on then," she said.

Mella enjoyed the drive up to Abisko.

It doesn't get any better than this, she thought. With the snow and the sunshine and everybody out and about on their snowmobiles and their skis.

Martinsson was in the passenger seat leafing through the preliminary investigation notes, reading and talking to Mella at the same time.

"You've got four children, haven't you?"

"Yes," said Mella, and started telling Martinsson about them.

Well, she's asking, she thought. So I'll answer her.

She told her about Marcus, who was in his last year at senior school. They did not see him all that often.

"Although of course sometimes he needs money. And sometimes he comes home to change. I don't think his clothes have had a chance to get dirty at all, but there's a hell of a lot of showering and changing and spraying. Jenny's thirteen and she's the same. Petter will be nine next week; he plays Bionicle and he really is a Mummy's boy. He's the complete opposite of the older two. He never goes round to see friends, he's always at home on his own. And that's no good either, of course. Then you start worrying about that."

"And then there's Gustav."

"Mmm," Mella said, stopping herself just in time before she started talking about the last time Robert had taken Gustav to nursery. There were limits. It was only other mothers who would find that kind of thing amusing.

There was silence. It was on the night that Gustav was born that Rebecka Martinsson had killed three men in a cottage in Jiekajärvi, in self-defence. She had been stabbed, and if Mella's colleagues had not got there in time, she would have died.

"Who likes kissing his old Mum," Martinsson said.

"But actually he's Daddy's biggest fan. The other day Robert was standing in the bathroom having a pee – I'm married to one of those men who think you'll turn into a homosexual if you sit down, and who's going to clean up when the boys do the same thing . . . Anyway, he was standing there having a pee, and Gustav was standing beside him with an expression of total admiration on his face. 'Daddy,' he said reverently, 'You've got a HUGE willy! It's like an elephant's willy!' You should have seen my husband after that. He kind of . . ."

She ended the sentence with a flap of her arm and a hoarse cock-crow.

Martinsson laughed.

"But it's Marcus who's your favourite, isn't it?"

"Oh, well, you love them all just as much in different ways," Mella said, keeping her eyes on the road.

How the hell could Martinsson guess that? Mella tried to go back a few sentences. It was true. She loved Marcus in a special way. They had always been more than just mother and son. Friends too. Although it was not something she ever allowed to show, or talked about; she hardly even admitted it to herself.

When they got out of the car at Kallis Mining's holiday house Mella felt almost as if she'd been conned. Rebecka Martinsson had got her to talk about herself, her family and the job all the way up. She hadn't said a word about herself.

Mella unlocked the door and showed Martinsson the kitchen, where the flooring had been ripped up.

"We're still waiting for the results from the lab, but we're assuming at this point that it was Inna Wattrang's blood in this little nick here. So we think she was killed right here. We've found traces of tape on her wrists and ankles, and on a chair like those ones."

She pointed to the dark oak kitchen chairs.

"And we're hoping to find out what kind of tape it was. And I'm also waiting for the medical examiner's report. Although provisionally he has said that she wasn't raped . . . but you know how it is, you wonder if she had had intercourse. That would suggest even more strongly that there was some kind of sex game involved . . ."

Martinsson nodded to show she was listening, and looked around.

If I'm waiting for someone, she thought, as the picture of Måns Wenngren took shape in her head, I put on my best underwear. What else do I do? Clean up, of course, tidy things away so that everything will be nice and cosy.

She looked at the dirty dishes in the kitchen. The empty milk carton.

"The kitchen's a mess," she said hesitantly.

"You should see what my place looks like sometimes," Mella said.

And I buy nice food, Martinsson continued her train of thought. And something to drink.

She opened the refrigerator. A few microwave meals.

"Was this all there was in the refrigerator?"

"Yes."

In that case it wasn't somebody new, Martinsson thought. She didn't need to make that kind of effort. But why the sports clothes?

She could not get it to make sense. She closed her eyes and started again.

He is on his way, she thought. For some reason I don't need to clean up and I don't need to shop. He calls me from Arlanda.

She thought about Wenngren's drawling voice on the telephone.

"Telephone," she said to Mella without opening her eyes. "Have you got her mobile phone?"

"No, we didn't find one. But we're checking her out with the networks, of course."

"Computer?"

"No."

Martinsson opened her eyes and looked out through the kitchen window towards Torneträsk.

"A woman like that with a job like that," she said. "She must have had both a laptop and a mobile. She was found in an ark out here. Don't you think you should send the divers down to check if the person who carried her to the ark dropped her phone through the fishing hole in the ice?"

"Good idea," Mella said without hesitation.

She ought to feel grateful, of course. Or say something complimentary to Martinsson. But she just could not do it. All she could feel was anger. Because she hadn't thought of it herself. And what the hell were her colleagues there for!

Mella looked at her watch. The divers would have time to search before dark if they came up right away.

By 4.15 on Monday afternoon a team of three divers had arrived, along with Stålnacke. They had sawn a hole in the ice. It was one metre in diameter. They had worked with an electric drill and chainsaws, and getting the thick block of ice out had been challenging. Mella, Stålnacke and Martinsson had all helped the divers with the lifting and carrying. The sun was beating down, and beneath their soaking wet jumpers their back muscles were aching from the exertion.

But now the sun was beginning to disappear, the temperature was dropping and they were starting to feel the cold.

"We'll need to make sure we cordon this off and mark it really clearly so nobody falls in," Stålnacke said.

"Still, it was lucky it was just here," the diver looking after the line said to Mella and Stålnacke. "It shouldn't be too deep; we'll see."

The reserve diver was sitting on a mat at the edge of the hole in the ice. He raised his hand in greeting as his colleague disappeared beneath the ice with a 75 watt flashlight. The lineman paid out the line, a few air bubbles floated to the surface, the diver swam below the ice towards the ark where Inna Wattrang had been found.

Mella shivered. Her wet clothes were drawing the warmth out of her body. She ought to run around to keep warm, but she just couldn't do it.

That was what Martinsson was doing. Running along the snowmobile tracks. It would soon start to go dark.

"She thinks we're complete Muppets, of course," Mella said to Stålnacke. "First of all she has to explain fission and fusion and exchanging capital investments, and now she has to teach us how to do our job."

"No, she doesn't," Stålnacke said. "She just happened to think of something before you got there. You can handle that, surely?"

"No," Mella said, only half seriously.

After twelve minutes the diver surfaced. He took the breathing tube out of his mouth.

"Nothing on the bottom, as far as I could see," he said. "But I found this, I don't know if it's anything important. It was floating under the ice fifteen metres from the hole, beneath the ark."

He threw a bundle of cloth onto the ice. The lineman and the reserve diver helped their colleague up out of the water while Mella and Stålnacke undid the bundle.

It was a man's beige poplin coat. Windproof, with a belt and a thin lining.

"Might not be anything," the diver said.

He had been given a mug of hot coffee.

"People sling all kinds of crap in the water," he said. "It's such a fucking tip down there. Old meatball packaging, plastic bags . . ."

"I think it is something," Mella said slowly.

On the left shoulder and the back of the coat there were faint pink stains.

"Blood?" Stålnacke said.

"From your mouth to the ear of God," Mella said, raising her hands and pretending to pray to a higher power. Let it be blood.

TUESDAY, 18 MARCH, 2005

The avenue of lime trees leading to Kallis' home, the Regla estate, ran a kilometre and a half from the main road. The trees were old ladies, some two hundred years old, gnarled yet slender, some of them as hollow as oaks. They stood there neatly, two by two, informing visitors that order had reigned here for many centuries. Here the residents sat nicely at table and observed a polite and civilized manner.

After a kilometre the avenue was interrupted by an iron gate. Four hundred metres further on there was another iron gate, set in a whitewashed brick wall surrounding the garden. The iron gates were cleverly crafted, two metres high, opened by means of a remote control in the residents' cars. Visitors, on the other hand, had to stop outside the first gate and use the entryphone.

The main building was a white house with a black slate roof, pillars on either side of the entrance, wings off to the sides, and leaded windows. The décor followed the style of the second half of the 18th century. Only in the bathroom had the owners gone for completely modern fittings – Philippe Starck.

Regla was such a beautiful place that Kallis could hardly bear it that first summer. It was easier in the winter. In the summer he was often struck by a sense of unreality as he drove or walked along the avenue. The light filtering through the tops of the lime trees, falling like a melody onto the road. He was almost revolted by the pastoral idyll in which he was living.

Kallis was lying awake in his bedroom on the second floor. He did not want to look at the clock, because if it was 5.45, he would have to get up in a quarter of an hour, which meant it was too late to go back to sleep. On the other hand, it might be an hour before it was time to get up. He looked at the clock; he always did in the end. 4.15. He had slept for three hours.

He had to get more sleep, otherwise anybody could see the whole thing was about to implode. He tried to breathe calmly, to relax. He turned his pillow over.

When he had managed to lull himself into a kind of half sleep, the dream returned.

In the dream he was sitting on the edge of his bed. His room looked exactly as it did in reality. Sparsely furnished, with the slender desk inlaid with wood, and the beautifully worn Gustavian chair with upholstered arms. His purpose-built dressing room in walnut and frosted glass, where his suits and perfectly ironed shirts hung in rows, his hand-made shoes in a special section with cedarwood shoe trees. The walls painted with linseed oil paint, pale blue with the faintest of colour variations; he had rejected borders and decorative paint effects when his wife was renovating the place.

But in the dream he could see Inna's shadow on the wall. And when he turned his head, she was sitting on the window seat. Behind her there was no glittering Lake Mälaren. Instead he could see the outlines of Terrassen, the apartment block where he grew up, through the window.

She was scratching and tearing at the watery mark around her ankle. The flesh was catching under her nails.

He was wide awake again now. He could hear the beating of his heart. Calm, calm. No, it was no good, he could not stand it, he would have to get up.

He put the light on, threw back the bedclothes as if they were an enemy, swung his legs over the edge of the bed and stood up.

Do not think about Inna. She has gone. Regla's still here. Ebba and the boys. Kallis Mining.

There was something wrong with him, of course. He tried to think about the boys, but it was no good. Their royal names sounded ridiculous and alien: Carl and Magnus.

When they were small they had lain in their expensive prams. He had always been away, travelling. Never missed them. Not that he could remember, in any case.

At that moment he heard a thud from the attic above. Then another thud.

Ester, he thought. She's at it again with her weights.

God, it sounded as though the entire ceiling was about to come down on him.

It was Inna who brought Ester into their lives.

"You have a sister," she says.

They're sitting in the S.A.S. lounge at Copenhagen airport, on the way to Vancouver. It looks like summer outside, but the wind is still cold. In a year she'll be dead.

"I have three," Kallis replies in a cool voice, indicating that this conversation does not interest him.

He does not like thinking about them. The eldest sister was born when he was nine. She was one when she was taken into care. They took him a year later.

He tries not to think about the time when he was growing up in Terrassen, the tower block in Kiruna where social services had apartments for people who could not get a rental agreement of their own. Harsh voices and the sound of quarrelling and screaming penetrated constantly through the walls, and nobody ever rang the police. The graffiti in the stairwell was never washed off. A feeling of hopelessness clung to the whole place.

And there are thoughts he never, ever thinks. The memory of a child crying, standing up in her cot. Mauri Kallis, ten years old, picks up his jacket and slams the front door behind him. He just cannot listen to her any longer. Her voice penetrates through the closed door, follows him down the stairs. The sound of his footsteps bounces off the concrete walls of the stairwell. Their neighbour is playing Rod Stewart. A sweet, stale smell comes from the rubbish chute. He has not seen their mother for two days, but he just cannot look after the kid any longer. And they have run out of porridge.

His middle sister is fifteen years younger than him. She was born while he was living with the foster family. Their mother was allowed to keep her for a year and a half, supported by social services. Then she got so bad she was taken into hospital, and the middle sister was taken into care as well.

Kallis met his elder sisters at their mother's funeral. He flew up to Kiruna alone for the funeral, he did not allow Ebba and the boys to go with him. Inna and Diddi did not offer to accompany him.

There was just Kallis and his two sisters, a priest and the consultant from the hospital.

Very appropriate weather, Kallis had thought as he stood by the coffin. The rain cascading down from the sky like grey chains. The water gouging into the ground, creating a delta of streams, carrying earth and gravel down into the grave. Like a weak brown soup at the bottom of the hole. His sisters were freezing standing there soaked to the skin in their poor, hastily assembled funeral clothes. They had black skirts and blouses, but a coat was too big an investment; one of them was wearing dark blue, the other didn't have one at all. Kallis gave them his umbrella, allowing the rain to ruin his Zegna suit. The priest was so cold he was shaking, his prayer book in one hand and his umbrella in the other. But he gave a good address, speaking very honestly about the difficulty when a person can't manage to fulfil the most important duty in life, taking care of their children. Then there were phrases such as "the inevitable conclusion" and "the road to reconciliation".

His sisters wept in the rain. Kallis wondered what they were crying for.

On the way to the cars they were hit by a hailstorm. The priest was running with the prayer book pressed against his chest. His sisters had their arms around each other so they would both fit under Kallis' umbrella. The hail was shredding the leaves on the trees.

It's Mum, thought Kallis, fighting down a rising sense of panic. She will never die. Pouring and hammering down. What am I supposed to do? Raise my clenched fist to the sky?

After the burial he invited his sisters to lunch. They showed him pictures of their children, said how lovely the flowers on the coffin had been. He felt extremely uncomfortable. They asked about his family, he answered as briefly as possible.

The whole time he was tormented by those aspects of their appearance that reminded him of their mother. Even the way they moved reminded him of her. The angle of the neck. The eldest sister had a way of screwing up her eyes when she looked at him. It made a dart of fear stab through him.

In the end, they got around to Ester.

"You know we have another sister?" his middle sister said.

Yes, they could tell him all about her. The girl was eleven now. Their mother got pregnant and had Ester in 1988. The father was another patient. Ester was taken into care immediately. A family in Rensjön looked after her. They sigh and say "poor little thing". Kallis clenches his fists beneath the table, while he asks politely if they would like something sweet with their coffee. Why was she a poor little thing? She didn't have to go through it all.

They seemed relieved when he said he had to leave. Nobody said anything stupid about keeping in touch.

*

Inna looks at him. The planes look like pretty toys out there, taking off and landing.

"Your youngest sister Ester," she says, "is only sixteen. And she needs somewhere to live. Her foster mother has just . . ."

Kallis raises his hands to his face as if he were splashing water on it, and groans.

"No, no."

"She can live with me at Regla. It's only temporary. She's starting her second year at the Idun Lovén Art School in the autumn . . ."

He never usually interrupts Inna. But this time he says "absolutely not". He cannot, he does not intend to have a living image of his mother wandering around the place. He tells Inna he can buy his sister an apartment in Stockholm, whatever she wants.

"She's sixteen!" Inna says.

And she gives him a pleading smile. Then she becomes serious.

"You're her only relative who . . ."

He opens his mouth to mention their other sisters, but she will not let him interrupt.

". . . who can take care of her. And right now your name is really hot . . . Oh, I forgot to tell you, *Business Week* is going to do a big feature on you . . ."

"No interviews!"

". . . but you ought to let them do a photo shoot. Anyway, if it comes out that you have a sister who hasn't got anywhere to go . . ."

So she wins. And as they board the flight to Vancouver, Kallis thinks that it doesn't really matter. Regla is not the kind of home that can be invaded. At Regla he has his wife and the boys and Diddi Wattrang with his pregnant wife and Inna. A lot of the company's corporate entertainment happens at Regla. They can hunt there, go out on a boat, give dinner parties.

He can feel that the recent media attention and the social whirl that has followed are taking their toll on him. Much more than work has ever done. All these people who want to shake his hand and talk to him, where do they all come from? He is making the maximum effort all the time in order to remain calm and friendly. Inna has been by his side constantly, whispering names and connections. Without her it would never have been possible. He can feel that he needs a rest. There are periods these days when he feels completely empty, it is as if everyone he meets takes a little piece of him. Sometimes he worries that all of a sudden he won't know where he is and who he is sitting in a meeting with and what it is about. Sometimes he just feels full of rage, like an animal that wants to growl, attack and satisfy itself. He gets irritated. By the way someone keeps their jacket buttoned to hide the fact that they are wearing yesterday's shirt. By the way someone else pokes at their teeth after a meal and puts the disgusting, used toothpick on the edge of their plate in full view. By the way one person thinks he is somebody, the way another person is too much of a crawler.

He is looking forward to the flight across the Atlantic. Because he is on the way somewhere, he does not feel restless. They are sitting still, reading, sleeping, watching a film, having a drink. He and Inna.

Kallis looked at himself in the mirror. The thudding noises above his head continued.

He had always loved the game. Closing the major deals. It had been his way of measuring himself against others. The one with the most money when he dies is the winner.

Now it felt as if all that did not matter at all. Something had caught up with him. Something heavy. It had always been close by, right behind him. Sucking him backwards, back to the tower block.

I'm losing it, he thought. Letting go.

Inna had kept the thing that was pulling him backwards at bay.

He did not want to be alone right now. It was two hours before his working day would begin. He looked up at the ceiling, heard the sound of a dumbbell rolling across the floor.

He would go up and chat for a bit. Or just be there for a while. He pulled on his dressing gown and went up to see his sister.

Ester Kallis is conceived in a secure psychiatric ward. It is the super-visor of ward P12 at the psychiatric clinic in Umeå who reports the matter at a team meeting. Britta Kallis is in her fifteenth week.

The other ward supervisors come to life and slurp a little coffee from their mugs. Best to drink it while it is too hot to taste. This is going to be interesting. And fortunately it is not their problem.

When the ward supervisor has finished speaking, Nils Gunnars-son the consultant puts his head in his hands. His mouth contracts into a wrinkled, hamster-like grimace.

"I see, yes, right, I see," he says thoughtfully.

Like a chicken in its eggshell, thinks one of his colleagues with a sudden pang of tenderness.

He looks such a sight. His white hair is far too long. He wears horrible old-fashioned spectacles with thick lenses, like the bottom of a bottle; he also has a habit of placing his finger on the lens to push them back into place when they have slipped too far down his nose. New employees at the hospital have been known to try to stop him leaving the ward, assuming he is a patient.

"Who's the father?"

"Britta says it's Ajay Rani."

A quick exchange of glances. Britta is forty-six, but looks sixty. She has smoked since she was twelve, and is on strong medication – that is what does it. Her bloated body on the sofa in front of the T.V. The slow, muddled thoughts. The involuntary movements of her mouth, her tongue suddenly poking out, her jaws moving from side to side.

Ajay Rani is thirty-something. He has slender wrists and white teeth. They still have high hopes of a recovery. He is training for work, and studying Swedish for immigrants.

Gunnarsson wonders what Ajay has said on this matter. The ward supervisor shakes her head and smiles apologetically. No, of course not. Who'd admit it? Britta is way down the scale as far as the patients go.

"What does she say? Does she want to keep the child?"

"She says it's a love child."

The consultant lets slip an "Oh God", and flicks through Britta's notes. Nobody says anything for a while. Their thoughts are touching shamefacedly on abortion pills and the compulsory sterilization of times gone by.

"We'll have to take her off the lithium," he says. "We'll have to try and get the little one out in as good a condition as possible, I suppose."

Who knows, they think. Perhaps Britta will begin to have regrets when she starts to feel worse, and will want to get rid of the child. That would be best for all concerned, really.

Gunnarsson attempts to close the notes and bring the matter to a conclusion, but the ward supervisor is not about to let him get away that easily. She has worked herself into a state before she has even begun to speak.

"I have no intention of having Britta on the ward without extra resources when she's off her medication," she says agitatedly. "She'll cause absolute havoc up there."

The consultant promises to do what he can.

The ward supervisor is not satisfied with that.

"I mean what I say, Nisse. I'm not taking responsibility for the ward if I have to have her there on a low-dose sedative. I'll quit."

The consultant notes dryly to himself that Britta is going to set the ward on fire. And the ward supervisor is her first victim.

Six months later, Britta is wheeled into the delivery room. Cursing and swearing. Midwives, junior nurses and the doctor in charge look at her with shocked expressions. Is she going to give birth like that? Strapped down? With her hands and feet shackled?

It is probably the only way, explains Gunnarsson, taking an enormous pinch of snuff.

The staff of the maternity unit watch in amazement as he wanders back and forth outside the delivery room like a parody of a father in the good old days, when men weren't allowed at the birth.

Two care assistants from the ward are in there with her; a guy and a girl, calm and resolute. They are wearing T-shirts; he has tattoos on his arms, she has a ring in her eyebrow and a stud in her tongue. This is not something they are going to hand over to just anybody. It's the delivery room staff who are degraded.

Britta is beside herself. During her pregnancy her condition has steadily worsened as she has been taken off the medication that would have harmed the baby. Her delusions have increased, as have the aggressive outbursts.

Now she is playing hell as much as she can between contractions. She is cursing everybody in the room, calling down the wrath of Satan and his hairy angels. They're all whores and dried-up old cunts and fucking fucking . . . as she searches for the next insult. From time to time she loses herself in incomprehensible exchanges with creatures only she can see.

But when the next contraction kicks in she screams "no, no" in terror, and the sweat pours out of her. When that happens, even the care assistants from her own ward look sympathetic. One of them tries to talk to her. Britta! Hello! Can you hear me? And the pains increase. She's dying, she's dying!

They all look at one other. Is she dying? Can she simply do that?

Then the pains abate and the rage returns.

Gunnarsson is listening to her through the door. He is so proud of her. How she grabs hold of her fury. That is all she has right now. Her ally against the pain, the powerlessness, the illness, the fear. She clings on tightly to it. It is getting her through all this, and she is screaming that it's their fault. The fucking doctor and the dried-up cunts. She saw one of the cunts grinning. Oh, yes she did. What's she grinning at, eh? What? Why doesn't she answer, fucking bully, answer me when I speak to you, fucking fucking . . . And the dried-up cunt feels compelled to attempt an answer of some sort, that she wasn't really smiling; the response is that she can take a scrubbing brush and shove it up her . . . But a fresh contraction interrupts the sentence.

Then the birth pains come. The midwife and the doctor are shouting: come on, Britta. And Britta tells them to go to hell. They shout that it's going really well, and Britta spits at them, trying her best to hit them.

The child finally arrives. It is taken into care immediately according to paragraph 2 § LVU and is carried out. The consultant makes sure Britta is given a tranquilliser and painkillers. She has been so good, fought her way through the birth, and the clinic has fought its way through her pregnancy.

She does not really seem to know what's happened. She has to stay strapped down while they stitch her up. She becomes calm at once, and is very tired.

Elsewhere the midwives are looking down at the newborn child. Poor little soul. What a start in life. They're all completely shattered.

They can see that her father must be Indian. To think their children are so much prettier than Swedish ones. The girl is absolutely beautiful, with her brown skin and all that hair and those dark, serious eyes. It almost makes them want to cry. It is as if she understands. Everything.

And nobody really thinks about it, but all those who were present at the birth are affected in one way or another during the following week. Britta has hurled her curses at them, heaped them on their heads. Most fell on barren ground, but some have taken root in their lives.

One of the nurses gets an abscess in her gum. The doctor is reversing in the parking lot and smashes one of her rear lights. Her house is broken into as well. Another person loses her wallet. The male care assistant with the tattooed arms loses his partner in a fire in their apartment.

That is how powerful Britta Kallis' gift is. Despite the fact that she is but a fraction of what she could have been, despite her own ignorance of what she does. Despite all this, her words gain a strange power when she is in a state half outside herself. There are various capabilities above and beyond what is normal on her mother's side of the family, but it is many generations since anyone has been aware of them.

And little Ester Kallis. She also has gifts. And Ester will get another mother, and will inherit also from that mother's side of the family.

My name is Ester Kallis. I have two mothers and no mother.

The person I call Mother in my mind married my father in 1981. She brought with her fifty reindeer. The majority of them were female, so my parents were hoping they would soon be able to support themselves by breeding reindeer. But my father always had to do other jobs. He drove the post van sometimes, worked on the railways. Temporary measures. He was never free.

They bought the old station house in Rensjön, and my mother made a studio for herself out of the old waiting room. The house was tucked in between Norgevägen and the railway line; the windows shook every time the train carrying ore went past.

The studio was freezing cold. In the winter my mother stood there painting in gloves and a hat. But still. She enjoyed the fragile light. Father painted the whole room white. It was before I came to them. At the time when he wanted to do things for her.

In 1984, Antte was born. They didn't really need any more children. Antte would have been enough. He could drive a snowmobile along a crack in the ice without going through, he had the right way with the dogs, that mixture of gentleness and reserve that made them work hard and put in the extra effort, running ten miles to bring back a straying reindeer; he was never cold, he went with Father and worked with the reindeer. He never moaned about wanting to stay at home to play video games like most of his friends.

And while Father and Antte were out in the mountains, my

mother painted and undertook commissions for Mattarahkka, the Sami craft co-operative: ceramic foxes, ptarmigans, elks and reindeer. She didn't answer the telephone. Forgot to eat.

Father and Antte would often come home to a freezing cold house with nothing in the refrigerator. It didn't matter, of course. The fact that they were tired and dirty, and had to get in the car and drive into town to go shopping before they could do anything else. She was useless in that way. When Antte and I were going to school, for example. We'd tell her beforehand, in plenty of time. On Thursday there's a trip to this place or that place. We have to bring a packed lunch. Then she wouldn't get anything ready. On the Thursday morning she'd be standing there rooting in the refrigerator while the school bus waited for us. And then we got given any old thing. For example, sandwiches made with sliced fish balls. At school, the other kids pretended to throw up when we got our packed lunches out. Antte was embarrassed. I could see it from his reddening cheeks, patches of carmine against his almost zinc-white skin, and his ears burning with the light behind them, shining through the blood vessels, slender threads of cadmium red. Sometimes he made a big point of throwing away what she'd given him. Spent the whole day hungry and furious. I ate mine. In that way, I was like her. Didn't really care what I shovelled down. Didn't care about my schoolmates either. And most of them left me in peace.

The one who was the worst was an outsider himself. His name was Bengt. He had no friends. He was the one who would yell, hit me on the back of the head and pick on me.

"You know why you're so thick? Do you, Kallis? Because your mother was in the loony bin. Took a load of pills that screwed your brain. Get it? And it was some curry-cock that gave her one. Curry-cock."

And he'd laugh and look sideways at the other boys. With his insipid blue eyes. A hunted look, the whole iris visible, a watercolour, cobalt blue. But it didn't do him any good. He stayed right there with me, way down at the bottom. Although it was worse for him, because he cared.

I didn't care. I'd already become like her. The one I call *eatnážan* in the Sami language, my little mother.

Completely obsessed with looking at things. Everything around me, all the people who are actually alive and filled with blood, all the animals with their little souls, every single thing and every plant, all the relationships between them – all these things are lines, colours, contrasts, compositions. Everything ends up inside the frame. It begins to lose taste, aroma, become a single dimension. But if I'm clever it regains everything, and more. The picture finishes up between me and what I see. Even if it's myself I'm looking at.

That's the way she was. Always take a step back to have a look. Driven. More or less absorbed. I remember several dinners. Father working away. She'd prepared something quick. Sat there in silence all through the meal.

But Antte and I were children, we usually ended up squabbling at the table. We might end up knocking over a glass of milk or something. Then all of a sudden she would sigh heavily. Sorrowfully, somehow, because we'd disturbed her thoughts, because she'd been forced to come back to us. Antte and I would fall silent and stare at her. As if a corpse had suddenly begun to move. She would wipe up the milk. Sullen and terse. Sometimes she just couldn't be bothered, and would call one of the dogs to lick it up.

She did everything she was supposed to do: cleaning, cooking, washing clothes. But it was only her hands that were occupied with these tasks. Her thoughts were far away. Sometimes Father would try complaining.

"This soup is too salty," he might say, pushing the bowl away.

But it didn't offend her. It was as if someone else had cooked the inedible food.

"Shall I make you a sandwich instead?" she'd ask.

If he complained that the place was a mess, she'd start cleaning. Perhaps that was why Father decided they should take me in. He probably told her they needed the money. Maybe he believed that himself. But when I think about it now, I think he was probably hoping subconsciously that a baby would force her back to this world. Like when Antte was tiny. She'd been there then. Perhaps another child could make her into a proper wife.

He wanted to open doors inside her. But he didn't know how. And he thought I would be the bridge that would lead her back to him and Antte. But it turned out to be the other way round. She painted. I lay on my stomach in the studio, drawing.

"What the hell's the matter with you? Get outside and get some fresh air!" he would say to me, slamming the door.

I didn't understand why he was so angry; I hadn't done anything wrong.

These days I understand his rage. I understood it then, but I didn't have the words. Although I did paint it. In my attic room at Mauri's I have almost all my paintings and drawings. There's an Elsa Beskow pastiche. When I did it, I didn't even know what pastiche meant.

It shows a mother and daughter picking blueberries. A little way off, between some gnarled mountain birch trees, a bear stands watching them. He's standing up on his hind legs, his head at a clumsy, sluggish angle. His expression is difficult to interpret. If I cover half his face with my hand, it has different expressions. One half is angry. The other half is sad.

My God, the bear is so much like my father I have to smile. It's like Antte too. I've only realized that now.

I remember Antte standing in the doorway of Mother's studio. He's eleven. I'm seven. Mother is choosing canvases. She's been given the opportunity to hang five pictures in a gallery in Umeå, and is finding it difficult to decide. She asks me what I think.

I consider and point. Mother nods and ponders.

"I think you should take these," says Antte, who has appeared at the door.

He points to completely different pictures from the ones I've chosen, looking at each of us in turn, challenging and defiant.

In the end Mother goes for the ones I picked out. And Antte stands there in the doorway, his bear's head drooping.

Poor Antte. He thought Mother was choosing between him and me. In fact she was choosing art. She would never have been able to include something that was less good, just to please him. That's how simple it was. And how difficult.

And it was the same with Father. He probably knew, deep down. He felt lonely in the reality that consisted of the house and the children, their bed, the neighbours, the reindeer, and the Sami council.

I remember before I started school, when Father and Antte had already left in the mornings. How I helped her look for her wedding ring in their big bed. She used to take it off at night when she went to sleep.

Now she's gone. When her body stopped obeying her, that must have been worst time.

Before that time came, she used to stand in the studio painting until late at night. Not very rewarding financially, compared with the commissions from Mattarahkka and a shop in Luleå that sold her silver jewellery and ceramic animals.

I would try to make myself invisible. I used to sit on the stairs leading up to our apartment, two rooms and a kitchen, looking into the old waiting room. Our home was full of different smells. Both old and new. You don't open the windows in the winter when it's minus 30°C outside. So there's a kind of shut-in smell, and wet dogs. There's the smell of cooked meat and the sharp odour of old reindeer skins, the way it gets when the fat in the skin has gone off slightly. She had so many things made of reindeer skin in the studio, from when she was little. Papooses and winter shoes, rucksacks and rugs. And in the quiet of the evenings, the smell of turpentine and oil paints, or a faint aroma of clay if she was working on her ceramics. I knew the staircase inside out, moving down little by little so that she wouldn't hear, avoiding every spot that creaked. I would push down the handle of the studio door so carefully, then sit out in the hall watching her through the gap. It was her hand I used to watch. How it moved over the canvas. Long, sweeping movements with the wide brush. The distinctive marking with the knife. The dance of the fine brush made of pine marten hair as she leaned forward shortsightedly, working on the small details: a blade of grass sticking up above the snow, or a reindeer's eyelashes.

She didn't usually notice I was there, or at least she pretended not to. Sometimes she'd say:

"It was bedtime a long time ago."

Then I'd say I couldn't sleep.

"Come and lie down here then," she'd say.

There was an old sofa in the studio. The arms were made of pine, and the cushions were of a speckled pink fabric. It was covered with lots of blankets to protect it from the dogs. I'd pull one of the hairy blankets over me.

Musta and Sampo would wag their tails in greeting as I wriggled my legs in between them so they didn't need to move.

In a cardboard box in the corner lay all my drawings, done in pencil, ink and chalk.

I longed to paint in oils. But it was too expensive.

"When you get a summer job and start earning your own money," she'd say.

I wanted to paint layer on layer. My longing was purely physical. Making a sandwich could take me ages as I spread the butter, trying as hard as I could to make it as smooth as newly fallen snow, or layered like snow that has drifted.

I tried to beg sometimes, but she was implacable.

She was painting a white landscape. I said:

"Can I paint something down there in the corner? You can paint over it afterwards. It won't show."

That aroused her interest.

"Why do you want to do that?"

"It'll be like a secret. Between you, me and the canvas."

"No, it would still show. You'd be able to see that the layers of paint were thicker and had a different structure just there."

I didn't give in.

"Even better," I said. "That'll make the person looking at the picture curious."

She was smiling now.

"It's a good idea, I'll give you that. Maybe we could do something slightly different."

She gave me several sheets of white paper.

"Paint your secrets," she said. "Then stick a sheet of white paper on top and paint something else on that."

I did as she said. I still have that picture in a box here in my room at my biological half-brother's house.

Mauri. He rummages through my pictures and canvases. Now Inna's died it's as if he's homeless. He owns the whole of Regla and more, but it doesn't help much. He comes up here to me and looks at my pictures. Asks a load of questions.

I pretend everything's fine, and talk to him. Work with my weights all the time. If a get a lump in my throat, I change weights or switch to the bench.

I did the picture the way my mother suggested. It was nothing special of course, I was a child after all. You can see a winter birch tree and a mountain. The railway winding through the landscape towards Narvik. The picture is stuck onto another sheet of paper. But the bottom right-hand corner is loose and has been folded back.

I rolled the corner of the paper around a pen so that it wouldn't lie flat against the motif underneath. I wanted the person looking at it to be seized by the desire to tear the sheets of paper apart to see the hidden picture. All you can see of that is a dog's paw and the shadow of someone or something. I know it's a woman with a dog, the sun shining on his back.

She was very pleased with the picture. Showed it to Father and Antte.

"The ideas she has," she said, fingering the rolled-up corner of the paper.

I was filled with an enormous emotion. If I'd been a house, the roof would have lifted off.

Morning briefing at Kiruna police station. It was 7.00 in the evening, but nobody seemed tired or reluctant to be there. The trail was still warm, and they had not ground to a halt.

Mella summed things up and pointed to the pictures on the wall.

"Inna Wattrang. Forty-four years old. She travels up to Kallis Mining's holiday place . . ."

". . . on Thursday morning, according to the airline," Olsson added.

"She took a taxi up to Abisko. Expensive trip. I had a chat with the driver. She was alone. I asked if they'd talked, but he said she was very quiet and seemed down."

Tommy Rantakyrö gave a little wave.

"I got hold of the woman who usually does the cleaning up there," he said. "She told me they always let her know in plenty of time if somebody's going to be staying at the house. She turns up the heating before they arrive, and does the cleaning while they're there. Nobody had informed her. She didn't know anybody had been in the house."

"Nobody seems to have known that she'd gone up there," Mella said. "The killer taped her to a chair in the kitchen and electrocuted her. She went into some kind of epileptic shock, chewed her tongue to pieces, clenched . . ."

Mella pointed to the pictures taken from the autopsy report, showing the palms of her hands with the livid marks of her nails.

"But," she said, "the cause of death is probably a penetrating blow to the heart with a long, sharp object. It went straight through her body. Not a knife, Pohjanen says. And at that point – although this isn't entirely clear – at that point she wasn't sitting on the chair, she was lying on the floor. Tintin found a mark on the ground under the flooring. The lab says the blood from that mark is Inna Wattrang's."

"Maybe the chair fell over," Olsson said.

"Maybe. Maybe somebody untied her and laid her on the floor."

"To have sex with her?" Rantakyrö said.

"Perhaps. There was no sperm in her body . . . but we still can't rule out sex, consensual or otherwise. After that the killer moved her to the ark."

"And the ark was locked, wasn't it?" Olsson asked.

Mella nodded.

"But it wasn't a difficult lock," Stålnacke said. "Any of our villains could deal with it."

"Her handbag was in the basin in the bathroom," Mella went on. "Her mobile and laptop are missing; they're not in her house at Regla either, we've asked our colleagues in Strängnäs to check."

"It's all so peculiar," Rantakyrö said.

There was silence for a moment. Rantakyrö was right. It was impossible to get a clear picture of the course of events. What had actually happened up there?

"Yes," Mella said. "We need to try and keep all our options open. It could be anything. A crime of hatred, a sex crime, a madman, blackmail, a kidnapping that went wrong. Kallis and Diddi Wattrang are keeping quiet about what they know about her, that's for sure. If it was a kidnapping, then these are the kind of people who won't involve the police.

"And we haven't found a weapon of any kind either. We've searched all around the cottage and Tintin has searched, nothing there. I definitely want the list of calls from her mobile network operator. Her address book would be brilliant too, but that's probably in the missing laptop and her phone. But the list of calls, please. Could you take care of that, Tommy?"

Rantakyrö nodded.

"And yesterday," Mella said, "the divers found this coat under the ice."

She pointed at a picture of the light-coloured poplin coat.

"It doesn't show up very well here," she said, "but there's a stain just here, on the shoulder. I think it's blood, Inna Wattrang's. But we've sent it to Linköping, and we'll see. I hope they can find a strand of hair or a trace of sweat or something from the inside of the collar. Then we might get the murderer's D.N.A."

"Do you really think it's the murderer's coat?" Rantakyrö said. "I mean, it's a summer coat."

Mella pressed her fingers against her forehead, a sure sign that she was thinking.

"Of course!" she said. "It's a summer coat. And if it's the murderer's coat, that means he came from the summer."

The others looked at her. What was she talking about?

"It's winter here," Mella said. "But in Skåne and the rest of Europe, it's spring. Pleasantly warm. Robert's cousin and her partner were in Paris last weekend. They were able to sit outside at pavement cafés drinking their coffee. What I mean is this: if he came from somewhere warm, then he wasn't from here, he was from somewhere far away. In which case he must have come by plane, mustn't he? And maybe hired a car? It's worth checking. Sven-Erik and I will go out to the airport and check if anyone remembers someone in a coat like this."

Kallis was squatting down in Ester's attic. He was looking through her paintings and drawings which were in two big cardboard boxes. Inna had provided paints, canvas, easel, brushes, watercolour paper. Everything was top of the range.

"Is there anything else you'd like?" she had asked a young Ester, standing there with her suitcases looking very small.

"Weights," Ester had replied. "Weights and a bar."

Ester was lying on her back using the bench press while Kallis rummaged through the boxes.

I was terrified the day she arrived, he thought.

Inna had rung to tell him that she and Ester and Ester's aunt were on their way. Kallis had wandered back and forth in his study, thinking about how he had felt at his mother's funeral. His sisters, who had reminded him of her. And now he was going to run the risk of bumping into his mother at any moment. It would feel like Russian roulette every time he poked his nose outside the bedroom door.

"I'm busy," he had said to Inna. "You show them round. I'll ring when you can come over."

In the end he had pulled himself together and rung.

And his whole body had become one huge sigh of relief when she walked in through the door. She was Indian. She looked Indian. Not a trace of their mother.

Her aunt had forced out the words:

"Thank you for looking after her, I only wish I could do it myself, but . . ."

And Kallis had seized hold of Ester's wrist, almost dizzy.

"Of course," he had said. "Of course."

Ester sneaked a look at Kallis. He was going through her pictures again. If she still drew, she would draw herself in her head, lifting her weights, and above her Kallis with the boxes in his arms. She was lifting him and his curiosity. Carrying both without showing any sign of it on the outside. Moving the pain to the pectoralis major, to the triceps bracchi. Lift, nine . . . ten . . . eleven . . . twelve.

But I still want him here, she thought. He needs to have a refuge here with me. Thats the way it's meant to be.

Kallis looked into a different life when he went through Ester's drawings. He wondered what would have become of him if he had been the one who ended up in the far north when he was very small. A trip to an alternative life.

The motifs were almost exclusively taken from her childhood home, the old railway station in Rensjön. He took out a few pencil drawings of her foster family. Her mother, busy with indoor tasks or with her ceramics. Her brother, in his blue overalls and baseball cap, tinkering with his snowmobile in the middle of summer, a riot of delicate wild flowers framing them both. Her foster father, cleaning the reindeer enclosure on the far side of the railway track down towards the lake, the pack reindeer standing by. And everywhere, in almost every picture, the sinewy little Swedish Lapphunds with their shiny coats and wagging tails.

Ester was struggling to get the bar back into its rest; her arms had gone limp. She took no notice of him at all, seemed to have forgotten he was there. It was nice to be able to sit here in peace for a while.

He took out the sketches of Nasti in his cage.

"I like this hamster," he said.

"It's a mountain lemming," Ester corrected him, without looking.

Kallis looked at the lemming. The broad head with the black button eyes. The little paws. Consciously or subconsciously, Ester had made them so human. They looked like little hands.

Nasti on his hind legs with his hands around the bars of the cage. Nasti's bottom as he bends over his food dish. Nasti on his back in the sawdust with his legs in the air. Cold and dead. As was so often the case in her pictures, those who were outside the motif were still there. A shadow. A fraction of a daily newspaper outside the cage.

Ester turned over onto her stomach and started doing back lifts. It was Father who came home with Nasti. He had found him out on the marsh. Soaked to the skin and close to death. Father put him in his pocket and saved his little life. For eight months he lived with them. You can learn to love someone in considerably less time than that.

I cried then, thought Ester. But she taught me what you can use a picture for.

"Paint him," says Mother.

Father and Antte haven't come home yet. I hurry to get out paper and a pen. And even after the first few strokes, the violent emotion is starting to calm down. The grief becomes muted, silent in my breast. The hand lays claim to the brain and the emotions, the tears must step aside.

When Father gets home I cry a bit more, mainly because I want the attention. The drawing of Nasti after his death is already right at the bottom of my box in the studio. Father comforts me. I'm allowed to sit on his lap. Antte doesn't care. He's much too grown up to grieve for a lemming.

"You know how it is," says Father. "They're so sensitive. Can't cope with all our germs. We'll put him in the woodshed and bury him in the summer."

Over the next few weeks I do three drawings of the woodshed. Thick snow covering the roof. The black darkness inside the barred windows, covered in frost. It's only my mother and I who understand that they're really pictures of Nasti. He's lying inside there, in a box.

"You should start painting again," Kallis said.

Ester changed the weights on the bar. She looked at her legs. Her thighs were starting to get noticeably thicker. Quadriceps femoris. She ought to eat more protein.

Kallis took out some of the drawings of Ester's aunt. Her foster mother's sister. In one she was sitting at the kitchen table, staring with resignation at the telephone. In another she was lying on her back on the kitchen sofa with a contented expression on her face, reading a novel. In one hand she was holding a Mora knife with a lump of dried meat speared on the end.

He was about to ask Ester whether she had heard from her aunt, but refrained. They were bloody awful people, both the aunt and the foster father.

Ester bent her knees beneath the bar. She looked at Kallis. At the brief furrow that appeared between his eyebrows. He shouldn't be angry with her aunt. Where could she go now when she needed a bolt hole? She was just as homeless as Ester.

Her aunt comes to Rensjön to visit them at regular intervals. It usually starts with a telephone call to Mother.

There have been calls all week. Mother has been walking around with the receiver clamped between her shoulder and her ear, trying to make the lead reach.

"Mmm," she says into the telephone, trying to reach the washing up and the slop bucket and the dogs' bowls; she can't just sit there doing nothing and talk, it's impossible.

Sometimes she says:

"He's an idiot!"

But most of the time she doesn't say anything. For long periods she simply listens. I can hear my aunt weeping in despair at the other end of the phone. Sometimes she swears.

I fetch the extension lead for Mother. Father is getting annoyed. He feels totally invaded by these endless telephone conversations. When the phone rings, he gets up and leaves the kitchen.

And then one day my mother says:

"Marit's coming."

"Oh, it's that time again, is it," says my father.

He pulls on his snowmobile overalls and disappears without saying where he's going. Comes home long after the evening meal. Mother heats up his food in the microwave. Silence. If it wasn't so cold in the rest of the house, Antte and I would escape to the studio, or up to the junk room in the attic where the washing hangs, frozen stiff, and the rime frost snakes across the windows like fronds of fern.

But instead we're sitting in the kitchen. Mother is washing up. I look at her back and at the clock on the wall. In the end Antte gets up and switches on the radio. Then he goes into the living room and switches on the T.V. and the computer, and plays a football game. The silence still manages to drown out all the rest of the noise. Father is glaring at the telephone.

But I'm pleased, at any rate. My aunt is a pretty creature. She has a whole suitcase full of make-up and perfume that you're allowed to try if you're careful. My mother is different when my aunt comes to visit. Laughs often. At the silliest things.

If I could still draw, I would re-do all my pictures of her. She would look the way she wanted to look. Her face like a little girl's.

Her mouth softer. Fewer lines between her eyebrows, and between her nose and the corners of her mouth. And I wouldn't bother putting in the fan-shaped network of fine wrinkles from the outer corners of her eyes down towards her high cheekbones. The delta of her tears.

She comes by train from Stockholm. It takes an afternoon, an evening, a night and half a day.

I'm standing in the living room upstairs, where my mother and father sleep at night on a pull-out bed. Antte sleeps on the kitchen sofa. I'm the only one who has my own space. A little cubby-hole with room for a bed and a chair. There's a little window that's so high up you have to stand on a chair to see out. I stand there sometimes watching the railway workers in their yellow overalls, working on the points. It's because I'm a foster child that I have my own room.

But at the moment I'm standing in the living room with my nose pressed against the window. I can see my aunt if I close my eyes.

It's the middle of winter. Stockholm is sepia and ochre on rain-soaked watercolour paper. Wet, black tree trunks, thin lines in ink.

I can see her on the train. Sometimes she goes to the toilet for a crafty cigarette. Otherwise she sits there looking out through the window. House after house after house. Forest after forest after forest. Her soul can feel that it's coming home.

She looks at her mobile from time to time. No network coverage. Perhaps he's tried to ring anyway. The pinging sound from the level crossings, the cars queuing to get across.

She can only afford a seat, not a berth. Pulls her coat over her like a blanket and falls asleep with her head against the window. The electric heaters are full on. There's a smell of burnt dust. Her feet and her narrow ankles in their nylon tights are sticking out from underneath her coat, resting on the seat opposite and suggesting something fragile and vulnerable. The train sways and sighs and rumbles. It's a lot like life before birth.

Mother and I meet her on the platform in Rensjön. My aunt is the only person who gets off. The snow hasn't been cleared, and we have to battle our way through. Dark blue afternoon twilight. Lumps of snow stick to the bottom of her suitcases.

She's wearing a little too much make-up and her voice is a little too cheerful as she chatters and trips along through the deep snow. She's going to be frozen in her Stockholm coat and her fine shoes. And she hasn't got a hat. I drag the case along. It gouges a deep track in the snow.

My aunt laughs happily when she sees the house. At one side the snowdrift reaches right up to the upstairs window. Mother tells her that my father had to climb out there, out of the upstairs window, the week before last, and that it took him and Antte four hours to dig out the front door.

My aunt has brought presents. An expensive watercolour block for me, with ready-pasted pages.

Mother tells me not to use it all up at once, then she tells my aunt off – it's too expensive.

At first my aunt wants the kind of food she and my mother used to eat when they were little. My mother makes *suovas* and blood dumplings and blood rissoles and elk, and in the evening my aunt carves thin slices of dried meat and eats as she talks. And they drink the wine and spirits my aunt brought with her as a present.

My father puts the heating on in the living room and watches T.V. in the evenings; my mother and my aunt stay in the kitchen, talking. She often cries, but we pretend not to notice that sort of thing in my family.

"You're having to move a lot," says my father when he comes into the kitchen to top up his whisky. "Maybe you should get yourself a caravan."

My aunt doesn't move a muscle, but I can see the pupils of her eyes become like two pinpricks.

"I'm bad at choosing good men," she says in a deceptively light tone of voice. "I think it's a family trait on my mother's side."

Every evening she puts her mobile on charge. She hardly dares go out skiing, because then the phone gets cold and the battery stops working.

One evening it rings, and it's the bastard. My aunt talks to him in the kitchen, very quietly. For a long time. My mother sends us out to play. We play in the dark for almost two hours. Dig a cave right into the snowdrift. The dogs dig too, like mad things.

We're allowed to come in when my aunt has finished talking. I listen while I'm taking off my dungarees and boots.

"I don't understand," my mother says. "How can you possibly take him back? All he has to do is click his fingers. It's such a waste of a woman's strength."

"'A waste of a woman's strength,'" says my aunt. "What's more important to devote your strength to than trying to catch a little bit of love before this life is over?"

That's what's difficult, thought Ester, fitting new weights to the bar. When Mauri comes up to my attic and looks at the pictures. Now I've started to think about my aunt, all the other memories will come too. At first you remember something that isn't dangerous at all, but behind it all the difficult stuff is pushing its way forwards.

The difficult stuff: my aunt and I are driving along Norgevägen on the way to the hospital in Kiruna. Darkness and snow. My aunt is gripping the steering wheel. She has a licence, but she's not used to driving.

The end is near. I don't even remember where Antte and my father are.

"Do you remember the fly?" my aunt asks me as we're driving along.

I don't reply. There's a huge truck coming towards us. My aunt brakes just before we pull level. That's the last thing you should do, even I know that. It's easy to go into a skid, and then you'll end up squashed. But she's scared and she does the wrong thing. I'm not scared. Not because of that, at any rate.

I don't remember the fly, but my aunt has told me about it before.

I'm two years old. Sitting at the kitchen table on my aunt's knee. The daily paper open on the table in front of us. A picture of a fly. I'm trying to pick the fly up off the page.

My mother is laughing at me.

"You can't do that," she says.

"Don't teach her that she can't do things," says my aunt crossly.

My aunt has a weakness for that particular trait from her mother's side of the family. The side that can staunch blood, and see things. She's probably a little bit annoyed with my mother, because she suspects that her sister has rather more of this ability than she lets on. She doesn't want my mother to teach me to put a lid on things. Even when I was a baby she used to look in my eyes and say to my mother: "You see, it's *áhkku*, it's Grandmother."

My father heard her once.

"Numbskulls," he said to them. "She isn't even related to us. She isn't Ester's grandmother."

"He doesn't understand a thing," my aunt said to me. Her voice was deceptively amused and she was completely focused on me, but after all I was a baby; it was my father who was meant to hear what she said. He thinks family is only to do with biology.

I try to pick the fly up from the picture in the newspaper. And suddenly it happens. It's buzzing around our heads, banging into my aunt's reading glasses, zooming down to the floor and crawling around, taking off clumsily and landing on my hand.

And I scream. A heartrending, terrified scream. My aunt tries to calm me down, but it's impossible. My mother chases the fly out through the window and it dies instantly in the cold. The fly is still there in the picture, but my aunt still stuffs the newspaper into the wood-burning stove and it is destroyed in the fire with a crackle.

"It was probably just a winter fly that had woken up," says my mother, choosing to be a realist.

My aunt says nothing. Now, fourteen years later, she asks me:

"Why did you scream like that? We thought you were never going to calm down."

I tell her I don't remember. And it's true. But it doesn't mean that I don't know. I know exactly why I screamed. The feeling is always the same when it happens, and it has happened to me later in life as well.

You become one with everything else. But at the same time, you're moving apart from everything. There's a feeling of disintegration. Like when a gust of wind whirls down into a valley and disperses the mist. Very frightening. Particularly when you're little, and you don't know it will pass.

Sometimes I know it's coming. It's as if my feet go to sleep, a thousand pinpricks. Then it feels as if there's a cushion of air between my feet and the ground. You're more at one with your body than you can imagine, and it's horrible to be separated from it.

I could say to my aunt: Imagine if gravity suddenly ceased to exist. But I don't want to talk about it.

I know why my aunt is reminding me about the fly as we drive along. It's her way of saying I'm related to my mother. That I have their grandmother within me.

Nobody really wants to know. Including my aunt.

I'm three years old. Once again I'm sitting at the kitchen table on my aunt's knee. She and my father have been sniping at each other for almost two weeks, and Father and Antte have gone up into the mountains. But on this particular day the telephone has rung. My aunt has booked her ticket home and packed her suitcase. Now she's showing me pictures. This man has a big sailing boat. She shows me pictures of the boat.

"It's in the Mediterranean," she tells me.

They're going to sail down to the Canary Islands.

"I remember," I say. "You sat here and cried."

I point at the prow of the boat.

My aunt laughs. She doesn't want to hear this. Ester doesn't have the gift.

"You can't possibly remember that, poppet. I've never even set foot on a sailing boat. This will be the first time."

Mother gives me a quick warning glance. They don't want to know, it means. That you can remember both forwards and backwards. Time goes in both directions.

Mauri doesn't want to know either, thought Ester, placing the bar across her shoulders. He's in danger, but it's pointless to try and tell him.

"You could paint me," he said with a smile.

It's true, thought Ester. I could paint him. It's the only picture I have left in me. Apart from that, the pictures are finished. But he won't want to see it. It's been here inside me since the first time I met him.

Inna meets my aunt and me at the door of Regla. Hugs my aunt as if they were sisters. My aunt relaxes. Feels her guilty conscience about me releasing its grip, I presume.

Personally, I feel really bad about being there. A burden to everybody. I can't paint. Can't provide for myself. Haven't got anywhere else to go. And because I don't want to be there, I keep disappearing. I can't help it. As my feet walk across two rugs towards Inna, I am two weavers, a man with his tongue stuck in a gap in his teeth the whole time, and a young boy. I brush against a wooden wall panel, and I'm the carpenter with his aching hip, planing the wood. All these hands that have turned and carved, woven and stitched. I get so tired, and I can't hold myself together. I force myself to hold out my hand to Inna. And I see her. She's thirteen years old, placing her cheek against her father's cheek. Everyone says she winds him around her little finger, but her eyes are so thirsty.

Inna shows us round. There are too many rooms to count. My aunt looks impressed. All the old furniture, polished wood with intricate legs. Urns with a blue Chinese pattern on the floor.

"What a place," she whispers to me.

The only thing she has a problem with are the dogs belonging to Kallis' wife; they're allowed to go anywhere they like, and they jump up on the furniture. She has to stop herself grabbing them by the scruff of the neck and heaving them out through the door.

I don't reply. She wants me to be happy about coming here. But I don't know these people. They're not my family. I've been carted off here.

Suddenly Inna's telephone rings. When she hangs up, she says I'm going to meet my brother.

We go into his room, a combined bedroom and study. He's wearing a suit, although he's in his own house.

My aunt shakes hands and thanks him for agreeing to look after me.

And he smiles at me. And says "of course". Twice he says it, looking me in the eyes.

And I have to look down, because I feel so happy. And I think that he's my brother. And that now I have a place here with him.

And he seizes my wrist and then . . .

Then the floor drops away. The thick carpet begins to writhe like a sea snake, trying to throw me off. There is a prickling feeling underneath my feet. I could do with something to hold onto, a heavy piece of furniture. But I'm already up near the ceiling.

The glass from the windows falls into the room like heavy rain. A black wind sucks the curtains inwards and tears them to pieces.

I have lost myself.

The room becomes almost completely dark, and shrinks. It's a different bedroom, long long ago. A bedroom that exists inside Mauri. A fat man is lying on top of a woman in a bed. There is no cover on the mattress, it's just dirty yellow foam rubber. His back is broad and sweaty, like a big smooth stone by the water's edge.

I realize afterwards that the woman is our mother, Mauri's and mine. The other one. The one who gave birth to me. But this is before I existed.

Mauri is so small, two or three years old. He's on the man's back, hanging round his neck and shouting Mummy, Mummy. Neither of them takes any more notice of him than if he were a mosquito.

That's my portrait of Mauri.

A pale little back, like a shrimp, above that great rock of a back in that dark, enclosed room.

And then he lets go of my hand and I'm back.

And then I know that I have to carry him. Neither of us has a place here at Regla. There is only a little time left.

Ester was doing lunges with the bar over her shoulders. Took a big step forward.

Mauri Kallis smiled at her and tried again:

"I can pay. There's plenty of money in portraiture. People who work in industry have egos as big as Zeppelins!"

"You wouldn't like it," she replied simply.

She glanced at him. Could see him trying to choose not to be offended. But what could she say?

At any rate, she couldn't bear him rummaging about among her pictures any longer. She bent her knees beneath the bar and he disappeared down the stairs.

"Yes, I do recall a customer wearing an overcoat like that."

Mella and Stålnacke were at Kiruna airport, talking to a man on the car rental desk. He was around twenty, frantically chewing gum as he searched through his memory bank. He had quite bad acne on his cheeks and throat. Mella was trying not to stare at a fully mature pimple, like white lava on its way out of a red-rimmed lunar crater. She held her mobile up to show him. It had a built-in digital camera, and was displaying a picture of the coat the divers had found beneath the ice of Torneträsk.

"I remember thinking he was going to be cold."

He laughed.

"Foreigners!"

Mella and Stålnacke did not say anything. Waited without asking questions. Better if he could remember by himself, rather than being pointed in a particular direction. Mella nodded encouragingly, and made a note in her memory: "foreigner".

"It can't have been last week, because I was off with flu. Just a minute . . ."

He tapped away at the computer, then produced a form that had been filled in.

"Here's the contract."

This is crazy, Mella thought. We're going to get him.

She could hardly wait to see the name.

Stålnacke pulled on his gloves and asked if he could have the form.

"A foreigner," Mella said, "what language did he speak?"

"English. That's the only foreign language I know, so . . ."

"Any kind of accent?"

"Mmm . . ."

He shifted the chewing gum around in his mouth. Placed it between his front teeth so that half of it was sticking out, then increased the rate of chewing. It made Mella think of a sewing machine, rattling its way around a scrap of white fabric.

"British, actually. Although not that kind of, like, posh English, more sort of . . . working class."

"That's it," he continued, nodding as if he were agreeing with himself. "Yes, because it didn't really go with the long trench coat and the shoes. He looked a bit haggard, I thought. Although he was very tanned."

"We'll hang onto the contract," Stålnacke said. "We'll get a copy to you, but don't talk to any journalists about this, if you don't mind. And we'll need all the information you've got on the computer, how he paid, anything at all."

"And we want the car," Mella said. "If it's out at the moment, you'll need to get it back. Give the customer a different one."

"This is about Inna Wattrang, isn't it?"

"Was he wearing the overcoat when he brought the car back?" Mella asked.

"Don't know. I think he left the key in our deposit box."

He looked at the computer again.

"Yeah, he probably took the evening flight last Friday. Or maybe early Saturday."

Then perhaps one of the flight attendants might have seen him without the coat, Mella thought.

"We'll put out a call for the man on the contract," Mella said to Stålnacke once they were back in the car. "John McNamara. Interpol can help us with the British contacts. Then if the lab can confirm that the blood on the coat is Inna Wattrang's, and if they can do a D.N.A. analysis of what's on the coat . . ."

"It might not be possible, it's been in the water."

"Then the Rudbeck lab in Uppsala can do it. It has to be possible to link this guy to the coat, it isn't enough that he happened to rent a car here at the time she was murdered."

"Unless we find something in the car."

"Forensics will have to go over it."

She turned to Stålnacke with a broad grin. Stålnacke pressed his foot to the floor of the car, automatically searching for a brake; he preferred it if she looked at the road while she was driving.

"Bloody hell, but we've worked fast," Mella said, flooring the accelerator with sheer joy. "And we've done it ourselves, without getting Stockholm involved, that's bloody fantastic."

Martinsson had her evening meal with Sivving Fjällborg. They were in his boiler room. Martinsson was sitting at the little Formica table watching Fjällborg prepare the food on the small hotplate. He placed slices of fish pudding in an aluminium pan and warmed them gently with a dash of milk. Almond potatoes were simmering in a pot alongside. On the table stood a basket of crispbread and a tub of extra salted margarine. The aroma of the food mingled with the smell of freshly washed woollen socks, hanging on the washing line.

"Quite a party," Martinsson said. "What do you say, Bella?"

"Don't even think about it," Fjällborg said quietly to the pointer bitch, who had been sent to her basket beside Fjällborg's bed.

Saliva was dangling from her jaws like two pieces of string. Her brown eyes told a tale of starvation and near death.

"You can have my leftovers," Martinsson promised.

"Don't keep chatting to her. She just takes it as permission to get out of her basket."

Martinsson smiled. She looked at Fjällborg's back. He was a wonderful sight. His hair had not thinned, just turned a silky white and somehow lighter, standing out around his head like a fluffy fox's brush. His combat trousers from the surplus store stuffed into thick woollen socks. Maj-Lis must have knitted a good stock for him before she died. A flannel shirt covering his big stomach. One of Maj-Lis' aprons that didn't quite meet at the back; instead he had pushed the ties into the back pockets of his trousers to hold it in place.

Up in the rest of the house Fjällborg had dutifully put up Christmas decorations in December; he had hung the Christmas stars in their respective windows, the orange paper star from the I.C.A. store in the kitchen, the hand-crafted straw one in the living room. He had got out the little Christmas elves and goblins, the Advent candlesticks and Maj-Lis' embroidered cloths. After Twelfth Night everything had been put back in boxes and carried up into the attic. The cloths had not needed washing. He never ate a meal off them, after all. Nothing got dirty up in the house.

Down in the boiler room where he lived nowadays, everything had remained the same. No cloths. No little goblins on the cupboard.

I like that, thought Martinsson. The fact that everything stays the same. The same pans and plates on the shelf on the wall. Everything has a purpose. The bedspread keeps the dog hairs off the sheets when Bella sneaks onto the bed. There is a rug on the floor because the floor is cold, not for reasons of decoration. She had got used to it, she realized. She no longer thought it was strange that he had moved down here into the cellar.

"What about all that business with Inna Wattrang," Fjällborg said. "It's all over the papers."

Before Martinsson could answer, her mobile rang. An 08 number. The law firm's exchange on the display.

Måns, she thought, and all of a sudden she was so nervous she stood up quickly.

Bella seized the opportunity and leapt up as well. In half a second she was over by the stove.

"Get away," Fjällborg grumbled.

To Martinsson he said:

"The potatoes will be ready in five minutes."

"One minute," Martinsson said, and dashed up the stairs. She could hear Fjällborg's "in your basket" as she closed the cellar door behind her and answered the phone.

It wasn't Måns Wenngren. It was Maria Taube.

Taube was still working for Wenngren. In another life, she and Martinsson had been colleagues.

"How are things?" Martinsson said.

"Disastrous. We're supposed to be coming up to the Riksgränsen resort to go skiing, the whole office. Hello! What sort of an idea is that? What's wrong with going somewhere warm, sunbathing and drinking something with an umbrella in it? And I'm so unfit! O.K., so I can at least borrow my sister's skiing gear, but I look like one of those new sausages they're advertising: "now even thicker", you know the kind of thing. And last Christmas I thought, O.K., after Christmas I'm going on a diet, and I thought I could lose half a kilo a week. And because I was going to go on a diet afterwards and get really really slim, I went a bit mad over Christmas. Then all of a sudden it was New Year, then January came and went in the blink of an eye, and I thought, well, I'll go on a diet in February, and if I lose a whole kilo a week . . ."

Martinsson was laughing.

". . . and now there's half a week left," Taube went on. "So do you think I can manage to lose ten kilos in that time?"

"Boxers usually go and sit in the sauna."

"Mmm, thanks for the tip. No, really. 'Died in the sauna. Just managed to call the Guinness Book of Records.' What are you up to?"

"Right now or at work?"

"Right now and at work."

"Right now I'm about to have dinner with my neighbour, and at work I'm doing a little bit of checking into Kallis Mining for the police."

"Inna Wattrang?"

"Yes."

Martinsson took a deep breath.

"By the way," she said, "Måns e-mailed me to say I ought to come up and have a drink when you're all up this way."

"Oh, I think so too! Please say you'll come!"

"Mmm . . ."

And what do I say now? Martinsson thought. Do you think I'm in with a chance there, or what?

"How is he?" she asked.

"O.K., I presume. There was a big hearing in that electricity company case last week. And it went well, so he's quite human at the moment. Before that he was . . . well, everybody was just creeping past his door."

"Apart from that? How's everybody else?"

"How should I know? Nothing happens here. Oh yes, Sonja Berg got engaged last Saturday."

Sonja Berg was the secretary who had been with Meijer & Ditzinger the longest. She was divorced with grown-up children, and over the past year the firm had enjoyed watching her being seriously courted by a man whose top-of-the-range car and expensive watch matched those of the partners. He was an agent selling calendars and stationery. Sonja referred to him as her "travelling salesman with papier mâché balls".

"Ooh, tell me everything," Martinsson said.

"What can I say? Dinner at the French restaurant in the Grand Hotel. As for the size of the stone, well you can imagine – she practically needed her arm in a sling. Are you coming up to the hotel?"

"Maybe."

Taube was good. She knew it was not about her, but about Martinsson. They had met twice since Martinsson had come out of hospital. It was when Martinsson was down in Stockholm selling her apartment. Taube had invited her round to dinner.

"I'll just do something simple," she had said. "And if you don't feel up to seeing people, or me, or if you just feel you want to stay at home and stub cigarettes out on your arms instead, just ring and cancel. That's absolutely fine."

Martinsson had laughed.

"You're crazy, you're not supposed to joke with me like that – I'm on the edge, you know! You have to be really, really nice and kind to me."

They had had dinner. And the evening before Martinsson went back up to Kiruna, they had gone to Sturehof for a few drinks.

"You don't fancy coming up to the office to say goodbye?" Taube had asked.

Martinsson had shaken her head. She was fine with Taube. Things were always easy with her. But the idea of presenting herself to the entire office was out of the question. And she had not wanted to see Måns either, not in that state. The scar running from her lip to her nose was still so obvious. Red and shiny. Her top lip had been pulled up a fraction, so it looked as if she had just taken a pinch of snuff, or as if she were slightly hare-lipped. They might operate on her, a decision had not yet been taken. And she had lost a lot of her hair.

"Promise me we'll keep in touch," Taube had said, taking hold of both of Martinsson's hands.

And they had. Taube rang from time to time. Martinsson was always pleased when she did, but never rang herself. And that seemed to be O.K. Taube did not stop calling because it was Martinsson's turn.

Martinsson ended the conversation and ran back down to the boiler room. Fjällborg had just placed the food on the table.

They ate, allowing the food to silence them.

She thought about Måns. The way his laugh sounded. How slender his hips were. How curly his dark hair was. How blue his eyes were.

If she had been a better flirt, someone who wasn't socially crippled and crazy, she would have taken him by storm a long time ago.

I'd never choose anyone else, she thought.

She wanted to go up and meet him. But what would she wear? Her wardrobe was full of smart suits for work. But this called for something else. Jeans, of course. She would have to buy some new ones. And what would she wear with them? She would have to get her hair cut too.

She continued to think about it all after she had gone to bed that night.

It mustn't look as if I've made an effort, she thought. But it has to look good. I want him to like what he sees.

WEDNESDAY, 19 MARCH, 2005

As usual, Mella was woken by Gustav kicking her in the back.

She looked at the clock. 5.50 a.m. It would soon be time to get up. She pulled him close, nuzzling his hair. Gustav turned to her. He was awake.

"Hello Mummy," he said.

On the other side of the boy, Robert grunted and pulled the covers over his head in a vain attempt to steal a few extra minutes' sleep.

"Hello little one," Mella said, besotted.

How could anybody be so cute? She stroked his soft hair. She kissed him on the forehead and the lips.

"I love you," she said. "You're the best thing in the whole wide world."

He stroked her hair in return. Then he suddenly looked very serious, and patted the area around her eyes very carefully; he said anxiously:

"Mummy, your face is all cracked."

From beneath the covers on the far side of the bed came a muffled shout of laughter, and she could see Robert's body heaving up and down.

Mella tried to kick her husband, but it was difficult with Gustav between them like a protective wall.

At that moment, her phone rang.

It was Inspector Fred Olsson.

"Did I wake you?" he asked.

"No, I've already had quite a wake-up call," she laughed, still trying to kick Robert while Gustav tried to burrow his way in under the covers on Robert's side.

Robert had tucked them under his body, and was resisting with all his might.

"You did say you wanted bad news straight away."

"No, no," Mella said, jumping out of bed. "I never said that, and besides I've already had some seriously bad news this morning."

"What on earth's going on there?" Olsson said. "Are you having a party, or something? Anyway, listen to this: the guy with the light-coloured coat . . ."

"John McNamara."

"John McNamara. He doesn't exist."

"What do you mean, he doesn't exist?"

"There's a fax here for you from the British police. The John McNamara who hired a car at Kiruna airport died eighteen months ago in Iraq."

"I'm on my way," Mella said. "Shit!"

She pulled on her clothes and patted the moving covers to say goodbye.

At 6.45 a.m., Mauri Kallis' security chief Mikael Wiik was driving up the avenue of lime trees to Regla. It took an hour to drive from Kungsholmen to Regla. This particular morning he had got up at 4.30 a.m. because he had a breakfast meeting with Kallis. But he was not complaining. Early mornings were nothing to him. And besides: the Merc he was driving was new. He had taken his partner to the Maldives for New Year.

Two hundred metres from the first iron gate he passed Kallis' wife Ebba on a black horse. He slowed down in plenty of time, and gave her a friendly wave. Ebba waved back. In the rear view mirror he saw the horse take a few little dancing steps when the gates were opened; the car had not frightened it.

Bloody horses, he thought as he drove through the second gate. They never know what's really dangerous. Sometimes they rear up just because there's a stick lying across the track that wasn't there yesterday.

Kallis was already in the dining room. A pile of newspapers beside his coffee cup: two Swedish, the others foreign.

Wiik said good morning and helped himself to coffee and a croissant. He had had a proper breakfast before he left home. He was not the type to sit there shovelling down porridge in front of his employer.

Nobody knows a man like his bodyguard, he thought as he sat down. He knew Kallis was faithful to his wife, if you disregarded the occasions when his business associates provided girls as a kind of digestif, so to speak. Or when Kallis himself was doing the providing, knowing that was what would get the fish to take the bait. But that was part of the job, and did not count.

Kallis did not drink much either. Wiik suspected more of that sort of thing had gone on with Kallis and Inna and Diddi Wattrang in the past. And it was true that during the two years Wiik had been working for him, he had had the odd drink with Inna – and one or two other things as well. But at work – no. When it came to working dinners or pub crawls, it was part of Wiik's job to have a word with (and pay) bartenders and the staff who were waiting on the tables to make sure Kallis was discreetly served alcohol-free drinks, and apple juice instead of whisky.

Kallis stayed in hotels with excellent sports facilities when he was away on business, and liked to work out in the hotel gym early in the morning. He preferred fish to meat. He read biographies and factual books, not novels.

"Inna's funeral," Kallis said to Wiik. "I was thinking of asking Ebba to organize it, so perhaps you and she could get together on that. We can't postpone the meeting with Gerhart Sneyers, he's flying in from Belgium or Indonesia the day after tomorrow, so we'll have a small dinner party then and hold the meeting on Saturday morning. Several people from the African Mining Trust will be there, you'll have a list tomorrow afternoon at the latest. They're travelling with their own security people, of course, but, well, you know how things are . . ."

I know, thought Wiik. The gentlemen on their way to Regla were well guarded and paranoid. And some of them had good reason to feel it.

Gerhart Sneyers, for example. He owned both mining and oil companies. Chairman of the African Mining Trust, an association of foreign company owners in Africa.

Wiik could remember Kallis' first meeting with Sneyers. Kallis and Inna had flown to Miami just to meet him. Kallis had been nervous. Wiik had never seen him like that.

"How do I look?" he had asked Inna. "I could change my tie. Or should I leave it off altogether?"

Inna had stopped him from going back up to his room.

"You look just perfect," she had assured him. "And don't forget: it's Sneyers who's asked for this meeting. He's the one who should be nervous about you. All you can do is . . ."

". . . sit back and listen," Kallis had said, as if he had learned it by heart.

They had met in the foyer of the Avalon. Sneyers was a well-preserved man in his fifties. His thick red hair peppered with grey. An attractive face, in a masculine, craggy way. White skin covered in freckles. He shook hands with Inna first, like a gentleman, then with Kallis. The bodyguards were ignored; they nodded almost imperceptibly at one another, professional colleagues in spite of everything.

Sneyers had two men guarding him. They were wearing sunglasses and suits, and looked like Mafioso. Wiik felt like a country boy in his mint-green jacket and cap. His internal defence mechanism was up and running with disparaging thoughts about the other two.

Fatso, he thought about one of the bodyguards. He would never manage more than a hundred metres. And he wouldn't even do that in a decent time.

Snivelling puppy, he thought about the other one.

They walked down Ocean Drive, the whole party, on the way to a boat Sneyers had hired. The wind was rustling in the palm trees, yet it was still so hot they were all sweating. The puppy kept on losing concentration, grinning suggestively at the body builders jogging along the beach to burn fat, their shorts tucked up into their bottoms to ensure a nice even suntan.

The boat was a Fairline Squadron, a 74-footer, a double bed on deck, double caterpillar engines and a top speed of 33 knots.

"It's what the celebrities want," said the puppy in his broken English, looking meaningfully at the double bed.

"It's not exactly meant for sunbathing," he went on.

Kallis, Inna and Sneyers had disappeared below deck. Wiik made his excuses and followed them.

When he got down below he positioned himself inside the doorway.

Sneyers was saying something, but paused briefly as Wiik slid in. Just long enough to give Kallis time to send him out. But Kallis said nothing, merely gave Sneyers a look to indicate that he should carry on.

A demonstration of strength, thought Wiik. Kallis decides who is here and who isn't. Sneyers is alone, Kallis has Inna and Wiik with him.

And Inna gave Wiik only the briefest glance. You're one of us.

Our team. The winners. Upstarts like Sneyers come running to us wanting meetings.

"As I was saying," Sneyers said to Kallis. "We've had our eye on you for a long time. But I wanted to see where you were going with Uganda. We didn't know if you were intending to sell once the prospecting was done. I wanted to see if you were made of the right stuff. And you were, no doubt about that. Cowards haven't got the nerve to invest in those areas, things are way too uncertain. But glory to the brave, isn't that what they say? My God, there are some fantastic deposits there! A snotty kid with a plank and a rag can extract gold there, just imagine what we can do . . ."

He paused to give Kallis the chance to speak, but Kallis said nothing.

"You own some large mines in Africa," Sneyers went on, "so we would be honoured if you were interested in joining our little . . . adventurers' club."

It is the African Mining Trust he is talking about. An association of foreign mine owners in Africa. Wiik is aware of them. He has heard Inna and Kallis talking about them. He has heard them talking about Sneyers too.

Sneyers is on Human Rights Watch's blacklist of companies who deal with dirty money from the Congo.

"His mine in western Uganda is mainly a money laundry," Kallis has said. "Militia groups plunder mines in the Congo, Sneyers buys gold both from there and from Somalia, and sells it on as gold from his own mines in Uganda."

"We have many common interests," Sneyers went on. "Building up an infrastructure. Security arrangements. The members of the group can be flown out from a pocket of unrest in less than twenty-four hours. From absolutely anywhere. Believe me, if you haven't encountered that kind of problem so far, you're bound to do so sooner or later – either you or your staff.

"We take a long-term view as well," he said, topping up Inna and Kallis' glasses.

Inna had finished her own drink, swapped her glass with Kallis' without anyone noticing, and finished his too. Sneyers went on:

"Our goal is to bring European, American and Canadian politicians onto the boards of our companies; many of the group's mother companies have former heads of state on their board. This also gives us a way of applying pressure. Influential people in countries providing aid, you see. Just to stop the blacks being difficult with us."

Inna excused herself and asked for the bathroom. When she had gone, Sneyers said:

"We're going to have problems in Uganda. The World Bank is threatening to freeze the aid in order to force through democratic elections. But Museveni isn't ready to let go of his power. And if he loses the aid, we'll have a new Zimbabwe. No reason to maintain good relations with the west any longer, and the overseas investors will be out on their ear. And then we'll lose everything. He'll take the lot. But I've got a plan. Although it'll cost money . . ."

"Oh yes?" Kallis says.

"His cousin Kadaga is a general in the army. And they've fallen out. Museveni has got it into his head that his cousin isn't loyal to him. Which is essentially true. Museveni is reducing Kadaga's power by not paying his soldiers' wages. They don't get any equipment either. Museveni has other generals whom he supports. It's gone so far that his cousin is staying away from Kampala. He's afraid he'll be arrested and accused of some crime. It's hell up there in the north right now. The L.R.A. and other groups are fighting with government forces over the control of the mines in the Congo. We'll soon be manoeuvred out of northern Uganda, and then they'll start fighting over those mines. In order to finance their wars, they need gold. If General Kadaga can't pay his soldiers, they'll desert. To whoever pays the best – other government troops or militia groups. He's ready to negotiate."

"What about?"

"He wants the financial resources to build up his forces again quickly. And to go into Kampala."

Kallis looked sceptically at Sneyers.

"A coup?"

"Not necessarily, a legal regime is better for international relations. But if Museveni were to be . . . eliminated. Then you could put up a new candidate in an election. And that candidate would need the military behind him."

"Who is this candidate? How do you know things would be better with a different president?"

Sneyers smiled.

"Naturally I can't tell you who he is. But our man will have the sense to keep in with us. He would know that we determined Museveni's fate, and can do the same with him. And General Kadaga will support him. And if Museveni is gone, the majority of the other generals will join him. Museveni is a dead end. So . . . are you in?"

Kallis was trying to digest what he had just heard.

"I'll think about it," he said.

"Don't think too long. And while you're thinking, move your money to a place where you can pay out without it being traced back to you. I'll give you the name of an extremely discreet bank."

Inna came back from the bathroom. Sneyers filled up their glasses again and fired his final salvo:

"Look at China. They couldn't give a damn that the World Bank won't lend money to undemocratic states. They go in and borrow billions for industrial projects in developing countries. And then they own enormous interests in the growing economies of tomorrow. I don't intend to sit on the sidelines and watch. We've got our chance in Uganda and the Congo right now."

Wiik's train of thought was interrupted by Ebba Kallis coming into the kitchen. She was still wearing her riding clothes, and gulped down a glass of juice in one go.

Kallis looked up from his newspaper.

"Ebba," he said. "Tomorrow night's dinner party, everything ready?"

She nodded.

"And then I was going to ask you to take charge of Inna's funeral," he said. "Her mother, well, you know how it is . . . It'll take her a year to come up with the perfect guest list. Besides which I presume I'm the one that's going to end up paying for it all, so I'd prefer it if you were dealing with things and not her."

Ebba nodded again. She did not want to do it, but what choice did she have?

He knows I don't want to take care of her funeral, she thought. And he despises me because I'll do it anyway. I'm his cheapest member of staff. And it'll be me that has to deal with her mother when she turns up with her impossible requests.

I don't want to organize any funeral, she thought. Can't we just . . . chuck her in a ditch or something?

She had not always felt like that. Inna had seduced her too, at the beginning. At first Ebba had been totally charmed.

It is a night at the beginning of August. Kallis and his wife are newly married, and have just moved into Regla. Inna and Diddi Wattrang have not moved there yet.

Ebba wakes up because somebody is staring at her. When she opens her eyes, Inna is leaning over her bed. She raises her finger to her lips to silence Ebba, her eyes shining with mischief in the darkness.

The rain is hammering against the window and Inna is soaked to the skin. Kallis mutters in his sleep, and turns on his side. Ebba and Inna look at each other, holding their breath. When his breathing is calm and even, Ebba gets up carefully and steals down the stairs to the kitchen after Inna.

They sit in the kitchen. Ebba fetches a towel. Inna dries her hair with it, but refuses dry clothes. They open a bottle of wine.

"But how did you get in?" asks Ebba.

"I climbed in through your bedroom window. It was the only one that was open."

"You're crazy. You could have broken your neck. But what about the gate? The guard?"

A local smith has just installed the remote-controlled iron gates. Inna does not have a remote in her car. The wall around the estate is two metres high.

"I parked the car outside and climbed. And Mauri might want to consider changing his security firm."

Lightning flashes across the sky. A second later the crash of thunder comes.

"Come on, let's go down to the lake for a swim," says Inna.

"Isn't it dangerous?"

Inna smiles, raising her shoulders up towards her ears.

"Yes."

They run down to the jetty. There are two jetties on the property. The old jetty is a little way off, you have to go through a dense wood. Ebba has been thinking of building a pool house down there. She has so many plans for Regla.

It is pouring with rain. Ebba's nightdress is sodden, clinging to her thighs. They strip naked on the jetty. Ebba is slender and flat-chested. Inna is as curvaceous as a film star from the '50s. Lightning splits the sky. Inna's teeth gleam white through the darkness and the rain. She dives from the jetty. Ebba stands there shivering, hesitating on the edge. The rain is whipping up the surface of the water so that it looks as if it is boiling.

"Jump in, it's warm," yells Inna, treading water.

And Ebba jumps.

The water feels strangely warm, and she stops shivering at once.

It is a magical feeling. They swim around in the water like two children. Back and forth. Down beneath the surface, puffing and panting back up again. The rain pelts down on their heads, the night air is chilly, but beneath the surface of the water it is warm and pleasant, just like a bath. The storm passes over them, sometimes Ebba hardly has time to count one elephant between the lightning and the thunder.

Perhaps I'll die here, she thinks.

And at that particular moment it does not really matter.

Ebba got herself a cup of coffee and a big bowl of fruit salad. Kallis and Wiik were talking about the security arrangements for Friday's dinner party. They were receiving overseas guests. Ebba stopped listening and allowed her thoughts of Inna to return.

They had been friends at first. Inna had made Ebba feel special.

Nothing unites two women like sharing experiences of their crazy mothers. Their mothers were obsessed with family, and collected rubbish. Inna had talked about her mother's kitchen cupboard. Stuffed with old East Indies china, held together with glue and metal clamps. Plus all the broken bits that could not be thrown away. Ebba had matched that with her tales of the library at Vikstaholm; you could hardly even get through the door. There were steel shelves crammed with old books and handwritten manuscripts that nobody could take care of, leaving everyone with a guilty conscience because they had handled them without gloves and the wasps were munching their way through the cellulose and they were in a worse state with every passing year.

"And I don't want her old crap," Ebba had laughed.

Inna had helped her ward off her mother's attempts to offload some of this cultural heritage in return for certain economic considerations; her new son-in-law had money, after all.

She was like a sister and a best friend, thought Ebba.

Things had changed later. When Ebba and Kallis had their first child. He was travelling more than he used to. When he was at home, he was always on the telephone. Or lost in his own thoughts.

She had been at a loss to understand it. The fact that he did not seem to care about his own son.

"You'll never have this time again," she had said to him. "Don't you understand that?"

She remembered her frustrating attempts at conversation. Sometimes she was angry, accusing. Sometimes calm, measured. He had not changed at all.

The renovation of Inna's and Diddi's houses was complete, and they moved into Regla.

Inna lost interest in Ebba at the same time as Kallis did.

They are at a cocktail party at the American Embassy. Inna is standing out on the terrace chatting to a group of middle-aged men. She is wearing a low-cut dress. One of her black stockings is torn. Ebba goes over to them, laughs at some joke, and whispers discreetly in Inna's ear.

"You've got a huge ladder in your stockings. I've got a spare pair in my bag, come to the Ladies and you can change."

Inna gives her a quick look, her expression impatient and annoyed.

"Don't be so insecure," she says crossly.

Then she turns her attention to the rest of the group, pushing her shoulder forward imperceptibly so that Ebba almost ends up behind her.

This effectively excludes her from the conversation, and she lopes away to look for Kallis. She longs to get home to her baby. She should not have come.

She has the strangest feeling that Inna stood there in the Ladies and tore her stocking deliberately. That huge ladder horrifies the women. But it does not bother the men. And Inna is as open and natural as ever.

It's a signal, thinks Ebba. That ladder in her stocking. It's a signal.

It is just that Ebba can't work out what kind of signal. And who it is aimed at.

Ebba got up to fetch another cup of coffee. At that moment there was a knock at the door, and they heard Diddi's wife Ulrika shout "hello" out in the hallway.

A second later she appeared at the door. She had the baby on her hip. Her hair was caught up in a pony-tail so no-one would notice that it had not been washed. Her eyes were red-rimmed.

"Have you heard from Diddi?" she asked in a voice that was on the point of breaking. "He didn't come home on Monday after you'd been to Kiruna. And he hasn't been home since. I've tried calling his mobile, but . . ."

She shook her head.

"Maybe I ought to call the police," she said.

"Absolutely not," said Kallis, without looking up from the paper. "The last thing I need is that kind of attention. On Friday evening representatives of the African Mining Trust are coming . . ."

"You're out of your mind!" yelled Ulrika.

The child on her arm burst into tears, but she did not appear to notice.

"I haven't heard from him, do you understand that? And Inna's been murdered. I know something's happened to him. I can feel it. And you're thinking about a business dinner!"

"It's those 'business dinners' that put food on your table and pay for the house you live in and the car you drive. And I know Inna's dead. Does it make me a better person if I lose my grip on everything and let us go under? I'm doing everything I can to hold myself and this company together. Unlike Diddi! Wouldn't you say?"

Wiik stared into his glass of juice and pretended he was not there. Ebba stood up.

"Come along now," she said, sounding like a mother.

She went over to Ulrika and took the sobbing child from her.

"He'll be home soon, I promise you. Maybe he just needs to be on his own for a while. It's been a shock. For all of us."

As she made the last comment she was looking at her husband, who was staring down at his newspaper without appearing to read a single line.

If I could choose between horses and people, thought Ebba Kallis, I wouldn't need to think about it for one second.

Mella looked around Martinsson's office for somewhere to sit.

"Chuck those on the floor," Martinsson said, nodding towards the files that were occupying the visitor's armchair.

"Haven't got the strength," Mella said, exhausted, and sat down on top of the files. "He doesn't exist."

"Santa Claus?"

Mella could not help smiling, despite the fact that she was so disappointed.

"The man who rented the car. The one who was wearing a light-coloured coat like the one the divers found in the water. John McNamara. He doesn't exist."

"In what way does he not exist? Is he a figment of somebody's imagination, or has he died?"

"Died, eighteen months ago. And the person who rented the car was using his identity."

Mella rubbed her whole hand over her face, up and down. She did that sometimes. Martinsson was fascinated by the gesture; it was so unusual for a woman.

"That means we can probably discount the idea of a sex game with somebody she knew that just went wrong," Mella said. "He came up here to kill her, right? Otherwise why would he use a false identity?"

"So his name wasn't John McNamara," Martinsson said. "But he was a foreigner?"

"The guy from Avis thinks he spoke English with a British accent. And it has to be him. He was wearing the same kind of coat as the divers found in the water under the ark."

"Have you heard anything from the lab?"

Mella shook her head.

"But it has to be her blood on the coat. It can't be a coincidence. How many people wear a summer coat like that in the winter? None."

She looked Martinsson straight in the eye.

"It was good that you had the idea of sending the divers down under the ark," she said.

"But that was to look for the mobile," Martinsson said, with a modest shrug. "And it wasn't down there."

Mella linked her hands behind the back of her neck, leaned back in the chair and closed her eyes.

"He didn't kill her straight away," she said, in a dream-like voice. "He tortured her first. Taped her to the kitchen chair and electrocuted her."

She chewed her tongue to pieces, Martinsson thought.

Mella opened her eyes and leaned forward.

"We have to choose which clues to work on," she said. "We don't have the resources to follow up everything."

"Do you think this was a professional hit?"

"Could have been."

"Why do you torture someone?" Martinsson said.

"To cause them pain, because you hate them," said Mella.

"Because you want information," Martinsson fired back.

"Because you want to . . . warn somebody."

"Mauri Kallis?"

"Why not?" Mella said. "Blackmail. Don't do this or this, otherwise this is what's going to happen to you and your family."

"Kidnapping?" Martinsson ventured. "And they didn't pay up?"

Mella nodded.

"I need to talk to Kallis and the brother again. But if it's to do with the company, they're not going to say a word."

She broke off and smiled, shaking her head.

"What?" Martinsson asked.

"These people. In this job you meet ordinary, middle-class people who think having anything to do with the police is rather unpleasant. Everybody has at least driven too fast at some point, so there's a kind of respect there mixed with fear."

"And?"

"Or you're dealing with villains who hate the police, but there's a kind of respect there too. But these people. It feels as if they think we're nothing but uneducated pond life whose job it is to keep the streets clean and stay out of their business."

Mella checked the time on her phone.

"Do you fancy some lunch? I was thinking of going to the stir-fry place in the old Tempo building."

On the way out Mella knocked on Stålnacke's office door.

"Do you want to join us for lunch?" she asked.

"Why not," Stålnacke said, trying to hide how pleased he was.

Shit, thought Mella. How lonely is he these days? Since that cat of his died he's always like a wilting plant.

That morning she had listened to the Thought for the Day on the car radio by mistake. Somebody had been talking about the importance of just stopping, the importance of silence.

A message like that must be a real slap in the face for so many people, thought Mella. It must be bloody silent around Stålnacke when he isn't working.

She promised herself that she would take the whole group out for some fun when this investigation was over. Not that she had any entertainment funds to speak of in the budget. But an evening's bowling and a pizza, at any rate.

Then of course she thought that Stålnacke could suggest they did something himself.

They walked along Hjalmar Lundbohmsvägen, turned up Geologgatan and went into the old Tempo building. Nobody seemed to have anything to say.

Martinsson was a lonely sort of person too, Mella thought. No, she'd much rather have her life full of kids who left their clothes in a pile on the floor and a man who has some kind of built-in fault that means he never actually finishes anything. If he cooks dinner, he doesn't clear away afterwards. And if he clears away after dinner, he never wipes the table and the draining board.

I'd never swap my life for hers, thought Mella as they were hanging their coats over the back of their chairs in the restaurant and going up to pay for lunch. Even if she does have an incredibly flat stomach and can give all her energy to her work. Although you could envy that ability to focus completely on the job.

There had been rumours about Martinsson when she had started in the prosecutor's office. That she snapped for no reason at the old misery-guts who worked there. That she sorted out all the case proceedings herself, wrote all the summons applications, and the old biddies in the office in Gällivare did not need to come up to Kiruna.

Mella's colleagues saw her in court sometimes when they were called as witnesses. Sharp and well prepared, they said. And they were pleased. They were on the same side in court, after all. The bloody defence lawyers had a fight on their hands.

Just wait till the kids have left home, Mella thought, spooning chicken and vegetable stir-fry with rice onto her plate. Then I'll be piling up completed investigations on her desk.

Her thoughts landed guiltily in the middle of a heap of investigations that had been put to one side because of the murder.

Then she pulled herself together and turned her attention to Martinsson and Stålnacke.

They were exchanging cat stories. Stålnacke had just been telling her something about Manne, and now it was her turn.

"They're such characters," she said, sprinkling soy sauce on her rice. "My grandmother's cats were all just called 'kitty'. But of course I still remember them. I remember a time when Grandmother had two dogs and Daddy had one, so there were three dogs in the house. And then we got a new kitten. Whenever we got new kittens they were fed on the worktop; they were so scared of the dogs at first, and were too nervous down on the floor. But this one! First of all he ate all his own food. Then he jumped onto the floor and emptied the dogs' bowls."

Stålnacke laughed as he worked his way through the hottest dish from the buffet.

"You should have seen them," she went on. "If he'd been a dog there would have been a fight, but they just didn't know what to do with this little thing. They looked at us as if to say: 'What's he doing? Can you take him away, please?' On the second day, he attacked the lead dog. Threw himself at him without a trace of fear, and ended up hanging from the skin of Jussi's throat. And Jussi! He was just so nice. It was beneath his dignity to acknowledge this minor irritation. He just sat there with the kitten hanging round his neck. The cat was doing his best to fight, scrabbling away with his back legs. And Jussi was trying to hang onto his pride. Completely miserable."

"'What's he doing? Can you take him away, please?'" Stålnacke repeated.

Martinsson laughed.

"Exactly. Then he started having toilet problems because of all the dog food he was bolting down. But he was so little he couldn't manage to climb into the litter tray, and so he soiled himself. Daddy rinsed him off under the tap, but he still smelled unpleasant. Then he went and lay down in the biggest of the dog baskets, and none of the dogs dared move him out, nor did they want to lie down next to Smelly-pants. We had two dog baskets in the hallway. The cat lay there on his own in the bigger of the two, snoring away in comfort. Our three big dogs piled in together in the smaller basket, looking mournfully at us as we walked past. That cat ruled the place until he died."

"How did he die?" Stålnacke said.

"Don't know, he just disappeared."

"That's the worst thing of all," Stålnacke said, mopping up the spicy sauce from his plate with a piece of bread. "Here comes somebody who certainly doesn't understand the first thing about cats."

Mella and Martinsson followed Stålnacke's eyes and saw Inspector Tommy Rantakyrö approaching their table. When Stålnacke's cat had disappeared, he had joked injudiciously with a grieving Stålnacke. Rantakyrö was blissfully ignorant of the fact that his sins had not been forgiven.

"I thought I'd find you here," he said.

He handed some papers to Mella.

"Inna Wattrang's incoming and outgoing calls on her mobile phone," he said.

"But," he went on, holding up another piece of paper, "this was the company phone. She also had a private subscription."

"Why?" Mella said, taking the paper.

Rantakyrö shrugged.

"How should I know? Maybe she wasn't allowed to make private calls from the mobile."

Martinsson laughed.

"Sorry," she said. "I forget you're employed by the government. So am I nowadays, nothing wrong with that. But I mean, how much did she earn a month? Almost ninety thousand kronor, before bonuses. That means you have a job that owns you. You have to be accessible all the time, and the fact that you can make private calls is probably the least of your fringe benefits."

"So why, then?" Rantakyrö said, slightly hurt.

"Kallis Mining can check the company phone," Mella mused. "She probably wanted a phone that was guaranteed to be private. I want the name, address and shoe size of every single person she's spoken to on this phone."

She waved the list from the private mobile.

Rantakyrö raised his index and middle fingers in a salute, indicating that her orders would be carried out.

Mella checked the printouts again.

"No calls in the days immediately before the murder; that's a shame."

"What kind of subscription was it?" Martinsson said.

"Comviq," Mella said, "so there's no network coverage up there."

"Abisko is small, though," Martinsson said. "If she's made any calls it has to be from the payphone in the tourist station. It might be interesting to compare the outgoing calls from there with the lists from the mobiles."

Rantakyrö looked exhausted at the thought.

"But that could be several hundred calls," he whimpered.

"I don't think so, actually," Martinsson said. "If she arrived on Thursday and was murdered some time between Thursday afternoon and Saturday morning, that's less than two days, so there can't be more than twenty or so calls. People are out skiing or sitting in the bar; I don't think they sit in a telephone box unless they have to."

"Check it out," said Mella to Rantakyrö.

"Red alert," Stålnacke said, his mouth full of bread.

Per-Erik Seppälä, a journalist with the local Norrbotten television station, was walking towards their table. Mella turned the printouts face down.

Seppälä said hello. He spent a little extra time taking in

Martinsson. So that was what she looked like. He knew she had moved back into town and started working for the prosecutor's office, but he had never met her. He found it difficult not to stare at the red scar running diagonally from her upper lip to her nose. She had really done herself some damage in that incident eighteen months ago. He had filmed a report, a reconstruction of the whole thing. It had been broadcast on the evening news.

He managed to take his eyes off Martinsson, and turned to Mella.

"Have you got a minute?" he asked.

"Sorry, I can't help you," Mella said sympathetically. "We'll be holding a press conference just as soon as we have any information that's of interest to the general public."

"No, it's not that. Well yes, it is about Inna Wattrang. There's something you ought to know."

Mella nodded to indicate that she was listening.

"Not here, if you don't mind," Seppälä said.

"I've finished," Mella said to her colleagues, getting up.

At least she had managed to eat half her lunch.

"I don't know if this . . . if it means anything," Seppälä said. "But I need to tell you about it. Because if it does . . . well, that's why I wanted this just between the two of us. I've no wish to die before my time."

They were walking down Gruvvägen, past the old fire station. Mella didn't speak.

"You know Örjan Bylund," Seppälä went on.

"Mmm," Mella said.

Örjan Bylund had been a journalist on the newspaper *Norrländska Socialdemokraten*. Two days before Christmas Eve, which was also his sixty-second birthday, he had died.

"Heart attack, wasn't it?" Mella said.

"That's the official line," said Seppälä. "But the fact is, he took his own life. Hanged himself in his study."

"I see," Mella said.

She was surprised she had not heard anything about it. Her colleagues always knew about that sort of stuff.

"That's what actually happened, anyway. In November he told me he had something big on the go to do with Kallis Mining. They've got concessions around here, as you know. Outside Vittangi, and on the marshes outside Svappavaara."

"Do you know what it was about?"

"No, but I just thought . . . I don't know, I just thought I ought to tell you. Maybe it's not just a coincidence, you know. First him and then Inna Wattrang."

"It's strange that I didn't know he'd killed himself. I mean, the police have to be called in if it's suicide . . ."

"I know. His wife will be completely devastated. She was the one who found him. And she cut him down and rang the doctor. You know how it is. He was well known in town, and there's always a lot of talk. So she rang a doctor she knew and the doctor signed the death certificate and didn't call the police."

"Bloody hell!" Mella said. "That means there was no autopsy either."

"I didn't know whether I ought to . . . but I had to tell you. I mean, you start thinking that maybe it wasn't suicide. If he was digging into Kallis Mining and so on. But the last thing I want is for Airi to get into any kind of trouble."

"Airi?"

"His wife."

"No, no," Mella promised. "But I need to talk to her."

She shook her head. How were they going to follow up everything? Put it all together and get an overview? It was beginning to feel overwhelming.

"If you find out anything else . . ." she said.

"Yes, of course. I saw Inna Wattrang at a press conference Kallis Mining held here in town before they floated one of the companies up here on the stock exchange. There was something magnetic about her; I hope you catch whoever did it. You will take it easy with Airi, won't you?"

Martinsson walked into her office. She felt upbeat. It had done her good not to have lunch alone, as usual.

She switched on the computer. Her heart gave a little leap.

A message from Måns Wenngren.

"You are coming, aren't you?" it said. Nothing else.

First she felt a little spurt of joy. Then she thought that if he had really cared, he would have written more. Then that if he didn't care, he wouldn't have written to her at all.

"He wasn't a particularly cheerful person. I know that. He was on anti-depressants . . . and tranquillizers too, sometimes. But still. I never thought . . . Would you like filter coffee or percolated? I can easily do either."

Örjan Bylund's widow, Airi, turned away from Mella and Stålnacke and put some Danish pastries in the microwave.

Stålnacke felt uncomfortable; he did not like this, poking and prodding at wounds that had only just begun to heal.

"Was it you who persuaded the doctor not to call the police?" Mella asked.

Airi Bylund nodded, still with her back to them.

"You know how people talk. But you mustn't blame Doctor Erlander. It was entirely my responsibility."

"It doesn't really work like that," Mella said. "But we're not out to put the blame on anybody."

Stålnacke saw Airi Bylund's hand move quickly up to her cheek to wipe away a tear that she would not allow them to see. He was seized by a desire to take her in his arms and comfort her. Then he discovered that his hand had been seized by a desire to get hold of that lovely broad bottom. He felt ashamed of himself, and pushed the thought away; for God's sake, that poor woman was standing there crying over her husband, who had hanged himself.

It was a pleasant kitchen, Stålnacke thought. There were several home-made rugs on the floor, which was done in imitation terracotta tiles. Along the wall was a sofa bed that was a little bit too wide and soft to sit on, but which would be very tempting if you fancied a doze after dinner. It was covered with lots of lovely comfy cushions, not those little hard ones that are just for decoration.

A few too many ornaments, but that's what women were like, not one empty surface. At least it wasn't some weird collection, elves, or hippos, or little glass bottles. He had once spoken to a witness whose entire house was cluttered with matchboxes from all over the world.

In the kitchen, pot plants and baskets were crowded along the windowsill. On the worktop stood the microwave and a stand made of bamboo that was used for drying mushrooms and herbs. Tiny pot holders that looked as though they might have been made by a grandchild hung on a hook. Nearest the stove stood a row of old porcelain jars with lids and ornate writing: "Flour", "Sugar", "Dried Fruit" and so on. One of them did not have a lid, and was where Airi kept her whisks and wooden spoons.

There was something about porcelain jars like that. Hjördis had been crazy about them too, and had taken them with her when she left him. His sister had some as well.

"Did he have a study?" Mella asked. "Do you mind if we take a look?"

If Airi Bylund's kitchen was cluttered, then at least it was clean and attractive. In her dead husband's study, teetering heaps of torn-out newspaper articles and reference books lay all over the floor. A thousand-piece jigsaw lay on a folding table, the pieces all the right way up and sorted according to colour. On the walls were a number of finished puzzles, glued onto sheets of masonite. Clothes and a blanket in a pile on an old sofa.

"I haven't exactly got around to . . . and I haven't had the strength," Airi said, waving a hand at the mess.

Lucky for us, Mella thought.

"We'll send somebody over to collect his papers and articles and that sort of thing," she said. "You'll get everything back. Didn't he have a computer?"

"Yes, but I gave it to one of the grandchildren."

She looked guiltily at them.

"His employer didn't say anything about wanting it back, so . . ."

"This grandchild who has got the computer . . ."

"Axel. He's thirteen."

Mella fished out her phone.

"What's his number?"

Axel was at home. He said the computer was fine, it was in his room.

"Have you cleaned the hard drive?" Mella said.

"No, it had already been wiped. But it was only 20 gigabytes and I want to be able to download stuff from Pirate Bay. So if you want it, I want a new one with a 2.1 gigahertz processor."

Mella had to laugh. What a negotiator.

"Forget it," she said. "But because I'm such a nice person, you can have it back when we've finished with it."

When she had finished talking to Axel, she asked Airi Bylund:

"Did you wipe the hard drive?"

"No," she said. "I can't even program the video."

She fixed Mella with her eyes.

"Make sure you learn how things like that work. All of a sudden you're on your own."

"Did anybody from the paper come here and do anything with the computer, then?"

"No."

Mella called Fred Olsson. He answered almost straight away.

"If somebody's wiped a hard drive, you can get the documents and cookies back, can't you?"

"Sure," Olsson said. "As long as you haven't E.M.P.-ed it."

"What?"

"Fired an electromagnetic pulse through it – there are specialist companies who do that. Bring it here, I've got some software that'll restore data from the hard drive . . ."

"I'm on my way," Mella said. "Don't go home. It'll take a while."

When she had finished speaking, Bylund was looking thoughtful. She opened her mouth and closed it again.

"What is it?" Mella said.

"No, it's probably nothing . . . But it was when I found him. It was here in the study, that's why the ceiling light is on the bed."

Mella and Stålnacke looked at the hook for the light fitting.

"The door to his study was closed," Airi went on. "But the cat was in here."

"And?"

"It wasn't allowed in here. We had another cat ten years ago, and it used to sneak in here and pee on his piles of paper. And in his sheepskin slippers. Since then all cats have been banned from his room."

"Perhaps he wasn't bothered about that when . . ."

Stålnacke broke off in mid-sentence.

"No, that's what I thought too," Airi said.

"Do you think he was murdered?" Mella said to her straight out.

Bylund was silent for a little while before replying.

"Perhaps I'm hoping he was. In some strange way. It's so difficult to understand."

Her hand flew up and covered her mouth.

"Although he wasn't a cheerful person. Never had been."

"So you've got a cat, then?" Stålnacke said, who had serious problems with Mella's direct approach.

"I have." Airi Bylund's face was lit up by a smile. "She's in the bedroom; come and have a look at something really cute."

On the crocheted cover on the double bed, a cat lay sleeping with four kittens in an untidy heap beside her.

Stålnacke fell to his knees as if he were at an altar.

The cat woke up immediately, but stayed where she was. One of the kittens woke up too, and came marching over to Stålnacke. She was a grey tabby, with an almost black ring around one eye.

"Doesn't she look funny," said Airi. "She looks as if she's been in a fight."

"Hi there, boxer," Stålnacke said to the cat.

She strolled confidently up his arm, using her needle-sharp claws to keep her balance, then ambled from one shoulder across the back of his neck to the other.

"Hello precious," Stålnacke said reverently.

"Would you like her?" Airi said. "It's difficult to find homes for them all."

"No, no," Stålnacke insisted, just as he felt the soft fur against his cheek.

The kitten jumped down onto the bed and woke up one of her siblings by biting the end of his tail.

"Take the cat and we'll go," Mella said.

Stålnacke shook his head firmly.

"No," he said. "They're such a tie."

They said their good-byes. Airi Bylund accompanied them to the door. Before they left, Mella asked:

"Your husband. Was he cremated, or . . . ?"

"No, he was buried in a coffin. But I've always said they can scatter me over Taalojärvi."

"Taalojärvi," Stålnacke said. "What was your maiden name?"

"Tieva."

"Aha," he said. "Twenty years or so ago I went by snowmobile up to Salmi. I was on the way to Kattuvuoma. And just opposite the village, on the eastern side of the sound by Taalojärvi, there was a little cottage. And I knocked on the door and asked the way to Kattuvuoma, and the woman who lived there said, 'they usually drive straight across the lake and over the marshes and then go to the left, and there's Kattuvuoma'. And we talked a little bit more and I thought she seemed a bit reserved, but I pulled myself together and started to speak Finnish instead, and then she thawed out."

Airi laughed.

"Oh yes, she probably thought you were a *rousku*, one of those bastards who can only speak Swedish."

"Exactly. So when I'd got back on the snowmobile and was just about to leave, she asked me, 'but where do you come from and whose boy are you, since you can speak Finnish?' So I told her I was Valfrid Stålnacke's boy from Laukkuluspa. '*Voi hyvänen aika!*' she said, clapping her hands. 'Good heavens. We're related, my boy. You mustn't go across the lake. There are lots of hollows and it's really dangerous. Go along the shore of the lake.'"

Stålnacke laughed.

"Her name was Tieva. Was she your grandmother?"

"No, she wasn't," Airi said, blushing. "She was my mother."

When they got out onto the street Mella set off like a soldier on a route march. Stålnacke scuttled after her.

"Shall we go and pick up the computer?" he asked.

"I want him up," she said.

"But it's the middle of winter. The ground's frozen solid."

"I don't care. I want Örjan Bylund's body up now! Pohjanen has to do an autopsy! Where are you going?"

Stålnacke had turned on his heel and was on his way back to the house.

"I'm going to tell his widow, of course. You go! See you at the station."

Martinsson got home at around 6.00 in the evening. The clouds had gathered, and it was beginning to get dark. Just as she got out of the car in front of her grey house, it began to snow. Feather-light stars glittered as they floated down through the glow of the lamp on the barn wall, and the light above the porch.

She stopped and stuck out her tongue, her arms at right angles to her body, her face turned upwards, eyes closed, feeling the soft flakes land on her eyelashes and her tongue. Although it did not feel the way it used to when she was little. Just like making angels in the snow, it was one of those things that was fantastic when you were a child. If you tried it when you were grown up, you just got snow inside your collar.

He is not for me, she thought, opening her eyes and looking down towards the river, enveloped in darkness, with a few lights showing from houses on the far side of the creek.

He doesn't think about me, the fact that he sends e-mails doesn't mean a thing.

During the afternoon she must have written twenty messages to Wenngren, then deleted them all. She did not want to seem too keen.

Forget it, she tried to tell herself. He's not interested.

But her heart was stubbornly contradicting her.

Look here, it said, calling up some pictures for her to look at. The two of them in the skiff. She is rowing. He is trailing a hand in the water. He has rolled up the sleeves of his white office shirt. His face soft and relaxed. Then: her on the floor in the living room in front of the open fire. Him between her legs.

When she got undressed to change from her work clothes into jeans and a jumper, she looked at herself in the mirror. Pale and slender. Her breasts were far too small. And weren't they a really odd shape? Not two little mounds, more like two upside down ice cream cones. She suddenly felt uncomfortable and unfamiliar with this body that nobody wanted, inside which no child had grown to full term. She quickly pulled on her clothes.

She poured herself a whisky and sat down at her grandmother's old drop-leaf table in the kitchen, taking bigger gulps than usual. Its warmth spread through her stomach, and her thoughts stopped tumbling over one another in her head.

The last time she had really been in love . . . it had been Thomas Söderberg, which ought to tell her something about her ability to pick a man. She would not think about it.

She had had the odd boyfriend after that, all law students at the university. She had not actually chosen any of them herself. She had allowed herself to be invited out to dinner, allowed herself to be kissed and somehow ended up in bed. Depressing and predictable from the start. Contempt had always been attendant. She had despised them all because they were such babies, upper-class boys, all convinced they would get higher grades than her if they could only be bothered to study. She despised their pathetic rebellion against their parents, which consisted of a moderate intake of drugs and a somewhat larger intake of alcohol. She despised their illusions of being different. She even despised their contempt for Philistines, until they started work and got married and turned into Philistines.

And now there was Wenngren. Take a little bit of boarding school, fine art, arrogance, alcohol and a sharp legal mind in a male body and shake.

Her father probably could not believe his luck when her mother chose him. That was how she imagined it had happened. Her mother chose her father, just as you pluck a piece of ripe fruit from a tree.

Martinsson was seized by a sudden desire to look at pictures of her mother. After her grandmother's death, she ripped all the photos of her mother out of Grandmother's album herself.

She pulled on her boots and ran across to Fjällborg.

There was still a faint smell of fried sausage in the air down in Fjällborg's boiler room. A newly washed plate lay on the string shelf, along with a glass, a pan and a frying pan, turned upside down on a red and white checked tea towel. Fjällborg was lying on top of the bed dozing, with the local paper over his face. There was a big hole in one of his socks. Martinsson was strangely moved when she saw him.

Bella leapt up, almost knocking the chair over in her joy at Martinsson's visit. Martinsson scratched her, and the rhythmic thumping of Bella's tail against the kitchen table and her ecstatic whimpering woke Fjällborg.

"Rebecka," he said happily. "Would you like some coffee?"

She said yes, and while he was measuring it out she explained her errand.

Fjällborg went upstairs, and after a while he came back with two albums under his arm.

"I'm sure there must be some pictures of your mother in here," he said. "Although it's mostly Maj-Lis and the kids, of course."

Martinsson flicked through the pictures of her mother. In one her mother and Maj-Lis were sitting on a reindeer skin on the snow in early spring, squinting and laughing at the camera.

"We're like each other," Martinsson said.

"True," Fjällborg said.

"How did she and my father meet?"

"I don't know. But I expect it was at a dance. He was a really good dancer, your father. When he had the nerve."

Martinsson tried to create pictures in her head. Her mother in her father's arms on the dance floor. Her father, with the self-confidence he has borrowed from a bottle, allows his hand to move across her back.

She was filled with an old emotion when she saw the pictures. A strange mixture of shame and anger. Fury to counteract the villagers' condescending sympathy.

They called her poor girl over her head. *Piika riepu.* Lucky she had her grandmother, they said. But how long would Theresia Martinsson be able to cope? That was the question. We all have our faults, that's true. But not to be able to take care of your own child . . .

Fjällborg looked at her sideways.

"Maj-Lis was very fond of your mother," he said.

"Was she?"

Martinsson heard that her voice was no more than a whisper.

"They always had plenty to talk about, they used to sit there at the kitchen table and laugh."

Oh yes, thought Martinsson. I remember that mother too. She looked for a photograph where her mother was not posing. Where she had not chosen the best angle for the camera and set her smile.

A real film star, by Kurravaara standards.

Two memories:

Memory number one. She wakes up in the morning in the two-room apartment in the town centre. They have moved from Kurravaara. Daddy is still living on the ground floor in Grandmother's house. The most practical thing is for Rebecka to live with her mother in town, they say. Close to school. She wakes up and everything smells fresh and clean. It is sparkling. And her mother has rearranged the furniture throughout the apartment. The only thing that is still in its old place is Rebecka's bed. Breakfast is on the table. Freshly baked scones. Her mother is on the balcony smoking a cigarette, and she looks really happy.

She must have spent the whole night cleaning and heaving furniture around. Whatever will the neighbours think now?

Rebecka slinks down the stairs like a cat, keeping her eyes firmly on the ground. If Laila from downstairs opens the door she'll just die of shame.

Memory number two. The teacher says: "Get into pairs."

Petra: I don't want to sit next to Rebecka.

Teacher: Don't be so silly!

The class listens. Rebecka stares down at her desk.

Petra: She smells of pee.

It is because they have not got any electricity in the apartment. It has been cut off. It is September so they are not cold, but they cannot use the washing machine.

When Rebecka comes home crying, her mother is furious. She drags her along to the local telecom offices and plays hell with the staff. It does not make any difference when they try to explain that she needs to contact the electricity company, that it isn't the same thing at all.

Rebecka Martinsson looked at the picture of her mother. It struck her that she was about the same age as she is now.

She was probably doing her best, Martinsson thought.

She looked at the smiling woman on the reindeer skin, and a feeling of reconciliation came over her. It was as if something inside her had found peace. Perhaps it was the realization that her mother was not very old.

What kind of mother would I have been if I'd chosen to have my baby? wondered Martinsson. My God!

And then it became the norm for my mother to leave me with Grandmother during periods when she could not cope. And I was here in Kurra for the summer holidays too.

And all the kids were grubby up here, she thought. We all probably smelled of pee.

Fjällborg interrupted her thoughts.

"I wondered if you could help me . . ." he began.

He always made sure he got her working. Martinsson suspected it was not so much that he actually needed help, but that he thought she did. A little bit of physical work to stop her brooding.

Now he wanted her to get up on the roof to knock down some overhanging snow.

"The thing is, it's going to come down any day now, and Bella might be underneath it. Or me, if I forget it's there."

She climbed up onto Fjällborg's roof in the darkness of the evening. The outdoor lighting was not much help. It was snowing. And the old snow underneath was hard and slippery. A rope around her waist and a shovel in her hand. Fjällborg had a shovel too, but only to lean on. He pointed and shouted out orders. Martinsson was doing it her way, and he was getting annoyed because his way was the best. That was the way things always were when they worked together. She was sweaty when she climbed back down.

But it did not help to distract her. When she got into the shower at home, her thoughts turned to Måns Wenngren again. She looked at the clock. It was only nine.

She needed something else to occupy her mind. She might as well sit down at the computer and carry on looking into Inna Wattrang.

*

At 9.45 there was a knock at Martinsson's front door. Mella's voice came from downstairs in the hallway:

"Hi there! Anyone home?"

Martinsson opened the door to the upstairs landing and shouted: "Up here!"

"There is a Santa Claus," puffed Mella when she reached the top of the stairs.

She was carrying a banana box. Martinsson remembered her joke from that morning, and laughed.

"I've been a good girl all year," she promised.

Mella laughed too. She found it easy to get on with Martinsson now they were working together on the Inna Wattrang case.

"These are papers and all kinds of stuff from Örjan Bylund's computer," Mella said after a moment, nodding towards the banana box.

She sat down at the kitchen table and explained about the journalist who had died, while Martinsson made coffee.

"He told a colleague he was working on something to do with Kallis Mining. Six weeks later he was dead."

Martinsson turned.

"How?"

"Hanged himself at home in his study. Although I'm not at all convinced about that. I've applied for permission to exhume his body and get an autopsy done. I just wish the authority would speed up with their decision. Here!"

She put a U.S.B. stick on the table.

"The contents of Örjan Bylund's computer. The hard drive had been wiped, but Olsson sorted it."

Mella looked around. It was a really comfortable kitchen. Simple, rustic furniture mixed with pieces from the '40s and '50s. Trays hanging from embroidered holders. Attractive, and slightly old-fashioned. It reminded Mella of her own grandmother and the way her house had been.

"It's lovely here," she said.

Martinsson poured her a coffee.

"Thanks. You'll have to have it black."

Martinsson looked around her kitchen. She was pleased with the way she had it. It was not some kind of mausoleum to her grandmother, but she had kept most things. When she had moved up here she had felt very strongly that she liked it just that way. She had stood in her apartment in Stockholm when she was discharged from the psychiatric ward and looked around. Looked at her trendy ant chairs and her Poul Hennings lighting. The Italian sofa from Asplund's that she had bought as a present to herself when she was elected to the Law Society. "This isn't me," she had thought. And so she had sold the lot along with the apartment.

"There's a payment to Inna Wattrang that I'm going to check on," Martinsson told Mella. "Somebody paid two hundred thousand kronor in cash into her personal account."

"Thanks," Mella said. "Tomorrow?"

Martinsson nodded.

This was brilliant, Mella thought. It was exactly this sort of thing she did not have time to do. Maybe she should ask Martinsson to come along when they went bowling. Then she and Stålnacke could talk about cats.

"Actually, I'm too old for this," Mella said, looking at her coffee cup. "When I drink coffee in the evenings nowadays I wake up during the night and my thoughts just go . . ."

She made a circular movement with her hand to show how her thoughts spun round in her head.

"Me too," Martinsson confessed.

They laughed, conscious that they had both had a cup anyway, just to get closer to each other.

Outside, the snow went on falling.

THURSDAY, 20 MARCH, 2005

It snowed throughout Wednesday night. But on Thursday morning the sky was clear and the sun was shining. Only minus 3°C. At 9.15 in the morning Örjan Bylund's coffin was dug up. The graveyard workers had cleared away the snow the night before, and put a heater on top of the grave.

Mella had argued with them about it.

"We need a decision from the authorities," they had said.

"To exhume the body, yes," Mella had replied. "But all I'm asking you to do is to put the heater on now, so that you can dig him up quickly when we get the decision."

By now the deep frost had gone from the ground, and they dug up the coffin with the graveyard's little Kubota.

There were a dozen or so photographers hanging about. Mella looked at them, and her thoughts flew guiltily to Airi Bylund.

But I'm working on a murder investigation here, she defended herself. That lot just want front page pictures.

And they got them. The filthy hole in the ground, the earth, the withered roses, the black coffin. And all around the sparkling early spring, newly fallen snow and sunshine.

Pohjanen and Granlund were waiting at the hospital to receive the body.

Mella looked at her watch.

"Half an hour," she said to Stålnacke. "Then we'll ring and ask how far he's got."

At that moment her phone buzzed in her pocket. It was Martinsson.

"I've checked that payment into Inna Wattrang's bank account," she said. "And there's something odd about it. On January 15th, somebody went into a small branch of Svenska Enskilda Banken on Hantverkargatan in Stockholm and paid in two hundred thousand kronor. On the paying-in slip, the person wrote: 'Not for your silence'."

"'Not for your silence'," Mella repeated. "I want to see the slip."

"I've asked them to scan it and e-mail it to you, so check your messages when you get in," Martinsson said.

"Leave the prosecutor's office and come and work downstairs with us instead," Mella said. "Money isn't everything."

Martinsson was laughing on the other end of the phone.

"I've got to go," she said. "I'm in court."

"Again? Weren't you there on Monday and Tuesday?"

"Mmm . . . It's Gudrun Haapalahti in the main office. She's stopped sending anybody else up here."

"You ought to complain," Mella said, in an attempt to be helpful.

"Actually, I'd rather die," laughed Martinsson. "See you later."

Mella looked at Stålnacke.

"Don't start," she said.

She rang Rantakyrö.

"Can you check on something for me?" she said, and without waiting for an answer she went on:

"Find out if any of the people Inna Wattrang spoke to on either of her mobile phones lives or works anywhere near the S.E.B. branch on Hantverkargatan in Stockholm."

"How exactly did I end up in this telephone hell?" Rantakyrö said. "How far back do you want me to go?"

"Six months?"

There was a groan on the other end of the phone.

"Start with January, then. The payment into her account was made on January 15th."

"Actually, I was just going to ring you," he said before Mella had time to ring off.

"Yes?"

"You asked me to check the phone at Abisko tourist station."

"Yes?"

"Somebody, and I reckon it has to be her, rang Diddi Wattrang's house late on Thursday night."

"He told me he didn't know where she was," Mella said.

"The conversation lasted exactly four minutes and twenty-three seconds. I reckon he's lying, don't you?"

Mauri Kallis was up in his study, looking down at the garden.

His wife Ebba was walking across the white gravel. Her riding hat under her arm, her new Arab stallion held loosely. Her black hair band was shiny with sweat, her head drooping; she looked tired but contented.

Ulrika Wattrang was coming from the opposite direction. She did not have the little boy with her. He was probably at home with the nanny.

The question was whether Diddi had come home yet. As far as Kallis was concerned, it did not matter. He could manage the meeting with the African Mining Trust just as well without him. Better in fact. You could not count on Diddi these days. Besides, Kallis could as easily get a monkey to do his job. You did not exactly need to exert yourself to find investors for Kallis' projects. Now people had lost faith in I.T. shares, and it seemed impossible to calculate China's appetite for steel, they were queuing up to join him.

He would get rid of Diddi. It was only a question of time before Diddi and his wife and their little prince were told to pack up and move on.

Ulrika had stopped to talk to Ebba.

Ebba glanced up at his window, and he stepped back behind the curtain. It moved, but you probably would not notice from outside.

I don't care about her, he thought frostily about Ebba.

When she had suggested separate bedrooms, he had agreed

without any discussion. It had no doubt been a final attempt on her part to provoke a row, but he had felt only relief. It meant he no longer had to lie there pretending not to notice that she was crying with her back to him.

And I don't care about Diddi, he thought. In fact I can't remember what I used to think was so fantastic about him.

I cared about Inna, though.

It is snowing. It is two weeks until Christmas Eve. Mauri and Diddi are in their third year at business school. Mauri is already working part time for a firm of brokers. He has started to follow trading in commodities as a special interest. It will be seventeen years before he ends up on the front cover of *Business Week*.

The area around Stureplan is like an advert. Or like one of those plastic globes that make a snowstorm when you shake them.

Beautiful women are drinking espresso in the cafés, with paper carrier bags from the N.K. department store on the floor beside them, full of packages. The snow is floating down.

Little boys and girls in cloaks and duffel coats, like miniature adults, hold onto the hands of their well-dressed parents, almost walking backwards so they can see all the Christmas displays in the shop windows. Diddi is making fun of the Christmas decorations in Östermalm.

"They've got such a London complex," he laughs.

They are on their way to Riche. Pleasantly tipsy, although it is only 6.15 in the evening. But they have decided it is time for their Christmas celebrations.

On the corner of Birger Jarlsgatan and Grev Turegatan, they bump into Inna.

She is walking arm in arm with an older man. Much older. He is bony, in the way that old men are. Death shadows him; his skeleton is pressing against his skin from the inside, saying: soon there will only be me left. The skin has very little resistance these days. It is stretched over his forehead where his cranium bulges outwards, without a hint of elasticity. His cheekbones are sticking out above his cheeks, which have collapsed inwards. The bones of his wrists are very prominent.

Not until afterwards does it occur to Mauri that Diddi was about to walk past without saying hello, but of course Mauri stops and introductions are necessary.

Inna is unflustered. Mauri looks at her and thinks she is like a Christmas present herself. Her smile and her eyes always look as though they are holding a lovely surprise.

"This is Ecke," she says, pressing herself affectionately against him.

All these pet names the upper classes have. It never ceases to amaze Mauri. There is Noppe and Bobbo and Guggu. Inna is actually called Honorine. And while a William is never known as Wille, a Walter is always Walle.

The man extends a bony hand covered with brown age spots from out of his expensive but shabby wool coat. Mauri finds it disgusting. He resists the urge to sniff at his hand to see if it smells dirty.

"I don't get it," he says to Diddi when they have said goodbye to Inna and her companion. "Is that Ecke?"

Inna has mentioned him from time to time. She cannot come out with them because she is off to the country with Ecke, she and Ecke have seen this film or that film. Kallis has pictured an upper-class young man with slicked-back blond hair. Sometimes he has wondered if he might be married, since they never get to meet him and Inna does not have much to say about him. But then she never says much about any of her boyfriends. Mauri has also thought that these men are probably older, and that Inna does not think they will have anything in common with her brother and Mauri, little boys who are still at school. But not that much older!

When Diddi does not reply, Mauri goes on:

"But he's an old man! What does she see in him?"

Then Diddi says, in a casual tone, but Mauri can hear him clinging onto his air of insouciance as it threatens to slip through his fingers, though he is holding onto it tightly, it is the only thing he has to hang onto:

"You really are naïve."

They stop there on the pavement outside Riche, everything looking like a Christmas card. Diddi flicks his cigarette away and stares intensely at Mauri.

He is going to kiss me, Mauri thinks, but does not have time to work out whether that scares him or not before the moment has passed.

Another time. Winter again. Snowing again. And Inna has a good friend, as she calls them. Although this is someone else. Things have been over between her and Ecke for a long time. She is going to the Nobel dinner with this man, and Diddi decides that he and Mauri must go round to her apartment on Linnégatan with a bottle of champagne to help her zip up her dress.

She looks amazing when she opens the door. A long, poppy-red dress, moist lips the same colour.

"O.K.?" she asks.

But Mauri is incapable of replying. He has discovered what the word breathless means.

He waves the bottle of champagne and disappears into the pantry to hide his feelings and to fetch glasses.

When he comes back she is sitting at the little dining table putting on more eye shadow. Diddi is standing behind her. He is leaning over her, supporting himself with one hand on the table. He has slipped his other hand inside her dress and is caressing her breast.

Both of them look at Mauri, waiting for his reaction. Diddi raises one eyebrow a fraction, but does not move his hand.

Inna is smiling, as if the whole thing were a joke.

Mauri does not move a muscle. He remains expressionless for three seconds, has total control over the fine network of muscles in his face. When the three seconds have passed, he raises his eyebrow, assumes an indescribably decadent Oscar Wilde expression, and says:

"My boy, when you have a hand free, I have a glass for you. Cheers!"

They smile. He really is one of them.

And they drink from her antique champagne glasses.

Ebba Kallis and Ulrika Wattrang met in the yard outside Regla. Ebba looked up at her husband's window. The curtain moved.

"Have you heard from Diddi?" Ebba said.

Ulrika shook her head.

"I'm so worried," she said. "I can't sleep. I took a sleeping tablet last night, although I don't really want to do that when I'm breast-feeding."

Echnaton pulled impatiently at the reins. He wanted to get into the stable, get the saddle off and be fussed over.

"He'll be in touch soon," Ebba said mechanically.

A tear seeped out from beneath Ulrika's thick eyelashes. She shook her head woefully.

Lord, I'm so tired of this, Ebba thought. I'm so tired of her crying.

"Don't forget he's going through a difficult period at the moment," she said gently.

Thinking waspishly, aren't we all.

Several times over the past six months Ulrika had turned up crying. "He just pushes me away, he's completely out of it, I don't even know what he's taken, I try asking if he doesn't at least care about Philip, but he just . . ." And she would hug the baby so hard he would sometimes wake up and sob inconsolably, and then Ebba would have to carry him about with her.

Echnaton laid his muzzle against her head and blew, ruffling her hair. Ulrika laughed through her tears.

"He's in love with you, I'm sure of it," she said.

Yes, he is, Ebba thought, glancing up at her husband's window. The horses love me.

She had got this particular stallion for next to nothing, when you looked at his pedigree. Simply because he was like the devil himself to ride. She remembered how excited she had been as they brought him out of the horsebox. Nostrils flaring, eyes rolling in that divine little black head. A back leg you needed to watch out for. It had taken three men to hold him.

"Good luck," they had laughed when they finally got him into his stable and could be on their way to carry on celebrating Christmas. The stallion had stood there, eyes rolling.

Ebba had not taken him to the paddock with a lunging whip and draw reins. Instead they drove the devil out of his body together. She let him run and jump, far and high. She put on a hard hat and a back protector and let him go, instead of reining him in. They had been covered in mud when they got back. One of the stable girls who helped Ebba had seen them and laughed. Echnaton had stood there waiting to go into his stable, his legs trembling with fatigue. Ebba had rinsed him down with warm water. He had whinnied with pleasure, and had leaned his forehead against her.

She had twelve horses at the moment. She bought foals and hopeless cases and broke them in. She intended to start breeding them herself, over time. Mauri used to laugh and say that she bought more than she sold. And she politely played along with the role of the housewife with two expensive hobbies. Racehorses and stray dogs.

"Regla is yours," Mauri had said when they got married.

As a compensation for the fact that Kallis Mining belonged to him alone, and to give her financial security.

But he bought and renovated Regla with borrowed money, and never repaid the loans.

If she were to leave Mauri, she would have to leave Regla. The horses, the dogs, the staff, the neighbours, her whole life was here.

She had made her choice. She smiled and received their guests when he entertained. She kept him informed about their sons' progress at school, and their hobbies. She organized Inna's funeral without protest.

I am like him, Ebba thought, looking at her horse. We are both slaves, freedom is not an option. If you make sure you are always exhausted, you can stop yourself from going crazy.

And just as she had finished thinking that very thought, Ester came bounding across the yard.

Anna-Maria Mella unlocked the door of her house at around lunchtime on Thursday, and said: Hello house. Her heart lifted when she saw that everything had been cleared away after breakfast and that the table had been wiped.

She got herself a bowl of cornflakes and a liver pâté sandwich, then rang Pohjanen's number.

"Well?" she said when he answered, without saying who she was.

There was a strange sound at the other end of the telephone, like a crow trapped in a chimney. You had to know Pohjanen to realize he was laughing.

"*Hätähousu.*"

"Give the *hätähousu* what she wants. What did Örjan Bylund die of? Did he hang himself, or was it something else?"

"What she wants?" Pohjanen's voice was suddenly creaking with annoyance at the other end of the line. "What's the matter with your colleagues? You should have sent him to me for an autopsy when you found him. It's remarkable how bloody useless the police are when it comes to following the rules. It's only the rest of us who have to do that."

Mella refrained from commenting acidly that the police had not even been called to the scene, since a doctor, one of Pohjanen's professional colleagues, had chosen to ignore the procedures and written heart attack on the death certificate and allowed the undertaker to collect the body. But it was more important to keep Pohjanen in a good mood than to make that point.

She muttered something that could be interpreted as an apology, and allowed Pohjanen to carry on.

"O.K.," he said in a pleasanter tone of voice. "It's a good job he was buried in the winter, because the soft tissue hasn't deteriorated. Although of course it's happening quickly, now he's thawed out."

"Mmm," Mella said, taking a bite of her sandwich.

"I can understand the assumption that it was suicide; the external injuries are consistent with the victim having hanged himself. There's the mark of a ligature around the neck . . . and he'd been taken down by the time the local doctor saw him, hadn't he?"

"Yes, his wife cut him down. She wanted to avoid the gossip. Bylund was a well-known person in Kiruna. He'd worked on the newspaper for thirty years."

"In that case it would be difficult to see if the injuries are consistent with the actual . . . hrrr . . . hrrr . . . method of hanging . . . hrrr . . ."

Pohjanen cleared his throat.

Mella held the receiver away from her ear while he got it over with. She did not mind talking about corpses while she was eating, but listening to a noise like that made her lose her appetite. He could talk about the police not following the rules! He was a doctor, and he smoked like a chimney. In spite of an operation for throat cancer a few years ago.

Pohjanen went on:

"I became a little suspicious as soon as I started a superficial examination of the body. There were a number of small bleeds in the conjunctiva of the eyes. Nothing much, just like tiny pinpricks. And then there are the internal injuries, bleeds at different levels, around the throat and in the musculature."

"Yes?"

"Well, if this is a hanging, you would normally expect the bleeding to be beneath and around the ligature mark, wouldn't you?"

"Right."

"But these bleeds are too big and too scattered. Besides which there's considerable damage to the thyroid cartilage and the tongue bone."

Pohjanen sounded as if he had finished and was about to hang up.

"Just a minute," Mella said. "What conclusions would you draw from all this?"

"That he was strangled, of course. You wouldn't expect these internal injuries to the throat from a hanging. I'd guess at strangulation. By hand. He'd been drinking too. A great deal. So I'd question the wife if I were you. They sometimes take the opportunity when the old man's had a bit too much."

"It wasn't his wife," Mella said. "It's bigger than that. Much, much bigger."

Mauri Kallis saw Ester come jogging across the yard. She nodded briefly to Ulrika and Ebba, then carried on down towards the little wood that lay between the old and the new jetties. She liked to run along that route, following a little path leading down to the old jetty, where Kallis' forestry manager kept his motor boat.

It was remarkable, this obsession with exercise that seemed to have replaced her painting. She read about proteins and building up muscles, lifted her weights and went running.

And it seemed as if she closed her eyes when she ran. It was like a challenge. Trying to run without bumping into the trees. Allowing her feet to find the path, even though she could not see.

He remembered a dinner party they had had not so long ago. Ebba's cousins from Skåne, Inna, Diddi and his wife and the little prince. Ester had just moved into the attic, and Inna had persuaded her to eat with them. Ester had tried to get out of it.

"I've got to exercise," she had said, staring at the floor.

"If you don't eat, it won't matter how much exercise you do," Inna had said. "Go for a run, then come in and eat when you're ready. You can go when you've finished. No-one will notice if you slip away a bit early."

In the middle of dinner, with the white linen tablecloth and the candelabra and the silver cutlery, Ester came down to the table. Her hair was wet and there were grazes all over her face; she was bleeding in two places.

Ebba had introduced her. White and concerned beneath her smile and words like "art school" and "acclaimed exhibition at the Lars Zanton Gallery".

Inna had found it difficult not to laugh.

Ester had eaten, intent and silent, with blood on her face, taking huge mouthfuls and leaving her napkin untouched beside her plate.

When they went out for a smoke on the veranda after the meal, Diddi said:

"I've seen her running down through the glade on the way to the old jetty with a blindfold over her eyes. That's when she gets . . ."

He made a claw-like gesture towards his face, indicating scratches and scrapes.

"Why does she do that?" one of Ebba's cousins had asked.

"Because she's crazy?" Diddi suggested.

"Exactly!" Inna agreed happily. "You must see that we have to get her to start painting again."

Ester cut across the lawn and almost ran over the top of Ulrika and Ebba and that black horse. Once she would have seen his slender little head, the line of him, his big beautiful eyes. Lines and lines. The sway of his back when Ebba practised his dressage turns in the paddock. The curves of his whole body: the throat, the hollow of his back, the legs, the hooves. And Ebba's line, straight back, straight neck, straight nose, the reins tight and straight in her hands.

But nowadays Ester did not bother about any of that. Instead she was looking at the horse's muscles.

She nodded in the direction of Ulrika and Ebba, thinking she was an Arab horse.

Light is my burden, she thought as she headed for the little wood between the estate and Lake Mälaren. She was beginning to know the path. Soon she would be able to run the whole way blindfolded, without bumping into a single tree.

It was the dogs that first realized Mother was ill. She was hiding it from Ester and Antte and Father.

I didn't understand anything, thought Ester as she ran with her eyes closed through the dense wood towards the Regla estate's old jetty. It's strange. Often, time and space do not constitute impenetrable walls, but are like glass; I can see straight through. You can know things about people. Big things, small things. But when it came to her, I saw nothing. I was so preoccupied with my painting. So happy that I could finally paint in oils that I didn't understand. Didn't want to understand why she was suddenly allowing me to hold the brush.

She ran faster. Branches scratched her face. It didn't matter, it was almost a relief.

"Right then," says Mother. "You've always wanted to paint in oils – would you like to learn now?"

She lets me stretch the canvas. I exert myself so much when I'm stretching it from corner to corner that I get a headache. Desperate for it to be right. I pull and fold and staple. My father has made the frame. He doesn't want my mother to buy cheap frames made from poorly dried wood that will warp.

My mother doesn't say anything, and I know that means I've stretched the canvas perfectly. She saves money by buying cheap canvas, but it has to be prepared using tempera. I'm allowed to do this. Then she draws guidelines using charcoal, and I'm allowed to stand beside her and watch. I think excitedly that when I'm allowed to paint all by myself, my own pictures, I won't draw one single line with charcoal. I'll just use the brush straight away. In my head I'm forming shapes using burnt umber or Venetian red.

My mother gives instructions, and I paint in the large areas of colour. The snow in dazzling white and cadmium yellow. The shadow of the mountain in cerulean blue. And the rock face, tending towards a dark violet.

It's difficult for my mother not to be holding the brush herself. Several times she snatches it out of my hand.

"Big brush strokes, stop hesitating like that, shaking like a leaf. More colour, don't be such a coward. More yellow, more yellow. Don't hold the brush like that, it's not a pen."

At first I resist. She knows what will happen, after all. When the colours are as harsh and unsettling as she wants them to be, the pictures are difficult to sell. It has happened before. My father looks at the finished painting in the evening, and says: "That won't do." And then she's had to change it. The contrasts have been made less disturbing. On one occasion I tried to console her by saying:

"The real picture is there underneath, though. We've seen it."

My mother carried on patiently painting, with the brush pressed hard against the canvas.

"It doesn't help," she said. "They're idiots, the whole lot of them."

She became more and more impatient, thought Ester, running between the trees. I didn't understand. Only the dogs understood.

Mother has made a thick meat soup. She places the big pan on the kitchen table to cool down. Later she will pour the soup into separate containers and freeze it. While it's cooling, she settles down in the studio to work on her ceramic birds.

A noise from the kitchen makes her wipe the clay from her fingers and go up there. Musta is standing on the table. She's knocked the lid off the pan and is fishing for bones in the soup. She burns her nose on the hot soup, but can't stop herself from trying again. Burns herself and barks angrily, as if the soup were burning her on purpose and needed to be told off.

"What on earth," Mother says, making a movement towards Musta to shoo her off the table or smack her.

Like lightning Musta goes for her. Snaps at my mother's hand, her lips drawn back over her teeth. A low, threatening growl comes from deep in her throat.

My mother pulls back her hand in shock. No dog has ever dared do anything like that to her. She picks up the sweeping brush from the corner and tries to drive Musta off the table.

Then Musta really goes for her. The soup is hers, and nobody's going to take it away from her.

My mother backs out of the kitchen. Just at that moment I get home from school, go up the stairs and almost bump into my mother on the landing. She turns around, her face white, her red, bitten hand clenched against her breast. Through the door behind her I can see Musta on the kitchen table. Like a little black demon, teeth bared, hackles up. Ears flattened. I stare at the dog, and then at my mother. What the hell has happened?

"Ring your father and tell him to come home," says my mother hoarsely.

My father arrives in the Volvo a quarter of an hour later. He doesn't say much. Fetches his shotgun and throws it in the boot. Then he fetches Musta. She doesn't have time to jump down from the table when she sees him, whimpers with pain and submissiveness as he grabs her by the scruff of the neck and the tail, carries her to the car and throws her in. She lies down on top of the gun case.

The car means outdoor work and fun, she doesn't understand what's going to happen. That's the last we see of her. My father comes home that evening without the dog, and we don't mention it.

Musta was a born leader. I'm sure my father was sorry to lose such an excellent worker and companion, out there in the mountains. She could set off across the mountain after a straying reindeer and return with it after two hours.

She could see what was happening to my mother. That she was growing weaker. Naturally Musta tried to take my mother's place as leader.

That afternoon my mother sat in the kitchen by herself. Snapped at me, so I kept out of the way. I understood that she was ashamed. Ashamed because she'd been afraid of the dog. Because of her fear and weakness, Musta was dead.

Stålnacke went round to see Airi Bylund in his lunch break. He had offered to do it, and Mella had been relieved that she didn't have to go. Sitting at Airi's kitchen table, he explained that her husband had not killed himself, but had been murdered.

Airi Bylund's hands kept moving, unsure of what to do with themselves. She smoothed out a crease in the tablecloth that was not there.

"So he didn't kill himself," she said, after a long silence.

Stålnacke unzipped his jacket. It was warm. She had been baking. There was no sign of the cat or her kittens.

"No."

A muscle near the corner of Airi's mouth was twitching. She got up quickly and put some coffee on.

"I thought about it so often," she said, with her back to Stålnacke. "Wondered why. I mean, he did have a tendency to brood about things, but just to leave me like that . . . without a word. And the boys. They're grown up, of course, but still . . . Just to leave us all."

She arranged pastries on a plate and put it on the table.

"I was angry too. God, I've been so angry with him."

"He didn't do it," Stålnacke said, looking into her eyes.

She gazed back at him. And in her eyes was all the anger, sorrow and pain of the past months. A clenched fist raised towards heaven, an impotent despair beneath an unanswered question, the search for her own guilt.

She had beautiful eyes, he thought. A black sun with blue rays against a grey sky. Beautiful eyes and a beautiful bottom.

Then she began to cry. Still gazing at Stålnacke as the tears poured down her cheeks.

Stålnacke got up and put his arms around her. Placed one hand behind her head, feeling her soft hair. The mother cat came strolling in from the bedroom, closely followed by her kittens who began winding themselves around Stålnacke and Airi's feet.

"Oh God," said Airi at last, sniffling and wiping under her eyes with the sleeve of her sweater. "The coffee will be going cold."

"Doesn't matter," Stålnacke said, rocking her gently. "We'll heat it up in the microwave later."

Mella walked into Chief Prosecutor Björnfot's office at quarter past two.

"Hi, Anna-Maria," he said cheerfully. "Glad you could come. How's it going?"

"Fine, I think," Mella said.

She wondered what he wanted, and wished he would get to the point.

Martinsson was there as well. She was standing by the window, and acknowledged Mella with a brief nod.

"And Sven-Erik?" asked the prosecutor. "Where's he?"

"I rang him and said you wanted to see us. I should imagine he's on his way. Do you mind if I ask what . . . ?"

The prosecutor leaned forwards, waving a fax.

"The lab has finished analysing the coat the divers found in Torneträsk," he said. "The blood on the right shoulder is Inna Wattrang's. They've managed to get D.N.A. from the inside of the collar. And . . ."

He handed the fax to Mella.

". . . the British police have found a match for the D.N.A. profile in their records."

"Douglas Morgan," Mella read.

"A paratrooper in the British army. In the mid-'90s he attacked an officer, was convicted of grievous bodily harm and dismissed. Started working for Blackwater, a firm that specializes in protecting individuals and property in various trouble spots around the world. He's been in central Africa, and was in Iraq pretty early on. While he was there, one of his close colleagues was taken prisoner and executed by an Islamic resistance group about a year ago. Guess what his colleague was called."

"John McNamara, perhaps," Mella said.

"Yep. He used his dead pal's passport when he came to Sweden and when he rented the car at Kiruna airport."

"And what about now? Where is he now?"

"The British police didn't know," Martinsson said. "He'd left Blackwater, that much is certain, but they refuse to say why, just insist it was at his own request. It's difficult to get security firms like this to answer questions and co-operate with the police. They're not too keen on being scrutinized. But Douglas Morgan's former boss at Blackwater said they thought he'd got a job with another company working in the same field, and gone back to Africa."

"We're looking for him, of course," Björnfot said. "But it's far from certain that we'll find him. It's really only if he comes back to England that . . ."

"So what do we do now?" Mella interrupted. "Just forget the whole thing?"

"Of course not," Björnfot said. "The kind of man who hires a car and travels on somebody else's passport . . ."

". . . got paid to kill Inna Wattrang," Mella said. "In which case, the question is by whom."

Björnfot nodded.

"One person knew where she was," Mella said. "And lied about it. Her brother. She rang him from the tourist station."

"You can take the early flight down there tomorrow morning," Björnfot said, looking at the clock.

There was a brief knock on the door and Stålnacke walked in.

"You need to go home and pack," Mella said. "Actually, no, we should be able to get the evening flight back tomorrow, otherwise we'll just buy a toothbrush each and . . . hang on, what have you got there?"

"Ah, well, I've just become a Daddy," Stålnacke said.

His cheeks were flushed. A kitten poked its head through the opening in his jacket.

"Is it Airi Bylund's?" Mella said. "Yes, I can see it is. Hi there, boxer."

"Oh look!" said Martinsson, who had come over to Stålnacke to say hello. "That's quite a black eye you've got there!"

She stroked the head of the kitten with the black ring around one eye. The kitten had no interest whatsoever in saying hello, she just wanted to climb out of Stålnacke's jacket to explore her new surroundings. She clambered up onto his shoulder, teetering recklessly. When Stålnacke tried to lift her down, she clung on with her claws.

"I'll look after her while you're away," Martinsson said.

Björnfot, Mella and Martinsson were all beaming, as if they were looking at the baby Jesus in his crib.

And Stålnacke was laughing. At the cat who clung stubbornly to his jacket, then started to climb down his back so that he had to bend forwards to stop her from falling off. The others had to loosen her little claws from his jacket.

They called her "boxer", "mischief", "little tinker" and "trouble".

Ebba Kallis was woken by somebody ringing the doorbell at 1.30 in the morning. Ulrika Wattrang was standing outside. She was shivering, wearing nothing but pyjamas and a dressing gown.

"Sorry to disturb you," she began in a despairing voice, "but have you got three thousand kronor? Diddi's just arrived in a cab from Stockholm, and the driver's going crazy because Diddi's lost his wallet and I don't have that much money in my account."

Kallis appeared on the stairs.

"Diddi's arrived," said Ebba, without looking at him. "By cab. And he can't pay."

Kallis made a small, resigned noise and went up to his room to fetch his wallet.

All three hurried across the yard to Diddi and Ulrika's house.

Diddi and the driver were standing by the cab.

"No," said the driver. "She's not coming back with me. You're both getting out here. And paying for the trip."

"But I don't know who she is," Diddi protested. "I'm going inside now for a sleep."

"You're not going anywhere," said the cab driver, grabbing hold of Diddi's arm. "Not until you've paid."

"Right," said Kallis, stepping forward. "Three thousand? Are you sure that's correct?"

He held out his American Express card to the driver.

"Listen, I've had to drive halfway round Stockholm dropping

people off, and it's been a hell of a job. If you want to see the details of the route, that's absolutely fine."

Kallis shook his head and the driver got in the cab to process the card. Meanwhile, Diddi fell asleep on his feet, leaning against the car.

"What about her, then?" said the driver when Kallis had signed the slip.

He nodded towards the back seat of the car.

Kallis, Ulrika and Ebba looked in.

A woman of around twenty-five was sitting there, fast asleep. Her hair was long and bleached blonde. Despite the fact that it was quite dark in the car, they could see that she was heavily made up, with false eyelashes and baby-pink lipstick. She was wearing patterned sheer stockings and white, high-heeled shoes. Her skirt was tiny.

Ulrika hid her face in her hands.

"I can't bear it," she sobbed.

"She doesn't live here," Kallis said coldly.

"If you want me to take her back it'll cost you," said the driver. "Same again. I've finished my shift."

Kallis handed over his card again without a word.

The driver got back in the car and swiped it again. Climbed out after a while, got the second slip signed. Nobody spoke.

"Can you open the gate?" said the driver as he got in the car.

As he started the engine and drove away, Diddi, who had been leaning on the car, crashed to the ground.

Ulrika cried out.

Kallis got him up on his feet. They turned him so his back was facing the outside light, and looked at the back of his head.

"He's bleeding a bit," Ebba said. "But I don't think it's anything to worry about."

"The gate," exclaimed Ulrika, dashing into the house to open it with the remote control.

Diddi grabbed hold of Kallis' arms.

"I think I've done something really stupid," he said.

"Make your confession to somebody else," Kallis said harshly, pulling away. "Coming here with some fucking tart. Did you invite her to the funeral?"

Diddi swayed on his feet.

"Fuck you," he said. "Fuck you, Mauri."

Kallis turned on his heel and walked quickly to the house. Ebba scurried after him.

Diddi opened his mouth as if to shout something after them, but suddenly Ulrika was by his side.

"Come on," she said, putting her arm around him. "That's enough now."

FRIDAY, 21 MARCH, 2005

Mella and Stålnacke parked their rented Passat outside the first set of gates on the track to Regla. It was 10.00 a.m. They had flown down from Kiruna that morning and hired a car at Arlanda.

"Quite a fortress," Mella said, gazing through the bars towards the next set of gates and the wall surrounding the estate. "How does this work?"

She looked at the telephone by the gate for a moment, then pressed the button with a picture of a phone on it. After a moment they heard a voice asking who they were and who they were there to see.

Mella introduced herself and Stålnacke, and explained why they were there. They wanted to speak to Diddi Wattrang or Mauri Kallis.

The voice on the other end asked them to wait. A quarter of an hour went by.

"What the hell are they doing?" Mella hissed, pressing the button again like mad, but this time nobody answered.

Stålnacke went and stood a little way off among the trees and had a pee.

What a beautiful place, he thought.

Gnarled oaks and deciduous trees he did not know the names of. No snow. Wood anemones and scilla beginning to emerge through the brown carpet of last year's leaves. It smelled of spring. The sun was shining. He thought about his cat. His cat and Airi. Airi had said she could look after Boxer whenever it was necessary, but

Martinsson had been so quick to offer this time. And that was probably for the best. What would Airi think if he took the kitten, then came back the very same day and asked her to look after it?

Mella called out from the iron gates.

"Somebody's coming!"

A Mercedes was driving down towards the gates. Wiik, Kallis' head of security, got out.

Next to the big gate was a smaller one that could be used by pedestrians. Wiik greeted Mella and Stålnacke perfectly pleasantly, but he did not open either of the gates.

"We need to speak to Diddi Wattrang," Mella said.

"I'm afraid that's not possible," Wiik said. "Diddi Wattrang is in Toronto."

"And Mauri Kallis?"

"I'm sorry. He's completely booked up for the next few days. Is there anything I can help you with?"

"Yes," Mella said impatiently. "You can help us to see Diddi Wattrang or Mauri Kallis."

"I'll give you the number for Mr Kallis' secretary. She can book an appointment for you."

"Right, I've had enough of this," Mella said. "Let us in. We're investigating a murder, for God's sake."

Wiik's expression hardened.

"You've already spoken to both Mr Kallis and Mr Wattrang. You have to understand that they're incredibly busy people. I can arrange for you to meet Mr Kallis on Monday, although that will be extremely difficult. I have no idea when Mr Wattrang will be back."

He passed a card through the gate to Mella.

"That's the direct number for Mr Kallis' secretary. Is there anything else I can do for you? I really do have to . . ."

He did not get any further. A car came driving along the avenue towards Regla. It was a Chevrolet Van with tinted windows. The car stopped behind Mella and Stålnacke's hired car. A man jumped out. He was wearing a dark suit and a black polo-neck.

Mella looked at his shoes. Sturdy but lightweight boots made of Gore-Tex.

Inside the car another man was sitting in the passenger seat. He had cropped hair and was wearing a dark jacket. She caught a glimpse of at least two men in the back, then the car door closed. Who were these people?

The man who had got out of the car said nothing, did not introduce himself, just nodded briefly at Mikael Wiik, who nodded almost imperceptibly back.

"If there's nothing else . . ." Wiik said to Mella and Stålnacke.

Mella was battling with her frustration. She had no way to overrule his refusal to let them in.

Stålnacke gave her a look. "No idea," it said.

"And who are you?" she asked the new arrival.

"I'll move so you can get out," was all he said, walking back to the Chevy.

The visit to Regla was over. Before Mella got in the car, she noticed a young woman on the other side of the wall. She was wearing a tracksuit, and was standing in the middle of a field of wood anemones.

"What's she doing?" she asked Stålnacke as she was reversing in order to turn round.

Stålnacke peered through the gate.

"Looking at the flowers," he said, "but she seems very disorientated. Hey, look out for those tree roots."

This remark was addressed to the woman in the tracksuit, who was walking backwards without looking.

*

Ester was looking at the ground. Suddenly there were flowers every-where. She had not noticed them before. Had all these flowers been here yesterday? She did not know. She looked around for a few seconds, not noticing the cars and the people over by the gate.

Then she looked through the oak trees.

And she could feel his presence. She knew he was there. Maybe a kilometre away. A wolf that had climbed up into one of the oaks.

He had them all in his sights. Keeping a count of how many came in and how many went out. He was looking straight at her at this moment.

She took a couple of steps backwards and almost stumbled over a tree root.

Then she set off. Galloped off, away from the forest and the flowers. This must be over soon.

It is early summer. Ester is fifteen years old, and has just finished school. She has been given a watercolour block and some water-colours as a present for taking her exams. There are flowers everywhere on the mountain, and she is lying on her stomach drawing in pencil. In the evening she comes home, covered in mos-quito bites and contented, and keeps her mother company in the studio, adding colour to the day's drawings. It is wonderful to have proper paper that takes the colour and does not buckle. Mother takes her time and looks: the delicate, pretty mountain wild flowers she found at Njuotjanjohka, the fine-leafed cloudberry, the plump yellow globe flowers. Ester has taken pains over the details. Mother praises her for the care she has taken to show the veins on the leaves.

"They're lovely," she says.

Then she tells Ester to make sure she adds the flowers' Latin names next to their Sami names.

"They like that sort of thing," she says.

"They." She means the tourists at the mountain station. Mother thinks Ester should frame the pictures in an adhesive mount, "it's cheap and it looks nice", and sell them at Abisko tourist station. Ester is not so sure.

"You can buy your own oils with the money," says her mother, and the decision is made.

Ester is sitting in the lobby of the tourist station. A train carrying iron ore is passing by on the way up to Narvik, and she looks out of the window. It is 10.00 in the morning. A group of mountain walkers are standing out in the sun, adjusting the straps of their rucksacks. A happy-looking dog is running around their feet. It reminds her of Musta.

Suddenly she becomes aware of someone looking at her pictures. She turns her head and sees a middle-aged woman. The woman is wearing a red anorak and putty-coloured Fjällräven trousers that look brand new. "They" spend thousands on clothes for their days out.

The woman is leaning over the drawings.

"Are these your drawings?"

Ester nods. She ought to say something, of course, but her mouth is stiff, she cannot produce a single thought or word.

The woman seems unconcerned by her silence. She has picked the drawings up now, and is examining them carefully. Then she examines Ester, narrowing her eyes.

"How old are you?"

"Fifteen." Ester manages to get the word out, staring at the floor.

The woman waves a hand and a man of the same age appears at her side. He fishes out his wallet and the woman buys three pictures.

"Do you paint anything else, apart from flowers?" she asks.

Ester nods, and somehow it is arranged that they will come to Mother's studio to have a look.

254

＊

They turn up that evening in a rented Audi. The woman has changed into jeans and a wool jumper that looks expensively simple. The man is still wearing spotless Fjällräven trousers, a shirt, and some kind of leather cowboy hat. He walks a few paces behind the woman. She is the first to extend her hand. She introduces herself as Gunilla Petrini, telling Mother that she is the curator at the Colour Factory, and is on the board of the national art council.

Mother gives Ester a long look.

"What's the matter?" Ester whispers to her mother while Petrini is going through the boxes that hold Ester's pictures.

"You said it was a tourist who wanted to come and look."

Ester nods. They are tourists.

Mother hunts around in the larder and finds half a packet of plain biscuits to offer them, and Ester looks on in surprise as she arranges them in a neat circle on a plate.

Petrini and her husband also look at Mother's pictures with polite interest, but she scrabbles in the boxes containing Ester's work like a hare in a ploughed field.

Her husband likes the pictures Ester drew when she and her mother went to the swimming baths in Kiruna. There is Siiri Aidan-pää drying her hair with her eyes closed. She has her curlers in, and is wearing silver earrings representing Sami symbols, although she herself is not Sami. Her ample bosom has been stuffed into a plain, sturdy bra of generous proportions; her stomach and bottom are also substantial.

"She's so beautiful," he says, looking at the seventy-year-old woman.

Ester has painted the enormous knickers salmon pink. It is the only colour in the picture. She has seen old, hand-coloured photographs, and was trying to achieve the same gentle tone.

Other pictures from the baths show middle-aged men swimming in a row in the exercise pool, the old changing rooms from the early '60s, built of dark wood, with a day bed and a little wardrobe, and the sign to the room before the showers with the words "ultra-violet lamp" written in silver letters. All the rest of the pictures are from Rensjön and Abisko.

What a small world, Petrini and her husband are thinking.

"As I said, I'm the curator at the Colour Factory," Petrini says to Ester's mother.

They are alone. Ester and Gunilla Petrini's husband have gone outside to look at the reindeer in the enclosure on the far side of the railway line.

"I'm on the board of the national art council, and I'm a buyer for a number of large companies. I have a considerable amount of influence in the art world in Sweden."

Mother nods. She has probably seen what is coming.

"I'm impressed by Ester. And I'm not often impressed. She's finished school; what's she intending to do now?"

"Ester's not much of a one for studying. But she's got a place to train as a care worker."

Petrini has to control herself. She feels like a knight in shining armour, riding in at the very last minute to save the girl. A care worker!

"You haven't considered allowing her to study art?" she asks in her gentlest voice. "She might be too young for art college, but there are preliminary training courses she could do. At the Idun Lovén Art School, for example. The principal and I are old friends."

"Stockholm," Ester's mother says.

"It's a big city, but I would look after her, of course."

Petrini has misunderstood. It is not anxiety at the thought of Ester going to the big city so young that she can hear in her mother's voice. It is restlessness. It is the fact that she is stuck here, stuck in her life with a family and children. It is all the unpainted pictures she carries deep down in her soul.

Later that evening they sit at the kitchen table with Father, telling him all about it.

"Of course they think you're exotic," says Mother, crashing dishes around. "An Indian girl in a Sami dress painting mountains and reindeer."

"I don't want to go," Ester says in an attempt to pacify her mother, although she has no idea what could be wrong.

"Of course you do," says her mother firmly.

Father says nothing. When it comes to it, Mother is the one who makes the decisions.

Mella and Stålnacke drove away from Regla. In the rear view mirror Mella could see Wiik opening the gate for the Chevrolet with the tinted windows.

"So who was that?" she said.

Just as she spoke, she realized. The practical boots, the friendly nod between Wiik and the driver of the Chevy.

"Security," she said to Stålnacke. "I wonder what's going on."

"I suppose they have these summit meetings. But unlike Swedish politicians, they have bodyguards."

Mella's telephone rang and Stålnacke grabbed the wheel while she rummaged in her pocket. It was Rantakyrö.

"Telephone exchange here," he said, pretending to sound upset.

Mella laughed.

"That payment into Inna Wattrang's account," he went on. "It was made from the bank's branch office on Hantverkargatan. There's a guy who's phoned Inna Wattrang's private mobile lots of times from an address near there."

"Could you possibly text me the address? Sven-Erik gets so stressed if I'm chatting on the phone and writing down addresses and driving at the same time."

She beamed at Stålnacke.

"No problem," Rantakyrö said. "Keep your hands on that wheel."

Mella passed the phone to Stålnacke. Thirty seconds later the name and address appeared on the screen.

"Malte Gabrielsson, Norr Mälarstrand 34."

"We might as well drive over there," Mella said. "I mean, we haven't got anything else to do."

An hour and ten minutes later they were standing outside the main door at Norr Mälarstrand 34, waiting. They managed to get in when a lady with a dog came out.

Stålnacke looked for Malte Gabrielsson's name on the board showing who lived in the building. Mella took a look around. In one direction was the outside door, in the other an inner courtyard.

"Look," she said, nodding towards the courtyard.

Stålnacke looked, but could not see what she meant.

"They've been getting all their paper ready for collection out there. Come on."

Mella went outside and started to rummage through the paper sacks.

"Bingo," she said after a while, holding up a golfing magazine with Malte Gabrielsson's name on the address label. "This bag belongs to Mr Gabrielsson."

She carried on digging through the sack, and after a while she passed an envelope to Stålnacke. On the back of the envelope somebody had written a shopping list in ink.

"Milk, mustard, crème fraîche, mint . . ." he read out.

"No, look at the handwriting. It's the same as on that paying-in slip. 'Not for your silence.'"

Gabrielsson lived on the third floor. They rang the bell. After a while the door was opened a fraction. A man in his sixties peered at them over the security chain. He was wearing a dressing gown.

"Malte Gabrielsson?" Mella asked.

"Yes?"

"Anna-Maria Mella and Sven-Erik Stålnacke, Kiruna police. We'd like to ask you a few questions about Inna Wattrang."

"Excuse me, but how did you even get in here? You need a security code to get through the outside door."

"May we come in?"

"Am I under some kind of suspicion?"

"Not at all, we'd just like to . . ."

"The thing is, I've got a terrible cold and I'm . . . well, I'm feeling pretty rough. If you've got any questions they'll have to wait."

"It won't take long," Mella said, but before she had finished speaking Gabrielsson had shut the door.

Mella leaned her forehead against the door frame.

"Give me strength," she said. "That's it, I've just about had enough of these bloody people treating me like someone else's Polish cleaner."

She hammered on the door.

"Open this bloody door," she roared.

She pushed open the letterbox and shouted into the apartment.

"We're carrying out a murder investigation here. If I were you, I'd talk to us now. Otherwise I'll be sending my uniformed colleagues to where you work to bring you in for interrogation. I'll be knocking on your neighbours' doors and asking questions about you. I know you paid Inna Wattrang two hundred thousand kronor before she died. I can prove that. It's your handwriting on the paying-in slip. I'm not going anywhere."

The door opened again, and Gabrielsson undid the security chain.

"Come in," he said, looking around the stairwell.

He was all at once amiability personified, hanging up their coats in the hall. It was as if he had never tried to fob them off.

"Can I get you anything?" he asked once they were settled in the living room. "I haven't managed to do any shopping, what with having such a cold, but perhaps a cup of tea or coffee?"

The sofas were white, the carpet was white, the walls were white. Large abstract oil paintings and *objets d'art* contributed colour to the room. It was a fantastically light apartment. High ceiling, huge windows. Not a thing was out of place. The plate on the door carried only his name, so he likely lived alone in this pristine space.

"We're fine, thanks," Mella said.

She got straight to the point:

"'Not for your silence', what was that all about?"

Gabrielsson fished a handkerchief out of his dressing gown pocket; he had folded it into a small pad, and wiped his sore nose with careful dabbing movements. Mella shuddered at the thought of picking up the snot-soaked hankie to put it in the washing machine.

"It was just a gift," he said.

"Do me a favour," Mella said pleasantly. "I did say I wasn't going anywhere until we sort this out."

"O.K.," he said. "I suppose it'll all come out anyway in the end. We were seeing each other for a while, Inna and I. And then we had a quarrel, and I gave her a couple of slaps."

"And?"

Gabrielsson looked sad and vulnerable, sitting there in his dressing gown.

"I think it's because I knew she'd grown tired of me. She would have left me anyway. I couldn't bear that. So I let myself . . . lose control, or however you want to put it. Then I could fool myself that that was why she'd left me. But she would have gone anyway. Somewhere inside, I knew that. I've thought about it a lot since then."

"Why did you give her the money?"

"Seemed like a good idea at the time. I left a message on her answer machine: 'This is not for your silence. I'm a pig. If you want to go to the police, then do it. Buy yourself something nice. A picture or a piece of jewellery. Thanks for the good times, Inna.' I really wanted it to be like that. That it was me who was a pig. And that I was the one who'd ended our relationship by raising my hand to her."

"Two hundred thousand is rather a lot for a couple of slaps," Mella said.

"The crime report would still say physical abuse. I'm a lawyer. If she'd gone to the police, I'd have been out on my ear."

He looked up at Mella and said sharply:

"I didn't kill her."

"You did know her, though. Is there anyone who really would have wanted her dead?"

"I don't know."

"What was her relationship with her brother like?"

"She didn't talk about him much. I got the impression that she was pretty fed up with him. I think she'd got tired of covering up his mistakes. Why don't you ask him about his relationship with her?"

"I'd love to, but he's in Canada on a business trip."

"Oh, so Mauri and Diddi are in Canada."

Gabrielsson dabbed at his nose again.

"They didn't spend much time grieving, then."

"Mauri Kallis isn't in Canada, just Diddi Wattrang," Mella said.

Gabrielsson stopped dabbing his nose.

"Just Diddi? I hardly think so!"

"What do you mean?"

"According to Inna, it's a long time since Mauri allowed Diddi to travel and take care of things on his own. He has no judgement. Made some really crazy decisions, quick and dirty. No, if he travels at all it's with Inna, well, not any more of course, but before, or with Mauri. Never on his own. He messes things up. Besides which, I don't think Mauri trusts him."

Back on the street, Stålnacke sighed.

"I feel sorry for some people."

"Sorry? For him?" Mella exclaimed. "Come on!"

"He's a really lonely person. He might be a lawyer earning a ton of money, but he's ill and there's nobody to shop for him. And that apartment, was that a home? He ought to get a cat."

"So he can put it in the washing machine or something? A man who beats up women, sitting there feeling sorry for himself because she would have left him anyway. And a couple of slaps – no chance. Oh, no! Anyway, what about something to eat?"

Inna Wattrang drives through the iron gates to Regla. It is December 2nd. She parks outside the old laundry, her home, and prepares to get out of the car. It is not easy.

She has driven from Stockholm, and now she is here her arms feel weak. She can hardly put the car into reverse and get the key out.

She does not really know how she got home. Jesus, she drove in the dark following the red rear lights of other drivers. One eye is completely closed, and she had to keep her head tipped back the whole time in case her nose started bleeding again.

She fumbles for the seat belt in order to undo it, but discovers that she had not put it on. She did not even hear the beeping noise that usually reminds you.

She has stiffened up; when she opens the car door to get out, she feels a sharp stabbing pain in her chest. And when she takes a deep breath because it hurts, it is even more painful. He has broken her ribs.

She almost has to laugh, because she is in such a mess. She

clambers laboriously out of the car. Hangs onto the car door with one hand, cannot manage to straighten up, stands there stooping, taking short jagged breaths because of her cracked ribs. She rummages for her door key, hoping her nose won't start bleeding again; she is very fond of her Vuitton bag.

Where's the fucking key? She cannot see a thing. She heads for the black wrought iron lamppost at the side of the house. And just when she is in full view under the light, she hears voices. It is Ebba and Ulrika. Sometimes they take the boat over to Hedlandet and meet up with some other "little wives" for wine tastings and girly dinners and quality time without the children. When they get back they usually cut across Inna's garden, it's the quickest way. She can hear them giggling and chatting.

They've had a nice evening too, thinks Inna with a wry smile.

For a moment she considers trying to make her escape, but what a sight that would be. Limping away like Quasimodo and disappearing into the shadows.

It is Ulrika who sees her first.

"Inna," she calls, a slight question in her voice; what's going on with Inna, is she drunk or something, why is she standing there in that strange, stooped position?

Ebba pipes up next.

"Inna? Inna!"

Their footsteps, hurrying across the gravel.

Masses of questions. It is like being trapped in a cupboard with a swarm of bees.

She lies, of course. She is usually very good at it, but right now she is a bit too tired and battered.

She whips up a quick story about being attacked by a gang of lads in Humlegården ... yes, they took her wallet ... No, Ulrika and Ebba are definitely not to ring the police ... Why not? Because she bloody says so!

"I just need to go and lie down," she says. "Can one of you get my bloody key out of this bloody bag, please?"

She's swearing instead of bursting into tears.

"Lying down can be dangerous," Ulrika says as Ebba scrabbles in the bag for Inna's key. "Did they kick you? You might have internal bleeding. We ought to ring a doctor at least."

Inna groans inside. If she had a gun she would shoot them, just to get a bit of peace and quiet.

"There's no internal bleeding!" she snaps.

Ebba has found the key. She unlocks the door and puts the light on in the hallway.

"But here's your wallet," she says, taking it out of the bag with an odd expression. Now they are in the light, they can see clearly what a mess Inna is in. They do not know what to think.

Inna forces a smile.

"Thanks. You're both . . . really sweet . . ."

Shit, she sounds as if they're a couple of teddy bears, she can't find the right tone, just wants them to go.

". . . we can talk about this tomorrow, I just really need to be on my own now . . . thanks. Please don't say anything to Diddi and Mauri, I'll deal with it tomorrow."

She closes the door on their shocked little fawn-like faces.

She kicks off her shoes and hauls herself slowly up the stairs. Roots around in the medicine cabinet, takes some Xanor, using her hand to scoop water from the tap so she can swallow them, then Imovane; she does not swallow those, but sucks patiently until the shell dissolves so they will work more quickly.

She wonders if she can make it down to the kitchen to fetch a bottle of whisky.

She sits on the edge of the bed and flops back, tasting the bitterness in her mouth as the Imovane kicks in. It is quick. Everything is fine now.

The outside door opens and closes, rapid footsteps on the stairs, her brother's voice:

"It's only me."

He always says that. He always opens the door and walks straight in with those very words. And since he got married it makes Inna feel like his concubine, with her own residence.

"Who was it?" is all he says when he sees her. The blood on her shirt, the swollen nose, the split lip, the closed eye.

"It was Malte," she says. "He got a bit . . . he kind of lost control."

She smiles at him, as mischievously as she can manage. There is no possibility of laughing with her ribs like this; they are still hurting, despite the painkillers.

"If you think I look bad, you should see the cream carpet in his bedroom," she jokes.

Diddi tries to smile back.

God, he has got so boring, thinks Inna. She wants to throw up all over him.

"How bad is it?" he asks.

"Getting better."

"Let me look after you," Diddi says. "Is there anything special you want?"

"Ice, I'm going to look like shit tomorrow. And a line."

He brings everything she wants. He gives her a whisky too, and she starts to feel pretty good, under the circumstances. She is not in so much pain now, and the whisky is making her feel warm and relaxed, while the cocaine is keeping her head clear.

Diddi undoes the buttons of her shirt and eases it off. He dips a flannel in warm water and washes the blood from her face and hair.

Inna holds a pack of ice wrapped in a tea towel against her eye, and tries out a few Rocky Balboa lines:

"I can't see nothing, you got to open my eye . . . cut me Mick

. . . you stop this fight and I'll kill you . . ."

Diddi sits down between her knees and slides his hands up beneath her skirt. Unfastens her suspenders and rolls down her stockings, kissing the inside of her knees as he does so.

His fingers move upwards again, caressing her inner thighs. They are trembling with desire. Inside her panties she is sticky with another man's sperm. It is incredibly sexy.

They usually laugh at her boyfriends, he and Kallis. She really does meet the most unlikely men. Where does she find them? He and Kallis often ask themselves that question.

Stick Inna on a bare rock out at sea, and some old guy in a wig and a dress will come sailing along, filled with dark desires that Inna can fulfil.

Sometimes she tells them all about it. To amuse them. Like last year, when she texted them from a luxury hotel in Buenos Aires. "Haven't been out of the room all week," it said.

When she got home, Kallis and Diddi were standing there like two expectant Labradors, hoping she might throw them a bone. "Tell us, tell us!"

Inna had laughed and laughed.

Her boyfriend had been a ship spotter.

"He travels around visiting the world's biggest harbours," she had explained. "Books into a top hotel with a view of the harbour, and sits there all week writing down details of the ships. Close your mouths while I'm talking, there's good boys."

They had closed their mouths.

"He films them too," she had gone on. "And when his daughter got married last year, he showed films of ships coming into and out of various harbours all over the world. For twenty minutes. The guests were moderately amused . . ."

She made a hesitant gesture with her hand to illustrate the wedding guests' level of interest.

"What did you do?" Kallis had asked. "While he was watching the ships."

"Well," she replied. "I read a whole load of books. Mostly he just wanted me to lie there and listen while he talked. You can ask me anything you like about tankers, though. I know everything there is to know."

They had laughed. But Diddi had thought with love that this was his sister. For her, everything was O.K. She found her peculiar companions. She loved them, found them interesting, helped them to make their dreams come true. And sometimes it was all harmless.

In fact, everything was harmless in her eyes.

We've always played innocent games, thinks Diddi as his fingers seek out Inna's vagina. Everything's O.K., as long as you don't hurt anyone who doesn't want to be hurt.

He longs for the feeling that used to surround him. The feeling that life is as fleeting as the ether. Every moment exists right now, and then it is gone. The feeling of being a wide-eyed child, gazing at everything in wonder.

He loses that feeling with Ulrika and the baby. He cannot really work out how it happened. How he ended up married.

He wants Inna to give him back that sense of being light-hearted, carefree. He wants to feel weightless, to float in life as if it were the sea. To be washed up on a beach. Wander along it for a while. Find a beautiful shell. Lose it. The tide takes him out again. That is how life should be, exactly like that.

"Stop it," Inna says crossly, pushing his hand away.

But Diddi does not want to listen.

"I love you," he mumbles against her knee. "You're amazing."

"I don't want to," she says. "Stop it."

And when he does not stop, she says:

"Think about Ulrika and the little prince."

Diddi stops at once. Moves a little distance away from her along the floor, placing his hands on his knees as if they were porcelain ornaments, each on their own pedestal. He waits for her to pacify him, to pour oil on troubled waters.

But she doesn't. Instead she digs out her cigarettes and lights up.

He sulks. Feels rejected and upset. Suddenly he wants to hurt her.

"What is it with you?" he asks, his voice making it clear that she is a hypocrite.

He has always loved his women, and a few men, with tenderness. He has never understood all that business of violence and treating them mean. But he has never felt the need to defend his position. If a partner wanted that kind of thing he had always declined politely, but wished them much pleasure. He even watched once. Just to be polite. And possibly because he did not have the energy to get up and go home.

But Inna. She has done most things. Look at her now. So what is it with her?

He asks her the question.

"So come on, what is it with you? Is it only the perverted stuff that gets you going these days? Do you need to be slapped around like some bloody drugged-up whore?"

"Stop it," she says, with something tired and pleading in her voice.

But by now Diddi is almost at his wits' end. He can feel that he is really losing her. Perhaps he already has. She has disappeared into a world populated by smelly old men with peculiar desires; his mind is filled with pictures of big, musty apartments in the expensive areas of Europe's capital cities. The still air carries the smell of layers of dirt from the drains and the toilets in the big bathrooms. Apartments where the heavy, dusty curtains are always kept closed against the sunlight.

"What is it with you and disgusting old men?" he asks, deliberately filling his voice with revulsion.

"That's enough."

"I remember when you were twelve and . . ."

"Stop! Stop it, stop it!"

Inna gets up. The drugs have taken care of the pain in her body. She drops to her knees in front of him, takes his chin in her hands and gazes at him with sympathy. Strokes his hair. Comforts him. While her soft voice says the most terrible things.

"You've lost it. You're not a boy any longer. And it's just so sad. Wife, kid, house, cosy dinners for two, invitations to country houses, it really suits you. And your hair's thinning. This long, stringy fringe is just pathetic. You'll be using it as a comb-over to cover your bald head soon. That's why you always need money nowadays. Can't you see it for yourself? You used to get everything for free. Company, coke. Now you've turned into a buyer."

She gets up. Takes a drag of her cigarette.

"Where do you get the money from? How much do you get through? Eighty a month? I know you've conned the company out of money. When Quebec Invest sold and the value of Northern Explore fell. I know it was you that fixed it. A journalist from *Norrländska Socialdemokraten* rang me and asked a whole load of questions. Mauri would go crazy if he found out about it. Crazy!"

Diddi was on the verge of tears. How had things come to this? When had things between the two of them got so bad?

He wants to rush out and leave her. At the same time, that is the last thing he wants to do. If he goes now, he can never come back – that is how it feels.

They have always been perfidious, he and Inna. Well, not perfidious – but they have never let anybody weigh them down. People come and go in life. You open yourself completely, then you let go when it is time. And the time to let go always comes. Sooner or later. But Diddi has always felt that he and Inna are the one exception for each other. While their mother has always been a cardboard cut-out obsessed with thoughts of money and social standing, Inna has been flesh, blood, life.

He isn't Inna's exception. He has slipped away from her. She has allowed it to happen.

"Could you go now, please," she says in her friendly voice, the voice that's for just anybody.

She is so very soft, so very pleasant.

"We'll talk about this tomorrow."

He shakes his blond head. Shakes his stringy fringe, feels it flopping against his forehead. They won't talk about this tomorrow. It has all been said, it is all over.

He shakes his head all the way down the stairs, across the yard, through the darkness and home to his wife and his little son.

Ulrika meets him in the doorway.

"How did it go?" she asks.

The little prince is asleep, and she moves in close to him. He forces himself to put his arms around her. Above her head, he meets his own gaze in the gilded mirror in the hall.

He does not recognize the person looking back at him. The skin is like a mask that is beginning to come unstuck.

And Inna knows about that business with Quebec Invest, that's bad, very bad. What was it she said? That a journalist from *N.S.D.* had been asking questions.

Inna lies on the bed holding the damp towel over her nose, which has started bleeding again. She hears the door downstairs open and close again. Kallis' voice this time.

"Hello."

She groans inside. Has not got the strength to explain. Has no intention of doing so either. Has not the strength to forbid them to call the police and the doctor.

At least Kallis knocks. First of all he knocks on the outside door, then on the door jamb downstairs as he calls up to her. He almost knocks on the banister as he calls out that he is coming up. And he knocks on the open bedroom door before tentatively peeping in.

He looks at her swollen face, her wrecked lips, her bruised upper arms, and he says:

"Do you think you'll be able to powder over that? You need to come to Kampala with me tomorrow to meet the Minister for Industry."

Inna has to laugh. She is absolutely delighted that Kallis is playing it cool and keeping the mask in place.

When Inna and Kallis disembark from the air-conditioned plane in Kampala on December 3rd, the heat and the humidity explode in their faces like an airbag. The sweat courses down their bodies. There is no air conditioning in the taxi, and the seats are plastic; their backs and bottoms are soon soaked through, and they try to sit on just one cheek some of the time in order to avoid contact with the seat. The driver is cooling himself down with a huge fan, singing lustily along with the songs pouring from the radio. The traffic is chaotic; from time to time the taxi is at a complete standstill while the driver hangs out of the window discussing the situation with other taxi drivers, or shouts and gesticulates at the children who pop up like jack-in-the-boxes wanting to sell this or that, or just to beg. "Miss," they say with pleading expressions, knocking on the window where Inna is sitting. Inna and Kallis are in the back with the windows closed; it is like being in a glass box, and they are sweating like pigs.

Kallis is angry, they were supposed to be picked up at the airport, but there was nobody there so they had to take a taxi. The last time he was in Kampala, he noticed the beautiful green parks, the hills around the town. This time he notices only the marabou storks, gathering in flocks on the roofs with their disgusting red wattles.

The air conditioning is working in the government building; it is only twenty-two degrees, and Inna and Kallis soon begin to shiver in their wet clothes. A secretary shows them into the building and the Minister for Industry comes to meet them as soon as they reach the top of the wide marble staircase with the red carpet and the banister made of ebony. She is a woman in her sixties, with big hips. She is wearing a dark blue suit, and her hair has been straightened and put up in a French pleat. Her black pumps are worn, you can see her little toe pushing the leather out into a bulge. She shakes hands with them, laughing and chatting and placing her left hand over their right hands. As they walk towards her office, she asks how the journey went, what the weather is like in Sweden. Asks them to sit down and pours them an iced tea.

She claps her hands and wonders with horror in her voice what happened to Inna.

"Girl, you look like someone who's tried to cross Luwum Street during rush hour."

Inna tell her the story of how she was attacked by a gang of boys in Humlegården.

"I'm telling you," she says to finish off the tale, "the youngest can't have been more than eleven."

It's the details that make the lie credible, thinks Kallis. Inna lies with such enviable ease.

"Whatever is the world coming to?" wonders the minister, pouring more iced tea.

Silence for a second. They are all thinking the same thing, but none of them admits it. The fact that a gang of little boys jump on a woman and beat her up and take her money is like a Sunday church service compared with the problems in northern Uganda, where military security forces and the L.R.A. are spreading terror among the civilian population. And the L.R.A. regularly recruits children as soldiers; they come in the night, aim a gun at the parents' heads, and force the child to kill the neighbouring family "or your mother will die", then take them away. There is no need to be afraid that they will run away after that. What would they be coming back to?

Every night, twenty thousand children walk from their country villages into the town of Gulu and sleep near churches, hospitals and bus stations, because they are afraid this will happen to them. In the morning, they walk home again.

But Kampala is an orderly town where people can sit outside the cafés conducting their business. They do not want to acknowledge the problems in the north. So neither Inna, Kallis, nor the minister says another word about children and violence.

Instead they begin to touch on the reason for their meeting today. That is another minefield. They would all like to come to an agreement. But not on the other party's terms.

Kallis Mining has closed the mine in Kilembe. Five months earlier, three Belgian mining engineers were killed when the Hema militia attacked a bus on the way to Gulu. The infrastructure is falling apart completely. Together with two other mining companies, Kallis Mining built a road from north-western Uganda to Kampala. Three years ago, it was new. Today it is practically impassable in places. Various militia groups have mined it, blockaded it and blown it up. They sometimes set up roadblocks once darkness has fallen, and then just about anything can happen. Eleven-year-olds, drugged to the eyeballs and spaced out, carrying weapons. And a little distance away, their older brothers-in-arms.

"I didn't build up the mine for it to fall into the hands of militia groups," Kallis says.

His security guards around the complex fled long ago. Now there is illegal mining going on there. It is not clear who is actually in charge of things, using the equipment the company did not manage to move out and running it into the ground. Kallis has heard rumours that they are groups which are allies of the government troops. It is therefore more than likely that it is Museveni who is stealing from him.

"It's a problem for the whole country," says the minister. "But what can we do? Our soldiers can't be everywhere. We're doing our best to protect schools and hospitals."

Bullshit, thinks Kallis. If they're not stealing from me, the government forces are fully occupied taking over mines in north-eastern Congo, plundering them and transporting the gold across the border.

The official line is, of course, that all the gold sold for export has been mined in Uganda in state-owned mines, but everybody knows the truth.

"You're going to have problems attracting foreign investors to your country," Kallis says. "They won't be too keen when they hear you can't control things in the north."

"We're very interested in foreign investors. But what can I do? We've offered to buy your mine."

"For nothing!"

"For the amount you paid."

"And since then I've invested over ten million dollars in the infrastructure and equipment!"

"But now all that's worthless! It's worth nothing to us, either. The region has many problems."

"You're telling me! And you don't seem to realize there's only one way to solve this problem. Protect the investors. You'd be rich!"

"Would we? How?"

"Infrastructure. Schools. Building communities. Jobs. Income tax."

"Really? During the three years you were running the company, it didn't turn over any profit. So there was no income from taxes."

"We had this discussion at the time! In the beginning you have to invest. Obviously you can't expect profits for the first five years."

"So we get nothing. You get the lot. And now you've got problems, you come to us wanting help from the military to protect your company. What I'm saying to you is: let the state come in as part-owner of the company. It would be much easier for me to find the resources to protect a company we have an interest in."

Kallis nods and appears to be considering this.

"Then perhaps we might be able to get some help with one or two other difficulties. Suddenly our discharge concession was no longer valid. And we were having a lot of problems with the union towards the end. Perhaps the president could also honour the commitments he made in our earlier agreement. When we acquired the mine, he promised to build a power station at the Albert Nile."

"Think about my offer."

"Which is?"

"The state will buy 50 per cent of the shares in Kilembe Gold."

"How much?"

"Oh, I'm sure we can come to some agreement. At the moment the president is concentrating on health care and education about A.I.D.S. We are an example to neighbouring countries. We could leave any future profits until the payment has been made."

The minister's tone is relaxed, as if they were old friends.

Despite the sharpness of his words, Kallis' tone is as always in the no-man's-land between expressionless and friendly.

Inna usually manages to lighten the atmosphere, but cannot bring herself to do it this time. Beneath their friendly, relaxed voices she can hear the clash of weapons.

Kallis and Inna drink several whiskies in the hotel bar. There is a ceiling fan and a really terrible pianist. Too many staff, too few guests. Westerners who know the prices are three times as high as in other bars in town, but tell themselves they don't care. It is still a fraction of what you would pay at home.

At the same time, there is an undercurrent of fury. A feeling of constantly being fleeced. Of always paying too much. Just because you are white. A constant haggling over prices, if you have the energy. And you still end up being conned.

And you are barely conscious of how irritating it is that one of the waiters is standing there flirting with one of the barmaids. Who is it who is here to enjoy themselves? The staff or the guests? Who is paying, and who is being paid?

Kallis drinks to make everything stop whirling around inside him. It is like muddy water in there. Something black and flaky that keeps being whipped up to the surface. He does not want to acknowledge it. He wants it to settle down. He wants to sleep, and think about all this tomorrow.

If only Inna had not been beaten up just then. Then perhaps everything would have been different. Then perhaps they would have talked this over together. She would have been able to get him to lighten up. She might even have been able to make him laugh and think: Oh well, swings and roundabouts.

But she hasn't the strength. She is drinking to ease the nagging ache in her face. And she is wondering whether she is going to get an infection in the cut on her lip or under her eye. They have not healed yet, and could turn into tropical sores that won't.

She has been subdued since it happened. Not really herself. For a number of reasons, as will become apparent.

And Kallis is woken at night by the whirlpools, the black layers breaking away from the edges.

The air conditioning has broken. He opens the window to the blackness of the night, but there is no coolness, only the constant chirping of the crickets and the sound of the fire-bellied toads.

How could he explain this to anyone? How would anyone understand?

When Inna comes dancing along, dragging his secretary behind him, and proudly shows him the cover of *Business Week*. And he sees his own face.

He does not share their happiness. Pride? Nothing could be further from the truth. The shame impales his body upon a spike.

He is everybody's bum boy. Could just as well be the challenge cup at a high security jail.

When Swedish Industry and the Association of Employers invite him to give a lecture, and take a fee of thirty thousand from each participant, and he fills the place – he is nothing but their whore.

They hold him up as proof that everybody has the same opportunity. Everybody can succeed. Everybody can get to the top if they really want to, just look at Mauri Kallis.

Thanks to Kallis, all the boys and girls in Tensta and Botkyrka, all those loafers in Norrland, they can all blame themselves. Stop their benefits, make it worthwhile working. Give people an incentive to be like Mauri Kallis.

And they pat him on the back and squeeze his hand and he will never be one of them. They have a surname that counts, they have families and old money.

Kallis is and will always be an upstart with no style.

He remembers the first time he met Ebba's mother. Invited to their fine manor house. It was of course incredibly impressive, until the day he saw the books and realized they ran conferences there so they could afford to hang onto the place, and not, as her mother had said in an interview in *Homes & Gardens*, because there was a cultural heritage there that belonged to everyone.

Anyway, that first time Kallis had turned up with a bunch of flowers and a box of Aladdin chocolates. A suit, despite the heat of the summer; it was the middle of July. He had not known what else to put on when he had been invited to visit someone who owned a place like that. It was like a palace.

Ebba's mother had smiled when he handed over the flowers and the chocolates. An indulgent and somewhat amused smile. The cheap chocolates were put out with the coffee. Lay there half-melting in their box. Nobody took a single one. The whole garden was full of roses and other flowers. There were magnificent arrangements in huge vases. He had no idea where his little bunch of flowers went. Presumably straight on the compost heap.

He and Ebba strolled down to the old bathing hut to say hello to her father. The pennant was flying over the bathing hut. A signal that Daddy was bathing, and not to be disturbed. But this was Ebba's boyfriend's first visit, and Daddy had said they should come down. The heat made Kallis take off his jacket. It was hanging over his arm. His top shirt button was undone, his tie rolled up in his pocket. The others were wearing light summer clothes that looked casual, but expensive.

Ebba's father was sitting on a sun lounger on the jetty. He got up and greeted them warmly. He was completely naked. Not bothered in the slightest. His little cock dangling limply.

But it was Kallis who was in the wrong.

Oh well, thinks Kallis as he stands there in the heat of the African night, with all of his life's insults and humiliations crowding around him. That was the last time Ebba's father appeared in front of him naked. Later on, when he came running along with his old friends wanting Kallis to invest their money, they were dressed in suits and inviting him to lunch at Riche.

He remembers the first time he flew over northern Uganda.

It was in a small Cessna; both Inna and Wattrang were with him. Kallis had started negotiations with the Ugandan government about buying the mine in Kilembe.

They had exchanged glances as they boarded the plane. The pilot was clearly under the influence of drugs.

"Some people are flying already," Inna said loudly.

But nobody understood Swedish.

They giggled as they climbed aboard. Clinging onto their light-hearted attitude. We laugh in the face of death.

At the beginning of the flight, Kallis was struggling with his fear. But then: he became completely enchanted.

Dense green rainforest covered the gentle curves of the mountains. And in the valleys between the mountains, freshwater rivers meandered. Shimmering green crocodiles were swimming in these rivers. And the mountains were full of red, fertile earth and gold that could feed everyone.

It was a spiritual experience. Kallis felt like a prince, spreading his arms wide and flying over his realm.

The noise of the plane's engine saved him having to talk to his companions. The feeling flooded his body, the sense of being at one with all this.

Who would he ever be in Canada?

Not to mention Kiruna.

The L.K.A.B. mining company would always be the biggest player up there. Even if he started prospecting, started up a mine, he would hardly be able to sell anything. The infrastructure was such a narrow sector. The railway line that transported the iron ore was fully occupied by L.K.A.B., not even they could transport as much as they could sell. You would end up standing there cap in hand all the time, putting up with being outmanoeuvred.

But here. He would become rich. Really rich. Whoever got in first here would make a fortune. And build towns, roads, railways, power stations.

Later he said to Diddi and Inna:

"The mine is actually nothing more than a muddy hole in the ground. They've got no equipment, they're hacking away and digging by hand. And yet they're still finding enough. There's unimaginable riches down there."

"And a load of trouble," Diddi had chipped in.

"Of course," Kallis said. "But if those problems hadn't existed, all the nervous investors would have been here already. I want to be the first. The Congo is too crazy, but this! At least Uganda has signed international agreements protecting overseas investors – M.I.G.A., O.P.I.C. . . ."

"Let's hope they value the money they get through overseas aid."

"They want a real mining industry here; they're sitting on treasure, but they haven't got the skills to get it out. Five years ago the Hema militia used dynamite in this very mine. They had a few poor geologists there who advised them against it, but nobody listened. And over a hundred people died like rats in a trap down there."

"There'll be trouble," Diddi repeated gloomily.

"Certainly," Kallis replied. "I'm expecting plenty. But that's what we do."

"You're my master," said Inna. "I think you ought to buy it."

Inna is sleeping off the pain in her battered face. Kallis is standing by the window in his hotel room, listening to the fire-bellied toads in the Ugandan night.

Gerhart Sneyers was right all along, he thinks.

"They don't have the capacity to extract their natural resources themselves," Sneyers says inside Kallis' head, tarring virtually all the African nations with one brush, "but they won't be able to tolerate the fact that we can do it either, and when that happens they're going to decide that the natural resources in their own country belong to them, of course. You can't reason with them."

At the time Kallis had found Sneyers' attitude rather sickening; he had thought it was prejudiced, and that Sneyers had completely forgotten Africa's history of colonialism. Besides which, Sneyers did not shy away from words like "darkies", and he called various states "backward".

But as early as July, when the Belgian engineers were killed, Kallis realized that Uganda's problems were not simply transitory. He mothballed the Kilembe project, took his western workforce home, and trained two hundred local men and women to guard the mining complex. One month later, he received reports saying they had left the mine to its fate.

In order to bring in other investors, Kallis Mining had promised a guaranteed minimum return on the project. These investors immediately contacted him, informing him of their imminent demands for payment.

After the meeting in Miami in May, Sneyers had set up an account for him and told him to put money aside to deposit there in the future.

"It mustn't be traceable," he had said.

As early as July Kallis has begun putting money into the account. Selling here and there. If nothing else, he might need the money in order to pay off future demands from the Kilembe investors. He cannot start panic selling in order to release capital then, that would seriously damage the reputation of the Kallis group on the market. And everybody would back off. He has also used some money to help build up Kadaga's forces in the northern part of the country. Kadaga has secured the areas around Kilembe, and around some other mines. But, Sneyers had said to him, this is not a long-term solution. Kadaga can sort out the mines, but not the infrastructure. So it's impossible to transport anything out of the mines safely. Besides which, mining at the present moment would be illegal for Kallis. The necessary permits from the authorities are no longer valid.

Today's meeting with the Minister for Industry has finally resolved the situation. Kallis may have been hesitating before, but not any longer. He has tried to be honest in a totally corrupt country. But he has had enough of being so naïve.

Sneyers is right. Museveni is a dead end.

Besides which, Museveni is a dictator and an oppressor. He ought to be court martialled. Getting rid of him is beginning to seem more and more like the only moral thing to do.

Kallis intends to protect his investment. He has no intention of going under.

Rebecka Martinsson was going through the files that had been on Örjan Bylund's computer. She was sitting in bed with the computer on her knees. She had put on her pyjamas and brushed her teeth, even though it was only seven o'clock. Boxer was investigating every nook and cranny in the room, coming back to Martinsson from time to time specifically to walk all over the keyboard.

"Listen, you," Martinsson said, lifting her down. "If you don't behave, I'll have to tell Sven-Erik."

She had lit a fire in the stove. It had caught well, and because she was burning fir, it sounded like a series of explosions. Boxer jumped every time, looking terrified and curious all at once.

What a monster, she seemed to be thinking. The fire glowed like a red eye through the half-open door of the stove.

What had Bylund been looking for? When Martinsson put Kallis Mining into Google, she got more than 280,000 hits. She scrolled through Bylund's cookie files to see which pages on Kallis Mining he had looked at.

Kallis Mining was the main owner of the mining company Northern Explore Ltd, which had been floated on the stock exchange. In September the shares had gone up and down like a roller coaster. First of all the Canadian investment company Quebec Invest had sold their entire holding. This had created a sense of unease, and the share price had plummeted. Then came reports of positive test results from drilling outside Svappavaara. The share price had jumped for joy, shooting upwards.

Who makes money on a share price roller coaster, she thought. The person who buys when the price is low and sells when it has gone up, of course. Follow the money.

One article that Bylund had looked at was about the mining company's new board, which had recruited an additional member since the Canadian company had sold its shares. A resident of Kiruna had been elected.

"Sven Israelsson on the board of Northern Explore", ran the headline.

She was interrupted by her phone, playing its little tune.

Wenngren's mobile number on the display.

Her heart was going through an Olympic gymnastics routine in her breast.

"Hello Martinsson," he said with his usual drawl.

"Hello," she said, trying to think of something else to say, but without success.

After thinking for an eternity, she came up with:

"How are things?"

"Fine, fine. We're all at Arlanda, just checking in."

"I see . . . cool."

He laughed at the other end of the line.

"Sometimes it's so bloody difficult to talk to you, Martinsson! But I'm sure it will be cool. Although nature is best on T.V. Are you coming up?"

"Maybe, but it's a bit far."

There was silence for a little while. Then he said:

"Come up. I want you to."

"Why?"

"Because I want to try and persuade you to come back to the office."

"I'm not doing that."

"That's what you say now. But I haven't even started trying to persuade you. We've booked a room for you from Saturday to Sunday. You can come up and show us how to ski."

Martinsson laughed.

"I probably will come," she said.

She realized with a sense of relief that it did not feel difficult to think of meeting people from the office. She would see Wenngren. He wanted her to come. She could not slalom, of course. They had not been able to afford that when she was little. And who would have taken her to the slalom course in town? But that didn't matter.

"Got to go," said Wenngren. "Promise you'll come?"

She promised. And he said in a deep, warm voice:

"Bye then, Martinsson. See you soon."

And she purred:

"Bye then."

Martinsson looked at the computer screen. On an international level, Quebec Invest's departure from Northern Explore had merited a small article in the English language specialist publication *Prospecting & Mining*. The headline was "Chicken Race". "We went too early," said the vice president of Quebec Invest Inc., commenting on the fact that shortly after the Canadian investment company had sold its shares, Northern Explore had found both gold and copper. He added that deficiencies in the analyses of sample drillings had been far too great, and that as part-owners of Northern Explore they had found it difficult to judge whether viable amounts were likely to be found. The vice president of Quebec Invest regarded it as "unlikely" that there would be any future co-operation between Kallis Mining and Quebec Invest.

Why? Martinsson wondered. Surely they ought to be keen to get a second chance, particularly when Kallis Mining has shown itself to be successful again.

And who was Sven Israelsson, the new board member? Why had Bylund done so many searches on his name?

She ran her own search. And found some interesting articles. She carried on reading.

Boxer was concentrating on a button hanging by a thread from Martinsson's pyjamas. She took a swipe at it, let it swing, grabbed it with both paws and sank her needle-sharp teeth into it. She was a lethal killer cat. The button was dead meat.

At 7.30, Martinsson rang Chief Prosecutor Björnfot.

"Do you know what Sven Israelsson did before he was elected to the board of Northern Explore?" she asked.

"No," Björnfot said, switching off the television. He had only been channel-hopping anyway, searching for something he could put up with.

"He was the boss of S.G.A.B. in Kiruna – they are a big chemical analysis company. They were very nearly taken over by an American company two years ago. But Kallis Mining went in and took a 50 per cent share, so they stayed in Kiruna. All very interesting, in view of the fact that a Canadian investment company, Quebec Invest, sold their entire holding in Northern Explore the previous year, just before Northern Explore announced that viable amounts of copper and gold had been found outside Svappavaara."

"I see . . . and the link to Israelsson is . . . ?"

"This is what I'm thinking: Israelsson is the boss of the company analysing samples from Northern Explore's test drilling outside Svappavaara. He presumably feels a strong sense of loyalty towards Kallis Mining, since they saved S.G.A.B. from being bought out by coming in as part-owners. They would all have lost their jobs, or been forced to move to the U.S.A. In one article I've found the vice president of Quebec Invest is complaining that the analyses of the samples from the test drilling were inadequate, and he thinks it "unlikely" that there will be any future co-operation between Quebec Invest and Kallis Mining. You have to wonder what he's sore about, don't you?"

"Do you?" Björnfot said. "They must have lost a lot of money through selling too early."

"Yes, but these investors are used to taking risks and losing money, without moaning when journalists ring up. And Israelsson is voted onto the board of the subsidiary company, Northern Explore. Now it takes a while to get the concession to start working the land, to actually start mining, but once that's gone through, Northern Explore is worth billions. Israelsson is a chemist working for a small firm of analysts. How did he manage to get onto the board of Northern Explore? It just doesn't make sense. But this is what I'm thinking: Israelsson had every opportunity to manipulate those results. I think he helped to cover up the samples that showed a positive result. I think he helped Kallis Mining to manoeuvre the second biggest owner out of the company. Maybe they sent some kind of signal to Quebec Invest, hinting that the results would be negative. And so Quebec Invest sold out in a bit of a panic, because they were afraid of making huge losses when the market reacted. When Quebec Invest sold, the share price fell. Just about a month later, Northern Explore released the news that the results were positive. Perhaps that's why Quebec Invest was sulking in the press and saying they couldn't see any possibility of working with Kallis Mining in the future. They feel they've been conned, but they can't prove anything. If anyone at Kallis Mining, or Israelsson, bought shares before the news of the positive results was made public, then it's insider trading. I think Israelsson was given a seat on the board, with all that entails in the way of salary and bonuses and so on, as a thank you for his help. And besides . . ."

Martinsson paused for dramatic effect.

". . . in November he bought a brand new Audi. By then the shares in Northern Explore had gone up by more than 300 per cent. Taken from the level they were at before the price fell."

"A new car," Björnfot said, getting up from the sofa and clamping the cordless phone firmly between his ear and his shoulder while he put on his shoes. "They always go for a new car."

"I know."

"See you in quarter of an hour," Björnfot said, pulling on his jacket.

"Where?"

"At Israelsson's, of course. Have you got the address?"

Sven Israelsson lived in a red-painted wooden house on Matojär-vigatan. Some children had already started work in a snowdrift, digging out a cave. The spades thrown carelessly aside bore witness to the fact that work had been abandoned with some speed when children's television programmes and dinner called.

Israelsson was in his forties. Martinsson was surprised. She had expected him to be older. He had thick brown hair, with a significant amount of grey. He looked fit and wiry, as if he swam or ran.

Björnfot introduced himself and Martinsson, using their full job titles. Chief Prosecutor and Special Prosecutor, that was enough to frighten anybody. Israelsson did not look afraid. It seemed more as though something else fleetingly crossed his face. Something like resignation. As if he had been waiting for a knock on his door. Then he pulled himself together.

"Come in," he said. "Keep your shoes on, if you like. The snow on the ground is clean, after all."

"You work for S.G.A.B., the chemical analysis company," Björnfot started off once they were all sitting around the kitchen table."

"That's correct."

"And Kallis Mining owns 50 per cent of the company."

"Yes."

"And last winter you became a member of the board of Northern Explore Ltd, a subsidiary company to Kallis Mining."

Israelsson nodded.

"Last autumn the investment company Quebec Invest sold a large amount of shares in Northern Explore; why was that?"

"I have no idea. I suppose they got cold feet. Didn't have the nerve to wait for the final test results from the drilling. Maybe they thought the shares would drop like a stone if the results were negative."

"The vice president of Quebec Invest said in an interview that he couldn't imagine working with Kallis Mining at any stage in the future," Martinsson said. "Why did he say that, do you think?"

"I have no idea."

"In November you bought a new Audi," Björnfot said. "Where did you get the money from?"

"Am I suspected of some crime?" Israelsson asked.

"Not officially, not at this stage," Björnfot said.

"There are circumstances surrounding this particular episode which might indicate significant insider trading, or aiding and abetting others to commit such a crime," Martinsson said.

She measured two inches between her thumb and forefinger.

"I'm this far from finding out who bought shares during the short period between Quebec selling and the publication of the positive test results," she said. "In insider trading, the buying is often done in small parcels through intermediaries and administrators. That shows up if the regulator does a routine check. But I'm going to follow up every single sale during that period. And if I find you or Kallis Mining are among the buyers, you can expect to be charged."

Israelsson shifted in his chair, and appeared to be trying to think of something to say.

"Regrettably, it's bigger than that," Björnfot said. "I have to ask you a question. Please don't lie; just remember we can check this information by other means. Did the journalist Örjan Bylund contact you and ask you questions about this matter?"

Israelsson said nothing for a while.

"Yes," he said eventually.

"What did you say to him?"

"Nothing. That he would have to take his questions to Kallis Mining."

And Inna Wattrang was head of information at Kallis Mining, Martinsson thought.

"Örjan Bylund was murdered," Björnfot said without preamble.

"What the hell are you talking about?" Israelsson said, agitated. "He died of a heart attack!"

"Unfortunately that isn't the case," Björnfot said. "He was murdered when he started digging into this particular story."

Israelsson went white. He grabbed hold of the edge of the table with both hands.

"So there we are," Björnfot said. "I don't believe you had anything to do with the murder. But you must understand how serious this is. Don't you think it would be better to tell us everything now? You'll find the pressure you're under will ease."

Israelsson nodded.

"There was a man at the lab," he said after a while. "And we found out he was leaking information to Quebec Invest."

"How did you find out?"

Israelsson gave a wry smile.

"Pure chance. He was sitting at home, chatting to the vice president of Quebec Invest on his home phone. And he had his mobile in his pocket; he'd forgotten to turn it off, and it rang the most recently dialled number, which was a colleague's. The colleague heard enough of the conversation to work out what was going on."

"And what did you do?"

"The guy who heard the conversation told me about it. And when the time was right, we supplied the first guy with false information."

"What, exactly?"

"The test drilling outside Svappavaara was at a critical stage. It was beginning to look as if Northern Explore wouldn't find anything there. They'd taken a lot of readings at a depth of more than seven hundred metres. The costs were soaring. Then they did some test drilling at almost a thousand metres. That was their last shot in this area. Everything depended on those results. It's only the biggest players who can afford to drill to that depth. God knows there are plenty of small companies who can only afford an initial survey from the air, then they send out foot patrols to dig up a few earth samples by hand."

"And they found gold."

"More than five grams per ton, which is fantastic. A couple of per cent copper as well. But I falsified a report, saying that we hadn't found anything and that it was now out of the question that viable quantities would be found in the area. And I made sure the guy who was leaking information saw it. Quebec Invest sold their shares in Northern Explore an hour later."

"What happened to your colleague?"

"I had a word with him . . . and after that conversation he handed in his resignation, and that was the end of that."

Björnfot sat for a few moments, thinking things over.

"Did you speak to anyone at Kallis Mining about this? About the leak? About giving out false information?"

Israelsson hesitated.

"Örjan Bylund has been murdered, and so has Inna Wattrang," Björnfot said. "We can't rule out the possibility that these events are related. The quicker the truth comes out, the greater our chance of catching the person who did this."

He leaned back in his chair and waited. This was a man with a conscience he had in front of him. Poor thing.

"I suppose it was Diddi Wattrang and I who came up with this together," Israelsson said eventually.

He looked at them with a pleading expression.

"He made it all sound so right. He called Quebec Invest swindlers. And he said what I've often thought about these overseas investors. That they're not actually interested in starting up a mine in this area. They're only interested in making money quickly. They're acting with permission and dealing with concessions, but they're not entrepreneurs. Even if you find viable quantities, nothing happens. The rights are sold on from one company to another, but nobody actually wants to get anything going. Either there isn't the money, I mean it costs at least a quarter of a billion to start up a mine, or some other fucking thing is missing. And all those overseas investors, they've got no feeling for this area. What do they care about job opportunities and the people here?"

He gave a slightly crooked smile.

"And he was the one who said that after all, Mauri Kallis does come from here originally. And he's got both the desire and the money and the entrepreneurial spirit. With Quebec Invest out of the way, the chances of the mine actually opening were 100 per cent greater. Don't get me wrong, I've thought about all this since. Every single day. But at the time it felt as if what we were doing was absolutely correct, morally speaking. After all, it was Quebec Invest who were the con men. They were the ones who had a spy in our company. Fucking bastards, we thought. Robbing the thief. Conning the con man. They were only getting what they deserved. And they couldn't expose us, because that would mean exposing themselves."

Israelsson fell silent. Martinsson and Björnfot watched him as the realization that it was all over hit home. The future began to take shape in his head. Losing his job. Being charged. People talking.

"When I was offered a seat on the board," he said, hastily wiping away the tears that had started to appear, "it just felt like a confirmation of the fact that Kallis Mining wanted to invest up here. They wanted local roots. But when I got the money . . . in an envelope, not paid into my account . . . then I didn't feel so good. I bought the car, and every time I've got in it . . ."

He broke off, shaking his head.

A man with a conscience, Alf Björnfot thought again.

"There you are then," Björnfot said as he and Martinsson left the house.

"We need to ring Sven-Erik and Anna-Maria and tell them what's happened," Martinsson said. "They can bring in Diddi Wattrang on suspicion of serious insider trading."

"Anna-Maria rang earlier. Diddi Wattrang's in Canada. But I'll call her anyway. When we've got the information about the sale of the shares, we can ask the Canadian police to help arrest him."

"What are you doing now?" Martinsson asked. "Do you want to come down to Kurravaara with me? I've promised to do some shopping for my neighbour. And he'll want me to stay for coffee afterwards. He'd be really pleased if you came along."

Sivving Fjällborg was delighted to see them. He liked talking to new people now and again. He and the prosecutor quickly established that although they were not actually related, they had a number of friends in common.

"This is all very cosy," Björnfot said, looking around the boiler room.

Bella was lying in her basket looking miserable, watching the others sitting at Fjällborg's Formica table enjoying the local bread with butter and cheese.

"Yes, I have a nice easy life down here," Fjällborg said philosophically, dipping his sandwich into his coffee. "What do you actually need? A bed and a table. And I've got the television down here as well, although there isn't much worth watching these days. And as for clothes, I've got two of everything. No more! There are those who get by with less, but I don't want to be stuck at home just because my clothes are in the wash. Actually, I've got five pairs of underpants and socks."

Martinsson laughed.

"But you shouldn't have that many," she said, looking meaningfully at the threadbare socks and worn-out underpants hanging on the line.

"Women!" laughed Fjällborg in turn, looking to Björnfot for support. "Who cares what I'm wearing underneath? Maj-Lis was just the same, she was always so concerned about having clean underwear on. Not on my account, mind you, but in case she got run over and ended up in hospital!"

"Quite right," laughed Björnfot. "What if the doctor was suddenly confronted with dirty underwear or a hole in a sock!"

"Come on," Fjällborg said to Martinsson. "Can't you turn off that computer? We're trying to enjoy ourselves here."

"In a minute," Martinsson said.

She was sitting with her laptop, checking out Diddi Wattrang's family's financial affairs.

"Maj-Lis," Björnfot said, "was she your wife?"

"Yes, she died of cancer five years ago."

"Look at this," Martinsson said, turning the computer towards Björnfot. "Diddi Wattrang always reaches his credit limit by the end of the month, minus fifty, minus fifty. It's been the same for several years. But immediately after Northern Explore found gold, his wife is registered as the owner of a Hummer."

"They always buy cars," Björnfot said.

"It would be nice to have one of those," Fjällborg said. "How much do they cost? Seven hundred thousand kronor?"

"Diddi Wattrang is guilty of insider trading. But I just wonder if there was any link to Inna Wattrang."

"Maybe she found out and threatened to expose him," said Björnfot.

He turned back to Fjällborg.

"So you and your wife were neighbours of Rebecka's grand-mother?"

"That's right, and Rebecka spent most of her childhood there too."

"Why was that, Rebecka? Did your parents die when you were little?" Björnfot said, coming straight to the point.

Fjällborg got up quickly.

"Would anybody like some egg on their sandwich? I've got some already hard-boiled in the refrigerator. They're from this morning."

"Daddy died just before I turned eight," Martinsson said. "He was driving a logging machine. He was out in the forest one winter, and got a leak in the hydraulic cable. We don't know exactly what happened, because he was on his own. But he got out and presumably felt at the cable, and it came loose."

"Oh, shit," Björnfot said. "Hot hydraulic oil."

"Yes, and the pressure's so great too. The oil must have hit him full on. They think he died instantly."

Martinsson shrugged. A gesture indicating that it all happened a long time ago. That it was all a long way from her now.

"Careless and clumsy," she said in a casual voice, "but we're all guilty of that from time to time."

Although he shouldn't have been, she thought, keeping her eyes fixed on the computer screen. I needed him. He should have loved me too much to be careless and clumsy.

"It could have happened to anyone," said Fjällborg, who had no intention of allowing Martinsson to discredit her father in front of outsiders. "You're tired and you get out of the machine and it's cold, it was minus 25°C that day. And no doubt he was stressed as well. If the machine breaks down, there won't be any money coming in."

"And what about your mother?" Björnfot said.

"They separated the year before my father died. But I was twelve when she died. She was living on Åland and was run over by a truck. By that time I was living here with my grandmother."

It is late winter, early spring. Rebecka Martinsson will soon be twelve. She has been out with some of the other children from the village, jumping off the roof of a barn. Straight down into the snow. Now she is soaking wet, right up her back, and her boots are full of snow. She needs to go home and change.

Home, that is Grandmother's house these days. At first after Daddy died she lived with her mother, but that only lasted a year. Her mother often works away. It was a bit of a mess at first; she kept leaving Rebecka with her grandmother, sometimes because she had to work, sometimes because she was tired. Then she would come and pick her up and be cross. Cross with Grandmother, although she was the one who had asked her to take care of Rebecka.

Today when Rebecka walks into the kitchen in her wet clothes, her mother is sitting at the table. She is in a really good mood. There are roses in her cheeks, and she has had her hair dyed properly at the hairdresser's, not by some friend the way she usually does.

She has met a new man, she tells them. He lives on Åland and he wants Rebecka and her mother to move there and live with him.

She says he has a lovely house. And there are lots of children living nearby. Rebecka will have plenty of friends.

Rebecka is getting cramps in her stomach. Grandmother's house is a lovely house. That is where she wants to live. She does not want to move.

She looks at her grandmother. Grandmother does not say anything, but she holds Rebecka's gaze.

"Never," Rebecka says.

And as soon as she has dared to utter that silent word, she can feel how true it is. She will never move, never move anywhere with her mother. She lives here in Kurravaara. And her mother is unreliable. One day she is the way she is now. And all Rebecka's friends think she is so pretty and she wears such lovely clothes, and she chats to the older girls in the playground. One of them sighed one day, so that Rebecka could hear her: "Wouldn't it be great to have a mother like that, one who understands stuff."

But Rebecka knows more about her mother. She can lie on the bed incapable of doing anything, and Rebecka has to run to the shops and live on sandwiches, and she dare not do anything, because whatever she does is wrong.

Her mother does everything she can to try and persuade Rebecka. She talks in her very best voice. Tries to give her a hug, but Rebecka slides away. She sticks to her guns. Keeps shaking her head. She sees her mother looking at Grandmother for support, calling upon her to agree when she says:

"It's too much for Grandmother to have you living here all the time, and I am your mother after all."

But Grandmother says nothing. And Rebecka knows that means she is on her side.

When her mother has been all sweetness and light for ages, she suddenly changes.

"Don't come, then," she snaps at Rebecka. "Please yourself. See if I care."

And she says she has been working overtime since Daddy died so that Rebecka can have a new winter coat; she could have been taking a course in something if it had not been for her responsibilities.

And still Rebecka and her grandmother say nothing.

They remain silent long after her mother has left. Rebecka keeps her grandmother company out in the barn. Holds the cow's tail while her grandmother does the milking. The way she used to do when she was little. They are silent. But when Mansikka belches, they have to laugh.

And then everything is almost back to normal.

Her mother moves house. Rebecka receives postcards telling her how fantastic life is on Åland. Rebecka reads them, and a stab of longing pierces her heart. There is not a single word to suggest that her mother is missing her. Or even that she cares about her. The postcards say they have been out in the boat, or that there are apple trees and pear trees growing in the garden, or that they have been off on a trip.

In the middle of summer, she receives a letter. You are going to have a little brother or sister, it says. Grandmother reads it too. She is sitting at the kitchen table wearing Daddy's old reading glasses, the ones he bought at the petrol station.

"*Jesus siunakhoon ja Jumal varjelkhoon,*" she says when she has finished reading. The Lord bless us and save us all.

Who told me she had died? Rebecka pondered. I don't remember. I remember so little of that autumn. But there are certain things I do remember.

Rebecka is lying on the sofa bed in the kitchen alcove. Jussi is not lying at her feet, because her grandmother and Sivving Fjällborg's wife Maj-Lis are sitting at the kitchen table, so Jussi is lying under the table. It is when Grandmother is in the barn or has gone to bed that Jussi usually comes to lie on Rebecka's bed.

Maj-Lis and Grandmother think Rebecka has gone to sleep, but she hasn't. Her grandmother is crying. She is holding a kitchen towel up to her face. Rebecka realizes it is to keep the noise down, so that Rebecka will not wake up.

She has never seen or heard her grandmother cry, not even when her father died. The sound makes her feel very afraid and uneasy. If Grandmother is crying, the world must be coming to an end.

Maj-Lis is sitting opposite her and making comforting noises.

"I don't think it was an accident," Grandmother says. "The driver said she looked at him and walked straight out into the road."

"It must have been tough, losing both parents when you were so young," Björnfot said.

Fjällborg was still standing by the refrigerator. Holding onto the eggs as if he did not know what to do with them.

When I think about the time immediately afterwards, I feel ashamed, thought Martinsson. I wish I had the right pictures in my head. A little girl standing by a grave, with tears on her cheeks and flowers on the coffin. Drawings of Mummy in heaven, or whatever. But I was cold.

"Rebecka," says her teacher.

What was her name again? Eila!

"Rebecka," says Eila. "You haven't done your maths homework again. Do you remember what we talked about yesterday? Do you remember promising me you were going to start doing your homework?"

Eila is nice. She has curly hair and a lovely smile.

"I do try," Rebecka says. "But then all I can think about is the fact that my Mummy's dead, and I just can't do it."

She looks down at the desk so that it will look as if she is crying. But she is only pretending.

Eila falls silent and strokes Rebecka's hair.

"I know, I know," she says. "I'm sure you'll catch up with the work sooner or later."

Rebecka is satisfied. She does not want to do her maths homework. She has succeeded.

Another time. She is sitting hiding in Grandmother's woodshed. The sun is filtering in through the gaps in the walls. Thin curtains of dust seem to be rising into the light all the time.

Fjällborg's daughter Lena and Maj-Lis are calling to her. "Rebecka!" She does not answer. She wants them to look for her forever. She feels angry and disappointed when they finally stop shouting.

And another time. She is playing down by the river. Pretending to hammer and bang on the jetty. She is building a raft. She is going to sail it down the river Torne. She knows that the river flows out into the Baltic. She is going to sail the raft across the sea and down the coast of Finland. To Åland. Then she is going to go ashore and hitch a ride to the town where her mother lived. Home to the house where that man lives. She rings the doorbell. The old guy opens the door.

He doesn't know what's going on. "Where's Mummy?" Rebecka asks. "She's gone for a walk," he replies. Rebecka runs. She is in a hurry now. At the very last second she grabs hold of her mother, just as she is about to walk out into the road. The truck thunders past, almost touching them. Saved! Rebecka has saved her. "I could have died," Mummy says. "My darling girl!"

"I can't remember being upset," Martinsson says to Björnfot. "I was living here with my grandmother, after all. And there have been so many good adults in my life. Unfortunately, I think I might have exploited it. Noticed that the adults felt sorry for me, and used it to get a little extra attention."

Björnfot looked unconvinced.

"Listen, kid," he said. "They had every reason to feel sorry for you. And you deserved a little bit of extra attention."

"The things you say," Fjällborg said. "You didn't exploit it at all. Try not to think about it. It was all so long ago."

Ester Kallis was sitting in her attic room at Regla. She was on the floor with her arms around her knees, getting herself ready.

She had to go down to the kitchen to fetch the pan of macaroni.

But it was difficult. The house and the whole estate were full of people and activity. There were specially hired waiters and waitresses, and a chef to prepare the food. Out in the yard stood men with walkie-talkies and guns. She had heard Mikael Wiik talking to them a while ago, standing just below her half-open window.

"I want armed guards on the gate when they arrive. Not because they're actually needed, but so the client's guests will feel safe and secure. You understand? They do a lot of travelling in areas of unrest, but even at home in Germany, Belgium or the U.S.A., they're used to being surrounded by security people. So when they arrive, I want two men on the gate and two up at the house. We'll reorganize once the guests are safely inside."

She had to go down and fetch the pan of macaroni. She had no choice.

Ester went down the attic stairs, passing Kallis' bedroom door, and on down the wide oak staircase to the hall.

She crossed the hall, walking over the Persian carpet and, without looking at herself, passing her own reflection in the heavy 18th-century mirror, then went into the kitchen.

Ebba was there discussing wine with the chef, and at the same time delivering instructions to the serving staff. Ulrika was standing by the marble worktop arranging flowers in an enormous vase. Both women looked as if they had come straight out of a glossy magazine, with their simply cut evening dresses protected by aprons.

Ebba had her back to Ester when she walked into the kitchen. Ulrika caught sight of her over Ebba's shoulder and raised her eyebrows at Ebba. Ebba turned around.

"Hi there Ester," she said in a friendly voice, accompanied by an extremely worried smile. "I haven't set a place for you, I didn't think you'd want to join us, it'll just be a lot of talk about business . . . deadly boring. Ulrika and I are under orders to attend."

Ulrika rolled her eyes to show Ester how tedious it was to have to be there.

"I just wanted to get my macaroni," Ester said quietly, her eyes fixed on the floor.

Her feet were prickling. She could not look at Ulrika.

"Oh, but of course we'll make sure you get something to eat," Ebba said. "We'll send a three-course meal up on a tray."

"God, that sounds wonderful," said Ulrika, "can't you do that for me as well? Then I can just lie there watching a film and eating something delicious."

They laughed, embarrassed.

"I just want my macaroni," Ester said.

She opened the refrigerator door and took out a big pan of cold cooked macaroni. A mountain of carbohydrate.

Then Ester looked at Ulrika. It was unavoidable. She was standing there when Ester closed the refrigerator door and turned around. Ulrika as white as paper. A red hole in the middle of her face.

A voice. Ebba's or Ulrika's.

"Are you O.K.? Don't you feel well?"

Oh yes, she felt fine. She just had to get back upstairs to her room in the attic.

She made her way up the stairs. A while later she was sitting on her bed. She was eating macaroni out of the pan with her hands, she had forgotten to bring a fork. When she closed her eyes she could see Diddi sleeping deeply in the matrimonial bed. He was fully dressed, although Ulrika had taken his shoes off when he got home last night. She could see Wiik positioning his men around the estate. He was not expecting any problems, just wanted the guests to see the guards and feel secure. She could see Mauri, wandering back and forth in his study, nervous about that evening's dinner party. She could see that the wolf had climbed down from the tree.

She opened her eyes and looked at her oil painting of Torneträsk.

I left her, she thought. I went to Stockholm.

Ester goes by train to Stockholm. Her aunt meets her at the station. She looks like a bookmark, or a hard-nosed film star. Her straight, black Sami hair has been curled and sprayed into a Rita Hayworth style. Her lips are red and her skirt is tight. Her perfume is sweet and cloying.

Ester is going to the art school for an interview. She is wearing an anorak and trainers.

At the Idun Lovén Art School, they have seen Ester's entry exam work. She is good, but she is far too young. That is why the board want to meet her.

"Now remember to talk," her aunt exhorts her. "At least answer when they ask you something. Promise!"

Ester promises, from within her numbed state. There is so much going on around her: the screeching and whistling of the underground train as it pulls into the station, words everywhere, posters advertising all kinds of things. She tries to read them, to work out what they are trying to sell, but she hasn't time, her aunt's heels are like drumsticks keeping a rapid rhythm through a crowd of people; Ester does not have time to look at them either.

She is to be interviewed by three men and two women. They are all well into middle age. Her aunt has to wait out in the corridor. Ester is invited into a conference room. There are large paintings on the walls. Ester's entry exam work is leaning against the wall.

"We'd very much like to talk to you about your pictures," one of the women says in a friendly tone.

She is the principal. They have shaken hands and explained who they are and what their names are, but Ester does not remember. She can only remember that the woman who is talking now said she was the principal.

There is only one oil painting. It is called "Midsummer's Eve", and it is a picture of Torneträsk, with a family just about to get into a boat by the shore. Midnight sun, and swarms of mosquitoes filling the air. A boy and his father are already sitting in the boat. The mother is pulling at a girl, who wants to stay ashore. The girl is crying. The shadow of a flying bird across her face. In the background the mountain, with the remains of the snow still lying on it. Ester has painted the water black. The reflections in the water have been enlarged; if you look only at them, you get the impression that the lake is nearer to the observer than the family is. But in the composition of the picture, the family is in the foreground. It worked well, making the reflections bigger. It makes the water look big and threatening. And beneath the surface of the water there is something white. But it could just be the reflection of a cloud.

"You're not used to painting in oils," one of the men says.

Ester shakes her head. Because it is perfectly true.

"It's an interesting picture," the principal says pleasantly. "Why doesn't the girl want to get into the boat?"

Ester hesitates.

"Is she afraid of the water?"

Ester nods. Why should she tell them? If she does, everything will be ruined. The white shadow beneath the water is the ghostly water horse that has awoken on midsummer's eve. When Ester was little, she read about the horse in a book from the school library. In the painting he is swimming down there, wishing for a child to fall in the water so that he can drag it under and eat it. The girl knows she is that child. The shadow of the bird across her face is the Siberian jay, *guovsat*, the bringer of misfortune. Her parents see only clouds in the sky. They have promised the boy in the boat he can steer, he wants to go.

They pull out other pictures. Nasti in his cage. Pencil drawings from her home in Rensjön, both indoors and outdoors.

And they ask about this and that. She does not know what they want to hear. And what can she say? After all, they've got the pictures right there in front of their noses, all they have to do is look. She does not want to explain and go into details, so she answers in monosyllables and becomes torpid.

Her aunt and her mother are sitting inside her head, conducting a lively discussion.

Mother: It's obvious that a painter doesn't want to talk about their paintings. You don't really know yourself where they've come from. And perhaps you don't want to know, either.

Aunt: Yes, but sometimes you just have to give something of yourself if you want to achieve a goal. Say something, Ester, you do want to get into art school, don't you? They're going to start thinking you're retarded in some way.

They are looking at all the dogs having a crap. It was Gunilla Petrini who chose which pictures Ester should send in. And she liked the dogs.

There's Musta, of course, madly kicking snow over her little pile with her hind legs.

The neighbour's pointer, Herkules. An austere, quite military hunting dog. Broad-chested, his muzzle slightly crooked. But when he wanted a crap, for some reason he always had to find a small fir tree. He had to do it with his bottom pressed against a tree. Ester herself is happy with the way she has captured his expression, pleasure and straining combined, as he stands there with his back arched over the little tree.

And then there is a picture she drew after a visit to Kiruna. It is a woman, pulling her Pekinese along on a lead. You can see only her calves from behind, they are quite thick, and her feet are stuffed into high-heeled shoes. The Pekinese is crouching, trying to have a crap. But it looks as if his mistress has grown tired of waiting, and is dragging him along on his walk. You see him from behind too, still in the position, the claws of his hind feet leaving marks on the ground.

They are asking her something. Inside her head, her aunt nudges her impatiently.

But Ester keeps her mouth firmly shut. What can she say? That she is interested in shit?

Her aunt wants to know how it went. How is Ester supposed to know? She does not like all that talking. But she tried. With the pictures of Nasti, for example. She realizes they are trying to see a deeper meaning in them. His captivity. His little dead body. Her father's words come out of her mouth: They're so sensitive, she said. They can cope out there on the mountain, but when they're exposed to our cold germs, for example . . . They all looked questioningly at her.

Now she feels like an idiot. Thinks she did too much talking. Although they think she hardly said a word, she knows that.

It went really badly, she thinks. She will never get in.

*

Ester put the empty pan down beside her bed. All she could do now was sit here and wait. She wasn't sure what for.

It will show itself, she thought. It's like falling. It happens all by itself.

She must not put on the light in her room. Must not give herself away.

Downstairs they were having dinner. Like a herd of reindeer, grazing. Unaware that the wolf pack is getting closer, blocking off their escape routes.

Pitch-black night outside. No moon. It made virtually no difference whether she closed her eyes, or opened them. A small amount of light from the lamp on the wall outside filtered into her room.

The dead were approaching. Or was she approaching them? She recognized several of them. Relatives on her mother's side that she had never met.

Inna too. Not as far away as you might think. Maybe she was worried about her brother. But there was not much Ester could do about that. She had her own brother to think about.

It was not too long since Inna had sat here in Ester's room. The swelling on her face had begun to subside. The bruises had changed colour, from red and blue to green and yellow.

"Aren't you going to get out your palette and paint me?" she had asked. "I'm so colourful at the moment."

She had changed recently. Stayed at home at the weekends. Was not as cheerful as she used to be. Sometimes she had come up and sat with Ester for a while.

"I don't know," she had said. "I just feel so tired of everything. Tired and depressed."

Ester had liked her like that. Depressed.

Why should a person always be happy? she had wanted to ask Inna.

These people. Happy and easy-going, lots of friends. That was the most important thing of all.

But still. Inna made that demand only of herself. Not of Ester.

In that way Inna was like Ester's mother.

They both let me be who I am, she thought. Mother. She promised the teachers in school that she would tell me to try harder. Try to learn the maths and writing. "And she's so quiet," the teachers said. "She hasn't got any friends."

As if it were some kind of illness.

But my mother let me be. Let me draw. Never asked if I had a friend I would like to invite home. Being alone was something natural.

At art school it was not the same. You had to pretend you were not alone. So that the others would not have to feel worried and weighed down by guilt.

Ester starts at the Idun Lovén Art School in Stockholm. Gunilla Petrini has a friend whose apartment in Östermalm is being renovated, and so the owners are spending the winter in Brittany. Little Ester can have one of the rooms, that's absolutely fine. The men working on the apartment arrive early in the morning and have finished for the day by the time Ester gets home.

Ester is used to being alone. She had no best friends in school. She has spent the whole of her fifteen years of life living on the fringes, sitting alone on school outings and munching her sandwich. She stopped hoping that somebody would come and sit beside her on the bus at a very early stage.

So of course it is her own fault. She is not used to making contact with people. Besides which, she is convinced she would be rejected if she tried. Ester sits on her own during break times. She does not initiate any conversations. The other students are very much aware of the age difference, and make the excuse to themselves that Ester must have friends of her own age to hang out with in her free time. Ester wakes up alone. Gets dressed and eats her breakfast alone. On the way out, she sometimes meets the men who are renovating the apartment, dressed in their blue overalls. The nod or say hi, but there are a million miles between them.

She is not particularly bothered by the fact that she is an outsider at college. She paints models in counterpose and learns by watching the older students on her course. When the others go out for a coffee, she often stays behind in the studio, walks round and takes a look. Tries to work out how this one got the lines to look so light, how that one found those colours.

When she does not have classes in life drawing, she goes for walks. And it is easy to be alone in Stockholm. Nobody can tell by looking at her that she is an outsider. It is not like Kiruna, where everybody knows who you are. There are lots of people walking here, all on the way to different places. It gives her a sense of liberation, to be one of the crowd.

In Östermalm there are old ladies who wear hats! They are even more entertaining than dogs. On Saturday mornings Ester pursues them with her sketch pad. She draws them in rapid lines, their frail bodies in thick nylon stockings and good coats. When it gets dark, they disappear from the streets like frightened rabbits.

Ester goes home and eats sandwiches and yogurt for dinner. Then she goes out again. The autumn evenings are still warm and black as velvet. She walks over the city's bridges.

One evening she is standing on Västerbron, looking down at a trailer park. A week later she comes back and watches a family who live there. The father is sitting on a camping stool, smoking. The family has hung up their washing between the trailers. The children are kicking a ball around. They are shouting to one another in a foreign language.

Ester catches herself longing to be part of them. That family down there that she does not even know. She could look after their children. Fold their washing. Travel down through Europe with them.

She tries calling home, but the conversation is hard work. Antte asks what it is like in Stockholm. She can hear from his voice that she has already turned into a stranger. She would like to tell him that Stockholm's not so bad. That the autumn is beautiful here, with the deciduous trees like friendly giants against the clear blue sky. Their yellow leaves, as big as Ester's hand, rustle dryly through the streets in flocks. And there is a little flower stall close to where she lives; she can stand there and watch. But she knows he does not want to hear any of that.

And her mother seems to be so busy all the time. Ester cannot work out what she can talk about so it won't feel as if her mother is about to hang up all the time.

And so the winter comes. Wind and rain in Stockholm. The old ladies are rarely seen now. Ester paints a series of landscapes. Mountains and rocks. Different seasons, different kinds of light. Gunilla Petrini takes some of them home to show her friends.

"They're terribly desolate," one of them says.

Petrini has to agree.

"Her drawings are very different. But she's not afraid of desolation. She really is comfortable with the realization that man is very small in relation to the world and to nature, don't you agree? She's like that as a person, too."

She shows them some of the drawings. They comment on what a driven artist she is. And how many artists can one say that about these days? It is as if Ester has been brought here in a time machine. They can see something of Gustaf Fjæstad's reflections in the water, Bror Lindh's wintry forests. And then they come back to the topic of desolation in her paintings of nature.

"She doesn't have a problem with being alone," Petrini says.

"That's a good quality for an artist to have," someone says.

They talk about her background. About the mentally ill woman who had a child by another patient. An Indian. About the little girl with the Indian appearance who has grown up with a Sami family.

One of the older men looks at the pictures, pushing his glasses up and down his nose. He owns a gallery in the Söder district of the city, and is well known for buying artists' work before they break through. He owns several pieces by Ola Billgren, and bought Karin Mamma Andersson early on. He has a ridiculously large Gerhard Richter on the wall at home. Petrini had something in mind when she invited him this evening. She tops up his glass.

"The lines of her mountains are interesting," he says. "There's always a gap, or a crack or a valley or a crevice in the landscape. Can you see? Here. And here."

"Another world behind this one," someone says.

"Narnia, perhaps," someone jokes.

And so it is decided. Ester is to have her own exhibition at the gallery. Petrini wants to jump up and down for joy. It will attract attention. Ester's age. Her background.

Martinsson drove Björnfot home to his overnight pad on Köpmangatan. There was no point in going to bed, he was not tired enough to go to sleep yet. Besides which, he felt a little too upbeat to sleep. The visit to Martinsson's neighbour had been very pleasant. He felt a strong sense of kinship with Sivving Fjällborg, who had chosen to move down into his boiler room.

That was why he felt so at home in his pad in Kiruna; he had what he needed, and no more. There was a sense of tranquillity in that. Things were different in the apartment in Luleå.

His skis were propped up against the wall in the hallway. He might just as well see to them now, then he would be ready to leave in the morning. He laid them over the backs of two chairs with the runners uppermost, put toilet paper over the fastenings and poured on the wax, waited three minutes and then wiped it off.

He managed to wax his skis, sort the pile of washing that was lying on the sofa and get the washing up done before the telephone rang.

It was Martinsson.

"I've been looking at Kallis Mining's sales over the past few months," she said.

"Are you working?" Björnfot asked. "Haven't you got a cat you're supposed to be looking after?"

Martinsson ignored his question and went on:

"Within a very short time they've sold a whole load of minority holdings in different projects around the world. And in Colorado the prosecution service have started a preliminary investigation into a subsidiary company of Kallis Mining with regard to significant financial irregularities. The subsidiary company has bought assets to the value of five million dollars. The prosecutor is of the opinion that this is a fictitious transaction, and the payment couldn't be traced to the alleged vendor in Indonesia, but to a bank in Andorra."

"Oh yes?" Björnfot said.

He had the feeling that Martinsson was expecting him to draw some kind of conclusion from what she had just said. But he had no clue as to what it might be.

"It seems as if Kallis Mining needs to get its hands on some cash. But they don't want to draw attention when they release capital. That's why they're selling minor holdings in different parts of the world. And they seem to have emptied the Colorado company of money. And they're moving money to a bank in Andorra, which has a strong code of confidentiality in its banking sector. So what I'm wondering is this: why does Kallis Mining need to release money? And why are they transferring it to a bank in Andorra?"

"Well, why?"

"Last summer, three engineers were killed by a militia group when they were on their way from a mine belonging to Kallis Mining in northern Uganda. Immediately afterwards, Kallis Mining shut down all operations in the area; there was just too much unrest. Then things just got worse, and the mine fell into the hands of various groups who fought over it. The same thing has happened to all the other mines in the northern part of the country. However, in January the situation was stabilized, to a certain extent. General Kadaga has taken control of most of the mining areas in the north. Joseph Cony and the L.R.A. have retreated up to the southern parts of the Sudan. Other groups have withdrawn into the Congo and are still fighting among themselves there."

Björnfot could hear Martinsson leafing through some papers.

"And this," she said, "is the really interesting part. For a long time there has been antagonism between the President and General Kadaga. A year ago, he was dismissed from the army. He has kept away from Kampala for fear that the President will have him arrested and brought to trial for some alleged crime. The President wants to get rid of him. Kadaga has managed as well as he could with a dwindling group of men. But now his private army has grown, and they've even managed to take over large areas in the north. And there's a report in *New Vision* which says that President Museveni is accusing a Dutch businessman of supporting Kadaga financially. The businessman is called Gerhart Sneyers, and he owns one of the mines in Uganda that was forced to shut down. These accusations are rejected out of hand by Sneyers, of course."

"Oh yes?" Björnfot said again.

"This is what I'm thinking. I think that Mauri Kallis and Gerhart Sneyers, and maybe other overseas businessmen, are supporting

316

Kadaga. Many people are in the process of losing their assets in the area. That's why they're releasing capital as discreetly as possible. They're financing his military operations, and in return he promises to leave their mines alone. Perhaps they're hoping they might be able to start up again if the situation stabilizes. And if a bank in Andorra is paying out money to commanders-in-chief, the payer's identity is protected by their code of conduct."

"Is it possible to prove any of this?"

"I don't know."

"O.K., well for the time being we've got Diddi Wattrang on suspicion of insider trading. We'll start there," Björnfot said firmly.

Kallis' dinner guests arrived just after eight on Friday evening. Cars with blacked-out windows drove along the avenue to the estate. Wiik's security staff met them down at the gates.

At the house, Kallis, Ebba and Ulrika received their guests: Gerhart Sneyers, mine owner and oil company owner, and chairman of the African Mining Trust; Heinrich Koch, vice president of Gems and Minerals Ltd, Paul Lasker and Viktor Innitzer, both of whom owned mines in northern Uganda, and former general Helmuth Stieff. Sneyers had heard about Inna, and offered his condolences.

"Some madman," Kallis said. "It still seems unreal. She was a loyal colleague and a good friend of the family."

Between handshakes he asked Ulrika:

"Is Diddi coming to dinner?"

"I don't know," Ulrika said, fixing Viktor Innitzer a drink. "I just don't know."

I am not a drug addict. This was something Diddi Wattrang had said to himself with increasing frequency over the past six months. Drug addicts inject themselves, and he was no drug addict.

Last Monday Wiik had dropped him off at Stureplan. He had gone on a bender that had lasted from Monday through to Thursday night, when he had come home in a cab. Now he had woken up in the darkness, his hair drenched in sweat. It was not until he had managed to switch on the bedside light that he realized he was at home at Regla. The past days and nights lay behind him like fragments of memory. Snapshots without any order. A girl, laughing loudly in a bar. Some guys he had started chatting to; he had gone to a party with them. His face in a bathroom mirror, Inna inside his head at that exact moment; he is standing in there wetting a piece of toilet paper, pouring amphetamine onto it, screwing it up into a ball and swallowing it. A steaming dance floor in some warehouse. Hundreds of hands in the air. He wakes up on the living room floor of the company's overnight apartment in Stockholm. Four people are sitting on the sofa. He has never seen them before. Does not have a clue who they are.

Then he must have sorted out a taxi. He seems to remember Ulrika helping him out of the taxi; she was crying. But that might have been some other time.

He was no drug addict. But anybody who had seen him right now, searching through the medicine cabinet, might have thought differently. He threw Alvedon and plasters and thermometers and Nezeril and a thousand other things on the floor as he hunted for tranquillizers. He searched through his drawers, and he looked behind a desk in the cellar, but this time Ulrika had managed to find the lot.

There had to be something. If not tranquillizers, then coke. If not coke, then speed. He had never been much of a one for hallucinogenic drugs, but right now he could imagine smoking some grass or dropping some E. Something. That could make this black thing inside him stop crawling and writhing.

Down in the kitchen he found a bottle of cough medicine in the refrigerator.

He gulped it down. And then there was someone standing behind him. The nanny.

"Where's Ulrika?" he asked.

She replied, unable to take her eyes off the medicine bottle in his hand.

The dinner. Oh my God. Mauri's dinner.

"What do you actually think of Mauri Kallis?" he asked her.

And when she did not reply, he said with exaggerated clarity: "What do you really think?"

And he squeezed her shoulder as if to squeeze an answer out of her.

"Let go of me," she said in an unusually firm voice. "Let go. You're frightening me and I don't like it."

"Sorry," he said. "Sorry, sorry. I'll . . . I can't . . ."

He could not breathe. It felt as if his throat had closed up, it was like breathing inside a suction pipe.

He dropped the cough medicine bottle on the floor. It smashed to pieces. He tugged at his tie in desperation.

The nanny pulled away. He slumped down onto a kitchen chair, trying to catch his breath.

Frightened? Was that what she said? She knows nothing. Absolutely nothing about being afraid.

He remembers when he told Kallis about Quebec Invest. That Israelsson had told him they had a leak at S.G.A.B.

"This guy is telling them about the test results in advance," he had said to Kallis.

Kallis had gone white. He was furious. You could see that, even though he did not say anything.

Everything is personal, thought Diddi. Kallis prides himself on being one of those guys who can say it's-just-business. But just below the surface is that sense of inferiority that turns everything into a personal insult.

Kallis had said they could turn this to their advantage. If the test drilling gave a positive result, then they could give the leak false information and buy shares when Quebec Invest sold and the value went down.

Diddi was to take care of it all, and keep Kallis' name out of it.

But it was idiot-proof, Kallis had said. Who was going to talk? Hardly Quebec Invest.

Diddi had hesitated. If it was that idiot-proof, why did he have to set it up, and not Kallis?

Then Kallis had smiled at him.

"Because you're so much better at persuading people," he had said. "We've got to have Sven Israelsson with us."

Then he had mentioned how much money could be involved for Diddi. Half a million at least, he thought. Straight into Diddi's pocket.

That had settled it. Diddi needed money.

Two weeks ago Inna had confronted him. It had been the last time she was at Regla. They were sitting on a bench on the south side of her house, leaning against the wall. Drowsy from the spring sunshine.

"It was Mauri, wasn't it?" she had asked him. "Who sorted the Quebec Invest stuff?"

"Don't start poking about in all that," Diddi had said.

"I'm just checking up on him," Inna had persevered. "I think he and Sneyers are supporting Kadaga. I think they're going to try and bring Museveni down. Or have him murdered."

"For my sake, Inna," he had said. "Just leave it alone."

Kallis and his guests were taking a stroll before dessert. Viktor Innitzer asked General Helmuth Stieff about Kadaga's chances of retaining control of the mining district in northern Uganda.

"The President can't allow it," the general said. "These are important resources for the country, and he regards Kadaga as a personal enemy. As soon as the election is over, he'll send his troops up there.

So will the other commanders-in-chief. They've only withdrawn temporarily."

"And as far as we're concerned," Sneyers said, "we need a calmer situation in the country if we're to run our businesses. A reliable power supply, a functioning infrastructure. Museveni won't let us back in; it would be naïve to expect it. Nobody has been able to work the mines over there for months and months. How long can you keep your investors sweet and convince them that it's only a temporary hitch? That it's 'care and maintenance', just for a little while? The problems in northern Uganda aren't going to be solved if we just sit and wait. Museveni is crazy. He puts his political opponents in jail. If he succeeds in taking over the mines, don't be under any illusions that he'll give them back to us. He'll claim that they've been abandoned, and therefore revert to state ownership. The U.N. and the World Bank won't lift a finger."

Koch went white. He had shareholders breathing down his neck, as Kallis did. Besides, he had so much of his own capital tied up in Gems and Minerals Ltd that he would be finished if they lost the mine.

Tomorrow there would be open discussion about the alternatives facing them. And Sneyers had stated clearly that they were no diplomats. They trusted each other, and spoke freely. For example, they would discuss who they thought might take over from the president if he were removed from power. And what possibilities they might have in the coming election if Museveni did not stand.

Kallis looked at Koch, Lasker and Innitzer. They were standing in an admiring little circle around Sneyers. Schoolboys surrounding the toughest boy in the playground.

Kallis did not trust Sneyers. He had to watch his own back. Koch and Innitzer in particular were in Sneyers' pocket. Kallis had no intention of joining them.

Turning to Wiik when all that business with the journalist,

Bylund, cropped up had been the right thing to do. Wiik had proved himself to be the man Kallis had hoped for when he employed him.

At the time when Diddi became crazy and threatening.

Diddi is wandering back and forth in Kallis' study. It is December 9th. Kallis and Inna have just got back from Kampala. Kallis is a different man from the one who left Sweden. He was furious after the meeting with the minister for industry, but now he is calm.

He is perching on the edge of his desk, almost smiling at Diddi.

"Do you understand what I'm saying?" Diddi says. "This Örjan Bylund has been asking questions about Kallis Mining and the business with Quebec Invest. I'm toast."

He presses his clenched fist against his abdomen; he seems to be in pain.

Kallis tries to calm him down.

"Nobody can prove anything. Quebec Invest can't talk, because they're just as guilty as we are. They'd be finished if this came out. And they know that! Same applies to Israelsson, besides which he's had a big juicy bone from his master. You need to chill. Don't rock the boat."

"Don't you tell me to chill," Diddi snaps.

Kallis raises his eyebrows in surprise. An outburst of rage from Diddi. He has not seen that since the time Diddi came to his student room demanding money. When that Spanish woman had dumped him. God, that was a whole lifetime ago.

"Don't think I'm going to take the blame if all this comes out," growls Diddi. "I'm going to point the finger at you, make no mistake."

"You do that," Kallis says icily. "But now I'd like you to leave."

He thinks for a while after Diddi has slammed the door behind him. Diddi has frightened him a little. But he is not going to panic. He knows he is acting rationally, thinking things through.

The last thing he needs right now is a journalist sniffing around the company's affairs. A little bit of searching will lead to the discovery that Diddi was one of those who bought shares in Northern Explore after Quebec Invest sold out, and sold them again after the report that gold had been found. If anyone follows the trail of payments from a number of transactions within the parent company and sees that they have gone to a bank in Andorra, they will be dangerously close. If they get hold of an arms dealer who lets slip that the payments for weapons for Kadaga have come from Andorra ...

So the next time Kallis is talking to his head of security, he says:

"I have a problem. And I could use someone discreet, a man of your capabilities, who could take care of my problem."

Wiik nods. He doesn't say anything, he merely nods. The following day he hands Kallis a sheet of paper.

"A problem solver," he says tersely. "Tell him you got the number from a close friend."

There is no name on the piece of paper. Just a number. The international code is Holland.

Kallis feels as if he is in some silly film when he calls the number the next day. It is a woman who answers; she says "Hello". Kallis listens tensely to her voice, the intonation, trying to make out background noises. He thinks she has a bit of an accent. And her voice is a bit gravelly. A woman in her forties from the Czech Republic who smokes?

"I was given your number by a friend," he says. "A close friend."

"A consultation costs two thousand euros," the woman says. "After that you'll get a quote for the job."

Kallis does not haggle over the price.

Wiik allows the security men to eat in shifts. There is no criticism of the arrangements surrounding the meeting. The Swedish guys he had recruited himself looked up to him. They envied him the job with Kallis, this was a peach of a job. He thought he noticed a difference in Sneyers' men too. More respect.

"Nice place," one of them said, jerking his head to signal the whole estate.

"Better than a medal from the French Minister of Defence," said the other.

So they knew about that. Hence the increased respect. It was also a sign that Sneyers was keeping his eye on the ball, with regard to both Kallis and those around him.

And they were right. It was better working for Kallis than for the Special Protection Unit.

"It must have been pretty tough down there, then? It takes a lot for the French to give a foreigner a medal."

"It was the boss who got the medal." Wiik attempted to brush the matter aside.

He didn't want to talk about it. His partner sometimes woke him up at night, shaking him. "You're screaming," she would say. "You'll wake the whole house up."

Then he would have to get up. Drenched in sweat.

The memories came crowding in. Taking hold when he was asleep. They had not faded with time. Rather the reverse. The sounds become clearer, the colours and odours more vivid.

There were sounds that could drive him mad. The sound of a fly, for example. Sometimes he could spend a whole morning trying to get them out of his partner's summer cottage. He would really have preferred to stay in the city in the summer.

Clouds of flies. Congo, Kinshasa. A village near Bunia. Wiik's group has arrived too late. The villagers are lying outside their houses, hacked to pieces, mutilated. Naked bodies. Children with their stomachs slit open. Three members of the militia group responsible are sitting leaning against the wall of one of the houses. They have not left with the rest of them. Out of it on drugs. They hardly seem to be aware that they are being spoken to. They seem unperturbed by the cloying smell of death or the clouds of buzzing flies around the bodies.

Wiik's commanding officer tries different languages: English, German, French. "On your feet! Who are you?" They remain sitting there, leaning against the wall, their eyes misty. In the end one of them grabs his gun; it has been lying on the ground beside him. He is perhaps twelve years old. He grabs his weapon and they shoot him on the spot.

Then they shoot his two companions. They bury them. Report back that all the militia forces had left the area when they arrived.

Sometimes it could be the rain against the window. If it started raining during the night, while he was asleep, that was the worst. Then he started to dream about the rainy season.

It pours down for weeks. The water gushes down the mountainsides, carrying mud along with it. The slopes disintegrate. The roads are transformed into red rivers.

Wiik and his colleagues joke with each other, saying they dare not take off their boots in case their toes get left behind inside. Every blister turns into a tropical sore. The skin loosens, turns white, comes away in great lumps.

The G.P.S. and two-way radios stop working. The technical equipment was not made for this kind of rain; it is impossible to protect it.

They are operating under French N.A.T.O. command; they are supposed to be securing a road, and now they are stuck at a bridge.

But where the hell are the French? There are only ten of them in the group, and they are waiting for support. The French are meant to be securing the road from the other side, but they have no idea who is over there now. Earlier in the day they saw three figures in camouflage gear disappearing into the jungle.

They are beginning to fear that a militia group is mobilizing around them.

Wiik pulled out a packet of cigarettes and offered them to Sneyers' lot.

It had ended in gunfire that time. He does not know how many he killed. He just remembers the fear as the ammunition was running out, old stories about what these madmen did to their enemies, that was what woke him up at night. It was for that battle they had been awarded medals.

It was a strange way to live. Staying in the towns between assignments, hanging out in bars with his colleagues. Knowing they were all drinking too much, but that they had never had to handle this much reality before. The little black girls, only kids, trying to sidle up to them, "mister, mister". You could fuck them for nothing. But you wanted a drink in peace with your mates first. So you chased them away like dogs, told the bartender you would go somewhere else if you were not left in peace. Then he would throw them out.

If you were interested, there were always several of them out in the street. Even if it was pouring with rain they would be standing there pressed against the walls of the houses, all you had to do was take them back to the hotel.

In one of the bars he met a retired major of the German Bundeswehr. He was around fifty, and owned a company that worked in the field of protection, both of people and property. Wiik knew him.

"When you've had enough of crawling around in the mud," the major had said, giving him a card with only a number on it. Nothing else.

Wiik had smiled and shaken his head.

"Take it," the major insisted. "You never know how things might turn out. We only deal with short, distinct assignments. Very well paid. And a hell of a lot easier that what you did the other week."

Wiik had stuffed the card in his pocket, mostly to put an end to the discussion.

"But hardly approved by the U.N., I imagine?" he had said.

The major had laughed politely, just to show he was not offended. He had slapped Wiik on the back and left.

Three years later, when Kallis came to Wiik and said he had a problem he wanted taken care of for good, Wiik had contacted the German major and said he had a friend who wanted to make use of their services. The major had given him a number for Kallis to ring.

It had been such a strange feeling, knowing that world still existed. Unrest, military commanders, drugs, malaria, children with empty eyes. It was all going on over there without him.

I got out in time. There are those who never manage to live a different kind of life. But I've got a partner, a real woman with a real job. And I've got an apartment and a good job. I can cope with everyday life, peace and quiet.

And if I had not given Kallis the telephone number, he would have got it from somewhere else. And how should I know what he used it for? Probably he didn't use it at all. I mean, he got it at the beginning of December. Long before Inna was murdered. And she . . . that can't have been a professional job. It was all so . . . messy.

Kallis pays fifty thousand euros into an account in Nassau. He receives no communication, either to say that the money has been received, or that any assignment has been carried out according to his wishes. Nothing. He has said he wants the journalist Bylund's hard drive wiped, but he does not know what happened about that.

A week after he has paid the money, he finds an item in the newspaper stating that Bylund has died. It sounds as if it were due to illness.

It was all so easy, and he could simply move on, thought Kallis, smiling as his wife shared a toast with Sneyers.

With Inna it had not been easy. A hundred times over the last week he has thought about alternative scenarios. And the whole time he comes back to the fact that there weren't any. It had been a necessary step.

It is Thursday, 13 March. In one day, Inna will be dead. Kallis is at Diddi's house. Diddi is upstairs in bed.

Ulrika had come round to Kallis and Ebba and rung the doorbell. She was crying, she had no coat on, just a sweater. She was carrying the baby in her arms wrapped in a blanket, like a refugee.

"You have to talk to him. I can't wake him up," she said to Kallis.

Kallis did not want to go. After Quebec Invest and after what Diddi told him about Bylund, they prefer not to have anything to do with each other. And definitely not just the two of them, alone. No, since becoming partners in crime they have used all their skill to avoid each other. Their shared guilt has not bound them together – quite the opposite.

Now he is standing here in Diddi and Ulrika's bedroom, looking at Diddi, who is asleep. He makes no attempt to wake him up. Why should he? Diddi has curled up into the foetal position.

Kallis is flooded with a grinding irritation when he looks at him.

He glances at the clock and wonders how long he has to stand there before he can go back. How long would it have taken if he had tried to wake him? Not very long, surely?

And just at that moment, as he is turning to leave, the telephone rings.

Thinking it is Ulrika calling to see how things are going, he picks up the receiver and answers.

But it is not Ulrika. It is Inna.

"What are you doing there?" she asks him.

He does not notice how different she sounds; he only thinks about that afterwards. He is so happy to hear her voice.

"Hi," he says. "Where are you?"

"Who are you?" she asks in her strange voice.

And now he can hear it. That this is a different Inna. Perhaps he already knows at this point.

"What do you mean?" he asks, although he does not want to know.

"What do I mean!"

She is breathing heavily at the other end of the phone, and then it comes.

"A while ago there was a journalist, a man called Örjan Bylund, asking questions about Quebec Invest quitting Northern Explore. And about a few other things. He died immediately after."

"Oh yes?"

"Don't give me that! I thought at first it was Diddi, but he's not smart enough. Just desperate enough for money to let himself be used, though. I've checked up on you, Mauri. It was easier for me than it was for the journalist. I'm part of the company, after all. You've emptied the company accounts, we're talking huge amounts of money! A whole lot of the payment invoices taking money out of the company are just thin air. The money is disappearing into a protected account in Andorra. And guess what? At roughly the same time as you started raiding the company accounts, General Kadaga started to mobilize his forces. A number of gangs joined him, because now there was financial support. Loyalty is just a matter of who's paying. In newspaper articles that nobody outside Central Africa reads, it says that weapons are being smuggled across the borders to these groups! By plane! How can they afford that? And they've taken control of the mining complex in Kilembe. You paid them, Mauri. Paid Kadaga and the military leaders who've joined him. So they'll protect your mine. So they won't plunder it and destroy it. Who are you?"

"I don't know where you've got these ideas . . ."

"Do you know what else I did? I met Gerhart Sneyers at the Indian Metal Conference in Mumbai. We had a few drinks one evening. And I asked him: 'So, you and Mauri will soon be getting things going again in Uganda?' Do you know what he said?"

"No," Kallis replies.

He has sat down on the bed next to the sleeping Diddi. The whole situation is unreal.

This isn't happening, he screams inside.

"He said . . . nothing! He said: 'What has Mauri said to you?' I was actually frightened of him. And for the first time he didn't keep on about the fact that Museveni is a new Mobutu, a new Mugabe. In fact, he didn't say a word about Uganda. I'll tell you what I think. I think you and Sneyers are providing Kadaga with money and weapons, and I think you're planning to get rid of Museveni. Am I right? If you lie to me I swear I'll spill everything I know to some really hungry media group, and they can sort out the truth."

Fear sinks its teeth into Kallis as if it were an animal.

He swallows. Takes a deep breath.

"It's company property," he says. "I'm protecting it. You're a lawyer, haven't you heard of *jus necessitatis*, the right of necessity?"

"Haven't you heard of child soldiers? You're giving those fucked up lunatics money for drugs and guns. These people who are protecting your property for money, they kidnap children. Kill their parents in cold blood."

"If the civil war in the north never ends," Kallis ventures, "if the unrest is just allowed to continue, then the population will never have peace. Generation after generation will end up as child soldiers. But now, at this precise moment, there's the chance to bring it to an end. The president isn't getting any aid, the World Bank has frozen everything. He's in a weakened position. The army's short of money. And the army is fragmented. Museveni's brother is busy plundering mines in the Congo. With a different regime, perhaps the children of tomorrow can be farmers. Or miners."

Inna remains silent for a long time. When she does speak, she does not sound angry any more. Her voice is almost tender. It is as if a couple, after all the arguments, finally decide to go their separate ways, and their thoughts turn from the current situation to the way things used to be. And it has not all been bad.

"Do you remember pastor Kindu?" she asks.

Kallis remembers. He was the pastor in the mining community near Kilembe. When the government started making life difficult, one of the first things that happened was that rubbish collections stopped. They said it was a strike, but in fact it was because the military were threatening the rubbish collectors. After only a week or so the whole place seemed to be lying beneath a blanket of the sickly stench of rotting rubbish. They started to have problems with rats. Kallis, Diddi and Inna went over there. They did not realize that this was only the beginning.

"You and the pastor sorted out a fleet of trucks and took the rubbish out of the town," Kallis said, a sorrowful smile in his voice. "You stank when you got back. Diddi and I put you up against a wall and sluiced you down with a hosepipe. The cleaning women stood at the windows laughing."

"He's dead. Those men you're paying, they murdered him. Then they set fire to his body and dragged it along behind a car."

"Yes, but that kind of stuff has gone on all along! Don't be so naïve."

"Oh, Mauri . . . I really respected you."

He tries. To the very last, he tries to save her.

"Come home," he begs. "So we can talk."

"Home? Is that Regla? I have no intention of ever coming back there. Don't you understand?"

"What are you going to do?"

"I don't know. I don't know who you are. That journalist, Örjan Bylund . . ."

"You don't seriously think I had anything to do with that?"

"You're lying," she says tiredly. "I did tell you not to lie."

He hears a click as she puts the phone down. It sounded like . . . it sounded like an old-fashioned public telephone. Where the hell was she?

He needs to think clearly. This could go really badly. If the truth comes out, then . . .

A series of pictures in his head. He becomes an international hate figure. No investors want to be associated with him. Even worse pictures: investigations involving Interpol. He ends up facing an international tribunal accused of crimes against human rights.

There is no point in regretting things you have done in the past. The question is, what has to be done now?

Where is she? A public telephone?

When he thinks back to the conversation, he could actually hear something in the background . . .

Dogs! A chorus of howling, singing, barking dogs. Sled dogs. A team of dogs, just before they set off.

And then he knows exactly where she is. She has gone to the company's house in Abisko.

He puts the telephone down carefully. He does not want to wake Diddi. Then he picks it up again and wipes it with the sheet from Diddi's bed.

Ester pushed the empty macaroni pan under the bed. It could stay there. She put on the black clothes she wore for her mother's funeral, a polo-neck jumper and a pair of trousers from Lindex.

Her aunt would probably have preferred it if she had worn a skirt, but could not quite bring herself to mention it. Ester had been quieter than usual. And it was not just grief. It was anger too. Her aunt had tried to explain:

"She didn't want us to say anything to you. She wanted you to paint for your exhibition. Not to be worrying about her. She wouldn't let us say anything."

So they said nothing. Not until it was absolutely necessary.

It is the private view of Ester's exhibition. Lots of people drinking mulled wine and eating ginger biscuits. Ester does not understand how they can actually see anything of the pictures, but perhaps that is not the idea. She is interviewed by reporters from two different newspapers, and has her photograph taken.

Gunilla Petrini introduces her to various important people. Ester is wearing a dress and feels odd. When her aunt turns up, she is really pleased to see her.

"This is amazing," whispers her aunt, impressed by what she sees.

She pulls a face when she discovers the mulled wine is alcohol-free.

"Have you spoken to Mother?" Ester asks.

And something shifts in her aunt's face. A hesitation, or perhaps it is the fact that she is avoiding Ester's eyes.

"What? What is it?"

And she wants her aunt to say: nothing.

But her aunt says:

"We need to talk."

And they go off to a corner of the room which is now full of people exchanging air kisses and handshakes taking a quick glance at Ester's pictures in between, and it is getting very loud and very warm and Ester is able to pick up only parts of what her aunt is saying.

"You must have noticed that she's started dropping things . . . and that she can't manage to hold the brush . . . was letting you paint the backgrounds . . . didn't want you to know, what with the exhibition and everything . . . a muscular disease . . . finally reached her lungs . . . won't be able to breathe any more."

And Ester wants to ask why, why nobody said anything. The exhibition! How can anybody think she cares about the damned exhibition?

Mother dies the day after Christmas Day.

Ester has said goodbye. She and her aunt have cleaned the house in Rensjön like mad things, visiting the hospital in Kiruna in between. Ester tries to find *eatnážan* behind the stiff mask into which the illness has transformed her face. The muscles beneath the skin have stopped functioning.

Her mother can talk, but it is slurred and she soon tires. She wants to know how the private view went.

"They don't understand a thing," her aunt snaps.

The exhibition attracted a few reviews. They were not good. Under the headline "Young, young, young" one reviewer wrote that Ester Kallis is certainly talented for her age, but that she has nothing to say. He is left unmoved by all her little nature pictures.

They are all the same. Ester Kallis is a child. What is the point of the exhibition? One of the reviewers questions both the gallery owner and Gunilla Petrini. She writes that Ester Kallis is not the young genius they would like her to be, and that unfortunately it is Ester who has to pay the price for their desire to attract attention.

Petrini rang Ester the day the first review appeared.

"Don't take any notice of it," she said. "The very fact that you've managed to get a review is good, lots of people never even get that. But we'll talk about this again. Take care of your mother now. Give her my best."

"What about this?" says her aunt, quoting from one of the reviews. "It says here that Ester Kallis 'grew up among the Sami'. What do they mean by that? It's a bit like Mowgli, growing up among the wolves, but he can't become a wolf because of his race."

Her mother looks at Ester with her strange, expressionless face, making a huge effort to find the words.

"It's good," she says sharply. "That you don't have a Sami name, that you don't look like a Sami. Do you understand? If they'd realized you were a Sami, none of them would have dared to criticize you. Your pictures would have been . . ."

". . . good, considering they were by a Lapp girl," her aunt adds.

But her mother wants to explain more clearly:

". . . an expression of our exotic culture, not real art. You would never have been judged by the same criteria. It gives you a small advantage, perhaps, in the beginning. A little bit of free attention. But then you can't get any further . . ."

". . . than Luleå," says her aunt, rootling in her bag for her cigarettes; she will need to go out on the balcony for a smoke shortly.

"Maybe they think they can't judge our art properly. Maybe that's why those who aren't much good get the same acclaim as the best. And that's fine for those who are mediocre, but you . . ."

". . . will compete with the best," her aunt finishes the sentence.

"For me it's been a cage. Nobody ever thought anything I did could be of interest to anybody apart from tourists or other Sami."

She looks at Ester. Ester cannot interpret her look.

"There's so much of our grandmother in you," she says.

"I know," says her aunt. "Just like *áhkku*. I've always said that."

Behind her, Ester hears her aunt begin to cry.

"At home in Rensjön," says her mother, "I remember watching you. The way you moved. How you were with the animals. Many times I thought: my God, that's just what my little granny used to do. But you never got to know her."

Ester does not know what to say. In her earliest memories, there were always two women in the kitchen. And the other one was not her aunt, she knows that. Her aunt does not wear a *jorbot*, the traditional cap that Sami women wear, nor does she have a flowery dress with buttons down the front, and an apron.

Then her mother dies. Not immediately after that conversation, but a week later it is over. And Father and Antte take her home. Now she is dead, she belongs only to them. Antte's mother, Father's wife. Ester is not allowed to be present at the division of their property. Neither is her aunt.

After the funeral her father and aunt have a quarrel. Ester can hear them through the door of the community centre kitchen.

"The house is too big for me and the boy," says her father. "And what do I want with the studio?"

He says he is going to sell everything. The reindeer too. He has a friend who owns a holiday village outside Narvik. He and Antte can go in as part-owners, and work there full time as well.

"But what about Ester?" her aunt hisses. "Where's she supposed to go?"

"She's got her own arrangements," her father says. "She's supposed to be going to that art school, isn't she? What can I do? You're not expecting me to move to Stockholm with her? And I can hardly hang onto all this just for her sake, can I? I was no older than her when I had to stand on my own two feet."

That evening at home in Rensjön, when they are sitting in front of the television – her aunt, her father, Antte and Ester – he takes out his wallet, removes the rubber band around it and takes out twenty five-hundred-kronor notes, which he gives to Ester.

"You'd better look in the studio to see if there's anything you want to take with you," he says.

"Bloody hell," says her aunt, getting up with such force that the coffee cups on the table rattle on their saucers. "Half of all this was hers. Ten thousand! Is that Ester's rightful share, do you think?"

Her father remains silent.

Her aunt rushes into the kitchen and turns the taps full on to do the washing up, and Ester and her father and Antte can hear over the running water and the crashing of the dishes that she is crying loudly.

Ester looks at Antte; his face is chalk-white, blue in the glow of the television. She tries to hold back. She does not want to know. But she is floating up towards the ceiling in the glow of the television as if she were floating through blue water. And from up there she looks down on Antte and her father. It is the same television, but a different room. Different furniture.

It is a small apartment. They are slumped on a sofa, gazing at the T.V. Antte is a few years older, and he has got quite fat. Her father has acquired lines of bitterness around his mouth. Ester can see that he was hoping to meet someone new. That he thought he would have a better chance working in a holiday village outside Narvik.

No woman, thinks Ester. No holiday village, either.

When Ester lands, she is standing in the kitchen. Her aunt has stopped crying and is smoking underneath the extractor fan. She talks about how things are going to be for Ester, about how angry she is with Ester's father. And then she talks about the new man in her life.

"Jan-Åke has asked me to go with him to Spain. He plays golf in the winter. I can ask him if you can come with us, before term starts. I mean, the apartment isn't very big, but we'll manage somehow."

"There's no need," Ester says.

Her aunt is relieved. Presumably the love between her and Jan-Åke is not the kind that can cope with a teenager.

"Are you sure? I can ask."

Ester assures her that she is quite certain. And her aunt keeps on about it until Ester is forced to lie and say she has friends in Stockholm, people who are on the same course, who she can go and stay with.

In the end, her aunt is satisfied.

"I'll call you," she says.

She exhales smoke and gazes out into the winter darkness.

"This will be my last time in this house," she says. "It's hard to believe. Have you looked in the studio, decided what you want to take?"

Ester shakes her head. The following day her aunt fills Ester's suitcase with tubes of paint and brushes and good paper. Even clay, which weighs a ton.

Ester and her aunt say goodbye at the central station. Her aunt has a ticket, and wants to celebrate New Year's Eve with that man, whatever his name was. Ester has forgotten already.

Ester drags her suitcase, heavy as lead, back to her room on Jungfrugatan. The apartment is silent and empty. The builders have taken some time off over the holiday. It is more than three weeks until the new term begins. She does not know anybody. She will not see a soul until then.

She sits down on a chair. She still has not cried about her mother.

But she would feel very insecure doing it here, in this situation. When she is so totally alone. She simply dare not do it.

And so she sits there like that in the darkness. She does not know for how long.

Not just now, she says to herself. Some other time. Maybe tomorrow. Tomorrow it's New Year's Eve.

A week passes. Sometimes Ester wakes up and it is light outside. Sometimes she wakes up and it is dark. Sometimes she gets up and puts water on to make tea. Stands there looking into the pan as it boils. Sometimes she cannot bring herself to take the pan off the hotplate, just watches it boil away. Then she has to start again with fresh water.

One morning she wakes up feeling dizzy. Then she realizes it is a long time since she had anything to eat.

She wanders along to the Seven-Eleven store. Going out is unpleasant. It feels as if people are looking at her. But she has to do it. The weather is grey. The tree trunks are damp and black. Wet gravel on the pavements. Disintegrating dog crap and rubbish. The sky dense and close. Impossible to imagine that the sun is up there. That the top of the cloud cover is like a snowy landscape on an early spring day.

Inside the store the smell of newly baked Danish and grilled sausages hits her. Her stomach contracts so violently that it hurts. She feels dizzy again, grabs hold of the edge of a shelf, but it is only the plastic strip they fasten the prices and the names of the items to, and she falls to the floor with the strip in her hand.

Another customer, a man who was standing over by the chilled goods counter, quickly puts down his basket and hurries over to her.

"Hey, what happened to you, love?" he asks.

He is older than her mother and father, but not old. His eyes are concerned, and he is wearing a blue woolly hat. For a moment she is almost in his arms as he helps her to her feet.

"Here, sit down. Can I get you anything?"

She nods and he comes back with coffee and a freshly baked Danish.

"Hey," he laughs as she bolts it down, drinking the coffee in great gulps although it is really hot.

She realizes she ought to pay, but then thinks that maybe she has not got any money with her. How could she leave home without thinking about that? She searches through her coat pockets and there is the money from her father. A roll of twenty five-hundred-kronor notes, held together with a rubber band.

She pulls it out.

"Jesus," the man says. "I'll stand you the coffee and the cake, but just use one of those at a time." He removes one of the notes from the bundle and places it in her hand. He pushes the rest of the money back into her pocket and zips it up carefully, as if she were a very small child. Then he looks at the clock.

"Will you be O.K. now?" he says.

Ester nods. The man leaves, and Ester buys fifteen Danish pastries and some coffee to take back to her room on Jungfrugatan.

The following day she goes back to the Seven-Eleven at the same time to buy more pastries. But the man is not there. He does not come the following day either. Nor the day after that. She goes back, hoping, four days in a row, then she stops going there.

She carries on sleeping through the days. It is hard when she is awake. She thinks about her mother. About the fact that she no longer belongs to anyone, or anywhere. She wonders if they have emptied the house in Rensjön yet.

Her aunt rings once on her mobile.

"How's things?"

"Fine," replies Ester. "What about you?"

Just as she is asking, she sees that her aunt takes the opportunity to cry when Jan-Åke is out playing golf.

It's so strange, Ester thinks. All of us who miss her so much. How did we end up being so lonely in our sorrow?

"Fine," says her aunt. "And of course Lars-Tomas hasn't called."

No, her father has not called. Ester wonders whether her father and Antte can talk to each other. No. Antte has been silenced by Father's "You have to look to the future" and "It'll all work out somehow."

One morning she wakes up, and as she is walking through the hallway to the kitchen to make some tea, she bumps into one of the workmen. He is wearing blue overalls and a thick jacket. "Hello there," he says. "You scare easily! I'm just here to pick up a few things. Plenty of snow out there."

Ester looks at him in surprise. Has it snowed?

"There must be at least a metre," he says. "Look out the window and you'll see. We should have been back at work here today, but nobody can get through."

Ester looks out of the window. It is another world.

Snow. It must have been snowing all night. Longer than that. She had not noticed anything. The cars on the street are visible only as small snow-covered mounds. Deep snow on the road. The street lamps are wearing thick white winter hats.

She totters out into the white world. A mother is toiling along in the middle of the street, pulling her child on a sledge. A man in a long smart black coat is skiing in the centre of the road. Ester has to smile; he is somehow managing to hold his ski pole and his briefcase in the same hand. He smiles back. Everybody she meets is smiling. They shake their heads; it is crazy, this much snow! Everybody seems to be taking it all very calmly. The city is so quiet. No cars can get through.

There are small birds in the trees, now that there are no cars, Ester can hear them. She has only seen jackdaws and pigeons, magpies and crows before.

It is proper fresh snow, *vahca* in the Sami language. Loose, cold, fluffy right down to the bottom. Not the kind with that slushy watery mess underneath.

She gets home an hour later. Her head full of snow pictures. Her grief has taken a step back.

She needs a canvas. A really big one. And loads of white.

Between the dining room and the old servant's bedroom in the apartment, the workmen have taken down a wall. It's lying there on the floor, more or less in one piece. Ester looks at it. It is an old wall. Old walls are made of stretched fabric.

Out in the hallway are several sacks of plaster, she knows that.

It is as if she catches fire. She becomes manic with the desire to do something, finds a plastic bucket and drags in one of the sacks of plaster. It is heavy, she is sweating.

She trickles the plaster through her fingers and stirs it with her arms; she is white right up to her elbows.

But if her body is in a fever, her head is full of ice-cold snow. Snow. And wind cutting across the mountains. The light is misty grey, lacking colour. You might be able to see a few spindly birch branches over to the right, down by the edge. In the centre of the picture lie an elk cow and her calf. They have slept in a hollow and the snow has covered them during the night. The fresh, deep snow insulates them from the cold.

Ester pours the plaster carefully over the big wall. She spreads it with her hands. She works in shifts, the picture is so big. The plaster sets, but before it has finished setting it becomes creamy, and you can draw in it. She draws with her fingers, using bits of debris and dust from the renovations to get some structure, tearing leftover wallpaper into strips to form the branches of the trees in the foreground.

It takes several days to complete the picture. Ester works hard. When the plaster has set, she hunts through the apartment for a base coat. The painters have put undercoat on the ceiling in the bedroom, and the paint is still there. It is perfect. Once she has done the base coat, she can add pigment without the plaster cracking. She takes her mother's colours out of her rucksack and paints in several layers; the first layers thin, thin, lots of turpentine and just a little pigment from the tube. No oil, she does not want it to be shiny. Matt, cold, blue. And the shadow in the hollow: yellow, brown, umber. She wants to show they are happy there, beneath the snow together.

She adds thicker layers of colour, less turpentine. She has to wait for it to dry. She sleeps in her clothes, wakes up and adds further layers of colour. It feels as if the painting wakes her up when it is ready for a new layer. She walks around it, munching whatever she can find in the kitchen. Drinks tea. She feels she cannot go out. Because out there the weather has changed and it has turned mild, everything has melted away. She must not see that. She is living in a world of snow. In her big white picture.

But one day it isn't the picture that wakes her, but Gunilla Petrini.

Term has started. The principal of the Idun Lovén Art School has called Petrini and asked about Ester. Petrini has called Ester's aunt. She has called Ester too, but Ester's phone needs recharging. Her aunt and Petrini have become very concerned. Petrini has called her good friends in whose apartment Ester has a room. The friends have given Petrini the name of the builder who is responsible for the renovations, and he has come along to unlock the apartment. He is standing in the doorway as Petrini sinks down onto Ester's bed, greatly relieved.

God, they have been so worried. They thought something had happened to her.

Ester remains lying on the bed. She does not sit up straight away. As soon as Petrini woke her up, the real world came back. She does not want to get up. She has no strength to get up and grieve for her mother.

"I thought you were with your family," Petrini says. "What have you been doing here?"

"I've been painting," Ester says.

And as she speaks she knows this is her last picture. She will not paint any more.

Petrini wants to see, so Ester gets up and they go into the dining room. The builder comes along too.

Ester looks at the picture and thinks with relief that it is actually finished. She did not know that, but she can see it now.

At first Petrini does not say a word. She walks around the enormous picture, lying there on the floor. Then she turns to Ester. Her expression is questioning, searching, strange.

"A portrait of you and your mother," she says.

Ester is incapable of replying. She carefully avoids looking at the picture.

"Nice," says the builder with feeling. "A bit on the big side, maybe."

He looks at the doorway and then at the window in despair, shaking his head anxiously.

"I want it out," Petrini says with the voice of total authority. "I want it out in one piece. You can pull down walls if necessary."

Where am I going to go? Ester thinks.

The realization that she will never paint again crashes down inside her like a heavy anchor.

No painting. No going back to art school.

Mella and Stålnacke were sitting in the Vanadis Hotel chatting. The room was traditionally decorated, with a fitted carpet and a flowery bedspread made of some synthetic material.

"Tomorrow we'll talk to Inna Wattrang's parents," Mella said. "And we'll try Diddi Wattrang again. I do wonder what happened at the cottage in Abisko. There's just so much that's odd about it all. Why was she wearing such fancy lingerie under her sports stuff, for example?"

Inna Wattrang is burrowing in her suitcase. It is March 14. She spoke to Kallis on the telephone last night, but she does not have the strength to think about that right now.

In two hours and five minutes she will be dead.

There are other jobs, she thinks.

And she thinks about her brother. She has to get hold of him. She will talk to Ulrika.

I'm going to stop closing my eyes to things, she thinks.

She is going to take a month's sabbatical, starting next week, and she is going to start doing some exercise. She has packed some sports things, but as she rummages through her case now, she realizes she has forgotten to pack any sports underwear. It doesn't matter. She can go for a run in what she is wearing, then rinse them through later.

She puts her trainers on.

She runs along the snowmobile tracks out on Torneträsk. People are lying outside their arks, fishing through holes in the ice. Or sitting on reindeer skins on the sledges behind their snowmobiles, their faces turned up to the sun. The sun is hot, and she is sweating. But she feels strong. The disappointment over Kallis drains away from her.

It is beautiful, she thinks. There is actually life outside Kallis Mining.

The mountain on the other side of the lake glows pink in the afternoon sun. Blue shadows in the ravines and precipices. A few scraps of cloud cling to the mountain tops; they look like woolly hats.

It'll be O.K., she thinks.

When she gets back the sun is setting. It almost looks as if there's a hole in it, and its glowing insides are pouring down over the sky towards the horizon. She is so preoccupied with looking at the sun that she does not notice the man standing outside the house until she is in the yard.

Suddenly he is there. He is wearing a light, thin coat.

"Excuse me," he says, and explains that his car has broken down up by the road, and that his phone has no reception.

Could he borrow hers?

She knows he is lying. She realizes it straight away. She can tell he is dangerous.

It is that deep suntan and the coat that is far too thin. It is that grimace that is supposed to represent a smile beneath the lifeless eyes. And it is the way he is getting closer to her all the time he is talking.

She does not have time to do anything. He sees the key in her hand. He has already reached her. He has not even finished speaking. It happens so quickly.

The man's name is Morgan Douglas. On the passport in his inside pocket it says John McNamara.

*

Morgan Douglas was woken by the sound of his mobile on the night of March 13th. The telephone's ring tone, the click of the bedside light, the familiar skittering across the floor as the cockroaches scuttled away from the light, the girl beside him mumbling something inaudible, flinging her arm across her eyes and going back to sleep, and then a voice on the telephone that he recognized.

The woman greets him politely and apologizes for disturbing him at this hour. And she quickly gets to the point.

"There's a job that needs taking care of now. Northern Sweden."

He is so bloody pleased to hear her voice, he makes a real effort to speak slowly when he replies so that he won't seem too eager. But he has been short of money for a long time now; he has had the odd little job, collecting debts and so on. But any black can do that kind of job, there is no real money to be made there. But this will pay well. He will be able to live well for quite a while, move out of this place and find something better.

"Payment as usual into your account once the job is done. A map, information, photo and travel expenses of five thousand euros are at the Coffee House at Schiphol. Ask for Johanna and say hello from . . ."

"No," he says. "I want all that at N'Djili Airport. How do I know this isn't some kind of bluff?"

She falls silent. It does not matter. Let her think he is paranoid. The truth is he cannot afford the ticket from Kinshasa to Amsterdam, but he is not going to admit that.

"No problem, sir," she says after just a second or two. "We'll arrange all that according to your wishes."

She ends the conversation by passing on greetings from the major. He likes that. She speaks to him with respect. These people know what it means, the fact that he was a paratrooper in the British

348

army. There are so many people who don't understand a damned thing. Who've never been there.

Douglas gets dressed and shaves. The bathroom mirror is mottled with age; soon it will be impossible to see a reflection at all. The water comes spluttering out of the tap, the pipes banging, and to begin with it is a brownish colour. One morning when he came in for a pee, there was an enormous rat. It turned round lazily and looked it him, then crawled under the bath, taking its time, and disappeared.

When he is ready he wakes the girl, who is still asleep.

"You have to leave," he says.

She sits on the edge of the bed, half asleep; he picks her clothes up off the floor and throws them at her. While she is putting them on, she says:

"My little brother. He must go to doctor. Sick. Very sick."

She is lying, of course, but he says nothing. Gives her two dollars.

"You have a little something for me, yes?" she says, looking longingly towards the chair where he had his glass pipe yesterday. He has already wrapped it in a piece of cloth and pushed it underneath his clothes. He will have to take whatever he needs in his coat pockets and under his clothes. He cannot take the case, otherwise the man on reception will make a huge fuss and insist he pays for the room, accusing him of trying to get out of paying, which is precisely what he intends to do. This place is crap, and they have not even cleaned the room during the weeks he has been living here. They can forget being paid.

"No, I haven't got anything," he says, pushing her out of the room.

He shushes her as they go down the stairs. The porter is asleep behind the counter; presumably he has another day job. No sign of the night watchman. He is probably asleep somewhere else.

The fluorescent light is humming and flickering coldly.

"I stay here," whispers the girl. "Until tomorrow. It's not safe on the streets, you know."

She points towards an armchair in the dreary lobby. It is so scruffy the stuffing is poking out of the upholstery.

Douglas shrugs. If the guy on reception wakes up before her he will take her money, but that's not his problem.

He takes a cab to the airport. After two hours a man comes in who looks as if he works for the diplomatic service. There are not many people in the waiting area. The suit comes straight over to him and asks if they have a mutual acquaintance.

Douglas gives the required answer and the suit hands him an A4 envelope and turns to leave in one single movement.

Douglas opens the envelope. All the information is there, and the advance payment is in dollars, not euros. Good. It is an hour and a half before his plane leaves. And it is a long journey.

He has time to do a little shopping. Just so he can relax on the journey. So that he will be able to cope afterwards. No doubt he is going to be on his feet and on the move for three full days. That is what he will need to do the job.

He takes another taxi out to one of the suburbs. It is still dark when he gets to his dealer. Who does not even have time to say "No credit" before Douglas manages to slip some unfolded dollar notes through the doorway.

And when morning comes and the air is rippling like hot glass, Douglas is sitting on the plane to Amsterdam. Speed balling. No tension. Calm happiness, that is all. He feels so bloody good.

In Amsterdam he buys two bottles of Smirnoff and drinks one on the plane to Stockholm. When everybody else stands up, he stands up too.

Then he is somewhere else. Lots of people going past, this way and that. Somebody takes his arm.

"Mr McNamara? Mr John McNamara?"

It is a flight attendant.

"Boarding time, sir. The plane to Kiruna is ready for take-off."

An hour and a half later he is standing in the men's lavatory sluicing the back of his neck with cold water. Time to pull himself together. He feels bloody terrible. He is at Kiruna airport, that's right. He hires a car and says to himself: "E10, travelling north." He will get this sorted in no time. He needs something to get him back on track, get him back to the way he was.

Douglas looks at Inna Wattrang. His feet are freezing. He has been waiting for ages. Had started to get worried. Got the idea the car would not start when he was ready to go back. But she is here now. Looks just like the photo. About one metre seventy, around sixty kilos. There are no problems. She has the key to the house in her hand.

He talks and gesticulates to distract attention from the fact that the steps he is taking towards her are swift and long.

In a second he has reached her. He steps behind her back, sliding his left arm around her neck at the same time. He lifts her, just enough for the pain to make her stand on tiptoe.

She feels as if her neck will break if she loses contact with the ground, so she stumbles backwards after him, half hanging over his hip.

He is moving towards the door now. She registers the fact that she is not even getting in the way of his feet. He unlocks the door with his free hand. She had not noticed he had taken the key from her.

This is no madman, she realizes. This is no rapist.

A pro, she thinks.

*

He looks around the hallway and as he begins to walk towards the kitchen, still holding firmly onto her, he slips a little. The snow beneath his shoes has formed a sole of ice. But he regains his balance and pushes her down onto a chair. He stands behind her, the pressure on her throat increases and she can hear the sound of tape being torn off a roll.

It happens incredibly quickly. He tapes her wrists to the arms of the chair and her feet to the legs. He does not cut it or tear it, but runs the tape from one hand to the other, down to the feet in one long piece, then drops the roll on the floor when he has finished.

He comes to stand in front of her.

"Please," she says. "Do you want money? I have . . ."

She does not get any further. He hits her across the face. It is like turning on a tap. Blood pours out of her nose, down her face and into her throat. She swallows over and over again.

"When I ask a question, you answer. Otherwise you keep your mouth shut. Understand? And if you can't manage that, I'll put the tape over your mouth. Then you can try breathing through a bleeding nose."

She nods and swallows again. She can hear her heart pounding in her head.

Douglas looks around. He would have killed her immediately if it had not been part of the job to find out if she had told anybody about . . . what was his name again, it was some German name he thinks. It is in the envelope.

He needs to frighten her so she will talk. It is easier to frighten women if you can show them pictures of their kids, but there were no pictures in the envelope. He should be able to scare her anyway. This should not take long.

He rummages through the kitchen drawers, hunting for a knife, but cannot find one.

He goes out into the hallway. There's a lamp on the desk. He pulls out the plug and rips the flex from the lamp. He checks in the envelope to see what he was supposed to ask about. 'Gerhart Sneyers', it says. And 'Uganda'.

He drags her chair close to a socket.

She watches him wide-eyed as he uses his teeth to open up the flex and remove the plastic sheath, then he separates the two copper wires and winds one around her ankle.

He is wearing ordinary shoes. As he bends down his trouser leg rides up, and Inna sees the marks on his ankle.

"I've got top-notch coke in my handbag," she says.

He stops.

"Where is it?"

"In the hallway."

He takes the bag into the bathroom. It is mostly habit. He has stood in hundreds of bathrooms and taken everything you can think of. When he lived in London they used to scare the little tarts, pretending to be undercover cops, pushing them up against a wall as they came from their dealers, taking their drugs and asking questions, always the same pattern: "did you see any weapons in there", "how many of them are there", pretending to be kind, letting them go with a "why are you doing this to yourself, get some help". Then it was straight into the nearest bathroom to take the lot.

Now he is hunting through Inna's Prada bag like an anteater who has found a termite stack. He pushes her phone into his pocket. That is from habit too: take everything that is easy to sell. Then he finds three small white packages. His heart jumps with relief and joy. Fine, pure snow. He lays out two lines on her hand mirror and takes the whole lot, no point in saving any. Two seconds, and he is in top form again.

He stands in front of the mirror feeling calm, his brain razor sharp.

Back into the kitchen. She is sitting there trying to free her hands from the tape. It is impossible, of course. Who does she think he is? Some amateur? He pushes the plug into the socket. But just as he is about to ask her if she has told anybody what she knows, he slips. The snow from both her shoes and his has melted. The water has made the floor slippery.

He falls hard. His legs fly up in the air. He has time to think about the water and the live cable, and he flounders like a fish as he tries to get back on his feet, terrified of electrocuting himself.

Inna Wattrang bursts out laughing. She might actually be crying, but it comes out like hysterical laughter. She laughs, and she cannot stop. The tears are pouring down her face.

It just looked so funny when he fell, as if somebody had pulled a rug from underneath his feet. And the way he scrabbled about, trying to get up. It's pure slapstick. Absolutely priceless. She laughs. She is hysterical. It's nice to be hysterical. She escapes from her fear into insanity. Into mad laughter.

He is frightened. And that makes him furious. He gets up feeling like a fool. And she is laughing. There is only one thought in his head: he is going to shut her up. He picks up the flex and pushes it against her throat. The circuit runs right through her body, down to her ankle. The laughter stops immediately, her head jerks forwards, her fingers spread, he presses and presses, he is going to shut her up. And when he takes the flex away, her head carries on jerking back and forth. Her hands clench and open, clench and open. And then she throws up on her jumper.

"Stop it," he says, because he has not had time to ask about that Sneyers guy yet.

The chair falls over. He jumps out of the way. He can see the whites of her eyes, her jaws are working and working and it takes a few seconds before he realizes she is chewing her own tongue to pieces.

"Stop it!" he yells, kicking her in the stomach as she is lying there.

But she does not stop, and then he realizes it is time to put an end to this. He will just have to report back that she had not told anybody.

Into the living room. The fireplace. There is an iron spit over the hearth. He runs and fetches it. When he gets back she is still lying on her back taped to the chair, twitching. He stabs her through the heart with the spit.

She dies immediately. But her muscles continue to contract.

He looks around, with a vague feeling that this has not gone too well. The instructions were that it should look like an opportunist attack. No suspicion that she might have known the perpetrator. She was not supposed to be found in the house.

This was unfortunate, but in no way a catastrophe. The kitchen is not too much of a mess, and the rest of the house is untouched. He can sort this out. He looks at the clock. Still plenty of time. It will soon be dark outside. He looks out of the window. He sees a dog running loose. He has seen several. If he leaves her outside somewhere, one of them will find her. And that could mean the police would be looking for him before the plane has taken off. But he is bound to come up with something . . . Down on the ice are those little houses on runners. He can carry her to one of those when it is dark. By the time they find her, he will be far away.

She has stopped moving.

Only now does he find the knives. They are hanging from a magnetic strip by the side of the stove. Good. That means he can cut her free.

Once darkness has fallen, Morgan carries Inna down to an ark on the ice. The snowmobile tracks are solid and easy to walk on. The ark is easy to open. He places her on a bunk inside. He puts a cover over the body. In his pocket he has a flashlight he found in a cupboard. When he shines the light on himself, he notices a red mark on the shoulder of his light-coloured coat. He takes the coat off, and when he lifts the trapdoor in the floor, he realizes it is covering a hole in the ice; there is just a thin crust of ice covering the water, and he can easily break that. He pushes the coat down into the hole; it will float away beneath the ice.

When he gets back to the house, he cleans up, whistling as he wipes the kitchen floor. He throws her laptop, the bundle of tape, the floorcloth and the spit into a plastic carrier bag, which he takes with him to the car.

On the road between Abisko and Kiruna he pulls over by the verge. Gets out of the car. The wind has got up. It is bloody freezing. He takes a step towards the forest to throw away the bag containing the laptop and all the rest of the stuff. Immediately he sinks into the deep snow, almost up to his waist. He hurls the bag in the general direction of the forest. The snowdrifts will cover it. It will probably never be found.

He also throws away her phone, which is in his pocket. What the hell was he thinking of, bringing it with him?

It is all he can do to clamber out of the ditch. Crawls back to the car, doing his best to brush off the snow.

The job is done. This is one hell of a cold country.

Martinsson had gone into the office for a little while after she had taken Björnfot home. When she got back to her own house, Boxer had attacked her as soon as she stepped into the hallway, sinking her needle-sharp claws into Martinsson's expensive sheer Wolford tights. She had quickly pulled on jeans and an old shirt. At 9.30 she rang Mella.

"Did I wake you?"

"No, no," Mella said. "I'm lying here in a nice clean hotel bed, dreaming of tomorrow morning's breakfast."

"What is it with women and hotel breakfasts? Scrambled egg, cheap sausages and Danish. I just don't get it."

"Move in with my husband and kids for a few days, then you'll get it. Has something happened?"

Mella sat up and switched on the bedside light. Martinsson told her about the conversation with Sven Israelsson. About Quebec Invest selling their shares in Northern Explore. About the fact that it seemed as if the Kallis Mining group had been bled dry of money in order to finance military activity in Uganda.

"Can you prove it?" Mella said.

"Not yet. But I'm 99 per cent sure I'm right."

"O.K., is there anything that will give us enough for an arrest or a search warrant? Or something I can wave about that will get us into Regla? Sven-Erik and I were there today, and they turned us away at the gates. They said Diddi Wattrang was in Canada. But I think he's at home, lying low. I want to ask him about the conversation he had with Inna the night before she was murdered."

"Diddi Wattrang is under suspicion of serious insider trading. You can ask Björnfot if you can arrest him; he's in charge of the investigation."

Mella jumped out of bed and began to pull on her jeans, the phone clamped between her ear and her shoulder.

"I'll do that," she said. "And I'll damned well go there now."

"Take it easy," Martinsson said.

"What for?" Mella said. "They've really annoyed me now."

*

As soon as Martinsson had hung up following her conversation with Mella, the telephone rang again. It was Maria Taube.

"Hi," Martinsson said. "Have you all arrived?"

"God, yes! Can't you hear? We might not be that brilliant on skis, but we know what to do in a bar!"

"I see, so Måns feels right at home then!"

"I should say so. He's parked himself next to the bartender, and Malin Norell is hanging round his neck. So I should think he's feeling pretty good."

A cold fist clutched at Martinsson's heart.

She made an effort to keep her voice cheerful. Cheerful and normal. Cheerful and casual. Only interested out of politeness.

"Malin Norell," she said. "Who's she?"

"Deals with company law. Moved over from Winge's eighteen months ago. She's a bit older than us, thirty-seven or eight, something like that. Divorced. Six-year-old daughter. I think there was something going on between her and Wenngren just after she started, but I don't know . . . Are you coming up tomorrow?"

"Tomorrow? No, I . . . there's just so much going on at work right now . . . and I'm not feeling too good . . . I think I might be getting a cold."

She swore to herself. Two lies is always one too many. You should only have one excuse if you are trying to lie your way out of something.

"Oh, no, that's terrible," Taube said. "I was really looking forward to seeing you."

Martinsson nodded. She had to finish this conversation. Now.

"See you," she managed to get out.

"What's the matter?" Taube asked, suddenly sounding worried. "Is something going on?"

"No, no. It's O.K. . . . I just . . ."

Martinsson stopped. Her throat was hurting. There was a lump there, getting in the way of the words.

"We'll talk more another time," she whispered. "I'll call you."

"No, wait," Taube said. "Rebecka?"

But she got no reply. Martinsson had hung up.

Martinsson was standing in front of the mirror in the bathroom. She was looking at the scar that ran between her lip and her nose.

"What were you thinking?" she said to herself. "What the hell were you thinking?"

Måns Wenngren was sitting in the bar of the Riksgränsen Hotel. Malin Norell was sitting next to him. He had just said something and she had laughed and her hand had landed on his knee, then she had pulled it back. A brief sign. She was his if he wanted her.

He really wished he did want her. Norell was pretty and smart and funny. When she had started working with the firm, she had made her interest very clear. And he had allowed himself to be captured, to be chosen. It had worked for a little while. They had celebrated New Year in Barcelona together.

But he had been thinking about Martinsson the whole time. Martinsson had been discharged from the hospital. When she was in there he had phoned, but she had not wanted to speak to him. And during his short relationship with Norell, he had thought that was for the best. He had thought that Martinsson was too complicated, too depressed, too much like hard work.

But he had been thinking about her the whole time. While he and Norell were celebrating in Barcelona, he had called Martinsson. Taken the opportunity when Norell had gone out for a while.

Norell was fantastic. She had not cried or played hell when their relationship ended. He had come up with a few excuses. And she had left him in peace.

And she was there if he wanted her. Her hand had landed on his knee.

But Martinsson was coming tomorrow.

The company were really meant to have gone to Åre. But he had made sure it was the Riksgränsen resort instead.

He thought about Martinsson the whole time. He could not help himself.

"Help me," Diddi said to the nanny.

He was sitting at the kitchen table looking lost as she picked up the broken medicine bottle from the floor, threw the pieces in the rubbish bin and wiped the floor with kitchen roll.

He realized he was just an old man in her eyes. She was so wrong, but how could he make her see that?

"Maybe you ought to go back to bed," she said.

He shook his head. Shook it because he was starting to hear voices inside it. They were not imaginary voices, nor fantasies, but memories. The memory of his own voice, shrill and urgent. Breathless and upset. And the memory of the soft but firm voice of an African woman. The Ugandan Minister for Industry.

He hated Kallis. Hated that smug little shit. He knew Kallis had killed Inna. He had realized it straight away. What could he do? He could not prove it. And even if he could turn Kallis in for financial misdemeanours, he himself was in it up to his neck as well. Kallis had been clever enough to make sure of that. And Diddi also had a family to think of.

He had nowhere to go. That had been the most powerful feeling when Inna died. There was grief. But mostly the panic-stricken feeling that he could not escape. The *Estonia* on her way down.

All the exits are blocked, the world tilts on its side and the water rushes in.

He had partied for three days. He had run from one bar to the next, one person to the next, one party to the next. The realization hot on his heels. The realization that Inna was dead.

He was beginning to remember more and more about those days.

"I can't avenge you," he had said to the dead Inna. Even though he had thought of a thousand ways to kill and torture Kallis, he had known he would never be able to do it. "I'm just a waste of space," he had said to her.

But now he was beginning to remember something in particular. It began with the voice of the Ugandan Minister for Industry.

He had wanted to get to Kallis. And he had done something insane. And very dangerous.

He had called the Ugandan Minister for Industry. It must have been yesterday. Or was it?

It was not difficult to get through. The Kallis Mining company name could still open doors. And Diddi told her Kallis was financing Kadaga's operation.

She had not believed him.

"These are bizarre claims," she had said. "We have complete faith in Kallis Mining. We have good relationships with all the investors in our country."

He remembers his voice becoming shrill. Agitated because she did not believe him. Desperate for her to take him seriously, he started babbling, and everything he knew just came pouring out.

"They want to bring about a coup. Or they want President Museveni murdered. They're making payments into a protected bank account. The money is paid out from there. I know this for a fact. He killed my sister. He's capable of anything."

"A coup? Who are 'they', these people who want to bring about a coup? This is all just loose talk."

"I don't know who they are. Gerhart Sneyers! He and Kallis and some others. They're going to have a meeting. They're going to discuss the problems they are having in northern Uganda."

"Who else is there besides Sneyers? I don't believe a word you're saying! Where's this meeting supposed to be taking place? In which country? Which city? You're just making it up to blacken the name of Kallis Mining. How can you expect me to take you seriously! And when? When is this alleged meeting supposed to be taking place?"

Diddi pressed his fingertips against his closed eyelids. The nanny took his arm tentatively.

"Shall I help you upstairs?" she said.

He jerked his arm away impatiently.

Oh God, he thought. Did I tell her the meeting was here? Did I say it was tonight? What did I tell her?

Uganda's Minister for Industry, Mrs Florence Kwesiga, President Museveni and General Joseph Muinde are sitting in a meeting which has been called at very short notice.

The minister has reported on her conversation with Diddi Wattrang.

She is pouring tea with lots of milk and sugar from a fine porcelain teapot. The president holds up his hand to refuse. General Muinde accepts a second cup. It amuses her to see her delicate little cups in his huge hands. He cannot get his finger through the handle, but balances the cup on his palm instead.

"What was your impression of Wattrang?" asks the president.

"That he was desperate and confused," Mrs Kwesiga says.

"Crazy?"

"No, not crazy."

"I've managed to confirm two things," General Muinde says. "One: Mr Wattrang's sister has been murdered. It's been in the Swedish press. Two: Gerhart Sneyers' plane has permission to land at Schiphol and Arlanda tomorrow."

"Less than twenty-four hours left," Mrs Kwesiga says. "What can we do?"

"We'll do what's absolutely necessary," the president says. "We don't know who's involved in this, apart from Sneyers and Kallis. This might be our only chance. In order to defend oneself, one must sometimes conduct a war on the other person's territory. If we've learned anything from the Israelis, it is that. Or the Americans."

"Different rules apply to them," Mrs Kwesiga says.

"Not this time."

"I made Mr Wattrang think I didn't believe him," Mrs Kwesiga says to the general. "I even laughed. He felt he wasn't being taken seriously. So he can't possibly be expecting us to take any kind of action. I thought if he regrets what he's done and tells somebody he's contacted us, they won't change their plans if he says I didn't believe him."

"You did absolutely the right thing," General Muinde says. "Well done."

He puts his teacup down carefully.

"Less than twenty-four hours," he says. "It's not much time. There will be a group of five. Not my own men. It's for the best, just in case of complications. We have guns at the embassy in Copenhagen. They can land there and travel to Sweden by car. That particular border crossing is risk free."

He gets up with a slight bow.

"I have a number of things to organize, so if you'll excuse me . . ."

He salutes. The president nods thoughtfully.

And the general leaves the room.

*

Diddi comes into dinner at Regla right in the middle of dessert. He is standing there in the doorway of the dining room. His tie like a loose piece of rag around his neck, his shirt half hanging out of his trousers, his jacket dangling from his index finger; perhaps he was intending to put it on, but he forgot, and now he is dragging it along behind him like an injured tail. The whole room falls silent, and everybody looks at him.

"Sorry," he says. "Forgive me."

Kallis gets up. He is furious, but controlled.

"I want you out of here right now," he says in Swedish, but in an extremely friendly tone of voice.

And Diddi stands there in the doorway like a child who has woken from a bad dream and comes to disturb his parents in the middle of dinner. He is quite touching as he asks, in careful English, if he might speak to his wife for a moment.

Then he adds in Swedish, in the same soft tone:

"Otherwise I'll make a scene, Mauri. And Inna's name will be mentioned, do you understand?"

With a brief nod Kallis indicates that Ulrika should go to her husband. She excuses herself and leaves the table. Ebba gives her a quick sympathetic smile.

"Domestic problems," Kallis says by way of apology to his guests around the table.

The men smile. This sort of thing happens everywhere, after all.

"At least let me change my shoes," Ulrika complains as Diddi sets off across the yard with her.

She can feel the dampness striking up through her sparkly, strappy Jimmy Choo sandals.

Then she starts to cry. She does not care about the fact that Wiik is sitting on the veranda in front of her house, and can hear her.

Diddi drags her away from the yard, away from the illumination from the outside light.

She is crying because Diddi is in the process of destroying their lives. But she does not say anything. There is no point, she has stopped trying. Kallis will kick him out of the company. Then they will not have anything to live on, or anywhere to live.

I have to leave him, she thinks. And that makes her cry even more. Because she still loves him, but this cannot carry on, it is just impossible. And what's he saying now?

"We've got to get out of here," Diddi says to her when they are a little way from the house.

"Please Diddi," Ulrika begs him, trying to pull herself together. "We'll talk about all this tomorrow. I'm going to go back and have my dessert and . . ."

"No, you don't understand," he says, grabbing her wrists. "I don't mean we've got to move house. I mean we've got to get out of here. Now!"

Ulrika has seen her husband stressed before, but now he is frightening her.

"I can't explain," he says with such despair in his voice that she starts crying again.

Their life was so perfect. She loves Regla. She loves their beautiful house. She and Ebba have become good friends. They know lots of nice people and do lots of fun things together. Ulrika was the one who landed Diddi Wattrang; God knows lots of girls had tried before her. It was like winning a gold medal at the Olympics.

And he is just letting it all go, destroying everything.

He is mumbling in her hair now. Holding her in his arms.

"Please, please," he says. "Just trust me. We'll leave now, we'll check into a hotel. You can ask me why tomorrow."

He looks around. Everywhere dark and silent. But a sense of unease is crawling inside his body.

"You need to get some help," she sobs.

And he promises that he will, if only she will come with him now. Quickly. They will collect their son and then they will take the car and get the hell out of here.

And Ulrika does not have the strength to resist him. She will do as he says now, and perhaps it will be possible to talk to him tomorrow. Dinner is ruined as far as she is concerned anyway. Just as well to avoid the look on Kallis' face when she comes back mumbling her apologies.

Ten minutes later they are sitting in the new Hummer on the way to the gates. Ulrika is driving. The little prince is sleeping in his child seat beside her. It takes two minutes to drive down to the gate, but when Ulrika presses the remote control to open the outer gates, nothing happens.

"They're playing up again," she says to Diddi, stopping the car a few metres away.

Diddi gets out. He walks towards the gate. He is in the beam of the headlights. Ulrika can see his back. And then he simply falls forwards.

Ulrika groans. She is so tired of this. She is tired of his drinking and getting high, his hangovers and his fears. Of his regrets, of how pathetic he is, of his diarrhoea and his constipation. Of the fact that he is over-sexed and the fact that he is impotent. She is tired of him falling over and not being able to get up. She is tired of taking off his clothes and his shoes. And she is tired of all those times when he cannot go to bed, the periods of manic wakefulness.

She waits for him to get back on his feet. But he does not. A violent rage floods her body. This is the fucking limit. She thinks she ought to just drive over him. Back and forth, several times.

Then she sighs and gets out of the car. A guilty conscience

over her unkind thoughts makes her voice gentle and considerate.

"Hey! What happened?"

But he does not reply. Now Ulrika is getting worried. She takes a few rapid steps towards him.

"Diddi, Diddi, what happened?"

She bends over him, places her hand between his shoulder blades and shudders. And her hand feels wet.

She does not understand. She never will understand.

A sound. A sound or something makes her look up and turn her head. A silhouette in the beam of the headlights. Before she has time to put her hand over her eyes to avoid being dazzled, she is dead.

The man who shot her whispers into his headset:

"Male and female out. Car. Engine running."

He points a flashlight into the car.

"There's an infant in the car."

On the other end, the group leader says:

"Mission as before. Everybody. Turn off the engine and advance."

Ulrika is lying dead on the ground. She does not have to experience it.

And in the darkness of her room, Ester is standing by the window and thinking:

Not yet. Not yet. Not yet. Now!

Rebecka Martinsson is lying in the snow outside her grandmother's house in Kurravaara. She is wearing her grandmother's old blue quilted nylon jacket, but it is not fastened. It is good to feel cold, it makes her feel better inside. The sky is black and studded with stars. The moon above her is a sickly yellow. Like a swollen face with pitted skin. Martinsson has read somewhere that moon dust stinks, that it smells of old gunpowder.

How can you feel this way about another person? she thinks.

How can you feel as if you want to die, just because he does not love you? He is just a human being, after all.

Listen, she says to her god. I don't mean to complain, but soon I won't want to be a part of all this any more. Nobody loves me, and that's really difficult to cope with. If the worst comes to the worst, I could live for another sixty years. What's going to become of me if I'm alone for sixty years?

I made it a little bit along the way, you saw that. I'm working. I get up in the mornings. I like porridge with lingonberry jam. But at the moment I don't know if I want all that any more.

Then she hears the sound of paws in the snow. The next moment Bella is at her side, galloping around her in a circle, then over the top of her, trampling all over her stomach so that it hurts, giving her a quick push with her nose, checking that she's O.K.

Then she starts barking. Reporting to her master, of course.

Martinsson hurriedly gets to her feet, but Fjällborg has already seen her. He rushes over.

Bella has already moved on. She is racing joyfully over the old meadow, the fresh snow spraying up around her paws.

"Rebecka," he shouts, failing to hide the concern in his voice. "What are you doing?"

She opens her mouth to lie. To joke and say she is looking at the stars, but nothing comes out.

Her face just cannot pretend. Her body makes no attempt to hide her feelings. She simply shakes her head.

He wants to make everything all right again. She can understand that he is worried about her. And who can he talk to, now his Maj-Lis is not around?

She just cannot cope with it. Does not want to see the longing in his face, wanting her to be cheerful and happy, for things to go well.

I haven't the strength to be happy, she wants to say. I can hardly even manage to be unhappy. Standing on my own two feet is my biggest project.

He is about to ask her to go for a walk with him. Or invite her in for coffee. In a few seconds he is going to say it. And she will have to say no, because it is just impossible. And he will hang his head, and then she will have made him unhappy too.

"I've got to go," she says. "I've got to call on a woman in Lombolo and give her a summons."

It is such an extraordinarily far-fetched and terrible lie that she feels outside herself. Another Martinsson is standing by her side and saying:

"Where the hell did you get that from?"

But Fjällborg seems to accept it. After all, he has no real idea of what she does at work.

"Oh yes," is all he says.

"Listen," she says. "I've got a cat in the house. Could you look after her for me?"

"Well, yes," Fjällborg says, "but are you going to be away for long?"

And as she is walking towards the car, he calls after her:

"Aren't you going to change your jacket?"

She pulls out onto the road to Kiruna. And she takes note of the fact that she is not wondering where she is going. Because she knows. She is going up to the Riksgränsen resort.

"What's that?" Mella says.

Stålnacke is sitting in the passenger seat, and he peers up towards the first set of gates to the Regla estate. In the beam of the headlights of their Passat he sees a Hummer facing in their direction, parked just inside the gates.

"Could be those security guys?" he says.

They stop outside the gate. Mella puts the car into neutral and gets out, leaving the engine running.

"Hello!" she shouts.

Stålnacke gets out of the car too.

"Jesus," Mella says. "Jesus Christ!"

Two bodies, lying face down. She reaches under her jacket for her gun.

"What the fuck has happened here?" she says.

Then she steps rapidly out of the beam of the headlights.

"Keep out of the light," she tells Stålnacke. "And turn the engine off."

"No," Stålnacke says. "Get back in the car and we'll get out of here and call for backup."

"Yes, you do that," Mella says. "I'm just going to take a look."

The outer gate blocks only the road. It is the inner gates further up the avenue that are set in a wall. Mella walks around the gatepost, but stops a short distance from the bodies. She does not want to go right up to them while they are still bathed in the light from their car.

"Move the car back," she tells Stålnacke. "I just want to take a look."

"Get into the car," Stålnacke growls, "and we'll call for backup."

So they end up quarrelling. They are standing there bickering, like an old married couple.

"I'm going to have a look, either get out of here or switch off the bloody engine," Mella snaps.

"There are procedures! Get in the bloody car!"

Unprofessional. They will think about that in the future. About the fact that they could have got each other shot. Every time a conversation turns to how cleverly you can react in a critical situation, their thoughts will come back to this moment.

And in the end Mella walks straight into the beam of the headlights. With her Sig Sauer in one hand, she feels for a pulse at the side of the neck in each of the bodies lying on the ground. No pulse.

Crouching down, she takes a few steps over to the Hummer and looks inside. A child seat. A child. A little dead child. Shot through its little face.

Stålnacke sees her lean against the windscreen, supporting herself with one hand. Her face is chalk-white in the Passat's headlights. She looks straight into his eyes with an expression so full of despair that his heart contracts.

"What is it?" he calls.

But the next moment he realizes he has not uttered a sound.

She bends forwards. It is as if her whole body is gripped by agonizing cramps. And she is looking at him. Accusingly. It is as if something is his fault.

The next minute, she is gone. She has bolted like a fox, and he does not know where she has gone. It is so bloody dark out there. Dense clouds are shutting out the moonlight.

Stålnacke leaps into the car and turns off the engine. Everything is black and silent.

He straightens up, and hears footsteps running towards the estate.

"Anna-Maria, for God's sake!" he shouts after her.

But he dare not shout too loudly.

He is about to run after her. But then he comes to his senses.

He rings for backup. Fuck her. The conversation takes two minutes. He is terrified as he is speaking on the phone. Afraid that someone will hear him. Someone who will come and shoot him in the head. He is crouched down beside the car throughout the entire conversation. Trying to listen. Trying to see something in the darkness. He takes the safety catch off his gun.

When he has finished, he runs after Mella. He tries to look inside the Hummer to see what made her react like that, but it is too dark now the headlights have been switched off. He cannot see a thing.

He keeps to the side of the road as he makes his way up towards the estate, running silently on the grass. If only his own breathing did not sound like a pair of bellows, he might be able to hear something. He is so scared he feels sick. But what bloody choice does he have? Where is the woman?

Ester can see someone in the mirror. Someone who looks like her. Science has come a long way, but there is nothing durable in us. A human being is a collection of vibrating chords. And the air around is also a collection of vibrating chords. It is remarkable that we do not walk straight through walls on a daily basis, melting into each other's being.

She has surrendered herself. To what, she cannot say. She simply knows it at a deeper level than her intellect. At every stage, the contract has been signed. She moved into Mauri's attic. She has trained her body. She has loaded her body with carbs. And now her head must follow her feet, and not the reverse.

Her head can rest as her feet run down the cellar stairs.

At that same moment, five men are advancing towards Regla. They are all dressed in black. The group leader is the one Ester called The Wolf in her mind. He and three of the others are armed with small machine-guns. The last man is a marksman.

The marksman lies down in the grass with Wiik in his sights. He should not need to lie down, his target is not moving at all.

Wiik is standing on the steps outside the house listening for sounds from the road. Diddi and his wife took the car and drove away from Regla. Presumably Diddi has had some kind of quarrel with Kallis. Bloody inconvenient, but Diddi is unpredictable these days.

He heard the car stop down by the outer gate, then they turned the engine off. He wonders why they did not keep going. Presumably they are sitting in the car having the row of the century.

I'm doing my job, Wiik thinks. And that isn't my job.

I'm not getting involved, he thinks. And I'm not involved. Not in the business with Inna, either. I gave Kallis that number. But whatever happened after that, I'm definitely not involved.

He had looked at Inna's body up in the morgue in Kiruna. There had been a terrible entry wound.

It cannot have been a professional, he convinces himself. She died for some other reason altogether. It had nothing to do with Mauri Kallis.

He takes a deep breath. The spring is woven through the night air. The wind is warm, carrying a scent of green. He is going to buy a boat in the summer. Take his partner out to the archipelago.

Then he stops thinking anything. As he falls forwards and hits the stone steps, he is already dead.

The marksman changes his position. Moves round to the other side of the house. Big dining room windows. Reads the room. Only one guard, standing by the wall in the dining room. The other guests are sitting ducks. He reports "all clear" through his headset.

Ester Kallis switches the electricity off at the mains. With a few rapid movements she unscrews the fuses for the three incoming phases. She throws the fuses under a nearby shelf. She hears them roll across the floor and stop. The darkness is solid.

She takes a deep breath. Her feet know their way up the stairs. She does not need to see. They are running along a black path.

And while her feet are following the black path, she herself is living in another world. You could call it a memory, but it is happening now. Again. It is happening just as much now as then.

She is standing on a mountainside with *eatnážan*. It is late spring. Only odd patches of snow left. Flocks of birds calling in the air all the time. The sun warms their backs. They have unbuttoned their cardigans.

They are looking down at a mountain stream. The melting snow has made it several metres wide. And it is a torrent. An elk cow makes her way into the water and swims across to the other side. Once she is on the bank, she stands there calling to her calf. She calls and calls, and eventually the calf finds the courage to get into the water. But the current is too strong. The calf does not have the strength to swim to the other side. Ester and her mother watch as the current takes it. Then the cow jumps back into the water and swims alongside her drifting calf. She swims around it, pushes it up against the current with her body, and they swim side by side. The current is strong, the cow's neck is stretched up above the surface of the water. She looks like a cry for help. When they reach the other side, she treads water, pushing against her calf so that it can scrabble its way ashore. At last they are both standing on the other bank.

Ester and her mother stand there watching them. They are overwhelmed by the elk cow's courage. By her powerful feelings for her calf. And by the calf's trust; it was so afraid of the current, but jumped into the water anyway. They do not say anything to each other as they stroll back to the reindeer herder's cottage.

Ester walks behind her mother. Tries to take long strides, so that her feet will land on exactly the same spot as her mother's feet.

Kallis is asking his guests what they would like with their coffee. Sneyers would like a large cognac, Koch and Lasker will have the same. Innitzer opts for Calvados, and General Stieff asks for a single malt.

Kallis tells his wife to stay where she is, and takes on the task of pouring drinks for his guests himself.

"I'll get some fresh candles," Ebba says, taking the candelabra up to the kitchen, slightly annoyed that the waiters have not noticed that they have almost burned down.

There is a security guard in the dining room. He works for Sneyers. When Kallis gets up and walks past him, he notices how discreetly the man has done his job. Kallis has not actually given a thought to the fact that he has been standing there all the way through dinner.

For that reason it is almost comical when the guard goes down, taking a 16th-century wall hanging with him. Kallis has time to remember a boy who fainted during the Lucia procession when he was at primary school. And at that same moment he becomes aware of the sound of breaking glass. Then there are two men in the doorway and the ridiculous popping sound of a hail of bullets.

And then all the lights go out. In the darkness he can hear Lasker screaming with pain. And somebody else screaming hysterically, then falling silent. The bullets stop, and after a second there is the beam of a flashlight, searching the room for the crawling, yelling, wriggling creatures trying to crouch down and make their escape.

General Stieff has got hold of the dead security guard's gun; he fires into the light, somebody falls to the floor and the flashlight goes out.

It is pitch black. Kallis discovers that he is lying down. And when he tries to get up, he cannot. His hand is wet, his shirt is wet.

I've been shot in the stomach, he thinks. But then he realizes he has got whisky all over him. Because he cannot see anything, sounds seem louder. There are women in the kitchen screaming with fear and then that popping noise and it goes quiet and Kallis thinks "Ebba" and he has to get out of there and that is the only thought in his head. He has to get out of there.

He can hear the intruders switching the mains on and off in the hallway, but nothing happens. The whole of Regla is in darkness.

And Lasker goes on screaming. Some of the men bump into each other underneath the table. It is a matter of seconds before the others are back in the dining room.

Kallis has been shot in the hip. But he can drag himself along using his hands. The dining room leads into the drawing room, and as the drinks cupboard is a wooden extension of the tiled stove in the drawing room, he knows he is close to the drawing room doorway. He drags himself across the threshold; this is where everybody would have had their coffee and after-dinner drinks. Two more metres, and his strength runs out.

That is when someone gently places a hand on his back. He hears Ester whisper in his ear:

"Keep quiet if you want to live."

The general is still shooting in the dining room, a random

barrage of shots comes from the doorway to the hall. One of the intruders stands in the hall holding the flashlight while the other fires. Lasker stops screaming. The general is firing, but less often. Not much ammunition left, soon they will be able to go in and finish off the lot of them.

Ester gets Kallis into a sitting position on a hard 18th-century sofa. Details about the bloodstains he leaves behind will appear in the preliminary investigation report, and there will be speculation about the probable scenario. Ester squats in front of him and picks him up in a fireman's lift.

Lift, she thinks. One, two, and three.

He is not very heavy. The drawing room leads into the library, which in turn leads into a room that has not been decorated yet, and is full of all kinds of things. It has a door leading out into the garden. She opens it and takes long strides out into the darkness.

She knows the way. She has run through the little wood down to the old jetty several times with her eyes covered. She has scratched her face to pieces on the trees, but she knows her black path. If she can just get across the yard and the grassy slope to where the trees begin.

The group leader shines his flashlight on the men in the dining room. The beam moves from face to face. General Stieff is dead, so is Lasker.

Koch is slumped against the wall. His hand is a lifeless claw above a spreading red stain on the front of his white shirt. He stares in terror at the man with the blackened face who is holding the flashlight in his left hand. His breath comes in short, rapid pants.

The group leader draws his Glock and shoots him between the eyes. This will make the two survivors more talkative. He takes note that Viktor Innitzer shouted out in horror.

It seems that Innitzer is completely unharmed, physically. He is sitting up against the wall with his arms pressed to his chest.

Sneyers is lying on his side underneath the table.

The group leader makes a movement with his head, and one of the men takes hold of Sneyers' feet and drags him over to the group leader. He lies there on his side, his knees slightly drawn up and his hands between his thighs. The sweat is breaking through the skin of his forehead. Gathering in beads and running down his face. His whole body is shaking, as if he were shivering.

"Your name?" the group leader asks in English. Then he changes to German.

"*Ihr Name*? And who were the others?"

"*Rot op*," replies Sneyers, and when he opens his mouth to speak, blood pours out.

The group leader bends down and shoots him too. Then he turns to Innitzer.

"Please don't kill me," Innitzer begs.

"Who are you? And who were the others?"

Innitzer tells him who he is, and says the names of the others as the beam of the flashlight falls on their dead faces. The group leader holds out a little tape recorder, and Innitzer speaks into it as clearly as he can, casting terrified looks up at the group leader the whole time.

"Is there anyone missing?" asks the group leader.

"I don't know . . . I don't know, if you could stop shining the light in my face . . . I . . . Kallis! Mauri Kallis!"

"Nobody else?"

"No."

"So where's Kallis?"

"He was standing just there!"

Innitzer points in the darkness towards the drinks cupboard.

The group leader shines his flashlight at the cupboard, and then at the doorway beside it. He aims his pistol at Innitzer's head: he is of no further use now, and fires. Then he signals to one of the others to go with him, and runs into the drawing room.

They search the room methodically with their flashlights. It looks like a well-rehearsed dance as they move back to back, round and round, forwards and backwards, the beams of the flashlights shining in different directions.

They are going to need better light, especially if Kallis has managed to get outside. They can only hope he is injured.

"Fetch the Hummer," says the group leader into his headset. "It can cope with this terrain."

Mella has just seen Diddi Wattrang's dead son in the family Hummer. She is running up to Regla. Although she is not really running, because it is so dark. She is trotting along, lifting her feet up so that she will not fall over anything: she has no desire to fall over while she is carrying a gun without the safety catch on.

What's happened here? she is thinking.

There are no outside lights on. The house itself is in complete darkness.

A little further on, she sees the beam of a flashlight. Somebody is shining it on the track in front of them and running towards her at high speed. She immediately turns aside and throws herself down into the ditch. Pulls off her jacket which is covered in reflective tags and flings it on the ground inside out. She does not have time to run any further away, or the person up there will hear her. She crouches down in the ditch; last year's grass is flattened and offers no protection, but there is a little bit of undergrowth, a few branches. If only the person does not shine the light in her direction, she will be O.K.

The water in the ditch is a hand's breadth deep. She can feel it penetrating her shoes and jeans immediately. She digs in the mud with her free hand and smears as much dirt on her face as she can, so that it will not show up as white in the beam of the flashlight. She has to look up, be ready to fire if the person catches sight of her and aims a gun at her. She holds the pistol in both hands. Then she keeps absolutely still and silent. Her heart is pounding like a jackhammer.

He passes by two metres from her. Does not see her. It is definitely a man. Once he has run past she takes a look and can make out a silhouette with broad shoulders. The sound of boots thumping on the gravel is gradually fading.

Friend or foe? She has no idea. Is he one of Kallis' security guys? Is he the one who just shot Diddi Wattrang and his family?

She does not know. And he is running down towards the gate, down towards the car with a dead child in the front seat. Down towards Stålnacke?

She gets to her feet and up onto the road, leaving her jacket in the ditch. Her knees and feet are soaked.

She runs after the man who is on his way towards the Hummer, keeping to the grass verge. If he draws his gun on Stålnacke. . . Well, there is only one thing she can do. She will put a bullet in his back.

The man reaches the Hummer. He gets into the car and starts it. The headlights come on, and suddenly the whole area seems to be bathed in a cold light. God, do two headlights really give that much light?

There's no sign of Stålnacke.

The man is reversing. She realizes he has no intention of wasting time turning the car around; he is going to reverse all the way up to the house.

Mella throws herself down into the ditch again. Lies flat on her stomach as the car passes by. Gets into a crouching position, watching him. He is too busy looking where he is going to glance in her direction. He is reversing at top speed, up the avenue to the house. Bloody hell, he's moving fast. Keeping dead centre on the road.

Then she realizes he is sitting next to the seat holding the child that has been shot through the head. It is a repulsive, disgusting thought. What kind of people are they?

"Sven-Erik," she calls quietly. "Sven-Erik!"

But there is no reply.

Stålnacke has just called for backup.

Now he's making his way along the grass verge. True, it is difficult when you cannot see anything, but his body remembers all those years in the forest. He has found his way many times when it has been pitch black. And he does not even have a birch bark basket on his back tonight.

His body has adopted a rapid loping gait, legs quite wide apart, knees bent. He can feel rather than see the road on one side and the lime trees on the other.

When the man with the flashlight comes running towards him, he does not splash down into the ditch, but hides behind a tree until he has gone by.

Without realizing it, Mella and Stålnacke meet. But they are on opposite sides of the road. Mella is running after the man with the flashlight. Stålnacke is going in the other direction, up towards the house. There is no more than four metres between them, but they do not see one another. And they hear only their own footsteps, their own breathing.

She is out in the garden. Ester is holding Kallis' arms and legs firmly; he is lying across her shoulders like a yoke. As she goes around the corner of the north wing of the house, she sees the flashlights' beams through the drawing room window. They are not far behind. But she is protected by the darkness now. She has to move silently. She cuts across the yard, avoiding the gravel.

She is going to go through the orchard and down to the dense wood. Through the dense wood down to the old jetty. Seven hundred metres of difficult terrain, carrying the weight of another person; as soon as she reaches the trees she can slow down.

She has almost reached the orchard when the Hummer drives into the yard. She sees it approaching like a red-eyed animal; it takes a second for her to realize they are the rear lights. It is reversing up the avenue.

And the headlights catch her. Suddenly she sees the gnarled trunks of the apple trees in the light, and takes a few rapid, heavy steps to get away. Keep going. Back to her dark path. Towards the trees.

The driver of the Hummer informs his colleagues via his headset that he has two escapees in his sights. He drives the car straight across the flowerbeds, out onto the grass and towards the orchard.

He has to stop before he reaches the orchard. The downward slope is too steep; he cannot drive down the steps of the stone terrace, he will get stuck.

He reverses a metre, changes gear, drives forward a little bit. Uses the car like a searchlight, checking the area methodically, telling his colleagues to get a move on. Two of them inform him they are on their way. The other two have gone to check out the other buildings. They have shot the nanny, who had just lit some candles in her living room and was aimlessly looking on the bookshelf for something to read, since the T.V. was not working.

Mella is out of breath. The Hummer has driven down through the garden and stopped on the edge of an orchard. In the beam of its headlights she can see a person carrying someone else over their shoulders, moving towards the wood. She sees them for a second, then they disappear out of the light. The Hummer turns skilfully and seems to be looking for them; the headlights are on main beam. Two people dressed in black appear beside the car, then stop briefly and look towards the orchard.

Mella crouches down, trying not to pant. She is no more than twenty metres from them.

They can't hear me over the noise of the engine, she thinks.

It happens in a split second: the person in the orchard is caught by the light again, and one of the men by the car lets fly a surge of bullets. The other raises a rifle to his shoulder, but does not have time to fire; the person in the orchard disappears into the darkness again. The Hummer reverses, turns, it takes a second.

The man with the machine-gun takes off across the terrace like a panther, following the poor bastards who are trying to get away. The marksman stays beside the car. Ready to fire from a standing position.

Mella tries to see something down there, but there are only tree trunks, spreading their winter-black branches in the ghostly glow of the headlights.

She does not think. Does not have time to make a decision.

But inside her is the absolute certainty that the people down there who are running away will be shot very soon if she does not do something. And in that car, turning and twisting with its murderous searchlights like a machine with a life of its own, in that car is a dead child.

There is a despairing rage in her footsteps as she runs towards the car with her gun in her hand. Her feet are digging into the ground, it is like a dream where you run and run and never reach your goal.

But she does reach her goal; in fact it only takes a couple of seconds.

They have not noticed her, all their attention is focused in a different direction. She shoots the marksman in the back. He falls forwards. Two rapid steps more and she shoots the driver in the head through the side window.

The engine dies, but the lights stay on. She does not give a thought to the fact that there might be more of them; there is no fear, she runs along the avenue of light down the terrace steps. Towards the orchard. Down between the trees. Following the man with the machine-gun who is following the person carrying some-one over their shoulders.

She has seven bullets left. That is all.

Stålnacke is crouching in the darkness when the Hummer comes reversing up towards the house. He watches it drive down towards the terrace and stop above the orchard, reverse and drive forwards, reverse and drive forwards. He does not see the person struggling through the apple trees with someone else on their back, but he does see the man with the machine-gun shoot at something then run down the terrace steps. He sees the marksman standing there ready to shoot beside the Hummer, watching for his target. He looks at his watch and wonders how long it will be before his colleagues arrive.

He hardly has time to grasp what he is seeing when he hears the shot and sees the marksman fall forwards, then someone shoots the driver. He does not realize it is Mella until he sees her running towards the apple trees in the headlights.

Stålnacke straightens up. He dare not shout to her.

Good God, she is exposed in the light. Totally insane. He is furious.

And in the middle of that feeling, the marksman gets up. Fear courses through Stålnacke's body like an electric shock. But she shot him. Then he sees that the man is wearing a bulletproof vest.

And Mella is running down there like a living target, right in the centre of the beam.

Stålnacke takes off. For his age and weight he moves very quietly and quickly. And as the marksman raises his gun and aims at Mella, Stålnacke stops and raises his gun. He could not get any closer.

It'll be O.K., he tells himself.

He holds the gun with both hands, takes a deep breath, feeling his whole body shaking with fear, exertion and tension. And he holds his breath as he pulls the trigger.

One of the machine-gun bullets hits Ester. She feels it penetrate her upper arm. It feels as if it is on fire. It misses the bone. It misses the main blood vessels. It goes into the tissue.

Only a few minor blood vessels are damaged, and they contract with the shock. It will take some time before she begins to bleed. The bullet goes through the arm and stops just beneath the skin on the other side. Like a callus. There will be no exit wound.

She will bleed to death from this injury. Small wounds and poor friends are not to be despised. But it will be a while yet. She will carry Kallis a little further.

My name is Ester Kallis. This is not my fate. This is my choice. I am carrying Mauri on my back, and soon we will be in the wood. Four hundred metres to go.

He is silent, but I am not worried. I know that he will live. I am carrying him, and it's the little boy I saw the first time we met that I am carrying. The two-year-old boy clinging to the back of a grown man who was lying on top of our mother. His skinny white back in the darkness. That's the child I'm carrying.

The stabbing pain in my arm is red, the colours are Venetian red and madder-lake in this darkness we are moving through. But I'm not going to think about my arm. I'm drawing pictures in my head as my legs carry us along the path they know from before.

I'm drawing Rensjön.

I'm doing a simple pencil drawing of my mother sitting outside the house preparing a reindeer skin, scraping off the hairs once the skin has been soaked until the follicles rot.

Mother in the kitchen with her hands in the washing up water and her thoughts far away.

I'm drawing Musta as she splits the reindeer herd as cleanly as a knife, brave as always, dashing between their legs, giving the slow ones a sharp nip.

I'm drawing myself. In the afternoon, when I finally get out of the school bus at home in Rensjön, the wind biting my cheeks as I run into the house. In the summer when I'm sitting on the shore drawing, and I don't realize until the evening how badly the mosquitoes have bitten me, and I sit there crying and scratching while my mother bathes the bites with lotion.

I'm getting pictures from Mauri too. It comes from the physical contact. I know that.

He's sitting in an office in another country. Because he's afraid of the men who are after us now, and of the men who sent these men, he'll have to stay in hiding for the rest of his life.

His hands are covered in the liver spots that come with age. The sun is bright outside. No air conditioning, only a fan. Out in the yard a few hens are scratching in the red dust. A bony cat scurries across the dried-up lawn.

There's a young woman. Her skin is soft and black. When he wakes in the night, she sings hymns in a low, dark voice. It calms him. Sometimes she sings children's songs in her native language. She and Mauri have a daughter.

The girl.

I am carrying her as well. She is still so small. Doesn't know it's wrong to open and close doors in the house without touching them.

I can see a police station in Sweden. Files piled up on top of one another. They contain everything that's known about the murder of Inna Wattrang, and about all the deaths at Regla. But no-one will be brought to account. They will never find anyone guilty. I can see a middle-aged woman with glasses on a cord around her neck. She has one year to go until she retires. She's thinking about this as she loads all these files containing murder investigations onto a cart and wheels it down to the archive room.

Soon we'll reach the old jetty.

I need to stop for a moment, it's getting dark inside my head.

I'll keep going, although I suddenly feel very dizzy.

I'm bleeding heavily from the back of my arm now. It's sticky, warm, unpleasant.

It's heavy. My footsteps are sinking. I'm so cold, and I'm afraid of falling. It's like trudging through deep snow.

One more step, I think. Just as my mother used to say when I was dead tired out on the mountain, and started whining. "Come on, Ester. One more step."

The snow is so deep. One more step, Ester. One more step.

Ebba Kallis is surprising herself. There is a window ajar in the kitchen. It got so warm in there when dinner was being prepared. When everything goes dark and she hears the shots, she does not even think for one second. She heaves herself out through the kitchen window. Inside they are all screaming in panic. And after a while they fall silent.

But by then she is already lying on the grass outside the window. She gets to her feet and runs until she reaches the wall that encircles the yard. Then she follows it down to the shore. She gropes her way along the shore to the old jetty. It is a slow process in her high-heeled shoes. She is shivering in her thin dress. But she is not crying. She thinks about the boys, who are with her parents, and she keeps going.

She reaches the old jetty. Clambers down into the boat and feels around in the storage box. If she can find a flashlight she can look for the ignition key. Otherwise she will have to row. Just as her hand closes around the flashlight, she hears steps on the track leading down to the jetty; they are very close.

And she hears a voice say something that sounds like "Ebba" or "Ebba he . . ." Or something.

"Ester?" she says tentatively, standing up in the boat and looking over the edge of the jetty. Although she cannot see anything in the darkness.

When she gets no reply, she thinks what the hell and switches on the flashlight.

Ester. With Mauri over her shoulders. She does not even seem to react to the light. And then she slumps to the ground.

Ebba pulls herself up onto the jetty. She shines the light on the two unconscious bodies.

"Oh my God," she says. "What am I going to do with you?"

Ester grabs hold of her silk dress.

"Run," she whispers.

Then Ebba sees the beam of a flashlight among the trees.

It is a matter of life and death now.

She grabs hold of Mauri's jacket and drags him across the jetty. Thump, thump, thump as the heels of his shoes are hauled across the planks.

She heaves him down into the boat. He lands with a thud; it sounds deafening to Ebba. She hopes he has not landed on his face. The beam of the flashlight is pointing in her direction. She will just have to forget about Ester. Ebba unties the boat and jumps down into the water. She wades behind the boat, pushing it out. In the end it is so far out it begins to drift. Ebba is strong, thanks to all the riding. But she only just manages to haul herself up and into the boat.

She takes hold of the oars. Slots them into the rowlocks. God, what a noise. The whole time she is thinking: we are going to be shot. Then she begins to row. She is well away from the shore. She is fit, and she keeps a cool head. She knows exactly where she can take Mauri. She is smart enough to know this has to be taken care of without hospitals or the police. Until he can tell her himself what he wants to do.

And the man with the flashlight who is on his way to the jetty never gets there. He gets the order through his headset that the mission is being aborted. Two members of the group have been shot, and the remaining three are leaving Regla. Before the police arrive they have disappeared.

It is snowing now. Ester plods on through the deep snow. Soon she will not be able to go on any longer. And then she thinks she has caught a glimpse of someone up ahead. Someone coming to meet her through the snowstorm, someone who stops a little distance away.

She calls to her mother. "*Eatnážan*," she calls, but the wind snatches her voice away and it disappears.

She sinks to the ground. The snow drifts over her, in a moment she is covered in a thin white layer. And as she lies there she feels something panting against her face.

A reindeer. A tame reindeer butting at her, blowing in her face.

Up ahead are her mother and another woman. Ester cannot see them through the snow whirling in the air, but she knows they are waiting for her. And she knows the other woman is *eatnážan*'s grandmother. Her *áhkku*.

She gets to her feet. Heaves herself up onto the reindeer's back.

Lies across it like a bundle. She can hear a familiar bark now. It is Musta, scampering around the two women. Musta's excited, demanding bark, she wants to be on her way. Ester is afraid they will go without her. Disappear.

Run, she says to the reindeer. Run. She grabs its thick coat with both hands.

And it begins to move forwards.

Soon they will catch up.

Mella discovers that she is fumbling around in a dark, silent wood. She stopped running long ago. She realizes she has no clue how long she has been wandering around, and she also realizes she is not going to find anybody here. She has the marked feeling that it is all over.

Stålnacke, she thinks. I must get back.

But she cannot find her way back. She does not really know where she is. She sinks down against a tree trunk.

I will have to wait, she thinks. It will be light soon.

The picture of the dead child comes into her head. She tries to push it away.

She is longing so urgently for Gustav. She wants to hold him, his warm body.

He is alive, she says to herself. They are all at home. If she had had her jacket she could have called Robert; her mobile is in her inside pocket, but her jacket is in the ditch.

She wraps her arms around her body, digging her fingers into her upper arms to stop herself from crying. And as she sits there digging and digging into her upper arms, she falls asleep in a second. She is exhausted.

When she wakes up, she notices that it has grown a little lighter. She gets up stiffly and begins to make her way up to the house.

There are three police cars in the yard, as well as a van belonging to the special operations squad. They have secured the area and are scattered about searching.

Mella comes walking up to the house with twigs in her hair and mud all over her face. All she feels when her colleagues point their guns at her is how tired she is. Hands up. They take her gun.

"Sven-Erik?" she asks. "Sven-Erik Stålnacke?"

One police officer is holding her arm loosely, a grip that can tighten if she starts playing up.

He looks troubled. He seems to be around the same age as Stålnacke. But he is taller.

"He's O.K., but you can't talk to him at the moment," he says. "Sorry."

She understands. She really does. She has shot two people, and God knows what else has happened. Obviously she has to be investigated. But she has to see Stålnacke. Perhaps mainly for her own sake. She needs to see somebody she cares about. Somebody who cares about her. She only wants him to look at her and give her a little nod, a sign that everything's going to be all right.

"Please," she says. "This was no picnic. I just want to know that he's O.K."

The police officer sighs and relents. How can he say no?

"Come with me, then," he says. "But remember. No exchange of information about what happened here tonight."

Stålnacke is leaning against one of the police cars. When he catches sight of Mella, he turns his head away.

"Sven-Erik," she says.

Then he turns to face her.

She has never seen him so furious.

"You and your fucking tricks," he shouts. "Fuck you, Mella! We should have waited for backup. I . . ."

He clenches his fists and shakes them in rage and frustration.

"I'm handing in my notice!" he shouts.

And at that moment Mella sees their colleagues over by the Hummer shining a light on the man with the rifle, the marksman. He is lying on the ground, and he has been shot in the head.

But I shot him in the back, thinks Mella.

"Right," she said absently to Stålnacke.

Then Stålnacke sits down on the bonnet of the police car and starts to cry. He thinks about Boxer, the cat.

He thinks about Airi Bylund.

He thinks that if Airi had not cut down her husband and got the doctor to lie about the cause of death, there would have been an autopsy on Örjan Bylund and they would have started a murder investigation and then perhaps none of this would have happened. And then he would not have had to kill anyone.

And he wonders if he can get over this so that he can love Airi. He does not know.

And he sobs his heart out.

Martinsson gets out of the car in front of the Riksgränsen Hotel. Her stomach is doing somersaults.

It doesn't matter, she says to herself. I have to do this. I have nothing to lose but my pride. And when she imagines what her pride looks like, she sees a worthless, worn-out thing, definitely the worse for wear.

In you go, she says to herself.

The bar is in full swing; as soon as she walks through the door she hears a tribute band playing an old Police track.

She stays in reception and calls Maria Taube. If she is in luck, Taube will have some man on the go and will be keeping an eye on her phone 24/7.

She is in luck. Taube answers.

"It's me," Martinsson says.

She is slightly out of breath because of her nerves, but she cannot let that distract her either.

"Can you find Måns and ask him to come out to reception?"

"What?" Taube says. "Are you here?"

"Yes, I'm here. But I don't want to see anybody, just him. Will you ask him, please."

"O.K.," Taube says hesitantly, realizing at the same time that she has missed something, that she has not understood. "I'll go and find him."

It takes a couple of minutes.

Just as long as nobody else comes out here, Martinsson thinks.

She needs a pee, she should have gone to the bathroom first. And so thirsty, how is she going to be able to talk to him when her tongue is sticking to the roof of her mouth?

She catches sight of herself in the mirror and discovers to her horror that she is wearing her grandmother's old quilted nylon jacket. She looks like somebody who lives out in the forest and grows everything organically, is on a permanent collision course with the authorities, and looks after stray cats.

She is seized by an impulse to run out to the car and drive away, but then her mobile rings. It is Taube.

"He's on his way," she says, and rings off.

And there he is.

Martinsson feels like an aquarium containing an electric eel.

He does not say "Hi Martinsson", or anything. It is as if he realizes this is serious. He looks so good. Exactly as he used to. He does not often wear jeans.

She steadies herself and tries to forget about her hair, which is way too long and needs styling, cutting, colouring. Tries to forget about her scar. And that bloody jacket!

"Come with me," she says. "I've come to take you back to my place."

She thinks she ought to say something else, but she cannot manage any more than that.

He smiles a little. But then his face grows serious. And before he has time to say anything, Malin Norell is standing behind him.

"Måns?" she says, looking from him to Martinsson. "What's going on?"

He shakes his head ruefully.

Martinsson doesn't know who he is shaking his head at. Her or the woman behind him.

But then he smiles at her and says:

"I just need to get a jacket."

But she has no intention of letting him go, oh no. Not for a second.

"Take mine," she says.

They are sitting in the car. The falling snow outside is like a white curtain, zero visibility. Martinsson is driving carefully. They do not say much. Nothing, in fact. Måns is studying the torn sleeves of the quilted nylon jacket he is wearing. It has to be the ugliest jacket he has ever seen in his life.

Then he looks at Martinsson. She really is something else. Crazy. And he begins to laugh. He cannot help himself.

She is laughing too. She laughs until the tears are pouring down her cheeks.

Much later. When she is resting in his arms, she starts to cry. It just overflows. And at first he jokes with her, and says:

"That good, was it?"

And that makes her laugh, but the tears come back.

Then he holds her tight. Holds her and strokes her hair, kisses the scar above her lip.

"It's O.K.," he says. "Just let it all out."

And she cries until she has finished crying. And he is full of good intentions. He is going to take care of her. She can move back to Stockholm and start working for the firm again. It will be fine.

During the night she wakes up and looks at him. He is sleeping on his back, his mouth wide open.

He is here right now, she thinks. I will try not to hold onto him so tight that he wants to get away. I will just enjoy it.

The fact that he is here right now.

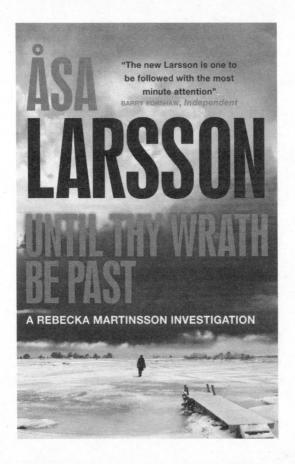